Crescent City Secrets

By
Madeline Kimmich

PublishAmerica
Baltimore

Hardcover 978-1-4560-5017-7
Softcover 978-1-4560-5016-0
PUBLISHED BY PUBLISHAMERICA, LLLP
www.publishamerica.com
Baltimore

Printed in the United States of America

This book is dedicated to my father and my dear Gram.

Chapter One

He felt the darkness of night swirling around him, closing in on him. His mind seemed a cloud but it was the clearness of it all that had him suffocating. The same air which had held such sweetness with each breath now only offered a nightmarish pain. Not a true physical pain but a mental pain. Pain that forced its way into every aspect of his being.

He still couldn't believe it. He had the whole world. He had the girl he loved. He had gotten accepted to Harvard. Why this? Why her? Barbara was so self-righteous, so controlling, so nasty.

Earlier that evening his life had changed. Barbara had called. She had to see him.

"John, I need to talk to you right away—in person," commanded Barbara.

Irritated John answered, "Barb, you know Janiene and I are back together. Why don't you stop calling?"

"Damn you, John. This is important. I have to see you!" she thundered.

"No, I don't think that would be a good idea."

"I must see you. I-I have something to tell you. I j-just can't tell you over the phone," she choked out.

John thought Barbara was about to cry. Damn, he hated when females used that tactic. It had always been a weakness for him. He couldn't stand it when a girl or woman cried.

"Okay, Barb. I've got to listen to the Presidential address at five o'clock. I'll run by your place around seven o'clock, okay?"

"You and your precious President Kennedy. I suppose I'll have to wait until seven, but don't come by the house. You know how Daddy feels about you. Meet me at City Park at our meeting place," Barbara ordered.

By the time seven o'clock rolled around John had already been waiting fifteen minutes.

City Park was a huge old southern park. Once part of the Louis Allard plantation, it was now a favorite gathering spot for New Orleanians on the weekends.

Their old meeting place was under a big oak tree known as McDonogh Oak. The huge oak was rumored to be nearly six hundred years old. Its branches spread out more than a hundred feet. Draped in Spanish moss, it had an eerie appearance. John thought it even more foreboding now, at dusk.

John looked at his watch. He didn't want Janiene hearing about his meeting with Barbara. He had only just proposed last week. He had felt so lucky when Janiene said yes. He didn't need Barbara screwing things up.

John looked at his watch again, fifteen after. It was just like Barb to be late. She thought the world revolved about her. John hated to admit it but a lot of it did. Barb had the beauty of Venus so most people didn't notice when Barb demanded everything her way. Her father was a judge from old southern money that gave his only child whatever she wanted.

John looked up when he heard the car door slam. Barb was a sight. Her long wavy golden hair was pulled back in a pony tail. Her tight peddle pushers, the latest style of pants, hugged her shapely hips. Her pink sweater, probably two sizes too small, showed just how well endowed she was. The catty girls at school had always said that Barb stuffed her bra. John knew firsthand that was not true. Barb's face was that of an angel with her deep midnight eyes, straight narrow nose and full pink lips.

It was too bad her personality isn't as sweet as her appearance, John thought.

"I wasn't sure if you'd come," Barbara said as she approached the giant oak.

"You weren't sure if I'd come? I'm not the one who's late," John said tersely.

"So shoot me. I'm sorry I'm late but I was sick."

"Should you be out in the night air?" John asked truly concerned.

"It doesn't matter what kind of air I'm in. This one's going to stick with me for awhile."

"We'd better sit down then. What's the matter? Do you have some sort of the flu or what?" He escorted her over to a park bench.

"I'll get to that but first I want to know if it's true," Barb said.

"If what's true?"

"If you asked Janiene to be your wife," she spat the words out like they were poison.

"You've got to be kidding! You dragged me out here to ask me that? I could have told you that over the phone. Yes, yes, a thousand times yes! You know I love Janiene. You weren't able to keep us apart. Not only did I ask her to be my wife—she accepted!" John bellowed.

"Congratulations are in order I suppose," Barbara said in a snide tone. "I guess you and I have nothing to discuss after all," she added.

"Great Barb, this was another one of your pathetic attempts to get back together with me, wasn't it? Well it won't work sweetheart. I'm in love with Janiene. She's going to be my wife."

"I was not trying to get you back, you bastard! I was going to tell you something that would have affected you. That is, if you had any sense of responsibility. I don't see any reason to ruin both of our lives though," Barbara cried.

She got up and started walking towards her car. John grabbed her by her upper arm and swung her around.

"What the hell are you talking about?"

"Never mind. You go on off and live happily ever after with that little—"

"Don't start, Barb or you'll get me really peeved," he interrupted.

"Big deal. With all I've got to worry about now, I don't give a shit if you're peeved."

"What are you talking about?" John boomed.

Barbara clasped her face in her hands and started to cry. Then to sob. She was nearly out of control when John put his arm around her.

She calmed down a little and whispered, "I'm-I'm pregnant."

"Is it mine?" John asked softly.

"Of course it's yours, you bastard. Why else would I tell you?" she managed to say between sobs.

"How? It can't be. I mean, I thought you said you were on that new pill, right?" John was in a state of shock.

"I was but I may have missed taking it for a day or two. I thought it didn't matter that much. I only missed one or two pills," she admitted.

"Wh-What?" he stuttered. "You did this on purpose; didn't you? You knew I wanted Janiene back. You knew how to use your body so I couldn't resist you. Thought you could get your hooks in me. Well forget it, lady. The jig is up. I'm not marrying you! I'm marrying Janiene," John yelled still whirling from the news.

"Drop dead you son-of-a-bitch. Sure, sure I got pregnant on purpose. I thought Daddy could use the publicity. I thought I'd enjoy being kicked out of my house. I thought how happy it would make my stepmomma. I especially liked the idea that I won't get to go to Loyola in the fall," she said sarcastically.

"I'm sorry Barb. I guess it's just the blow. What are you going to do? I hear there are safe ways of getting rid of a pregnancy."

"Kill my baby? Is that what you want? I'm supposed to go in some dark ally and hope it's safe? Forget it! You can walk away if you want to but, like it or not, I'm having your child!" Barbara's tone was shrill but the sobbing had caused her voice to come out in uneven spurts.

John didn't know how he had gotten home that night. He prayed this was all a dream. That he'd wake up. He prayed that at the very least it was a lie; a cold calculating lie. That Barb would call any second and tell him the truth—that she wasn't really pregnant. That wouldn't happen. He knew in his gut that it was real. It was true.

John hadn't quite decided how he was going to tell his parents. He had spent half the night tossing and turning.

Trying to figure out an easy way to break it to them. They had always been so open, so honest with him.

He had no choice. He had to tell them. Any publicity would not only be a blow to Barb's father but also to his own.

His father was a highly respected businessman. He owned the most profitable chain of antique stores in the state of Louisiana.

His father was Creole and Irish. His mother was French, actually Cajun. They lived together with John in a Creole town house in the French Quarter.

The house, mansion really, had been passed down from his great-grandfather, Henri Sommier, to his grandfather and then to his father. It was Henri's last request that this town house, built in 1850, remain in the family.

So the Sommier's had stayed. Stayed when it was no longer fashionable. Even when the poorer European immigrants moved into the area. Even when his grandfather had been snubbed as being too cheap to move out west of the city into one of the newer areas of wealth. They had stayed.

Now his father, a millionaire in his own right, had stayed too.

Many of the French Quarter town houses had been turned into apartments or small hotels or sectioned off with businesses on the ground floors and apartments on the upper floors.

Theirs was one of the few town houses still owned and occupied by the descendants of the original family.

John loved this place. It was hard to imagine it had ever been out of style. It had been a stylish place to live for as long as John could remember. He used to love impressing his friends with its size and splendor.

John looked up at the grandfather clock as it chimed the hour. It was time.

John had asked his parents to meet him in the sitting room at four o'clock.

He went into the sitting room and readied himself.

The sitting room was a dark masculine looking room. Two large wing-back chairs sat opposite a burgundy leather tufted sofa. A massive

9

cherry wood coffee table sat between the chairs and sofa. A large hearth fireplace dominated the room.

John always thought of this room as his father's room. While the drawing room was his mother's.

As his parents walked in he greeted them.

"John darling, you look tired," said his mother.

"Yes son, you do. You know you really need to get to bed at a more reasonable hour. I saw your light on at one o'clock this morning. Now that you're going off to Harvard you need be more reasonable about such things," added his father.

His father was a tall man, broad of shoulder, with dark hair and dark eyes. Even in middle age the man was striking.

His mother was a tiny thing, though she had put on weight the last few years. She had long black hair, which she always wore braided like a crown around her head, and beautiful green eyes.

John took after his father with one exception. He had his mother's eyes.

"I suppose you want to talk about the wedding," his father said.

"Yes, dear John, there's nothing to worry about. We know Janiene's parents aren't people of wealth. We will pay for whatever they will allow," said his mother.

"It's not about the wedding, mother." John frowned thoughtfully.

"Well, if it's school—"

John interrupted his father, "No Dad, it's not about school. If you'll just let me talk, I'll explain. It's hard enough to tell you anyway," John said grimly.

"What could be so terrible, John? You look as if you've lost your best friend," said his father.

"I did, I mean I will when Janiene hears about this," John said softly.

"What on earth are you talking about?" asked his mother.

"I'm sorry, Mom, Dad. I don't think there is an easy way to tell you so I'll just tell you." John sighed. "Barbara Cartwright is pregnant with my child."

John's mother fell back in her chair and his father looked like a smoldering mountain.

"How could you, John? How could you cheat on Janiene like that? I thought you loved her. Simply because Janiene would not sleep with you was no reason to be unfaithful," his mother cried.

John knew his mother and Janiene were close. He didn't realize they discussed his sex life though.

"Mom, it's not like that. Please, try to understand. When Janiene broke it off with me nearly four months ago was when it happened. Janiene had said she wasn't right for me. That she was holding me back. She wouldn't listen to reason. I thought it was over. Barb was there when I needed someone," John explained.

"Did you have to sleep with her? Why John? Why?" His mother looked confused.

"Catherine, calm down, your heart," his father gently took his mother's hand and patted it.

"You know son, the Cartwrights are not our type of people. They are dangerous. Judge Jefferson Cartwright is purported to be a high ranking member of the Klan or some other White supremacist group. He'll have your head on a platter or your hand in marriage for his daughter," his father said sharply.

"I've already told Barb, I won't marry her. That I love Janiene. I asked her to get rid of the pregnancy but she refused." John shook his head in disbelief.

"You told her what? Do you really think Janiene would have you while another woman carries your child? I cannot believe what you suggested to Barbara. It's not legal or safe, not to mention moral, to abort this child!" Henri yelled at his son.

"Now it is you who must calm down, Henri," said Catherine.

"Your father is right. I know Janiene will not have you now. I know too, that it is only proper and right for you to marry Barbara," finished his mother.

"You know our family secret must never be shared with Barbara. She is not like Janiene. She and her father could and probably would harm us publicly and, perhaps, privately if they knew," Henri warned.

"Oh, Dad, that happened over a hundred years ago. That doesn't matter now." John unconsciously rolled his eyes.

"It matters still. My grandfather knew it mattered, my father knew it mattered, I know it matters and you must know it matters. You had better learn that now. You cannot afford to take any chances; you cannot tell Barbara until we know she is really a part of this family. You will be the first in three generations that will be unable to share this with his wife-to-be," said Henri in stern tones.

Chapter Two

The wedding had been the society event of the season. All the upper crust, old money families, had been in attendance.

Barbara had looked the perfect virginal angel in her cloud of white fluff. John, the dashing handsome groom. They had looked more like the stereotypical knot tiers than the porcelain figurines that topped their cake.

The wedding was held at a friend's antebellum mansion out on old River Road. It looked as if it were the perfect fairy tale wedding. It would have been too, John thought, if the angel in white had been Janiene instead of Barbara.

The wedding night had been one of passion. Barb certainly had a gorgeous body and knew all the ways to use it. Her body was almost enough to make John forget he was in love with Janiene. Almost. John thought it would have been nice to make love on his wedding night rather than just having sex. Even if the sex was phenomenal.

Two months had passed since the rushed wedding. Barb was no longer sick but she was starting to show now. Not just in her belly either. Her breasts were even fuller than before and her bottom seemed rounder.

She wanted sex all the time now. John didn't mind accommodating her. It helped him forget what a witch his wife could be. It helped him forget that he was in love with another woman.

"John, darling, I don't understand why we have to live in this tiny apartment. Both of our folks have more than enough money to help us get a house," Barb complained as she rolled over to him in bed.

"We've been over this before. Since you refused to go to Harvard with me for my undergrad work, we have to stay here."

"If you had gone to Harvard, we'd still be in some tiny little depressing rat hole. You know Daddy still gives me four hundred dollars a week allowance. We can easily afford a house in the Garden District, Gentilly or wherever you'd like."

"No! Barb, I will not live off your Daddy's money. Hell, I won't live off my own father's money. What I earn doing the books for my father can just sustain this household. I can't afford a larger place. Relax, after I get out of Law School you'll have everything you want, Lady Barbara."

Barbara knew he was really mad now. He only called her 'Lady Barbara' when he was really steamed or when he was in one of his black moods. The moods he had when he was thinking of Janiene.

"Don't get angry, darling. You know we'll need a larger place when the baby comes."

"So you've said, time and time again. Just drop it, okay?"

"No, it's not okay. I'm not going to drop it just because you might get in one of your black moods. Just because you might start comparing me to that little slut of yours."

"What slut of mine? You don't mean Janiene, I know. Honey, you're the one who's five months pregnant and only two months married."

Barbara slapped him as hard as she could. There was a red hand print on his cheek when she pulled her hand back.

He grabbed her wrist and glared into her eyes with pure fury.

"I've never once hit a woman in my life. However, if you ever strike me again, I assure you, I will strike you back."

"How dare you?" Barbara screamed.

"How dare you? You slapped me for telling you the truth!"

"You called me a slut!" she said.

"I most certainly did not. I merely pointed out that you're the one who got pregnant before she got married."

"It's not like I got pregnant all by myself."

"No, but I don't recall having to force your legs apart."

God, he was getting nasty. When would she learn? John always got nasty and defensive whenever she brought up Janiene. She didn't want him going to school mad at her.

"I loved you then, John. I do love you. You were my first and only lover," Barbara said sweetly.

"Come on Barb, I wasn't raised on lies. I knew about some of your birthmarks, in some very private places, from Tad Overthall before I ever saw them. Don't lie about it. Don't you think I could tell you weren't a virgin? Why lie? I wasn't a virgin either. I'm no hypocrite. What's good for the goose is good for the gander," John said.

"Well, in a way I wasn't lying. You were the first man I loved that I shared myself with. You must feel something for me too or you wouldn't have married me."

John nodded in agreement. Yes, John thought, he felt something all right. He felt trapped.

"Sweetheart, you're my wife. What more do you want?"

"Your confession of undying love," Barbara said only half teasingly.

"I've got to get to school. What are you doing today?"

John pulled the covers back.

Barbara noticed the quick change of subject but decided not to pursue it. She did, after all, have John while Janiene only had his love.

"I'm going shopping for baby clothes and baby furniture," Barbara answered.

"Again? Don't we have enough baby clothes? When are you going to decide on a crib anyway?"

"Sugar, I can't pick a crib just like that." Barbara snapped her fingers to demonstrate. "Our son or daughter will be spending the first two years of his or her life in that crib. It has to be perfect."

"Okay, okay, I get the picture. I've got to get a move on. I'm in the shower and then I'm off," John said as he jumped up from bed.

John had found he liked Tulane University. He especially liked the location. It sat right across the street from Audubon park.

Between classes, weather permitting, John would study in the park. The sprawling park stretched all the way from St. Charles avenue, where

Tulane sat, to the mighty Mississippi. It was a most conducive spot for study. John often saw his fellow classmates in the park.

John finished with his classes and was headed over to the park when it happened. He had seen her. Janiene. Her long straight chestnut hair flowing in the wind. Her ivory face glowing with radiant color. Her body so tiny, so slender yet so shapely. Her brown eyes were sparkling. Sparkling, that is, until she caught sight of him watching her. Her eyes lost their sparkle. Her face, its glow. John tried to speak to her but she still would not speak to him. Janiene had not spoken to him since that night, almost three months ago, when he told her about Barbara.

God, he still loved her. When he looked at her he was glad of one thing. He was glad he had never made love with Janiene. If he had, he doubted if he'd have any contentment at home.

After seeing Janiene, John had wandered around the park for hours. It was starting to rain. He knew he should head home but after seeing Janiene he just wasn't up to seeing Barb. John decided to go to the library instead.

* * *

Barbara had spent the day shopping as she said she would. She did however, make a detour coming home.

All the black moods John had over that little tramp. Barbara never could see what he saw in Janiene. Barbara had a better body, a better face and she was much more cunning than Janiene. After all, she did have John after setting her sights on him only six months ago. Janiene had him for over three years and couldn't even hang on to him. Stupid girl, Janiene didn't even know how to use her body to keep a man. Of course, the little bitch didn't have much of a body.

Barbara had waited in her car until she saw Janiene pull up in her father's beat up old Ford.

"Hey, Janiene, I've got to talk to you," Barbara said as she hopped out of her white shiny Cadillac.

"I don't have time Barbara; I have to get ready for work," Janiene said.

"You don't start for three more hours," answered Barbara.

"How do you know that? What are you doing, having me followed?" Janiene asked.

"My God, you're paranoid. I know a girl you work with. I needed to find a time I could talk with you so my friend told me your hours."

"Fine. Talk," Janiene said quickly.

"Outside? Standing up? It even looks like rain." Barbara looked to her rounded stomach. "Maybe you don't realize how hard it is on a pregnant woman."

Gee, she's sinking low, Janiene thought. "Come on inside then but we'll have to go through the back so my mother doesn't see you. She wouldn't welcome you into our home, pregnant or not."

Barbara followed her through the back door and up the back stairs up to Janiene's room.

Janiene's room was not at all cluttered like some childhood rooms. It smelled of fresh jasmine. No wonder John liked jasmine so damn much, Barbara thought.

Janiene sat on the end of her mahogany canopy bed. She pointed to a ladder back rocking chair.

"Have a seat, Barbara and say what you've come to say," Janiene said quietly.

"Thanks. I know you think I stole John away from you but I really didn't," Barbara started.

"Funny that he's not my husband then," Janiene said sharply.

"I didn't say I didn't have him. I said I didn't steal him. You see, John came to me shortly after you dumped him, his heart broken. I had just stopped dating Tad. He needed someone and so did I. We started kissing I told him it couldn't go any further. He made me feel wanted again though. I told John that I was a virgin and that I didn't have any protection. He said not to worry. He said I couldn't get pregnant the first time. He was wrong," Barbara said with profuse regret.

Janiene knew a lot of the kids in high school had thought a girl couldn't get pregnant the first time. John had never said it to her but she had never let things go beyond kissing.

If Barbara was telling the truth, and she sounded like she was, this must have been terrible for her.

Janiene always thought Barbara was fast and easy. Maybe she was wrong. Maybe the rumors about Barbara had been lies. Barbara had been the most beautiful girl in high school. The rumors could have been made up by jealous girls or boys who had been shunned by Barbara.

Janiene didn't know what to believe anymore. Barbara seemed to be telling the truth. She seemed like she was just another victim in this whole mess.

"If you were a virgin," Janiene tried to find the words.

"Well, John wouldn't, I mean, he didn't force you. Did he?" Janiene asked.

"No. He just strongly encouraged me." Barbara secretly smiled as she thought how it really happened.

"Is that all? Is that all that you came to tell me?" Janiene felt sorry for Barbara but she felt even sorrier for herself. She wanted Barbara out of her house.

"Yes. I just didn't want you thinking I had done this on purpose or to hurt you. I know we never ran in the same circles. Still, I wouldn't do anything to intentionally hurt you or anyone," Barbara said with a genuine tone.

"Thank you for telling me. I'm sorry I thought the worst of you. John isn't the type to kiss and tell. He just told me that you were pregnant by him. I hope everything goes well for you. John too. You really better go now. My mother wouldn't be happy at all if she found you here. She really loved John. She was hurt too." Janiene walked Barbara out.

"Thanks for hearing me out, Jan. I'll see you around." Barbara's heart skipped a beat as she slipped into the car.

The entire drive home Barbara smiled. She never thought it would be this easy. The stupid bitch had actually believed her. Now John would have no chance of getting Janiene back. Not now. Not now that Barbara had Janiene's sympathy.

When John finally arrived home, Barbara had his dinner waiting.
"Where have you been? You're late," Barbara snapped.
"Sorry. I went to the library after classes. Did you find a crib?"
"No, but I think I'll find one soon."

Barbara had already eaten so after she served his dinner she went into the bedroom. She slipped off all of her clothes and put her silk white robe on. The robe she had worn the first night they made love. It barely fit now with her big belly in the way. Still, it always seemed to entice him.

She thought back to the first night. She had called him that night...

"Hello John?" Barbara asked.

"Hey Barb. How are you doing?" John inquired pleasantly.

"Not too good. I-I don't know who to turn to. Tad's your friend. Maybe you can talk to him," she cried.

"What is it Barb? What's he done?"

"He said some, oh, some terrible things to-to me," Barbara had really begun to cry.

"I'll go talk to him now," John said.

"No, don't! I mean I could use a friend right now if you'd come over. My Daddy and Stepmomma aren't even here so I have no one to talk to," Barbara said sounding truly distraught.

"I'll be right there, Barbie. You try to pull yourself together. See you soon." John hung up and headed over.

Barbara smiled. Her plan was finally working. She had dated that sap, Tad, so she could befriend John. She had convinced Janiene's best friend that John was too upper class for their type. That he'd eventually hurt her or else Janiene would just hold him back. Janiene had believed her friend too. She had broken up with John. After three years she just dumped him.

Stupid tramp. Barbara would never dump a gorgeous hunk like John. If he's half as good in bed as he looks, he'll be incredible, Barbara thought with a wry smile.

The doorbell rang. It was John. She answered the door in her white silk robe. She had smeared mascara under her eyes for effect. John looked at her face and then to her breasts. This was going to be easier than she first thought.

"Come in, John. Why don't you come into my room? Daddy would have a fit if he found a boy alone in the house with me. Just bring your bike into my room. If Daddy comes home you can leave out my veranda," Barbara said in a soft, coaxing tone.

"I don't know, Barb. If your Dad would get peeved and all," John said.

"Please John, I need a friend." Tears welled up in Barb's eyes.

"Okay, for a little while," John sighed.

She led him into her bedroom. Barbara put his bike near her French doors. With any luck he would have to use those doors to get out, she thought.

"What did Tad say that upset you so much?" John asked.

"He was such a brute." Barbara threw herself on the bed and started crying.

John didn't know what to do. He sat on the edge of her bed and started rubbing her back trying to comfort her.

That's when he was sure that she didn't have a bra on. At the door he could see something looked softer, more rounded, different about her breasts. Now he knew what.

Barb turned over, her robe gaping open so he could see most of both breasts except the nipples and all of one long creamy white shapely leg.

She didn't seem to notice. She was too upset. Tears were still welling up in her eyes.

John could feel something welling up in him too. Desire.

"John, just hold me," Barb begged.

"It's okay, Honey, you'll have lots of other beaus," John said.

"Do you think so? Do you really think so?" Barbara asked.

"Of course, with looks like yours you'd have to."

"I'm not sure I know what you mean."

"You know full well what I mean. You're gorgeous."

"I don't feel even the slightest bit pretty. What about me is pretty?"

She still lay looking up at him with her deep pools of blue overflowing with tears. Her robe still gaping.

He tried not to look down. He saw a blonde triangle where her robe was pulling apart at her thighs. Just a glimpse had his blood hot.

"Well, sweetheart, you have the face of an angel. Your eyes are like looking into an azure sea." John's voice grew husky as he gazed upon her breasts. It took all of his self control not to look further down her body.

"John, do you like my body?" Barbara asked suggestively as she sat up fully exposing both breasts.

"Yes, uh, yes," John choked out.

John lost all control. He took her gently and laid her back down. John began kissing her softly at first but as his desire increased so did the force of his kiss.

John's mind was spinning. The taste of her was so hot, so sweet. John let his hands roam her body as he felt hers roam his own body.

John pulled back abruptly, "Oh shit, damn it! We can't do this."

"Why not? I want to. I really want you to make love to me. To be part of me."

"Shit. I want that too. More than anything right now but I don't have anything with me. I don't have any protection."

"Is that all? Sugar, I'm on that pill. I have to take it to regulate my, well, for female reasons. As long as you don't have VD or anything, we're both safe." Barbara slipped her robe off her shoulders seductively.

A smile curved Barbara's mouth as she thought back to that night in detail. That night had been one of more than a dozen. In only two weeks time too! Barbara had had very little doubt that she'd become pregnant. By the time Janiene had decided she could not live without John, Barbara knew John was hers.

Barbara came out of her daydream to the feel of John's hands all over her body.

"You've finished your supper already?" she asked.

"Uh huh," he said still caressing her.

"I love you John Jackson Sommier," she whispered.

"Show me," John said huskily.

This was going to be a wonderful night, Barbara thought as she turned off the light.

"John are you awake? John! John, wake up," Barbara urged.

"What? What is it? Are you okay?" John asked groggily.

She took his hand and placed it on her stomach. The baby was really kicking up a storm. Up until now, only she could feel the little flutters. Barbara felt sure even John could feel these.

"Wow! I can feel it. They're just soft little movements," John said in awe.

"Little movements? That babe of yours is doing a full gymnastic routine," she said.

It was still dark out. John didn't have to go to school for at least a couple more hours. Barbara hoped for a repeat of last night. John had been wonderful. So tender, so loving, so passionate. She just knew he'd be in love with her soon.

Soon, yes, soon. Soon that little tramp, Janiene, would be a faded memory.

John was still feeling the baby when she leaned over and kissed him. He kissed her back. A soft kiss, no passion.

"John, honey, you have some time before you go to school," Barbara reminded him.

"That's right but I really need to finish that Poli Sci paper. I was planning on getting up early anyway."

John sat at the small kitchen table trying to finish his paper. He could not concentrate, Barb had awakened him from a blissful dream about Janiene. It was amazing to feel his child moving but he resented being taken away from his sweet Janiene.

In his dream Janiene had worn a white flowing blouse over form fitting slacks. Her hair danced in the wind. They were walking, talking and laughing along the riverfront. Janiene delighted in seeing all the boats and barges making their way up and down the river. They walked hand in hand back to and through the French Quarter. Janiene was a vision of loveliness, of happiness. Then they were at his house. In his bedroom. He went to draw the shades. Lovely Janiene was wearing a white silk robe, the white silk robe. Her body lay mostly exposed to his gaze. He moved to touch her, to kiss... she was slipping away. Then there was only Barb's voice. That's when he woke up.

He couldn't fathom having sex with his wife this morning. He felt like making love. Like making love to Janiene.

Damn, he thought, squinting over his paper in the dull light, he had to forget about Janiene. He was married now. He would not break his vows to his wife. Not unless, of course, she broke hers to him.

"Sugar, can I get you some breakfast? Why don't you turn on the living room light on so that you can see better?" Barbara asked.

"The light's fine in here. If you're fixing something for yourself, I'll have some. Otherwise, I'll just pick something up at school or maybe I'll go to Acme for lunch.

Barbara liked the idea of John going to Acme for lunch. It was an oyster bar. A cozy, smoky, French Quarter establishment where people sat at tables or stood at the bar sucking down raw oysters. Most people got a cold beer to wash them down.

Barbara had read that oysters were an aphrodisiac. She knew that beer always improved John's moods.

"No, Sugar, I wasn't going to fix anything for myself," she said in her sweetest drawl. "Why don't y'all go over to Acme."

Barbara would be more than ready for John by the time he came home from lunch.

John knew Barb wanted something. He just didn't know what. Her sugar coated southern drawl was reserved for those times when she wanted something.

Maybe she wanted the afternoon to herself. Why else would she want him to go to the Quarter for lunch. Well, he'd give her the afternoon free from him if that's what she wanted.

It was a typical day at school. John's classes were really going great. If he could keep his grades up, his unit load up and go to summer school, he'd be finished with his undergrad work in only two and a half years. He was really anxious to get on to Harvard.

John was glad now that Barbara had been so stubborn. She had refused to go with him to Harvard. She had said it was a waste of money when he could do his undergrad work anywhere. He knew she just didn't want to leave Louisiana but her arguments had been right. Still, he would not have stayed if his mother hadn't gotten so upset. Originally, John had decided to go to Harvard anyway. He would see his wife on holidays. He would come home for the birth of his child. He had planned it all out.

Everything changed when his mother found out. His mother had flipped her wig when she found out about John's plans. She had asked what kind of man would leave his pregnant wife alone. She had told him that even if he did not love Barbara that she was still his wife. Barbara was Barbara Sommier and she would be treated as all Sommier women have always been treated. Barbara must be treated with love, respect and tenderness his mother had told him.

His mother had been right of course. His wife had been right too. His parents had saved money on his undergrad work. The money they had saved they promised to give John upon graduation. Barbara had her friends here and didn't always need John. Then there was Janiene. He had seen Janiene. That alone had made his choice all worth while.

John arrived shortly after two o'clock at the Acme Oyster Bar. He loved the neon light reflecting off the dark wood paneling and picture-window sized mirrors. The strong smell of the sea mixed with that pungent pepper sauce, Tabasco, and beer to fragrant the air. He and Janiene had loved this place.

Janiene had panicked when she saw John come into the restaurant. She had run into the restroom. She still loved him so much. Just the sight of him made her heart ache. She felt ill every time she saw him because of that love.

Janiene had seen him many times on campus but she was always careful so that he did not see her. Careful, that is, until yesterday. She knew he sat outside on the grass after chemistry class. How could she have forgotten? Did she forget? Maybe her heart had taken her where her mind would not.

She had been devastated when he spoke to her. Then to come home to find Barbara waiting for her. It had been nearly all she could do to keep her composure. She had wanted to scream, to cry. Yet all the while she had wanted to touch Barbara's stomach. To feel the baby.

The entire time Barbara had talked, Janiene had wanted to feel the baby. To feel John's child. Maybe to gain a sense of what it would feel like to carry John's child. No, that wasn't it. It was as if she already loved John's child. It didn't even matter who the mother was. Janiene would love any part of John. Even the child that forced them apart.

Janiene couldn't stay in the restroom. What was she going to do? If she didn't go out there soon her friend would come in after her. She had no choice. She had to face facts. She needed to stop being so immature. She would talk to John.

Janiene saw him when she came out of the restroom. He was still the most handsome boy she had ever laid eyes upon. Except now he was no longer a boy. He was a man. His face had lost the boyish look. His shoulders had broadened over the year. His muscles were so well defined.

His dark soft curls fell in a rakish manner about his face. His bright white smile was flashing as he spoke to Joe behind the counter. As she approached him, his emerald eyes came upon her. They seemed surprised yet intrigued.

"Janiene," John whispered.

"Hello, John Jackson," Janiene said quietly.

"Janiene."

John could feel his heart slamming against his ribs. It was pounding so hard and loud that he was sure everyone could hear his heartbeat.

"John Jackson, I want to wish you and Barbara well."

"Thanks. I'm sorry—"

"John Jackson, don't," Janiene interrupted. She spoke quickly before he could reply, "how is your mother? And your father?"

"They are both doing well. Dad's shops are really busy right now. I'm doing the books for all the stores. Mom is doing her painting. Haven't you talked to Mom recently? You two used to spend hours on the phone," John said surprised.

"Of course not," she replied.

"Why not? Mom would love to hear from you."

"That wouldn't be fair to your mother. She couldn't remain close with her son's ex-girlfriend and still show respect to his wife."

John hadn't thought of that. God, he had messed up a lot of relationships. He knew why Janiene's mother didn't want to see him anymore. He didn't think about Janiene's relationship with his mother. After all, Janiene hadn't done anything wrong.

"I still think Mom would love to hear from you at least once in awhile," John commented.

"Maybe I'll call her or drop by to see her soon."

Janiene's friend who had been waiting at the end of the table walked up to them. Janiene introduced her to John. Janiene's friend made up some excuse about having to leave. Her friend pointed out to John that they had not yet eaten. Her friend, Stacy, then suggested that John fill in as lunch companion. Janiene was going to kill Stacy. Stacy apparently thought she was playing cupid. Stacy didn't know she had dated John for three years. Stacy didn't know John had betrayed her.

"You want the usual?" John said with ease.

"You don't need to buy my lunch. I'll get it myself," Janiene said firmly.

John didn't reply to her. He looked at Joe. "Hey Joe, half a dozen shucked and a Coke for the lady."

"Here John, take this. It will cover my lunch," Janiene said as she pushed a couple of dollars into John's hand.

John didn't want to take her money. Janiene seemed adamant about it so he took the money.

They didn't have a long wait. The oysters were open and served in a matter of minutes.

"Since we were speaking of Mom earlier, I thought that you might like to know that I'm going to see her right after lunch," John said.

"Great, you can tell her I said hello."

"I've got a better idea. Why don't you walk over with me? It's only a couple blocks from here."

"I know how far it is. I just don't think that it's such a good idea."

"Nonsense! She'd love to see you. She hasn't gotten out lately due to her heart. I know she loves to have guests. Please come with me. Please?" John begged.

Against Janiene's better judgment, she went with John. John was like the pied piper to Janiene. Instead of using a pipe, John used his eyes. He had always been able to get her to do just about anything he wanted when he pleaded with those sparkling emeralds. Surrounded by long black lashes, his eyes looked like huge emeralds on a bed of black velvet. Mesmerizing.

As they approached his parents house Janiene began to feel nervous. Walking over had felt like old times. For a moment she had forgotten that he was not hers. She had forgotten that he made another woman pregnant. That he had married that other woman.

When they came upon the stoop John allowed Janiene to go up the steps first. She waited for him as he pulled the cord.

John's parents' house still had a system of cords and bells. The system dated back to when the house was first built. Cords could be pulled from nearly every room in the house. From the sound of differing bells the slaves had been able to determine where they were needed. Originally all the bells had been in the carriage way. Now most of the bells were in the kitchen and the upstairs hall.

Oliver opened the door. He was their one and only servant. Oliver had gone to work for John's grandfather when Oliver was just a boy. Not much older than John's own father. He had been with them ever since.

Oliver was always very loving yet he remained quite reserved.

"Well, well, well! It sure be nice to see you M'selle Janiene," Oliver said with a big smile, his Cajun accent thick.

Oliver's smile faded when he saw John. Something that looked like worry took its place.

"Hello M'seur John," Oliver said dryly.

"Come in, come in," he commanded.

"Your Momma be in de drawing room. She be doing some of that painting of hers, yes. I was fixin' to get her some tea. How about you helping me with dat, M'seur John? M'selle Janiene, you go right 'head to de drawing room," Oliver said.

Janiene went to the drawing room while John followed Oliver to the kitchen.

"What you mean by dis, M'seur John? You a married man now. You can't be bringing any young ladies to dis house 'cept your wife. You know your Momma has a weakened heart. Why you tryin' to worry her dis way?" Oliver scowled at John.

27

"I ran into Janiene at Acme. I was coming over here and I thought Janiene might like to see Mom. It's purely innocent." John said sheepishly.

"Well it surely don't look innocent, no. I can see de way you look at de girl. Dat surely ain't de way you look at your wife."

"Oliver, relax. It's no big thing. C'mon lets just take the tea out."

"No sir! I'll take de tea out. You'll wait here. You'll wait here until M'selle Janiene has gone. Your Momma won't know y'all came together, no. Don't you come out there, ya hear?" Oliver said harshly and carried the tray from the kitchen.

When Janiene entered the drawing room she noticed the lovely antique chairs and big armoire. She used to love this room with its light yellow paint and floral wall paper. The room smelled strongly of gardenias. Just as it always had when she had visited.

Janiene saw Mrs. Sommier sitting near the French doors that opened onto the courtyard.

Catherine Sommier looked as if she should be in a painting. She was so beautiful, so dignified, so regal yet she had a soft approachable look to her. She was like a beautiful delicate rose. Like a rose, Mrs. Sommier could have thorns. She was fiercely protective of those she loved.

"Hello Mrs. Sommier! You look absolutely stunning today." Janiene crossed the room.

Catherine Sommier's face lit up when she saw Janiene. She simply adored Janiene.

"Oh, Janiene, don't tease. I'm fast becoming an old woman. You are the stunning one. You truly are. Come here and give me a hug." Catherine Sommier stretched out her arms to Janiene.

"Old, ha, you're far from old. I, however, have started to feel as if I am old. Between work and school it seems I never get any sleep."

"At eighteen you should be feeling an endless supply of energy. You must manage your time better so that you get plenty of sleep. We don't want you getting sick. Now do we?"

"Don't worry about me," Janiene said as she walked around the easel so that she could view the painting. "That is lovely. The colors so true to life. Mrs. Sommier, I think you've really outdone yourself."

"Thank you. I've always wanted to do a study of birds. When I saw this photograph in a magazine I just knew I'd have to paint it. Of course, no one will ever mistake it for an Audubon but I am enjoying myself so."

"The painting you did for me hangs prominently in our dining room. I admire it daily. I think of you each time I see it."

Catherine Sommier put her arms around Janiene. "I think of you often, dear. I miss our long talks. No one shows as much interest in my paintings as you did. You have always been a boost to my old ego. I'm sorry I couldn't call you. I hope you understand."

"Yes. I do understand. I just wish sometimes that things were different, Mrs. Sommier."

"Things are what they are. Some things cannot be changed no matter how much we might wish it. Other things can be changed. I can think of one thing we can change right now. Please start calling me Catherine."

"Oh no! I could never do that Ma'am. That would be disrespectful."

"It most certainly would not be. If things had been different you would be calling me Mom now. Janiene, you are very special to me. The daughter I never had. You are more than that though. You are my friend. You would honor me if you call me be my given name."

Janiene felt tears come to her eyes. She wanted to cry. She had thought of the Sommiers as family for years. Just six months ago, she had thought how she was so lucky. She had had two mothers that loved her. Janiene couldn't let her tears fall and risk upsetting Catherine Sommier.

"If that is your wish, I will not disrespect you by not honoring it. It will take some getting used to," Janiene said quietly.

Oliver walked into the drawing room carrying a tray with a sterling silver tea service and two delicate porcelain cups. Oliver placed the tray on the low table and began to pour.

"Let's see, two cubes sugar, one squeeze lemon. I remember, no?" Oliver looked to Janiene.

"Exactly right! Thank you," Janiene said as she took the tea cup.

"Madam Catherine, M'seur John called not ten minutes ago. He said he was held up at de school. He be here shortly." Oliver looked to Janiene while he spoke to see if she had said anything about her coming with John.

"Merci. I mean, thank you, Oliver," Catherine answered.

Being Cajun, Catherine grew up speaking a form of French. Oliver's father was Cajun. His mother was Negro. He was raised mostly by his father's people. Oliver spoke English fluently but he preferred to speak French. It was his first language. So when Catherine and Oliver were alone together they spoke French. Sometimes one of them would forget and speak French in front of others. Since most of the people Catherine knew here in the city did not speak French she had to constantly watch herself so she would not be rude.

Janiene knew right away why Oliver had taken John into the kitchen. How stupid she had been to come here with John. What that must have looked like to Oliver. Thank God he had prevented her from seeing Catherine with John. She would have looked like a harlot that was after another woman's husband. Or worse, an adulteress. She felt so stupid, so ashamed.

"Mrs.,uh, Catherine, I really must be going. It was great to see you again."

"I completely forgot John was coming over when I saw you. He called before his school to say he'd be by. I know it would be uncomfortable for you to be here with him." Catherine walked Janiene to the front door.

Oliver had let John out through the carriage way so John could ring the front bell again. Catherine Sommier was a smart woman. She might not question about not hearing the telephone ring but she would definitely notice the absence of both the telephone and the door bells.

John had a nice visit with his mother. Her spirits were surely bright after seeing Janiene. His mother had not, however, told John about her visit with Janiene. John thought it prudent not to bring Janiene up at all.

Barbara was furious when John walked through the door.

"Where have you been, you asshole?" Barbara greeted him.

"What's wrong with you? Hormones again?" John asked dryly.

"Don't play games with me John Sommier! I wondered where you were when you didn't come right home from lunch. So I called Acme to see if you were still there. The guy on the phone said a guy matching your description left with a woman."

"Why would you think I'd come home right after lunch? Think, Barbara, use your brain! If I didn't need to stay out then why the hell would I have lunch out? I would have come home for lunch!" He boomed.

"What about the bimbo you were seen with?"

"I went to my mother's right after lunch. She'll tell you I was alone. Call her and see."

"I'm supposed to call your mother? Yeah, right. Like she wouldn't lie for—"

"Shut up Barb. Shut up now. My mother does not and will not lie for me or anyone. The Sommiers aren't like the Cartwrights. We aren't a family of liars," John said harshly.

"You bastard!" Barbara screamed.

"I told you to shut up," he said.

"Big deal. What if I don't? What's the big man going to do if I don't?"

"I'll spend the evening elsewhere. Maybe even the whole night."

Barbara started to yell at him but noticed the stoniness of his face. He was serious. He would spend the evening or the night out if she didn't shut up.

Barbara wanted him there. She had wanted him there all day.

"Can I fix you something to eat?" Barbara asked in a soft voice.

"No, thanks."

"I'm sorry, John. When the man said he saw someone that looked like you leave with a woman I was crazy with jealously."

John didn't say anything. He just sat there with his arms crossed.

Barbara moved over to him. He knew that look in her eyes. No wonder she wanted him home for lunch. This lady was insatiable. Well, she was his wife, he reasoned. He couldn't allow that beautiful body suffer.

"Come here," John said opening his arms.

Barbara saw the desire in his eyes. She was ready. Boy, was she ready.

Chapter Three

The weeks seemed to be flying by. School was going great. John felt sure he'd pull off all A's. That was damned good considering he was carrying twenty-one units and Barbara had let him get very little sleep this semester.

Lately, however, Barbara was letting John sleep. But only because she had to; she was nearly nine months pregnant.

When the doctor told them to refrain from sexual relations Barbara had been furious. John still couldn't believe she had actually argued with the doctor. She had asked if the baby could be hurt if she was on top! That had been embarrassing. When they left the doctor's office that day the doctor stopped John. With a huge grin on his face the doctor slapped him on the back and whispered that he wished he had a wife like Barbara.

John was glad to have the reprieve. He needed his sleep if he expected to sail through his final exams.

John had seen Janiene once since that day they went to his parent's house. She had been cordial but obviously uncomfortable with him. John wished he could learn to love Barb the way he loved Janiene or at least stop loving Janiene so much.

Janiene was so soft and gentle while Barb was all hell fire. Janiene had never called John a nasty name. Not even when he told her Barb was pregnant. Not even when he told her he would be marrying Barb. Barbara on the other hand...whew! She could make the dock hands on the river blush.

Almost daily Barbara greeted John with some malediction. He had to give her credit though. She had a way of combining her oaths that was downright ingenious. At times her oaths almost elicited laughter rather than anger. He never heard anyone with a mouth as foul as his wife's. Barbara was, however, always the genteel lady in public. When they went out he could depend on his wife to be the epitome of the perfect Southern belle.

Barbara looked at her nude body in the mirror. She slowly turned sideways. God, she was huge. Even if the doctor hadn't forbidden making love she was sure John wouldn't want to. She couldn't blame him, she found her own body repulsive.

She had hated ruining her perfect figure. But, it had been the only way. She knew she would have never gotten John away from Janiene if she hadn't been expecting a baby.

A baby. Barbara hadn't given much thought to an actual baby until now. Damn, there really would be a baby soon. She had prayed for a miscarriage right after they had been married. She had even considered an abortion but couldn't risk John finding out. Besides, she thought, she had probably been too far along by then anyway. So there would be a baby.

Barbara was certain about one thing. No matter what John said, like it or not, they would have a nanny. Preferably a wet nurse.

Barbara didn't much like children. She didn't believe that old axiom about it being different because it was yours. She had little doubt that it would make a difference just because the child was her own. Anyway, her daddy was excited enough for the both of them. Barbara would use that to work in her favor. She felt sure she could get Daddy to pay for the baby nurse.

She thought about money. She couldn't afford a nurse. Not that she didn't receive a generous allowance but she would need every penny once the baby came. As soon as she got her figure back she would order all new clothes. Now that she was married she could order all the black lingerie she wanted to. Her stepmother couldn't say, 'Nice young ladies would never wear something like that.' She would be able to get those low cut dresses too. The pretty silk ones with the chiffon over top. She wouldn't have to depend upon tight sweaters to show off her figure. Finally, she could show as much cleavage as she wanted. At least in evening wear. She would have to see to it that John took her out a lot.

Barbara was glad for one thing about the baby. It was due shortly after Christmas. That would give her time to get her figure back and have her evening gowns made. All before the Mardi Gras balls started. Yes, she thought, everything was working out perfectly.

Well, almost perfectly. She still had to get this damn baby out of her body. Barbara never had a high threshold for pain. She had told the doctor that she wanted to be completely under when he delivered the baby. He had argued but only a little. He told her that there were ways that she would feel little to no pain and still be awake to see the miracle of birth. Blah, Barbara thought. She didn't want to see any bloody, disgusting, crying baby.

She'd see the baby when John saw the baby. When he or she was clean with a diaper and clothes on. That way if the little brat cried John could hold it.

The time was upon him, finals. John wasn't worried about the three finals he had today even though two of them counted for one half of his grade. John had studied so many hours he could practically quote his texts verbatim. He carried an A in all his classes. He wasn't too worried about receiving A's on his finals as well. He was just anxious to get them out of the way.

John was in the bathroom shaving when he heard Barbara cry out.

He ran into the bedroom, his angular chin spotty with white foam. "Barb, what is it? Are you okay?"

"John, call the doctor! I think my water broke and there's so much—" Barbara let out an ear piercing scream.

John ran to telephone the doctor as Barbara swore loud enough for the neighbors to hear.

"Sounds like it's time. Bring her in." The doctor chuckled as he heard more curses in the background.

"It can't be time. She's not due until after Christmas. I've got finals today," John pleaded.

"Bring her in boy. Babies don't care none about due dates or finals. Bring her in, ya hear?" the doctor said impatiently and hung the phone up with a thud.

Barbara seemed to know she had to go to the hospital even before John told her. She had her bag packed and was moving towards the front door.

"Come on, John. Grab my car keys. I'm not riding in your Beetle in my, oh my God, in my condition. Hurry up you bastard!" Barbara was half screaming, half panting.

John drove like a maniac to get Barbara to the hospital. All her screams had him a nervous wreck. The time had come, he was going to be a father in a mere matter of hours.

The doctor hadn't been able to put Barbara under because of some reason John hadn't completely understood. John had been too nervous to listen to the doctor while his wife's cries were echoing off the walls.

Barbara held up considerably well. The nurses tried to ease John's embarrassment by telling him that they had heard far worse than the curses Barbara had uttered. John didn't think that was possible. He could hear her clearly, loudly, two doors down in the waiting room. Yet, after fourteen long hours the nurse came in the room to tell John that his wife had given birth.

John was in awe of the beauty of his son. Dark hair, lots of it, pink skin and blue eyes like his mother's. He was a Sommier all right. He weighed nine pounds seven ounces and was twenty-three inches long. Barbara insisted they name their son after John. John Jackson Sommier Junior. They would call him John Jr..

"My Daddy will be coming by later today. I can't believe all the flowers I've gotten," Barb said with her face glowing. "And the gifts, did you see all the gifts?"

John had never seen Barb more beautiful. He thought she glowed with excitement of having a baby, his baby.

Barbara truly was glowing. Glowing from all the gifts. There were silver cups, spoons, bowls and wonderful silk dressing gowns for her.

But she was especially glowing with the news that Daddy had found a suitable wet nurse.

"My parents will be here tonight. They sure are anxious to see John Jr.. I think Mom cried when I told her she had a big healthy grandson," John said.

"Daddy was nearly the same way. Why he went right out and got me a nurse for the baby."

"Barb, I thought we agreed. I thought there would be no nurse for the baby."

"No, John, we did not agree. You decided for us, for me really. I have decided that I do need help. You'll be at school most of the time." Barbara saw a deep frown etch his face. "John please. Please don't go into one of you moods."

"I'm not."

"Oh really? Then why the sour puss?"

John tried to smile but a furrow was still etched between his brows. "I'm sorry, I just realized I missed my finals yesterday. I've also got three more finals tomorrow."

"Oh no. Can you make them up? Surely they'll understand when you tell them your wife had a baby."

"I don't know. Not too many professors smile upon students being married. They think you should get an education first. I mean it's okay for you girls, you don't have to support your families. One professor, Professor Burton, says a smart man never marries before he's at least thirty. I'm fairly sure he won't allow a make up."

"Well that's the most ridiculous thing I've ever heard. You just tell that old son of a bit—"

"Let's not worry about that now. Barbara, you're going to have to start watching your language in front of the baby. As far as that nurse business goes, we will give it a whirl. You are the one who will be with John Jr. twenty-four hours a day."

Not her, thought Barbara, the nurse. Barbara was going to spend all her mornings out. She'd start by going to the ladies gym.

Judge Cartwright arrived with all the pomp and circumstance he was known for. He came with a three foot teddy bear in one arm and a mink stole in the other.

"Hi Darlin'! Where's my new grandson?" Judge Cartwright boomed.

"Hi Daddy. I'll ring for the nurse and have her bring him. Why that's the biggest teddy bear I've ever seen."

"The bear is for my grandson but this stole is for you." he said and handed her the mink.

"Oh my, it is gorgeous. Whatever are you giving it to me now for? It's not Christmas yet."

"It's not your Christmas gift either. It's a thank you for giving me a grandson."

The nurse walked in with John Jr.. John followed them in. He had been down getting some coffee.

"Whoa, give him to me, that's right. He's a mighty big fella. Right cute too. Hi there John Jr.. I'm your Granddaddy." Cartwright cooed at the baby.

"Hello Judge." John stood along the side of Barb's bed.

"You must be proud of my daughter for the beautiful boy she bore you'" Judge Cartwright said gruffly.

"Yes sir. My son is a beauty. Look at the size of him. He's all Sommier," John goaded.

"Well son, I'm no small man myself," Judge Cartwright countered.

"I was speaking more of strength and length rather than girth." John eyed the Judge's protruding gut.

"Will you two stop it? Don't you think you could be civil for just one day?" Barbara asked.

"Well Sommier, you have to admit one thing," Judge Cartwright said with a smile.

"What's that, sir?"

"Those eyes are the eyes of a Cartwright."

John had to agree with that.

"John, oh John, look what Daddy brought me. Isn't this stole just the thing? It's wonderful and it's not even my Christmas present,"

Barbara beamed. "Oh, he brought the teddy bear for John Jr.," she added as an after thought.

"That's real nice sweetheart. That bear is really something. We'll have to watch it or John Jr. will be spoiled rotten," John said.

"I intend him to be!" Judge Cartwright boomed.

"Sorry Judge, I can't have my son growing up thinking the sun rises and sets only for him," John said.

"Why the hell not? If I had my way, it would. You don't know how lucky you are to have a son. Why if you were any sort of man at all you'd give that boy of yours the world on a silver platter," Judge Cartwright barked.

"Really? What kind of man would I truly be if I did that? I'd be up robbing my own son of his manhood. One day John Jr. will want to go out there and get the world for himself. That's what I want. I want to raise a man, not a weak pathetic excuse for one," John answered through clenched teeth.

"Okay, okay, calm down. Point taken," Judge Cartwright said thoughtfully.

"I believe I asked you two to try and be civil," Barbara said annoyed.

Tiny John Jr. squirmed in his Granddaddy's arms. That brought an enormous grin to the face of the judge. In the judge's arms, John Jr. looked so small and so pale. Judge Cartwright had a bright pink coloring as if he always had a severe sunburn. John Jr.'s color certainly couldn't compare with that.

"I'll have that wet nurse in tomorrow, Darlin'," Judge Cartwright said as he continued to look at his grandson.

"Wait a minute. You didn't say anything about a wet nurse!" John's eyes bore down on Barbara.

"Well, John I've got a problem. We have to have a wet nurse," Barbara said evenly.

"What problem?" he demanded.

Barbara had to think fast. She couldn't tell him the truth. She couldn't tell him that she didn't want to be bogged down with having to feed the baby. She didn't want to worry about embarrassing wet spots. She didn't want to take a chance that the added weight from the milk would cause her breasts to sag. Hell, she didn't want to have to fool with bottles either.

She motioned for John to come closer so she could whisper. "The doctor said since my breasts are so large that the extra weight from the milk would be too hard on my back."

John believed her explanation. He had been there when the doctor had told her if she wanted to breast feed she'd have to take extra precautions due to her breast size. The doctor didn't push breast feeding too much anyway. Bottle feeding was all the vogue right now.

John turned to Judge Cartwright. "I'll want to know a lot more about this woman before I'll let my son suckle at her breast," John said seriously.

"I can tell you everything you need to know, Sommier. You don't think I'd let just anyone be wet nurse to my grandson, do you?" Judge Cartwright asked. "What's say you and I go down and get some food. Barbie and my grandson can rest whilst you and I talk."

"Oh Daddy, don't go," Barbara pleaded.

"I'll be back soon, Darlin'. Get yourself some shut eye." The judge handed her the baby.

Apparently the judge had been very hungry. He bought out half of the cafeteria. John decided some gumbo and a piece of crusty bread would be enough for him.

They seated themselves under the bright florescent lights in the stark hospital cafeteria. The judge had been picking at his food all the way to the table. He wasn't even seated before a quarter of his food was devoured.

"What do you want to know, son?" Judge Cartwright asked, his mouth full.

John swallowed his food before he answered. "Who is this 'nurse'? Is she really a nurse? Is she of high moral fiber? Is she-?

"Whoa there! You've gotta give me time to answer, Boy," Judge Cartwright interrupted.

"Let's see now if I can remember all your questions. Her name's Lacy Washington. No, she's not trained as a nurse but she's a Colored and I expect she's been caring for young ones all of her life. She's nineteen, a real looker if you know what I mean. She acts right respectful like she should. Let's see what else? Oh yeah, she's not married. She had a bastard some two and a half years ago. Her momma's been looking after that one and Lacy's been wet nursing ever since. Is she of high moral fiber? Well—she's a Colored girl and a wet nurse, need I say more? Like I said, the girl is right respectful. Knows her place. That's what's important when you're dealing with her kind." Judge Cartwright finished.

John was about to pop a gasket. He hated the damn racists of the South. He knew some were truly ignorant and could be educated. Those people didn't bother him much. He hated the ones that thought they were superior. The ones who felt it necessary to always belittle someone. The ones who were always tooting their own horns at the expense of someone else.

John had found out long ago the biggest racists were the people who were the most insecure. Those people claimed there was an inferior race. They always needed to put someone down in order to put themselves up. Others who were insecure would readily agree with them. While still more agreed out of ignorance or fear of someone that looked or sounded different from themselves. It was easy for people to believe they were superior. It did wonders for the ego. So hatred filled the South. Hell, John thought, it filled all of America.

"I can see by your face that you're upset, What is it? Don't you want a colored girl feeding your boy? I thought you were one of them bleeding heart liberals. Your type preaches equal rights but wouldn't let one of their kind in your house to clean it," Judge Cartwright said.

John had to take a few deep breaths. He had to calm down before he responded to this old bastard. He didn't want to make a scene.

"I'm going to try to make this as clear as possible. I don't care for your remarks, sir. You're right, I am a liberal. If because I care about others that makes me a bleeding heart, so be it. And you're right again, I wouldn't have a Negro in my house to clean—"

"See, boy, I was right about—" Judge Cartwright tried to interrupt.

"Let me finish, damn it. I wouldn't let a Negro clean my house because I've got your daughter to clean my house," John said smugly.

John could see the fury welling up in his father-in-law but he continued, "I don't see what Lacy Washington's race has to do with her moral fiber. If I hadn't married Barbara, John Jr. would be a bastard right now. Does that mean all White princesses are of low moral fiber? I doubt it."

"Now you wait a damn minute. You aren't gonna to compare my daughter to a Colored girl. Don't you see the difference, boy? You married Barbara because you're White, because we aren't like animals. We don't fornicate like dogs. If one of ours gets pregnant, we take responsibility. Their kind doesn't. Hell, Lacy's baby is half White. She knew no White man would ever marry her. Still she lay with him. Just like a bitch in heat," Judge Cartwright said with conviction,

"If I hadn't married your daughter would you be telling your friends that Barb laid with me 'like a bitch in heat'? Come on, I didn't have to marry Barb. I sure as hell didn't marry her to save her good name. I married her for the sake of my child. What does that say for the bastard who fathered Lacy's child? This man is supposed to be better than Lacy? I think he's the one who's like a dog." John threw his spoon down in his half eaten gumbo. "There's no point of arguing this with you," John said disgustedly. "You are too narrow minded to see the truth. What kind of judge are you? You judge Lacy but not her child's father. Where is the fairness to that?"

"I'm a damn good judge! I'll not allow you to attack my character!" Judge Cartwright yelled.

Cartwright's face had turned two shades of purple. He pushed his chest and his huge gut out like a rooster ready to crow.

John didn't care. He was sick of hearing attitudes like Cartwright's. Why couldn't people apply their reasoning to both races? John couldn't understand why it was if a Negro did something wrong or immoral it's because they're inferior. John was sick of that argument besides it wasn't what they had come down here to discuss.

"Judge, I could argue with you 'til I'm blue in the face but it wouldn't do any good," he said with a sigh. "It's my son's first day of life. I don't want to spend it arguing with you. I will meet Lacy myself. I'll decide if she'd be good with my son, understand?"

John got up and slammed his chair into the table. He started to walk away but then, suddenly, turned back.

"You'll start showing me some respect too. You may call me John or Mr. Sommier. You will stop calling me boy or just Sommier. If you don't, I won't allow you to see John Jr.," John said firmly.

"Well, you're as touchy as a Colored man 'bout what you're called," Judge Cartwright said tersely.

"I don't think it's a matter of race. It's a matter of respect. You show people respect and they won't complain about not getting respect. That's not such a difficult concept, is it?," John scowled at the judge.

John wanted to get back upstairs to his son. He also wanted to calm down before his parents came. He knew where to go to calm his mind.

John stopped by the nursery. Seeing his son would surely improve his mood. His eyes searched through the window until he came upon John Jr.. He was filled with pride. John stood there for a long time admiring his son. So big for a newborn yet so tiny. John couldn't believe how much he loved his boy. His whole heart was filled with love.

The six other babies were no match for John Jr.'s size and color. Every parent wanted to believe that their baby was the smartest or the best looking. John decided that his son really was the best looking. John hoped his son would prove to be the smartest too.

John Jr. was squirming. The nurse went to him and began changing his diaper. John tapped on the glass.

The nurse finished changing the baby. She put John Jr. down and motioned to John to walk over to the door. The nurse stepped out of the nursery. "May I help you, Sir?" she said.

"I see my son's awake. Can you bring him to my wife's room now? My parents will be here shortly to see John Jr.." John beamed.

"Your son is John Sommier, right? Let me check his chart," the nurse said before she walked back into the nursery. The nurse checked the chart. She popped her head back out the door. "Mr. Sommier, your son has to be fed right now. I'll bring him by the room after he's been fed. He'll probably be sleeping by then."

"That's okay. Thank you." John said softly.

John walked back to the room. When he walked in Barbara was sleeping peacefully.

John could really use some sleep too. If he expected to make it though his finals tomorrow he'd need some sleep soon.

John hoped that old fat windbag had already come and gone. John was too tired to go another nine rounds with the judge.

John eased into the chair next to Barb's bed. It wasn't long before he had drifted off.

"Thank you, Mother and Father." Barbara said as she took the baby blanket.

John began to stir at the sound of voices.

"Hi Mom and Dad. What do you think of your grandson?" John said through his fingers which covered his openmouthed yawn.

John got up stretching his arms over his head and offered his mother his chair with a sweeping motion of his hand.

Catherine Sommier took the chair. "He's simply beautiful. He's—"

"John Jr. is one of the best looking babies I've ever seen. He's all Sommier too!" John's father interrupted his mother.

"You haven't seen him awake yet. Have you? John Jr. has blue eyes like Barb's." John said.

"Yes. His eyes are Cartwright eyes. They are just like mine. They are as blue as the midnight sky." Barbara said proudly.

"You had blue eyes John when you were a baby too. Your eyes changed when you were about eight months. Your father used to tease me until your eyes changed. You see, no one on either side of the family had blue eyes. Our milkman did have blue eyes. See what a terrible man your father was? Suggesting such an impropriety of his wife." Catherine Sommier chuckled.

"That's true. If your eyes hadn't changed to green I was going to change milk services." John's father teased.

"You'll have to wait and see. The baby's eyes could change at any time until he's a year or so." John's mother said.

"Barb's father was here. Did you have a chance to see him?" John asked his parents.

"Daddy came back and said his good-byes before you got back, John." Barbara answered for them.

Good. John had hoped he wouldn't have to see that pompous racist again today. He was glad his parents didn't have to be subjected to the judge either. They didn't like Cartwright any better than he did.

John's parents left after a short visit. They said they didn't want to tire Barbara or the baby out. John Jr. had been returned to the nursery for the night. Barbara looked like she hadn't slept in days.

"Barb, I'm going to get out of here for the night. I'll be back after my finals tomorrow." John promised.

"Do you have to go now? Can't you stay with me a little longer?" Barbara whimpered.

"Sure, Barb, why not?"

John thought Barbara probably felt pretty alone at the hospital. He'd wait until she fell asleep before he left. He didn't have a long wait.

The rest of John's finals had gone without a hitch. John felt sure he would get A's in those classes. John was trying to get make up exams for the finals he missed.

So far he was fifty-fifty. His Poli Sci professor had given him a green light. The exam only counted for twenty-five percent of his grade. The professor graded on a curve. He had told John, even if he didn't make up the final he would still probably get an A. Probably. John would make it up.

His Art of Speech professor hadn't been so generous. The exam had counted for fifty percent of his grade. The professor informed John that the grade on his final was an automatic F. No explanations necessary. The grade would stand. Luckily that professor graded on a curve too. John might pull off a B rather than a C.

Now John was headed to Professor Burton's office. At first John thought he'd be wiser if he just let the grade stand. Professor Burton was notorious for his speeches on ethics. Understandably so, Professor Burton taught Ethics. Of course, he did not grade on a curve. At least, John thought, Professor Burton averaged the letter grade thus far with the final letter grade like his other teaches did. If John couldn't make up the exam he'd definitely get a C in the course.

John knocked upon the Professor's outer office door. There was no answer but the light was on. John knocked again.

"Lilian, Lilian get that door!" Professor Burton growled.

There was still no answer so John continued knocking.

Professor Burton walked into the outer office to find his secretary gone for the day. He must have lost track of time again.

"Stop that incessant knocking! I'm coming. Just a minute." Professor Burton said irritably.

When the professor opened the door he did not seem surprised. Quite the contrary, he looked as if he had been expecting John.

"Come in Mr. Sommier. Come back into my office." Professor Burton stopped to clear a stack of books from a chair for John to sit in. "What is it that I can do for you, Mr. Sommier?" Professor Burton inquired.

"Well, Sir, as you know I missed my final exam the day before yesterday. I would like to explain my situation in the hope that you will allow a make up exam." John nervously tapped a pencil on his knee.

"You have been a good student all semester, Mr. Sommier. I'll hear your explanation as long as you, Sir, are not tedious. It has been a long day." Professor Burton frowned before he continued, "I will warn you however, you have little chance of gaining a make up exam from me."

"Thank you for at least hearing me out." John continued determinedly, "My wife gave birth to our son on the day of your final. I had to take her to the hospital early in the morning. She was in labor all day."

"Congratulations are in order then." Professor Burton said without feeling. "If I am to even consider a make up exam you will have to answer some questions for me."

"Yes, Sir, anything you'd like to know." John replied.

"You seem awfully young to have a wife that's having a child. Are you a freshman, just out of high school?"

"Yes Sir."

"How long have you been married, Mr. Sommier?"

"For the better part of a year, Professor." John answered as he wondered where this was going.

"It's the end of December. You got out of high school in May yet you've been married for the better part of a year. So your parents allowed you to marry while you were in high school?"

"No sir, they did not. I didn't say I had been married the better part of a year but rather the year. Starting school at Tulane has been the better part of my year."

"Ah, Sir, semantics. You must be more straightforward or our conversation, and your make up chances, are finished right now. Straightforward now! Exactly how long have you been married?" Professor Burton questioned.

"Since the end of June."

"Yet your wife had a baby two days ago. Was the baby early?" Professor Burton arched his right brow.

"Yes, the baby was early." John paused. He could see what the professor was getting at. "The baby came almost two weeks early." John added quietly.

"So you impregnated your wife before you married her. You then had to get married, I suppose. Is that correct?"

"I fail to see where any of this is any of your business, sir!" John said irately.

"Don't you? Mr. Sommier, I teach Ethics. Do you feel it's ethical for me to allow you to make up your exam under your circumstances?"

"I worked hard all semester in your class. With the exception of the final exam, I never missed your class."

"You cannot make exception there. That, Sir, is why you are here."

"Yes, but if it hadn't-

Professor Burton cut him off, "Do you think your situation is ethical?"

"Perhaps not, but I still fail to see that as a basis for your decision."

"On what else would I base my decision? The validity of any excuse must be based on ethics. Do you understand what I mean?"

"Yes, I suppose."

"Would it be fair for me to allow a man who broke society's rules to, then, bend university rules because of his first action?"

"Well, one doesn't necessarily affect the other."

"This one has affected the other. If you had staid your intimacy until after marriage you would not be in my office now. Tulane University does not accept all who come to her doors. I cannot bend the rules and lower the school's standards. Your request is denied."

"Professor Burton if I can't make up this exam I'll get a C." he pleaded.

"Sometimes our actions have ramifications well in to the future, Mr. Sommier. You could not have known all the ways your actions would affect you. You still probably do not know. My class could not begin to teach all the consequences of unethical behavior. It seems, Sir, you will gain a fair understanding though life experience."

"That's it? Your answer is no."

"Mr. Sommier, did you come to Tulane to learn or for the grades?" Professor Burton asked.

"Both." John answered truthfully.

"Good. I believe that you have learned something and I will give you a grade, a C."

John left the professor's office. John surprised himself, he wasn't angry. The professor had been right.

John had known the ramifications for his actions were long reaching. He had married a woman he didn't love. He had messed up many relationships. He had a son that he'd have to raise and support. He wasn't able to go to Harvard for his undergrad work. He would never have guessed this would have affected his finals. He had learned something. Something valuable.

Chapter Four

The weeks seemed to be flying by. School was going great. John felt sure he'd pull off all A's. That was damned good considering he was carrying twenty-one units and Barbara had let him get very little sleep this semester.

Lately, however, Barbara was letting John sleep. But only because she had to; she was nearly nine months pregnant.

When the doctor told them to refrain from sexual relations Barbara had been furious. John still couldn't believe she had actually argued with the doctor. She had asked if the baby could be hurt if she was on top! That had been embarrassing. When they left the doctor's office that day the doctor stopped John. With a huge grin on his face the doctor slapped him on the back and whispered that he wished he had a wife like Barbara.

John was glad to have the reprieve. He needed his sleep if he expected to sail through his final exams.

John had seen Janiene once since that day they went to his parent's house. She had been cordial but obviously uncomfortable with him. John wished he could learn to love Barb the way he loved Janiene or at least stop loving Janiene so much.

Janiene was so soft and gentle while Barb was all hell fire. Janiene had never called John a nasty name. Not even when he told her Barb was pregnant. Not even when he told her he would be marrying Barb. Barbara on the other hand...whew! She could make the dock hands on the river blush.

Almost daily Barbara greeted John with some malediction. He had to give her credit though. She had a way of combining her oaths that was downright ingenious. At times her oaths almost elicited laughter rather than anger. He never heard anyone with a mouth as foul as his wife's. Barbara was, however, always the genteel lady in public. When they went out he could depend on his wife to be the epitome of the perfect Southern belle.

Barbara looked at her nude body in the mirror. She slowly turned sideways. God, she was huge. Even if the doctor hadn't forbidden making love she was sure John wouldn't want to. She couldn't blame him, she found her own body repulsive.

She had hated ruining her perfect figure. But, it had been the only way. She knew she would have never gotten John away from Janiene if she hadn't been expecting a baby.

A baby. Barbara hadn't given much thought to an actual baby until now. Damn, there really would be a baby soon. She had prayed for a miscarriage right after they had been married. She had even considered an abortion but couldn't risk John finding out. Besides, she thought, she had probably been too far along by then anyway. So there would be a baby.

Barbara was certain about one thing. No matter what John said, like it or not, they would have a nanny. Preferably a wet nurse.

Barbara didn't much like children. She didn't believe that old axiom about it being different because it was yours. She had little doubt that it would make a difference just because the child was her own. Anyway, her daddy was excited enough for the both of them. Barbara would use that to work in her favor. She felt sure she could get Daddy to pay for the baby nurse.

She thought about money. She couldn't afford a nurse. Not that she didn't receive a generous allowance but she would need every penny once the baby came. As soon as she got her figure back she would order all new clothes. Now that she was married she could order all the black lingerie she wanted to. Her stepmother couldn't say, 'Nice young ladies would never wear something like that.' She would be able to get those low cut dresses too. The pretty silk ones with the chiffon over top. She wouldn't have to depend upon tight sweaters to show off her figure. Finally, she could show as much cleavage as she wanted. At least in evening wear. She would have to see to it that John took her out a lot.

Barbara was glad for one thing about the baby. It was due shortly after Christmas. That would give her time to get her figure back and have her evening gowns made. All before the Mardi Gras balls started. Yes, she thought, everything was working out perfectly.

Well, almost perfectly. She still had to get this damn baby out of her body. Barbara never had a high threshold for pain. She had told the doctor that she wanted to be completely under when he delivered the baby. He had argued but only a little. He told her that there were ways that she would feel little to no pain and still be awake to see the miracle of birth. Blah, Barbara thought. She didn't want to see any bloody, disgusting, crying baby.

She'd see the baby when John saw the baby. When he or she was clean with a diaper and clothes on. That way if the little brat cried John could hold it.

The time was upon him, finals. John wasn't worried about the three finals he had today even though two of them counted for one half of his grade. John had studied so many hours he could practically quote his texts verbatim. He carried an A in all his classes. He wasn't too worried about receiving A's on his finals as well. He was just anxious to get them out of the way.

John was in the bathroom shaving when he heard Barbara cry out.

He ran into the bedroom, his angular chin spotty with white foam. "Barb, what is it? Are you okay?"

"John, call the doctor! I think my water broke and there's so much—" Barbara let out an ear piercing scream.

John ran to telephone the doctor as Barbara swore loud enough for the neighbors to hear.

"Sounds like it's time. Bring her in." The doctor chuckled as he heard more curses in the background.

"It can't be time. She's not due until after Christmas. I've got finals today," John pleaded.

"Bring her in boy. Babies don't care none about due dates or finals. Bring her in, ya hear?" the doctor said impatiently and hung the phone up with a thud.

Barbara seemed to know she had to go to the hospital even before John told her. She had her bag packed and was moving towards the front door.

"Come on, John. Grab my car keys. I'm not riding in your Beetle in my, oh my God, in my condition. Hurry up you bastard!" Barbara was half screaming, half panting.

John drove like a maniac to get Barbara to the hospital. All her screams had him a nervous wreck. The time had come, he was going to be a father in a mere matter of hours.

The doctor hadn't been able to put Barbara under because of some reason John hadn't completely understood. John had been too nervous to listen to the doctor while his wife's cries were echoing off the walls.

Barbara held up considerably well. The nurses tried to ease John's embarrassment by telling him that they had heard far worse than the curses Barbara had uttered. John didn't think that was possible. He could hear her clearly, loudly, two doors down in the waiting room. Yet, after fourteen long hours the nurse came in the room to tell John that his wife had given birth.

John was in awe of the beauty of his son. Dark hair, lots of it, pink skin and blue eyes like his mother's. He was a Sommier all right. He weighed nine pounds seven ounces and was twenty-three inches long. Barbara insisted they name their son after John. John Jackson Sommier Junior. They would call him John Jr..

"My Daddy will be coming by later today. I can't believe all the flowers I've gotten," Barb said with her face glowing. "And the gifts, did you see all the gifts?"

John had never seen Barb more beautiful. He thought she glowed with excitement of having a baby, his baby.

Barbara truly was glowing. Glowing from all the gifts. There were silver cups, spoons, bowls and wonderful silk dressing gowns for her.

But she was especially glowing with the news that Daddy had found a suitable wet nurse.

"My parents will be here tonight. They sure are anxious to see John Jr.. I think Mom cried when I told her she had a big healthy grandson," John said.

"Daddy was nearly the same way. Why he went right out and got me a nurse for the baby."

"Barb, I thought we agreed. I thought there would be no nurse for the baby."

"No, John, we did not agree. You decided for us, for me really. I have decided that I do need help. You'll be at school most of the time." Barbara saw a deep frown etch his face. "John please. Please don't go into one of you moods."

"I'm not."

"Oh really? Then why the sour puss?"

John tried to smile but a furrow was still etched between his brows. "I'm sorry; I just realized I missed my finals yesterday. I've also got three more finals tomorrow."

"Oh no. Can you make them up? Surely they'll understand when you tell them your wife had a baby."

"I don't know. Not too many professors smile upon students being married. They think you should get an education first. I mean it's okay for you girls, you don't have to support your families. One professor, Professor Burton, says a smart man never marries before he's at least thirty. I'm fairly sure he won't allow a make up."

"Well that's the most ridiculous thing I've ever heard. You just tell that old son of a bit—"

"Let's not worry about that now. Barbara, you're going to have to start watching your language in front of the baby. As far as that nurse business goes, we will give it a whirl. You are the one who will be with John Jr. twenty-four hours a day."

Not her, thought Barbara, the nurse. Barbara was going to spend all her mornings out. She'd start by going to the ladies gym.

Judge Cartwright arrived with all the pomp and circumstance he was known for. He came with a three foot teddy bear in one arm and a mink stole in the other.

"Hi Darlin'! Where's my new grandson?" Judge Cartwright boomed.

"Hi Daddy. I'll ring for the nurse and have her bring him. Why that's the biggest teddy bear I've ever seen."

"The bear is for my grandson but this stole is for you." he said and handed her the mink.

"Oh my, it is gorgeous. Whatever are you giving it to me now for? It's not Christmas yet."

"It's not your Christmas gift either. It's a thank you for giving me a grandson."

The nurse walked in with John Jr.. John followed them in. He had been down getting some coffee.

"Whoa, give him to me, that's right. He's a mighty big fella. Right cute too. Hi there John Jr.. I'm your Granddaddy." Cartwright cooed at the baby.

"Hello Judge." John stood along the side of Barb's bed.

"You must be proud of my daughter for the beautiful boy she bore you'" Judge Cartwright said gruffly.

"Yes sir. My son is a beauty. Look at the size of him. He's all Sommier," John goaded.

"Well son, I'm no small man myself," Judge Cartwright countered.

"I was speaking more of strength and length rather than girth." John eyed the Judge's protruding gut.

"Will you two stop it? Don't you think you could be civil for just one day?" Barbara asked.

"Well Sommier, you have to admit one thing," Judge Cartwright said with a smile.

"What's that, sir?"

"Those eyes are the eyes of a Cartwright."

John had to agree with that.

"John, oh John, look what Daddy brought me. Isn't this stole just the thing? It's wonderful and it's not even my Christmas present,"

Barbara beamed. "Oh, he brought the teddy bear for John Jr.," she added as an after thought.

"That's real nice sweetheart. That bear is really something. We'll have to watch it or John Jr. will be spoiled rotten," John said.

"I intend him to be!" Judge Cartwright boomed.

"Sorry Judge, I can't have my son growing up thinking the sun rises and sets only for him," John said.

"Why the hell not? If I had my way, it would. You don't know how lucky you are to have a son. Why if you were any sort of man at all you'd give that boy of yours the world on a silver platter," Judge Cartwright barked.

"Really? What kind of man would I truly be if I did that? I'd be up robbing my own son of his manhood. One day John Jr. will want to go out there and get the world for himself. That's what I want. I want to raise a man, not a weak pathetic excuse for one," John answered through clenched teeth.

"Okay, okay, calm down. Point taken," Judge Cartwright said thoughtfully.

"I believe I asked you two to try and be civil," Barbara said annoyed.

Tiny John Jr. squirmed in his Granddaddy's arms. That brought an enormous grin to the face of the judge. In the judge's arms, John Jr. looked so small and so pale. Judge Cartwright had a bright pink coloring as if he always had a severe sunburn. John Jr.'s color certainly couldn't compare with that.

"I'll have that wet nurse in tomorrow, Darlin'," Judge Cartwright said as he continued to look at his grandson.

"Wait a minute. You didn't say anything about a wet nurse!" John's eyes bore down on Barbara.

"Well, John I've got a problem. We have to have a wet nurse," Barbara said evenly.

"What problem?" he demanded.

Barbara had to think fast. She couldn't tell him the truth. She couldn't tell him that she didn't want to be bogged down with having to feed the baby. She didn't want to worry about embarrassing wet spots. She didn't want to take a chance that the added weight from the milk would cause her breasts to sag. Hell, she didn't want to have to fool with bottles either.

She motioned for John to come closer so she could whisper. "The doctor said since my breasts are so large that the extra weight from the milk would be too hard on my back."

John believed her explanation. He had been there when the doctor had told her if she wanted to breast feed she'd have to take extra precautions due to her breast size. The doctor didn't push breast feeding too much anyway. Bottle feeding was all the vogue right now.

John turned to Judge Cartwright. "I'll want to know a lot more about this woman before I'll let my son suckle at her breast," John said seriously.

"I can tell you everything you need to know, Sommier. You don't think I'd let just anyone be wet nurse to my grandson, do you?" Judge Cartwright asked. "What's say you and I go down and get some food. Barbie and my grandson can rest whilst you and I talk."

"Oh Daddy, don't go," Barbara pleaded.

"I'll be back soon, Darlin'. Get yourself some shut eye." The judge handed her the baby.

Apparently the judge had been very hungry. He bought out half of the cafeteria. John decided some gumbo and a piece of crusty bread would be enough for him.

They seated themselves under the bright florescent lights in the stark hospital cafeteria. The judge had been picking at his food all the way to the table. He wasn't even seated before a quarter of his food was devoured.

"What do you want to know, son?" Judge Cartwright asked, his mouth full.

John swallowed his food before he answered. "Who is this 'nurse'? Is she really a nurse? Is she of high moral fiber? Is she-?

"Whoa there! You've gotta give me time to answer, Boy," Judge Cartwright interrupted.

"Let's see now if I can remember all your questions. Her name's Lacy Washington. No, she's not trained as a nurse but she's a Colored and I expect she's been caring for young ones all of her life. She's nineteen, a real looker if you know what I mean. She acts right respectful like she should. Let's see what else? Oh yeah, she's not married. She had a bastard some two and a half years ago. Her momma's been looking after that one and Lacy's been wet nursing ever since. Is she of high moral fiber? Well—she's a Colored girl and a wet nurse, need I say more? Like I said, the girl is right respectful. Knows her place. That's what's important when you're dealing with her kind." Judge Cartwright finished.

John was about to pop a gasket. He hated the damn racists of the South. He knew some were truly ignorant and could be educated. Those people didn't bother him much. He hated the ones that thought they were superior. The ones who felt it necessary to always belittle someone. The ones who were always tooting their own horns at the expense of someone else.

John had found out long ago the biggest racists were the people who were the most insecure. Those people claimed there was an inferior race. They always needed to put someone down in order to put themselves up. Others who were insecure would readily agree with them. While still more agreed out of ignorance or fear of someone that looked or sounded different from themselves. It was easy for people to believe they were superior. It did wonders for the ego. So hatred filled the South. Hell, John thought, it filled all of America.

"I can see by your face that you're upset, What is it? Don't you want a colored girl feeding your boy? I thought you were one of them bleeding heart liberals. Your type preaches equal rights but wouldn't let one of their kind in your house to clean it," Judge Cartwright said.

John had to take a few deep breaths. He had to calm down before he responded to this old bastard. He didn't want to make a scene.

"I'm going to try to make this as clear as possible. I don't care for your remarks, sir. You're right, I am a liberal. If because I care about others that makes me a bleeding heart, so be it. And you're right again, I wouldn't have a Negro in my house to clean—"

"See, boy, I was right about—" Judge Cartwright tried to interrupt.

"Let me finish, damn it. I wouldn't let a Negro clean my house because I've got your daughter to clean my house," John said smugly.

John could see the fury welling up in his father-in-law but he continued, "I don't see what Lacy Washington's race has to do with her moral fiber. If I hadn't married Barbara, John Jr. would be a bastard right now. Does that mean all White princesses are of low moral fiber? I doubt it."

"Now you wait a damn minute. You aren't gonna to compare my daughter to a Colored girl. Don't you see the difference, boy? You married Barbara because you're White, because we aren't like animals. We don't fornicate like dogs. If one of ours gets pregnant, we take responsibility. Their kind doesn't. Hell, Lacy's baby is half White. She knew no White man would ever marry her. Still she laid with him. Just like a bitch in heat," Judge Cartwright said with conviction,

"If I hadn't married your daughter would you be telling your friends that Barb laid with me 'like a bitch in heat'? Come on, I didn't have to marry Barb. I sure as hell didn't marry her to save her good name. I married her for the sake of my child. What does that say for the bastard who fathered Lacy's child? This man is supposed to be better than Lacy? I think he's the one who's like a dog." John threw his spoon down in his half eaten gumbo. "There's no point of arguing this with you," John said disgustedly. "You are too narrow minded to see the truth. What kind of judge are you? You judge Lacy but not her child's father. Where is the fairness to that?"

"I'm a damn good judge! I'll not allow you to attack my character!" Judge Cartwright yelled.

Cartwright's face had turned two shades of purple. He pushed his chest and his huge gut out like a rooster ready to crow.

John didn't care. He was sick of hearing attitudes like Cartwright's. Why couldn't people apply their reasoning to both races? John couldn't understand why it was if a Negro did something wrong or immoral it's because they're inferior. John was sick of that argument besides it wasn't what they had come down here to discuss.

"Judge, I could argue with you 'til I'm blue in the face but it wouldn't do any good," he said with a sigh. "It's my son's first day of life. I don't want to spend it arguing with you. I will meet Lacy myself. I'll decide if she'd be good with my son, understand?"

John got up and slammed his chair into the table. He started to walk away but then, suddenly, turned back.

"You'll start showing me some respect too. You may call me John or Mr. Sommier. You will stop calling me boy or just Sommier. If you don't, I won't allow you to see John Jr.," John said firmly.

"Well, you're as touchy as a Colored man 'bout what you're called," Judge Cartwright said tersely.

"I don't think it's a matter of race. It's a matter of respect. You show people respect and they won't complain about not getting respect. That's not such a difficult concept, is it?," John scowled at the judge.

John wanted to get back upstairs to his son. He also wanted to calm down before his parents came. He knew where to go to calm his mind.

John stopped by the nursery. Seeing his son would surely improve his mood. His eyes searched through the window until he came upon John Jr.. He was filled with pride. John stood there for a long time admiring his son. So big for a newborn yet so tiny. John couldn't believe how much he loved his boy. His whole heart was filled with love.

The six other babies were no match for John Jr.'s size and color. Every parent wanted to believe that their baby was the smartest or the best looking. John decided that his son really was the best looking. John hoped his son would prove to be the smartest too.

John Jr. was squirming. The nurse went to him and began changing his diaper. John tapped on the glass.

The nurse finished changing the baby. She put John Jr. down and motioned to John to walk over to the door. The nurse stepped out of the nursery. "May I help you, Sir?" she said.

"I see my son's awake. Can you bring him to my wife's room now? My parents will be here shortly to see John Jr.." John beamed.

"Your son is John Sommier, right? Let me check his chart," the nurse said before she walked back into the nursery. The nurse checked the chart. She popped her head back out the door. "Mr. Sommier, your son has to be fed right now. I'll bring him by the room after he's been fed. He'll probably be sleeping by then."

"That's okay. Thank you." John said softly.

John walked back to the room. When he walked in Barbara was sleeping peacefully.

John could really use some sleep too. If he expected to make it though his finals tomorrow he'd need some sleep soon.

John hoped that old fat windbag had already come and gone. John was too tired to go another nine rounds with the judge.

John eased into the chair next to Barb's bed. It wasn't long before he had drifted off.

"Thank you, Mother and Father." Barbara said as she took the baby blanket.

John began to stir at the sound of voices.

"Hi Mom and Dad. What do you think of your grandson?" John said through his fingers which covered his openmouthed yawn.

John got up stretching his arms over his head and offered his mother his chair with a sweeping motion of his hand.

Catherine Sommier took the chair. "He's simply beautiful. He's—"

"John Jr. is one of the best looking babies I've ever seen. He's all Sommier too!" John's father interrupted his mother.

"You haven't seen him awake yet. Have you? John Jr. has blue eyes like Barb's." John said.

"Yes. His eyes are Cartwright eyes. They are just like mine. They are as blue as the midnight sky." Barbara said proudly.

"You had blue eyes John when you were a baby too. Your eyes changed when you were about eight months. Your father used to tease me until your eyes changed. You see, no one on either side of the family had blue eyes. Our milkman did have blue eyes. See what a terrible man your father was? Suggesting such a impropriety of his wife." Catherine Sommier chuckled.

"That's true. If your eyes hadn't changed to green I was going to change milk services." John's father teased.

"You'll have to wait and see. The baby's eyes could change at any time until he's a year or so." John's mother said.

"Barb's father was here. Did you have a chance to see him?" John asked his parents.

"Daddy came back and said his good-byes before you got back, John." Barbara answered for them.

Good. John had hoped he wouldn't have to see that pompous racist again today. He was glad his parents didn't have to be subjected to the judge either. They didn't like Cartwright any better than he did.

John's parents left after a short visit. They said they didn't want to tire Barbara or the baby out. John Jr. had been returned to the nursery for the night. Barbara looked like she hadn't slept in days.

"Barb, I'm going to get out of here for the night. I'll be back after my finals tomorrow." John promised.

"Do you have to go now? Can't you stay with me a little longer?" Barbara whimpered.

"Sure, Barb, why not?"

John thought Barbara probably felt pretty alone at the hospital. He'd wait until she fell asleep before he left. He didn't have a long wait.

The rest of John's finals had gone without a hitch. John felt sure he would get A's in those classes. John was trying to get make up exams for the finals he missed.

So far he was fifty-fifty. His Poli Sci professor had given him a green light. The exam only counted for twenty-five percent of his grade. The professor graded on a curve. He had told John, even if he didn't make up the final he would still probably get an A. Probably. John would make it up.

His Art of Speech professor hadn't been so generous. The exam had counted for fifty percent of his grade. The professor informed John that the grade on his final was an automatic F. No explanations necessary. The grade would stand. Luckily that professor graded on a curve too. John might pull off a B rather than a C.

Now John was headed to Professor Burton's office. At first John thought he'd be wiser if he just let the grade stand. Professor Burton was notorious for his speeches on ethics. Understandably so, Professor Burton taught Ethics. Of course, he did not grade on a curve. At least, John thought, Professor Burton averaged the letter grade thus far with the final letter grade like his other teaches did. If John couldn't make up the exam he'd definitely get a C in the course.

John knocked upon the Professor's outer office door. There was no answer but the light was on. John knocked again.

"Lilian, Lilian get that door!" Professor Burton growled.

There was still no answer so John continued knocking.

Professor Burton walked into the outer office to find his secretary gone for the day. He must have lost track of time again.

"Stop that incessant knocking! I'm coming. Just a minute." Professor Burton said irritably.

When the professor opened the door he did not seem surprised. Quite the contrary, he looked as if he had been expecting John.

"Come in Mr. Sommier. Come back into my office." Professor Burton stopped to clear a stack of books from a chair for John to sit in. "What is it that I can do for you, Mr. Sommier?" Professor Burton inquired.

"Well, Sir, as you know I missed my final exam the day before yesterday. I would like to explain my situation in the hope that you will allow a make up exam." John nervously tapped a pencil on his knee.

"You have been a good student all semester, Mr. Sommier. I'll hear your explanation as long as you, Sir, are not tedious. It has been a long day." Professor Burton frowned before he continued, "I will warn you however, you have little chance of gaining a make up exam from me."

"Thank you for at least hearing me out." John continued determinedly, "My wife gave birth to our son on the day of your final. I had to take her to the hospital early in the morning. She was in labor all day."

"Congratulations are in order then." Professor Burton said without feeling. "If I am to even consider a make up exam you will have to answer some questions for me."

"Yes, Sir, anything you'd like to know." John replied.

"You seem awfully young to have a wife that's having a child. Are you a freshman, just out of high school?"

"Yes Sir."

"How long have you been married, Mr. Sommier?"

"For the better part of a year, Professor." John answered as he wondered where this was going.

"It's the end of December. You got out of high school in May yet you've been married for the better part of a year. So your parents allowed you to marry while you were in high school?"

"No sir, they did not. I didn't say I had been married the better part of a year but rather the year. Starting school at Tulane has been the better part of my year."

"Ah, Sir, semantics. You must be more straightforward or our conversation, and your make up chances, are finished right now. Straightforward now! Exactly how long have you been married?" Professor Burton questioned.

"Since the end of June."

"Yet your wife had a baby two days ago. Was the baby early?" Professor Burton arched his right brow.

"Yes, the baby was early." John paused. He could see what the professor was getting at. "The baby came almost two weeks early." John added quietly.

"So you impregnated your wife before you married her. You then had to get married, I suppose. Is that correct?"

"I fail to see where any of this is any of your business, sir!" John said irately.

"Don't you? Mr. Sommier, I teach Ethics. Do you feel it's ethical for me to allow you to make up your exam under your circumstances?"

"I worked hard all semester in your class. With the exception of the final exam, I never missed your class."

"You cannot make exception there. That, Sir, is why you are here."

"Yes, but if it hadn't-

Professor Burton cut him off, "Do you think your situation is ethical?"

"Perhaps not, but I still fail to see that as a basis for your decision."

"On what else would I base my decision? The validity of any excuse must be based on ethics. Do you understand what I mean?"

"Yes, I suppose."

"Would it be fair for me to allow a man who broke society's rules to, then, bend university rules because of his first action?"

"Well, one doesn't necessarily affect the other."

"This one has affected the other. If you had staid your intimacy until after marriage you would not be in my office now. Tulane University does not accept all who come to her doors. I cannot bend the rules and lower the school's standards. Your request is denied."

"Professor Burton if I can't make up this exam I'll get a C." he pleaded.

"Sometimes our actions have ramifications well in to the future, Mr. Sommier. You could not have known all the ways your actions would affect you. You still probably do not know. My class could not begin to teach all the consequences of unethical behavior. It seems, Sir, you will gain a fair understanding though life experience."

"That's it? Your answer is no."

"Mr. Sommier, did you come to Tulane to learn or for the grades?" Professor Burton asked,

"Both." John answered truthfully.

"Good. I believe that you have learned something and I will give you a grade, a C."

John left the professor's office. John surprised himself, he wasn't angry. The professor had been right.

John had known the ramifications for his actions were long reaching. He had married a woman he didn't love. He had messed up many relationships. He had a son that he'd have to raise and support. He wasn't able to go to Harvard for his undergrad work. He would never have guessed this would have affected his finals. He had learned something. Something valuable.

Chapter Five

Lacy Washington had proved to be indispensable in the first few months once Barb and the baby came home.

Lacy was a beautiful girl with skin the color of café au lait. Her eyes were like onyx. Bright and shiny eyes in which you could see your own reflection but could read nothing of her emotions. Her body was long and svelte and she had the grace of a swan.

Not only did she take care of John Jr., but she cooked and cleaned. She did a far better job than Barb ever had. She was a better cook too. She had an abundance of energy.

Lacy's disposition was always bright around John Jr.. In fact, her disposition was bright around everyone. Everyone, that is, except Barbara and her father.

Barb and the, so called, honorable Judge treated Lacy like she was the dirt beneath their feet.

Yet Lacy never cowered to them. She never looked angry with them either. She just looked as if she expected such behavior. She looked at the Cartwrights as if they were below contempt. Maybe they were.

While Barb's behavior may not have bothered Lacy, it sure as hell bothered John. He had argued many times with Barbara about it.

This morning was typical. Lacy had made breakfast. Barbara was on the warpath.

That's when things got ugly.

"Lacy you are so lazy. I wanted my eggs sunny side up. You just scrambled them all because John always wants his eggs that way. Did

you even think to ask me? No! You just made them the easy way!"
Barbara shrieked.

"One way isn't any easier than the other." Lacy said calmly and
continued buttering the toast.

"Don't you mouth off to me! You remember who pays your wages
missy!" Barbara yelled.

"You gonna wake John Jr. if you don't stop your hollerin'. You
oughta lower your voice."

"Don't you dare tell me to lower my voice! You'd do well to
remember your place. This is my house! My son! I will not have you
telling me to lower my voice!" Barbara roared.

John had just come out of the shower when he heard Barbara yelling.
He was sick of starting his school days like this. He was going to put
an end to this once and for all.

"Barbara, come in here please." John said quietly from the bedroom.

"I'm busy John. Just a minute." Barbara replied.

"No. Now. Get your fanny in here right now." John said restraining
his anger.

Barbara sauntered into the bedroom as if she were the Queen of
England.

She certainly wasn't prepared when John grabbed her by both arms
and glared into her face. "Since you seem to think Lacy's beneath you
and cannot tell you what to do, let me. This is not only your house.
John Jr. is not only your son. They are ours. Ours, you understand? I
will not have you screaming at the top of your lungs in our house. You
will not wake our baby with your ranting. Do you understand me?"
John said between clenched teeth.

"You have no right to—"

"I have every right. You're my wife. You promised to love, honor
and obey me. I don't give a damn about the love but you will honor and
obey me. I don't want to hear you berating Lacy anymore. Hell, I don't
want you berating Lacy whether I can hear you or not. Is that clear?"

"You don't even know what happened yet you take her side. She's
lazy just like all of them. I wanted my eggs sunny side up! Did she
think to ask? No! She just made—"

"Lazy? That's a lie. You calling someone lazy is like the pot calling the kettle black. Lacy is John Jr.'s wet nurse. She is not our maid nor our cook. That's your job. It seems to me that your the one who's lazy. What do you do all day anyway? Never mind, I don't give a damn. I will solve this breakfast problem for you." he said as he released her.

"Will you talk to Lacy about breakfast then?"

"Yes."

"Thank you John. I know she'll listen to you."

"I don't think that you will be happy with what I say to Lacy."

"Why? What are you going to say?"

"Only that from now on I want my wife to make my breakfast. Since you'll be making my breakfast you can go ahead and make your own." John said with a dashing smile.

"That's not fair. You are just—"

"What Barb? Don't you want to make your own husband breakfast? Don't you love me, dear? John asked sarcastically.

"I'll make your breakfasts, you son-of-a-bitch."

"More like husband of one." he murmured under his breath.

John was meeting Tad Overthall for lunch at the French Market.

John, Tad and Janiene used to come here all the time when they were in high school. They would get their food at one of the vendors in the French Market and then they'd walk along the river. They would usually go on the weekends or after school.

John hadn't talked to Tad in nearly a year. Not since Tad found out John had slept with Barbara. John figured Tad had been in love with Barb. He understood. He really missed his friendship with Tad but he understood.

John saw Tad standing under the arched entrance to the Market. He ran up to meet him.

"Hey Tad. I'm glad you called. It's good to see you." John said enthusiastically.

"John. It's been a long time." Tad said dryly.

They walked through the semi-open air market, its roof protected its visitors from sudden showers but there were no walls to stop any blowing rain.

John loved the French Market with its many selections of fruits and vegetables in wooden crates and card board boxes lining either side of a singular aisle. Strings of garlic and peppers hung from support beams.

John noticed the hand written and painted signs that claimed all the vegetables were Creole; Creole onions, Creole tomatoes, Creole corn and even Creole green beans. John wasn't sure what made a vegetable 'Creole' and was about to make a joke about it when realized Tad had gone ahead of him and was already ordering his food at the hot foods counter.

They didn't speak again until they had gotten their food and walked up on the levee.

The day looked bleak and dark. It would probably rain soon. John thought the day went perfectly with the mood Tad was setting.

"What's up Tad? Like I said, I'm glad you called. I'd like to think we can still be friends." John tried to remain cheerful.

"I don't give a damn what you think after what you did. For some reason however, Janiene does. She asked me to talk to you." Tad said coolly.

"Is something wrong with her? What is it? Is she okay?"

"Shit John, I hope you're as devoted to your wife. You sound like you still love Janiene."

"I do."

"Then why the hell did you take Barbara from me? Why did you sleep with my girlfriend? You knew I was in love with her."

"She called me. She was all broken up."

"Of course the only honorable thing to do was to comfort her. To screw her, right?"

"Don't get nasty Tad. You're talking about my wife now."

"Yeah, but she was my girlfriend at the time."

"Not quite. You had broken it off with her."

"What the hell are you talking about? I never broke it off with Barb. Sure, I was peeved when I found out she'd slept with Mike Callahan.

I even called her a few choice names but she promised it wouldn't happen again."

"What are you talking about? You never told be about Callahan."

"Didn't have a chance. You were the next guy to climb into Barb's bed," Tad said icily.

"Barb told me that you two had broken up."

"Sure she did." Tad's eyes were filled with disbelief.

"When have I ever lied to you? I swear I thought it was over between you two."

"You knew I loved her."

"No I didn't. You talked about your sexual exploits with her to all the guys. Like she was a tramp. I really never guessed you loved her until later. From the way you talked, I thought Barb was just a roll in the hay for you. Hell, we all thought that."

"How else could I act? She had me by the balls. All she had to do was bat her eyelashes. I'd come running. I didn't want the guys to find out she had turned me into a spineless jellyfish. I loved Barb as much as you loved Janiene. I thought you and I were close enough that you knew how I felt about Barb."

John could hear the pain in his friend's voice. One more casualty from his reckless behavior.

"Anyway guy, Janiene asked me to meet with you so you wouldn't find out from a stranger. Janiene and I are dating. It's starting to get serious. We're talking about marriage. But we're going to wait until we have our degrees before we take the plunge."

John felt like someone had dropped a ton of bricks on him. He couldn't breathe. He couldn't think. He wanted to get up. He wanted to run, to run away from the truth.

John hadn't thought about Janiene having relationships. Sure, he was married. Sure, he had sex with his wife. Still, he had thought Janiene was his. His—until the day they died.

"John, John are you listening to me?" Tad cut into his thoughts.

"Yeah, congratulations. I'm happy for you." John made a dour attempt at a smile.

"Yeah right. You sound happy. What were we supposed to do? Pine away for a married man, a married woman? We had to get on with our lives. Janiene was there when I lost Barbara. I hadn't even told her you slept with Barb, remember? You and Janiene were back together. I never told Janiene why I had broken off my friendship with you. She figured it out once you told her about Barb being pregnant." Tad paused looking at the river before he continued. "Janiene would call me every night in the first few weeks after you broke up. She'd cry for hours. After a while, there were no tears left and we'd just talk for hours. We already loved each other. Good friends always do. It was a natural step to start dating."

John was burning with jealously. Were they sleeping together? John had to know. If they got married they would have to sleep together. They weren't married yet. Tad was the type known for his sexual prowess. John wanted to kill Tad. He had to ask. He had to know.

"Are you sleeping with her?" John asked darkly.

"Go to hell."

"Are you?"

"You have no right to ask that question. If you wanted Janiene to be pure and untouched, except by you, you should have remained faithful to her."

"Then you are sleeping with her," John goaded.

"It's none of your damned business. You have no right to be jealous. Think of Barb, for God's sake. She just had your baby a few months ago and you're going to be jealous of Janiene and me. Why don't you get your priorities straight?"

John sat quietly for a moment. He was considering his friend's words. He was feeling the loss of Janiene all over again.

"I'm sorry. Forgive me. Forgive me for everything. I'm really sorry about Barb too. Barb really did tell me that you two had broken up."

"Barb lied. That's neither here nor there now. You're forgiven."

Tad extended his hand. The two old friends shook hands and then grabbed each other in a big, yet slightly tense, bear hug.

On the way home, John felt ill. He wanted to drive by Janiene's. He wanted to whisk her off to some unknown island. He didn't think the two of them needed anyone or anything. Then John remembered. He did need someone else. There was a new little life. A little life that John couldn't live without. There was John Jr..

John stopped his crazy thoughts. He loved his son. He loved his son with an all consuming love. His love for Janiene was as great but it was different. His son needed him. He needed his father to love his mother. John could try. He sure as hell could try.

John decided he'd pick up some roses for Barb. Then if Lacy could stay with John Jr. he'd take his wife out to dinner.

John had a long drive. They had gotten a new house a few months earlier. Well, they rented it. They moved to a new housing division on the outskirts of New Orleans proper, near Kenner. Barbara had insisted they get a house right after the baby was born.

John felt pretty good by the time he walked in the door. He had thought of all the good things about his wife. He hadn't realized that most of the good things about her took place in the bedroom. He was only aware that his mood was no longer bleak.

"Barb, hey Barbie, I'm home." John called out.

"Hi Sugar. Oh my God! Are those for me? What's the occasion? You've never brought me flowers before." Barbara grinned.

"Does a man have to have an occasion to bring his wife flowers? Where's Lacy? If she can stay this evening, we're going out."

"Really John? Where?"

"Let's ask Lacy first. Then we'll decide where."

"I'll go ask her. Why don't you get yourself a beer."

John grabbed a beer. He sat on the sofa and kicked his feet up.

Barb was back in a flash.

"Yes, she said yes. Now, where are we going?" Barbara begged.

"You just go put one of your fanciest dresses on. It'll be a surprise. Oh yeah, sweetheart would you iron my best suit?

"I would but it doesn't need it. It's just back from the cleaners two days ago."

Barbara nearly floated out of the room.

Maybe she wasn't such a witch. Maybe she just needed to be treated with love. Maybe.

John was finished dressing first as usual. He got another beer and waited for Barbara.

When Barbara finally entered the room she was a vision of loveliness. She wore a deep blue silk crepe dress which complemented her eyes. It was a sleeveless number with a low cut V neckline that showed off a lot of cleavage. The dress was a tight fitting sheath that fell just to the top of Barb's perfectly shaped calves. She wore the same color blue fabric pumps. Even her purse was a perfect match. She had her hair pilled atop her head in a mass of blonde curls. Her make up was done perfectly. She had added a black beauty mark near her left eye.

All the bedroom memories on the way home had put the wood in his fireplace and Barb's sexy dress was a book of matches to that wood.

"You look beautiful. Do we have to go out?" John said with lust in his eyes.

"Yes, I spent over an hour getting ready."

"Come here so that I can at least kiss you."

"You'll muss my make up, Sugar," Barbara said in her sweetest drawl.

"I won't kiss your face."

John walked over to Barbara. He bent his head as if he were going to kiss her mouth but then went lower. He nuzzled and kissed her exposed cleavage.

"Stop it, what if Lacy walks in?" Barbara fought back a giggle.

John raised his head and smiled, "I'll tell her you lost a contact lens. Just helping you find it."

John gripped Barbara's hips and went back to his kiss. Barbara thought she would melt. Her knees were starting to buckle. If she didn't make him stop soon they really wouldn't be going to dinner. Barbara couldn't stop him. It felt too good.

John picked Barbara up as if she were weightless. He carried her into the bedroom and kicked the door closed. He gently laid her on the bed.

"What about Lacy?" Barbara whispered.

"I'll be right back. Don't move a muscle. Don't change a thing."

As John walked out of the room Barbara smiled dreamily. John finally loved her, she thought. She was the happiest woman on earth.

"Lacy's gone." John said as he walked back over to the bed.

"What did you tell her?"

"I told her that you had a headache."

John striped off his tie and shirt and crawled into the bed with the grace of a panther.

A headache, Barbara thought. That was the first time she had ever heard of someone using a headache as an excuse to make love.

Chapter Six

John and Barbara pulled up in the Beetle on Rue Royal. They were lucky to find parking in front of the shop called Past Into Present or PIP as it was known by the locals. It was the first of the Sommier's antique stores. It was also the busiest.

Barbara had surprised John a week earlier by expressing her desire to work. He had thought she was the socialite type not the type that works. She had been insistent about work so he called his father about a position for her. She was in luck. Dana, a longtime sales clerk was graduating with a degree in art history. She was leaving to work in administration at the New Orleans Museum Of Art.

Barbara was actually qualified for the opening. Not surprisingly, Barbara had an extensive understanding of antiques. The homes of the wealthy were often filled with such things. To keep up, or compare, with the Jones's or Rockerfellers one had to be familiar with all the expensive antiques. Barbara grew up knowing how to recognize a Chippendale, Sheffield, Limoges, etc.. She would be a natural sales girl since she not only knew her antiques but she loved antiques as well.

John's father had been reluctant to hire Barbara especially since the Rue Royal shop was the one he spent most of his time at. In the end John talked his father into giving Barb a try.

John was finding out there were a lot of things he had assumed about his wife. She really was turning out to be a different person than he once thought. Her desire to work proved that.

John and Barbara climbed from the yellow Beetle. Barbara was trying to force a smile. She was a little apprehensive about working.

Though it was better than having to stay home with a baby. With John Jr. nearly weaned, Barbara had worried that John would want to get rid of Lacy. That's when she came up with the idea of work. Anything would be better than cleaning house and caring for a baby.

She loved John Jr.. But she didn't want to be bothered with him all the time. The diapers, the feedings and the baths were all nurses work anyway. Barbara didn't understand why John wanted her to do all those things. If he wanted to be married to poor white trash then he shouldn't have married her. He almost did marry trash. He was lucky she saved him from that life.

A little bell above the door rang out as they opened the heavy door. Once inside there wasn't much room to walk. Narrow pathways winding through the antiques were hard to follow with the eye.

The eye was caught by sparkling crystal, gilded antebellum furniture, mahogany chests, fine porcelain lamps and curios, delicate slipper chairs and so much more. The back wall was lined with three massive armoires. Several crystal chandeliers hung from the fourteen foot high ceiling. On the left side of the store was the check-out counter. It was, in itself, a thing of beauty. A mass of rich dark wood with locked display cases that held fine hand-blown perfume bottles. On top of the counter sat a black antique register with golden scrolls painted on it. The bright artificial light caused the polished wood to shine and the gold and crystal to shimmer.

The total effect of the shop made Barbara feel as if she were in a pirate's den full of booty.

Barbara thought the way everything glimmered and sparkled was enough to make anyone believe everything in the shop was brand new. The only thing that betrayed the store's inventory was the smell of age. A dank musty smell that was only slightly overpowered the smell of lemon furniture polish.

John's father had been in the back room and hadn't heard them come in.

"Have you been here long? Why didn't you come back and get me?" Henri asked his son.

"I wanted to give Barb a chance to look around," John answered.

74

Barbara's face shown brightly. She was in awe of everything she saw there. The Sommier's must have even more money than she imagined. The things in this shop alone had to be worth close to half a million dollars and they had five shops!

"I take it you like our little PIP here, Barbara," Henri observed.

"Oh my, yes. The pieces in here are exquisite. I've never seen a collection quite like this. None of the pieces are flawed either," Barbara said in surprise.

"No. This is not a garage sale. We try to restore all our pieces to their original grandeur before they go out to the showroom. I'll be showing you all aspects of the business today. That is, if I can get rid of my son."

"Okay, Dad. I can take a hint. Even if it's as subtle as that," John teased.

"You're not staying?" Barbara sounded worried.

"None of the employee's spouses come to work with them. You have never come to work with John when he does the books, have you?" Henri tried to calm his daughter-in-law.

"No but I thought—"

"You'll be fine, Dad doesn't bite or at least he hasn't bitten anyone in years." John winked at his father. "I'll be back at six."

"Come to the back with me, Barbara," Henri said. Henri held the thick door open for Barbara to walk ahead of him.

The 'back' consisted of a large room behind the showroom and the upstairs section of the building. This section was hot. Apparently, Barbara thought, the air-conditioner was not turned on for this part of the business. Barbara covered her nose with her hand, the back smelled of varnish, stripper, dust and mildew.

There were several pieces of furniture in varying degrees of repair. Silver and brass pieces were black from tarnish. Copper pots and dishes were corroded and green. There were chairs without cushions and still more chairs with ripped or soiled cushions.

Barbara could tell that once all the pieces had been fine pieces of the well-to-do but frankly nothing looked salvageable to her.

"You won't be working back here, Barbara. However, I want you to know all the aspects of the antique business so pay attention. What do you think of the front of the store?" Henri had noticed Barbara crinkle her nose to the items in varying degree of repair in the back room.

"I love it! Everything is so beautiful," Barbara answered cheerfully.

"And what do you think of the back of the store?" Henri asked.

"Well, it smells terrible and there's an awful lot, well, a lot of junk back here." Barbara looked around as she spoke.

"One man's trash is another's treasure. When I shop for pieces to bring into one of my stores I see the finished product in my mind. Most of the furniture you saw up front looked like the things back here when I first acquired them. As long as the wood isn't rotted, it is repairable."

Henri walked across the room with a glow in his eyes.

"Take this desk for instance. Yes, this coat of ugly red paint will have to be stripped. It will have to have to be rubbed with an oil stain many times before it will finally be restored. You must let the oil dry before it is rubbed again. The whole process will take many months. Come here and look closely."

Barbara did as she was told. As she followed the lines of the desk she realized she was looking at a Chippendale.

Henri saw the recognition come into her face. "Yes, that's right. It's a Chippendale. I paid two dollars for this desk but it will sell for two hundred when it is restored. That is what gives me the most pleasure about my business. Not the profits, though that's nice too. It's that we save irreplaceable pieces of furniture. After the War Between the States so much of the South's finer things were sold to people who didn't appreciate their worth. I see it as our job to truly bring that glorious furniture back to life. In other words, bring the 'Past Into Present'."

Barbara was really going to like this job. Her father-in-law's fervor for his business was catching. Barbara could feel it too. She was enthralled by antiques and like most rich Southerners she did not want to let the glory of the past go.

To the side of the back room was a courtyard filled with many pieces of fine furnishings that were obviously placed there to accelerate the drying process. So numerous were the items in the courtyard that Barbara could hardly see the brick with it's mossy mortar that formed the walls of the courtyard.

Barbara walked out into the courtyard as far as the works in process would allow. Iron trellis twenty feet above her head doubled as a clothesline of sorts. Numerous rugs and tapestries, attached to the trellis by large metal clips, were swaying in the gentle breeze.

"Upstairs we have the crystal, porcelain, curios and things of a fragile nature. We usually do not purchase broken fragiles. If we do, we repair them but sell them as damaged," Henri paused as he decided not to take Barbara upstairs. "They are more for window dressing than anything else since the bulk of our profits come from furniture."

Barbara walked back into the back room noting the difference between the items there and the items in the courtyard. She was taking everything in when she felt the strong hand close around her upper arm.

"Be careful, Barbara. Those Emerson Electric fans work wonders in this heat but they can easily cut a hand off if don't watch yourself."

Barbara looked directly in front of her and saw the three foot black metal fan. It looked like an antique in its own right. It didn't have a protective grill to speak of, only four small bars that crossed the front of the fan to protect the blades of the fan if it fell over. Barbara could feel the hot air being stirred by the giant fan and was surprised that she hadn't noticed it before.

"We have three Emersons back here, so watch yourself. We wouldn't want you getting hurt. Let's go back up front and I'll show you how to write up a sale, work the register and verify with the banks on larger checks."

They walked up to the front just after the bell rang. Barbara knew the woman and her daughter coming into the store. It was Misty Fontain and her mother. Two truly arrogant socialites.

"Go and wait on them," Henri told her.

Barbara was so embarrassed. She didn't want them thinking she had to work for money. Gracious, she thought, they would tell everyone that she was working as a sales girl.

Barbara must have hesitated too long because her father-in-law brushed past her and was going up to the Fontains.

"Hello Mrs. Fontain. Misty," Henri gave them a brilliant smile.

"Hello Mr. Sommier. How are you doing this fine day?" Mrs. Fontain gushed. She had been coming here for years and had always flirted with Henri Sommier.

"Why, I am doing wonderfully today. You probably know my daughter-in-law Barbara. Misty went to school with her and John." Henri motioned for Barbara to come over.

Barbara's face was flushed. She had to think of a lie fast. She couldn't have all of society knowing she was a sales girl.

Henri saw the panic in Barbara's eyes and spoke before she had the chance to. "You know my son is going into law. He isn't able to help me like he used to. So Barbara, dear girl that she is, offered to help me buy and help our more important customers," Henri smiled.

"That's just marvelous, Mr. Sommier. I'm sure she will be invaluable," Mrs. Fontain drawled sweetly.

"Please excuse me, I have some things in the back that require my immediate attention, I'll leave you in good hands." Henri turned to Barbara, "If you need to write up a sale just call me."

Barbara appreciated how her father-in-law had spared her any embarrassment. Misty had even commented on how lucky Barbara was to be helping in the family store. She said it must be wonderful to have your pick of all the finest things. Barbara didn't tell her that it didn't work that way. Let her think it. If there must be gossip then let it be good.

All in all, Barbara's first day had gone quite well. She had even made a sale. When John came to pick her up she was very tired.

At home that evening she was beaming as she told John about her new job.

"John, you should have seen it. Under all these coats of ugly red chipped paint was a Chippendale desk. Your father said he only paid two dollars for it!" Barbara told him.

John didn't remind her that he had grown up with the shops. He knew all the ins and outs of the PIP stores. It was good to see Barbara so involved in something.

Barbara began parking in the Sommier's carriage way and walking over to the store with her father-in-law. Parking was hard to find in the Quarter. It was metered and only available on one side of the narrow Rue Royal.

Barbara enjoyed her walks with Henri. He was a strong man. Not at all loud like her own father yet he was still very outspoken.

Many of their talks on the way to work had caused stern disagreements. Her father-in-law never got visibly angry at her though she knew he was capable of such anger since she had witnessed John receive his father's wrath. But with her he was always controlled.

This morning was yet another disagreement that Barbara had inadvertently started with an offhand comment.

"No, Barbara, people are not inferior simply due to their race. Certainly, some individuals are smarter than others," Henri told her.

"All you have to do is look at all the nig, uh, Negroes. They are a slower, lazy people," Barbara replied seriously.

"I wish we could do just that. Look at all the Negroes. I'm afraid you are judging a whole of people by the few you see. It is like beauty. Not all people are given the gift of beauty. Say I see only ugly people of the White race. Even though I have seen a small representation of Whites would it be fair for me to say that all White people are ugly?"

"That's not the same thing. You can see the Negroes hanging around the liquor stores. They just stand around doing nothing."

"So, you've never seen Whites hanging around liquor stores loitering?" Henri asked.

"Well sure, but most of us don't do that. Most of us are at work or at home taking care of the family."

"What makes you think that you are seeing 'most' of the Negro population when you see the people who are loitering? Doesn't it stand to reason that if Negroes are at work or at home caring for families that you would not see them on the street?"

Barbara was silent for a few minutes while she thought about his words. He had made a good point. She had no way of knowing how many Negroes were actually working or were at home with their young. Her Daddy had always pointed them out to her around town saying that they were a lazy people. It was true that she had seen many White people loitering but her father had never once pointed them out.

"I suppose if someone is working or at home that I wouldn't see them on the street. That still doesn't mean that most of them aren't lazy," she said.

"Most Negroes do work. All you have to do is look at the unemployment numbers. Yes, there are more unemployed Negroes but that is because they are not given the same opportunity as Whites are." Henri looked down into Barbara's eyes.

"Oh no! Not that old tired argument." Barbara rolled her eyes. "They have their own community. They can work within it. Now, thanks to the federal government, they can go to our schools. If they were as smart as they claim to be then they would build their own businesses instead of trying to ride on our coat tails."

Henri knew he was getting a good dose of Judge Cartwright's beliefs. "What if the Negroes do start to build their businesses. Many do, you know. They are still a people that are greatly out numbered in terms of race. I don't know how many times I've seen a Negro burned out or lynched because his business was getting too big for the likes of the bigot. Quite a few White people say that the Negroes can build their own businesses and almost in the same breath they say they should 'know their place'. These two thoughts cannot coexist." Henri pulled a big brass key ring, jangling with keys, from his pocket.

Barbara didn't have a chance to reply. They had arrived at the store. They were expecting a shipment of purchases that Henri had made in Jackson the week before. They received the shipment in the early afternoon.

In the shipment were two boxes of crystal. Henri was overseeing the large furniture pieces so that no more damage was done to them. Since the furniture often looked like junk, movers tended to be hard on it if they weren't watched.

Henri had given the key to the upstairs to Barbara and asked her to let the mover in and for her to unpack the crystal.

Barbara had been working at PIP for over a month yet she had never seen the upstairs. Henri had told her that in addition to the breakables they kept some family heirlooms that were damaged in a fire right off the carriage way at the Sommier house in a storage area. They had been damaged many years ago but somehow they just never managed to go through the things to see what could be salvaged.

After the mover left the boxes, Barbara began to look around. Henri had never said the upstairs was off limits to her but neither had he showed it to her.

Though the windows didn't have curtains on them the room was still rather dark. The buildings in the French Quarter tended to sit one atop another so the sunlight was blocked. The room had a strong odor of dust and a faint odor of smoke.

It was insufferably hot, much hotter than then downstairs un-airconditioned section. Heat definitely rises, Barbara thought. The combination of the June heat and the high humidity made Barbara feel as though she were melting. Perspiration from her scalp trickled in a continuous stream down her spine like a small waterfall.

She found the switch for the overhead fan. When she pushed up the toggle she noticed a box directly below the switch. It was labeled in big black letters; Fire And Water Damage 1954, books and writings of Henri Sommier.

Her curiosity was overwhelming. Barbara's father-in-law had some ideas that were pretty different from her own. She wondered what kind of books he would read, what kind of things he would write.

Slowly, as if the slightest sound might give her away, she opened the box. The smell of smoke and mildew assaulted her nostrils. The strong aroma only enticed her further. Carefully she sifted through the books. There were works by Shakespeare and Plato along with many other writers she had never heard of.

Barbara examined the bindings since they all appeared to be leather bound but many were cracked and separating from their spines. Each of the books had once been gilded and the leathers were thick and fine. Barbara thought her father-in-law must have had the books since childhood.

She was halfway down the box when yet another worn leather binding caught her attention. Etched in gold across the front cover was the name Henri P. Sommier. The book had obviously been handled in much the same way repeatedly because all of the gold had been rubbed off the last three letters in Sommier and the letters themselves were no longer etched deeply like the rest of the name.

It struck Barbara as strange for the middle initial to be 'P'. She thought for sure her father-in-law's middle name was Dubois after his mother's maiden name.

The muscles across her shoulders tightened when she opened the journal. It was a thick book, about three inches or so and apparently it was full with his memories. She nearly fell over when she saw the date of the first entry, April 1837!

This must be John's grandfather's, no, his great grandfather's journal, Barbara thought. Hot blood began pulsing through her temples. She held the diary of a man who had made his first entry one hundred and twenty-five years before!

Barbara sat down on the dusty wooden floor and started to read.

April 1837
It is the 25th day of the month. Uncle Jean brought me these wonderful blank books back from France when he returned last month. Up until now I have had nothing worth writing. Now I have something very exciting upon my heart. Tomorrow Papa is taking me to the city with him. Just me, not any of the other children. Since I am the youngest I have never been to the city alone with Papa. Of course, the girls never go to the city without Maman but where is the need in that? I must learn the way so that I may travel there alone one day. Papa says since I will be eight years old in three months that it is time I started to learn the responsibilities of a man.

Luc was very happy for me and told me many things about the city since Papa has taken him many times. Luc also told me of a mistress Papa keeps in the city. I am not sure what this means but Luc said because of it I will be allowed to stay in the park alone and go and buy candy while Papa is entertained. I shall write again upon my return from the city.

Barbara had turned to the next entry when she heard someone on the stairs. She rushed over to the new shipments and pretended to be inspecting the new arrivals.

She sighed in relief when she saw it was only the mover with another box.

She held her curiosity in check and forced herself to finish unpacking the boxes. When the last one was finished she grabbed the journal, turned off the ceiling fan and headed downstairs.

She held the journal behind her back as she passed Henri and the other men. She crossed her fingers, hoping Henri wouldn't notice her. Luckily as she walked towards the door to the showroom Henri was much too busy to notice anything other than the movers.

Barbara was relieved when she entered the chill air of the showroom. She quickly slipped the journal in the bottom drawer behind the counter. That was the drawer Henri had told her to keep her lunch, and other things of a personal nature, in. No one ever went into that drawer except her. She would be able to read the journal whenever Henri was gone and she didn't have any customers.

Barbara felt a little guilty about taking the journal but not enough to put the journal back. After all, she was a Sommier too, she reasoned with herself.

Barbara hadn't had much time to read the journal over the course of the week. The store had been too busy. She really hadn't thought too much about it either. That is, except, at night.

Every night she'd imagine all the things a young man of the last century would have to write about. Barbara had already looked at the date of the very last entry. It was June 1858. She could hardly wait to read it. Henri P. Sommier had made entries for over twenty years. She wondered if he had written about his loves, his enemies, his family and his business ventures.

Tomorrow she would be able to spend at least an hour reading. If the store wasn't busy then she could read even longer. Her father-in-law was up in Natchez at an auction. Girod and Jim, who did most of the refinishing, never came up front.

Barbara arrived at work early. It was still fairly cool out when she opened up.

She stocked the front window with the antique jewelry that was put in the safe each night. She went into the back and made a fresh pot of coffee. Now she was ready.

Barbara took the journal out of the back of her lunch drawer. She settled in a cream and gold slipper chair behind the counter. The fabric of the chair had pictures of the French aristocracy and gardens in a repeating pattern on it.

Barbara opened the journal to where she had last left off.

Sept. 1837

In two days I shall return to the city with Papa. This will be my fourth trip alone to New Orleans with Papa. I hope I see that boy whose face favors Papa's so much. Out of the seven children that Maman and Papa have not even one wholly favor Papa in looks. Luc does favor Papa in deeds but not in looks. Maman often said she tried to give Papa a son that looked like him.

When I saw that boy on the second trip with Papa I thought I would die from excitement. I tried to talk to the boy but he ran from me. I think the way I came running at him scared him. When we went last, I saw the boy again. His colour is darker than Papa's. He is probably in the sun more than Papa because his skin is of an olive tone. I told Papa of the boy. Papa got upset with me. He said I was probably daydreaming while I sat in the park. He told me to make no mention to Maman or the other children. He said they need not be bothered with my daydreams. If only I can find that boy and take him to Papa. He would see that I do not daydream.

Barbara shifted position before she read the next entry. She was so engrossed she didn't notice the jangle of the bell when the customer walked in the store.

Sept. 1837

I talked to the boy yesterday. His name is Jean-Claude. He is seven years old but he said his eighth birthday is approaching soon. I told him that I turned eight last month. He said his birthday is in February. I do not think his birthday is very close at all. I suppose he wishes he were eight years old like I am.

Jean-Claude lives in New Orleans all year—even during fever season. I told him of our town house on Rue Burgundy. He said he lives on Rue Rampart. I do not think I've been to Rue Rampart. Jean-Claude said that his house is near Congo square where the slaves gather on Sundays to sing, dance, and play drums. I have heard their drums but I have never seen their dances. Jean-Claude says that he sees them every week. He asked if we had slaves. I told him we had two hundred slaves. Papa says slavery is a necessary evil. Without the slaves we could never harvest the sugar cane. When I asked Jean-Claude if they had slaves he looked at me funny. He finally said they only had two servants that his father gave his mother. His mother gave them their freedom so they are servants not slaves. I do not see that there is much difference if they still work for them.

"Excuse me. Miss, excuse me," the customer called out to Barbara.

Barbara was so startled she nearly spilled her coffee when she jumped up to wait on the elderly lady.

She could hardly wait to get the customer on her way. Then there had been one more customer and another and another. It wasn't until she had closed up the store that she was able to complete the entry she had begun midmorning.

I did not have the chance to ask Jean-Claude to meet Papa. Marie-Anna who lives on a plantation near to ours came up to us. She is my age. She is always smiling and batting her lashes around the boys. Papa says she is much like her Maman. Marie-

Anna was really acting silly around Jean-Claude. She kept giggling and dropping her kerchief so that Jean-Claude would pick it up for her. Her Maman was in the textile shop buying fabrics when she came running out of the store like a mad woman. She grabbed Marie-Anna and she slapped Marie-Anna's mammy. In front of everyone! She yelled at Marie-Anna for flirting with a boy like that. She pointed at Jean-Claude and asked him where he belonged. Jean-Claude ran from Madam Folliers. I would have too if she hadn't caught my arm. She demanded to know if he were ours. I told her that he was not my brother. I can understand her thinking he was my brother because he looks so much like Papa. Still, I think Madam Folliers must be losing her mind. She has known all the Sommier children for all of our lives.

Barbara wanted to start a new entry but it was already starting to get dark. John would be home alone with John Jr.. Maybe he'd have the baby in bed before she got home. Barbara was anxious to spend some time with John.

She hadn't thought he'd go to summer school. John said he wanted to get into law school as quickly as possible.

Barbara thought she didn't get to spend enough time with John during the regular school year. Summer session was a nightmare. He went to school everyday and then he'd study up until he went to bed. Summer session had been hell on her love life. Tonight, she thought decidedly, was going to be different.

Chapter Seven

After making love with John, Barbara usually slept. Tonight, however, she wasn't able to sleep. The journal kept popping into her mind.

Henri P. Sommier had only been eight years old when he made the entries she had read so far. It was understandable why he hadn't put everything together.

Barbara lived in New Orleans all of her life. She knew the history of the area well. Henri had written that Jean-Claude lived on Rue Rampart. Young Henri's father had a mistress. Jean-Claude looked like Henri's father only Jean-Claude had olive skin. Unless Barbara missed her guess, she knew exactly who Jean-Claude was... and what he was.

Barbara knew about the actions of the Creole gentry of the last century. It was not uncommon for a wealthy Creole gentleman to have three households. His plantation to the north or west of the city, his town house in the city and his mistress's house, also in the city. Technically, the last house would belong to the mistress but the gentleman could come and go as he pleased.

The mistress agreed to this arrangement because included in the bargain was her freedom. Mistresses were often slaves. Yet some were half-breeds or quadroons, daughters of the mistresses of pleasure.

Not only would the mistress receive freedom in these pacts, her children would also be free. The Creole gentleman would send any sons she bore him to Europe to be educated. Most of the sons from these unions remained in Europe as they were more readily accepted as equals.

The Creole gentlemen usually bought a town house for the mistress and any children she might bear him. Most commonly, these houses were on Rue Rampart.

The pieces all fit together perfectly. Jean-Claude must have been Henri's father's bastard offspring.

No wonder the woman had been so upset by her daughter's flirtation. Barbara knew that she would have probably acted the same way. If John Jr. ever thought about dating a Negro, she would kill him. Of course the little girl was probably like young Henri. She didn't realize Jean-Claude was a Negro. If she had, Barbara was sure the little girl would not have even spoken to Jean-Claude let alone flirt with him.

The next few weeks had been busy at the store yet Barbara had found time to read the journal everyday.

She had been right about Jean-Claude. Though, Henri didn't discover the truth until he was ten years old. By then he had already formed a close friendship with Jean-Claude.

From the descriptions in Henri's journal, Jean-Claude looked remarkably like her own John. The same black hair and light green eyes. Barbara had already read up to the boy's fourteenth year. She was anxious to read more about both the boys. Each day at lunch she settled in the slipper chair with the journal. Today was no different.

March 1844

I rode today to meet Jean-Claude. He promised to take me to a brothel. Jean-Claude need not go to the brothels, he is so popular with the ladies. I fear the way the Creole ladies are always giving me notes for him that he may end up with his neck stretched. Since he is a Negro he would not be called out. He would not be given the chance to defend himself.

Jean-Claude goes to the ladies homes when no one of importance is there save the lady. I think he is a rogue though he is careful not to deflower any young maid. He goes instead to the bored, married, ladies. He has even been with some friends of Maman. To me these women are too old to appeal yet Jean-Claude says charm has no age.

He says he does it in part for the pleasure and in part for the way he is treated because he is a half-breed. He is far smarter than any young man I know yet all the Creoles treat him as if he was stupid. He has taught himself to read even though it is illegal for the Negro in Louisiana.

I must write of my experience at the brothel lest I forget even a moment. Now I see what Jean-Claude raves about. Of course, I have had the dreams but they do not compare to the actuality.

I entered the raised cottage in the country with Jean-Claude. It was not a large cottage yet it was elegant in decoration. The Madam was dressed in a black dress with a high neckline. She looked as if she would fit better at a convent. I thought we might be in the wrong place but then she led us to a room full of women. Many of the women were in their under garments. Blonde heads, red heads, brunettes and black haired ladies filled the room. They were all shapes, sizes and colours. Enough variety that any man might find what pleases him. Jean-Claude had gone off with a blonde busty lady almost at once.

I felt very uneasy to be alone in my selection. Madam made some suggestions but my eyes fell upon a lady with long dark tresses and skin the colour of a perfect cup of cafe au lait. She was slender but with a full bosom, Madam introduced her as Annette. Annette led me off to her upstairs chamber. Her boudoir was dark and had a musty odor. I asked Annette to pull the curtains so that I might see her. She looked like she was sixteen or seventeen in the sunlight. Her eyes were like coal and she had light rouge on her cheeks and lips.

The room had only two pieces of furniture in it. A large canopy bed of carved mahogany sat in the very center of the room. Then there was a dresser with an ornate mirror above it.

The ropes of the bed barely let out a squeak when I sat down. Annette asked me how I preferred to love. I told her it was my first time and that she should choose whatever is most pleasurable for us. She began to undress me. I was afraid my trembling was going to give away my nervousness but she did not seem to notice. When she had all but my long under things off, she began to undress herself. Her breasts were full with tight little buds at the tips. The buds looked to be made of bittersweet chocolate. Immediately I felt the urge to taste them. She continued her undressing and revealed a small waist and full shapely hips. Her hair below was straight black and shiny. I could feel the strain of my maleness against my under things. I completed my undress. She came to me and eased the lamb skin around me. Then she eased herself atop me. Her breasts were pendulous around my face as I laid my back against the bedding. She arched her back so that I could taste them.

I felt her heat around me and began a rhythm that was both foreign and natural to me. The sensations I felt were unlike any I have felt before. It is no longer a mystery to me why Jean-Claude takes the risks that he does.

I could barely walk when we left the brothel. I was still shaking from excitement.

I am sorry I did not experience this sooner. Papa offered me a slave girl when I turned twelve. Jean-Claude had talked me out of taking pleasure with her. He said it was wrong to be with any female that was not willing. Be it for coin or pleasure, he said she must be willing. I told him that she was willing. He said that was only because she had no choice. He told me to ask her if she did have a choice what it would be. I did ask her. She told me she wanted to wait until she jumped the broom. Jean-Claude had been right.

I only wish Jean-Claude had introduced me to brothels sooner. I will visit again soon. Jean-Claude says if I were not so shy around the ladies then I would not have to pay for the loving. I will gladly pay for this! It is better than the lightheadedness caused by the best liquor or the delight from the sweetest confection.

Barbara smiled to herself. The description of young Henri's lovemaking had aroused her. Too bad it was only lunch time.

As Barbara heard the customer come in she quickly put the journal in the drawer. The thought of what she had been reading made her flush.

While Barbara was showing the customer some wine tables, Henri had come forward. When he noticed Barbara's half eaten sandwich on the counter he went to put it away for her. The customer must have required immediate attention. Barbara was not usually so messy. Henri re-wrapped the leftover sandwich and wiped crumbs from the wood counter top. He leaned down and opened the drawer to put the sandwich away. Staring up at him from the drawer was the name Henri P. Sommier!

Henri opened the drawer wider. It was his grandfather's journal. The journal had a bookmark in it. So, Henri thought, she was reading it. Where was the other one? Henri searched the drawer but only saw the one journal.

He placed the sandwich in the drawer and closed it. He rushed to the back to go upstairs.

He went to the box in which his grandfather's things from the fire was kept. He pushed books aside quickly looking for the journal etched Henri P. Sommier, Vol. II. Henri was sweating as much from his own nervousness as the heat while he searched for the book. He did not stop looking to turn on the ceiling fan. He hoped to God that Barbara did not have the Vol. II of his grandfather's writings. That could bring trouble upon the whole family if Barbara read that.

At last Henri fell back with relief. He saw it. Henri picked it up and took it with him as he left the upstairs.

Henri put the book in a small box before he walked though the front of the store.

The customer was gone. Barbara seemed to jump when he opened the door to the front show room. He guessed that she was reading the journal.

Let her read it, he thought. There was nothing in the first journal that could damage the Sommier family name.

"Barbara, take care of the shop. I have to run over to the Carollton location. I need to help Margaret with a small shipment they received this morning," Henri told her and walked out of the shop.

Henri walked as quickly as he could. He had to talk to Catherine. She would know what to do. She always kept a cool head in critical situations.

Oliver opened the door before Henri had a chance to turn the key.

"M'seur Henri, you are home early." Oliver took note of his employer's expression. "Is everything right by you, M'seur?"

"No, no it's not, Oliver. Where is Mrs. Sommier?"

"Madam, she is in de courtyard," Oliver answered.

"Thank you." Henri walked out to the courtyard. He pulled the journal out of the box.

"What a lovely surprise. I did not expect you to be home until late this evening. Henri, is everything all right?" Catherine studied his face before she saw the journal in his hands.

"Barbara has the first journal in her lunch drawer. It had a bookmark in it so I assume she's reading it." Henri paced the floor.

"Did you take that from her drawer?" Catherine asked.

"No. This is volume two. Thank God above! Apparently, she did not find this journal. I don't think she would have left it behind if she had seen it."

"How did she find the first one? Weren't they together?" she asked.

"Yes, I'm sure they were in the same box. I still had them upstairs at the Rue Royal store. They were with the fire damaged things. I found this one at the bottom of the box. She's only been upstairs once. When I returned from my trip to Jackson, I had Barbara escort the mover to the upstairs area. I asked her to unpack some boxes up there."

"Don't worry, Henri. She only has the first journal. The private information is in the second journal, right?"

"Yes, but at the end of the first journal Grandpere says that he will continue in his second volume."

"You have the second volume. How can she continue? She has done this in secret so she cannot ask us where the second volume is. Besides which, if she goes though the box again she will probably think that it burned in the fire," Catherine said with authority.

"Yes, of course, you are right. To ensure just that, I will send her up to bring some crystal down in a month or two. By then she should be ready to search for the second volume."

"It's a good thing Barbara is a married woman. I remember much of what your Grandpere wrote in his first journal made me blush," Catherine said with a giggle.

"You forget, our Barbara was not the blushing virgin that you were when she married," Henri said coolly.

"Oh Henri. That isn't nice at all. For all we know, John could have been her first lover," Catherine scolded.

"He wasn't. I asked him before they ever married. He said a few boys had claimed to have been with Barbara."

"Yes, I'm sure. She's a beautiful young woman with an astonishing figure. Many boys would want to be with her. You know how young boys like to brag. Even if they have to make something up."

"Do you think Tad Overthall would make things up?"

"Oh my." Catherine threw her hands up in surprise. "Well now, it's none of our business."

"No. I was just trying to point out that she wouldn't be blushing at my grandfather's words. She'll probably even enjoy his escapades," Henri assured her.

"I didn't say I didn't enjoy what I read. I merely said that it made me blush," Catherine said coyly.

"My, my, I've been married to you twenty years and never realized how brazen you are." Henri walked over and kissed his wife.

Catherine wrapped her arms around his neck. "You have no idea how brazen I can be. If you will join me upstairs, I will be glad to show you," Catherine smiled.

"Lead the way. Lead the way." Henri was glad he had rushed home about the journal.

Barbara had nearly jumped out of her skin when she saw her father-in-law come up front. She had just pulled the journal out of the drawer. Thank goodness he had been on his way out to the Carollton store. That would give her time to read some more.

Barbara felt a little nervous. After she helped the customer she had returned to the counter. Something didn't seem right but she couldn't put her finger on what it was. She had seen Henri out of the corner of her eye when she was helping the customer select a wine table. At first she had worried that she hadn't put the journal away. That wasn't it. The journal had been in the drawer with her lunch.

With her lunch...that was it! That was what was different. She hadn't put her lunch away. She had left it on the counter top. Her customer hadn't given her a chance to put it away. She had thought she'd slip it under the counter if she had to write up a sale. She had forgotten that she hadn't put her lunch away.

Henri must have put it away for her. She wondered if he saw the journal. No, he couldn't have. He was not a mousy sort of man. If he saw the journal he would have asked her what she was doing with it. She always pushed the journal to the back of the drawer anyway. He must not have seen it. He would have mentioned it to her.

That had been close. Barbara didn't want him to know she had been snooping around in his things. They were just beginning to like each other. She would have to be more careful in the future.

***

John was pleased Barbara was working. It gave him time to get his homework done. He didn't have to listen to her pick apart Lacy. As a mater of fact, he thought, he hadn't heard her cuss him out in quite awhile either. Work was good for her.

When John arrived home he was greeted by Lacy and his round smiling son.

John Jr. was seven months old now. He was starting to crawl everywhere. He was a fast little ankle biter too.

"Mr. John, I was wonderin' if I might could have a word with you," Lacy said.

"Lacy you've been with us for over half a year. How many times do I have to tell you to call me John?" John smiled.

"Well, sir, that just wouldn't be propra. Besides, Miss Barbara would pitch a fit," Lacy warned.

John knew Lacy was right about that. "Well, if you ever feel comfortable with calling by my chosen name, feel free to do so. What was it you wanted to talk to me about?"

"My Mama can't take my boy everyday no more. She ain't as young as she usta be. Would it be okay if I brought my boy here one or two days a week?" Lacy said softly.

"Surely. How old is he? What's he called anyway? You don't talk much about him."

"My boy will make three this month. His name be Jamal but we call him Jammy. I don't like to bring my personal life to work with me." Lacy gave a hearty laugh. "I guess I can't avoid bringin' my personal life to work now. My life don't get more personal than my Jammy. I thank ya, sir. Jammy won't cause no trouble for y'all," Lacy said gratefully.

John sent Lacy home for the night.

Barbara didn't usually get home until after six-thirty. John was in the habit of bathing his son after Lacy fed him. He really enjoyed his time with John Jr..

Barbara arrived after John had finished bathing John Jr..

John thought he better break the news to her about Jammy. He wasn't sure how she would respond but he knew it would not be good. With the exception of John Jr., Barbara didn't seem to like kids all that much.

"How was your day?" John observed the tense look about her.

"It was fine. How was your day? Where's John Jr.?" Barbara asked quickly.

John thought it might not be the best time to break the news about Jammy. He'd fix her a drink first.

"I'm getting a beer. Can I get you a glass of wine or something?"

"Sure, I'll take a double martini. Thanks," she said in a clipped tone.

John wondered what could be bothering her. Barb didn't usually drink the hard stuff unless it was with dinner. She was a woman with few inhibitions and alcohol caused her to have none.

She had gotten drunk and been talked into doing a strip tease for a group of boys when they were in high school. Luckily a friend of the judge had seen Barb at the park with the group of boys. Her father found her at the park completely naked. The boys had fondled and groped her body while she screamed for them to stop. Judge Cartwright fired a warning shot in the air. The boys ran. She never forgot that night. She had nearly been gang raped. Ever since, Barb was careful to limit her intake of alcohol. Even when we're alone, John thought.

Barbara drank down the martini and asked for another. She just couldn't shake the feeling that she had been caught with the journal. She knew it had been close. That she hadn't really been caught. But she had a tugging in her stomach, a nagging feeling. She didn't want to lose her father-in-law's trust. More importantly she didn't want to lose her job there. She didn't want to take care of John Jr.. That was Lacy's job.

The second double martini was starting to really kick in. Barbara remembered the words of Henri P. Sommier. The words that made her flush earlier. The thoughts of what he had written combined with the martinis made Barbara's skin start to feel as if it were on fire.

"John, can you put the baby to bed? I want to get changed." Barbara swished and swayed into the bedroom.

John put John Jr. in his crib with a bottle. He went into the bedroom to see how his wife was doing.

"Hi, Johnny. Why don't you help me with this?" Barbara slurred her words as she tried to unfasten the buttons of her blouse.

"Sure, honey. Why so much to drink tonight? Did you have a problem at work?" John undid her blouse and helped her slip out of it.

"My day was fine. Except there was this old hag who kept having me pull different jewelry out for her. Then she'd tell me she had one just like it. I'm sure she did. She was an antique herself." Barbara leaned into John. "Did I ever tell you that you have very sexy eyes? Would you undo the hooks on my bra for me?"

John didn't think he had ever seen Barb like this. She was always sexy and could be quite seductive. Now she was being seductive without even knowing it.

"Johnny, do you want to make love? You have that look in your eyes." Barbara licked her upper lip and gently bit her bottom lip.

John didn't answer her. He picked her up and carried her to the bed. He began kissing and fondling her when she suddenly stopped him.

"Johnny, let's try something different." Barbara unzipped his pants.

John lay awake after their lovemaking. It had been a different experience for him. He had never known a girl who had done the things she'd done. Hell, John thought, Barb's never done those things before herself. She really didn't have any inhibitions when she was drunk. What worried John was the reason why she had gotten drunk.

He slipped out of bed to call his father. He wanted to know if his dad had had a fight with Barb. He had to know what was going on.

Oliver said his father was out but he went to get his mother.

"John?" his mother picked up the phone.

"Hey, Mom. Sorry to bother you this evening. I was trying to reach Dad. Do you know where he is?"

"He's out at the Carollton store. They got a shipment in and he went out there to sort it out for Margaret."

John was really worried now. Whenever there was a shipment to one of the other stores his father went out to them in the early afternoon. What had kept him from going earlier? John hoped Barb hadn't caused any problems.

"Was the shipment late?" John hoped that was all it was.

"Not that I know of."

"Is Dad okay? I mean why is he at the shop tonight? Why didn't he go this afternoon?"

"He came to talk to me this afternoon."

"Why didn't he just call you? Was everything okay?" John asked nervously.

"I don't know why he didn't just call. Maybe your father actually enjoys my company—"

"Sorry, Mom, I didn't mean it like that," John interrupted.

"What is it John? What's wrong?"

"Nothing I guess. I just thought maybe Dad and Barb had a fight," John confided.

"Why would you think that? Did Barbara say something about a fight to you?"

"It wasn't what Barb said. It's what she didn't say. She hit the sauce pretty hard when she came home. That's not like her at all."

"As a matter of fact, when your father came home today it did concern Barbara. I don't want to discuss this over the phone. Come over tomorrow after your classes and we'll talk. Good night my son." Catherine hung up.

Catherine wondered about Barbara's behavior. Maybe she had realized Henri knew what she was up to. How could that be? Catherine knew that this girl was trouble. At least she had given them John Jr..

Hopefully John Jr. would make Barbara feel some sort of loyalty to the Sommier family. Just in case she ever did find out.

After classes John went straight to his parents' home. He had wondered all morning what this was all about. What had Barbara done? Maybe it was something she had said. John was anxious to find out what the problem was.

Catherine awaited her son in the drawing room. She had instructed Oliver to bring coffee and cookies to her as soon as John arrived.

"You look lovely as usual, Mom," John said genially.

"Thank you. Can I get you some coffee? Cookies?"

John nodded his head in the affirmative. He grabbed a couple of cookies while his mother mixed his coffee and hot milk with sugar,

"John, I don't know how to broach this subject gently. Barbara has been prying. She went though at least one of the boxes from the fire damaged things."

"Is that the problem? I must say, I'm not surprised. Barb has a nosy streak in her a mile wide. I'll talk to her about going through your things. It won't happen again," John assured her.

"I wish that were the only problem. Barbara found one of your great grandfather's journals. There was a bookmark in it so we assume she's been reading it. Merci Dieu, it is only the first journal. There is nothing about the family in that one that is damaging. Your father has the second volume so she won't be able to read it. I don't want you saying anything to her about her snooping. Henri will send her back to where the fire damaged things are in a month or so."

"I'm not quite following you. Why don't you want me to say anything to her? She shouldn't be going through your things. Are you sending her back to where she found the journal in hopes that she will put it back? If so, if you let me talk to her I can guarantee she'll put it back. Not in a month or so either. Now!" John was disgusted with his wife's actions.

"No, John we hadn't really thought about how she would return the volume. The first volume makes mention that he will continue his writings in a second volume. Your father thought she would want to search for that one. I think she will assume it was burned in the fire."

"I don't understand why you don't want me to have a talk with her."

"John, if you confront her it will damage her relationship with us. Furthermore, what if she then asks us if she can read the journal? It is part of her son's heritage. I do not wish to lie to her about the second volume. It is easier to let her assume that the second volume was destroyed."

John's mind was working frenziedly. Since Barb had done this on the sly she really couldn't talk about it. What if she did read the second volume? She would have to keep her reactions a secret or expose herself as a sneak. Then John could tell her about the family secret himself. It would seem to her that he had confided in her. Also, he wouldn't have to deal with her anger or shock then because she would already know.

John proposed his plan to his mother.

"I don't know about that, John. I'd prefer if Barbara never knew. I don't think she'll necessarily keep quiet about it just because she found out covertly," Catherine frowned thoughtfully.

"It is part of my son's history. I'll have to tell John Jr. someday. I can hardly forbid him from telling his own mother about it." John argued.

"Look at the Kennedy's history, Mom. Their family started with illegal activity and no one even cares now."

"Indeed but you have many years before you have to tell John Jr.. Perhaps Barbara will be more firmly rooted in the family by then."

"There is no way of knowing if Barb will feel more committed to the family with the passage of time. I was only three years old when Dad told me. I think it helped influence my social development. I want to tell John Jr. while he's still young enough that he hasn't been influenced by his peers."

"I see your point, John. You must try to see mine. If the Sommier secret gets out it can have repercussions far reaching. It could damage the family business. It could endanger our lives."

"I don't know why you and Dad believe that. Even if the secret were out, publicly, it would not change who we are. We are still the same people. It happened so long ago anyway."

"John, you are so young. So naive about the ways of the world. Some people do judge the Kennedy family about their past. You know things aren't so different now, that your great grandfather's actions would be ignored."

"Maybe not, but I still think we should let Barb read the second journal. Trust me; she would be hard pressed to tell anyone about it. She would think it would reflect badly on her."

"Now that is probably true. I will talk to your father about it. I think you may be right. In the meantime, don't let on to Barbara that we know anything."

Chapter Eight

Judge Cartwright had received the notification he had been waiting for. He had been nominated for Pegasus.

Jefferson Cartwright had long been a member of White Wings. A political organization that advocated the divine supremacy of the White race.

Unlike the Klan, White Wings accepted Catholics into it's organization. Jefferson came from a long line of Irish Catholics. He was recruited for White Wings when he first started college and had been with them ever since.

White Wings saw itself as different from the other White supremacist groups. White Wings, or the Wings as it was widely known, did not condone hatred of Negroes or other minorities. They believed God had created the minorities as he did all the other animals. The White man was put on earth to reign supreme.

The Wings felt that minorities should count themselves lucky and stop trying to gain more rights. After all, as inferior beings they had no right to demand anything.

The Wings felt a responsibility toward the Negro. Like all the beasts put on the earth, the Negroes were theirs to rule but also theirs to watch over. Cartwright wished that Lincoln hadn't freed the slaves. He was sure the Negroes had been a damned sight easier to manage back then.

At least the government had been smart about the Indians. They were off on their own little parcels of land. They didn't bother anyone much.

The Wings did not like to use violence as a means for control. They would use violence as a last resort. When they had tried and tried to reason with someone and could not, then violence was often the only answer. There were those Negroes that got so uppity that they practically begged to be struck down.

Jefferson Cartwright jumped in his car and headed over for the 'hanger'. The hanger is where a group of not more than twenty-five White Wings would meet. Each group had its own pilot and copilot. Every area had a leader called The Eagle. The Eagle usually had between ten to twenty-five hangers under him. Cartwright had been The Eagle for the New Orleans area for over four years.

The time had come. He would be Pegasus. Pegasus was the leader for the state.

As Pegasus, Judge Cartwright would be able to implement new laws, organize new strategies and command a group of thousands. He had worked and waited for this for a long time.

"I just heard the news. Congratulations," a White Wing greeted the Judge when he walked through the door.

"Thanks. Let's hope I get it. Have you seen Jamison?" Cartwright asked.

"Yeah, he's in the back with the new kid."

Jefferson Cartwright went in search for Thomas Jamison. Jamison had been the pilot of the hanger nearest to Cartwright for about two years. As The Eagle, Cartwright had to visit all the New Orleans area hangers' pilots and copilots on a regular basis but he liked Jamison the best.

Cartwright found Jamison passing out stacks of recruitment flyers to the college age men in the group.

"How y'all boys getting along today?" Cartwright paused for the pleasantries. "Jamison, can I have a word with you?" Cartwright was eager to talk to his friend.

"You bet. Just one second. Let me give Buker his instructions. Have you met Buker? He's our latest recruit. Buker, this is The Eagle for our area, Judge Jefferson Cartwright."

"Good to meet you Buker. Is that your last name or some sort of nickname?" Cartwright extended his hand to the young man.

The young man shook Cartwright's hand vigorously. "It's a pleasure to finally meet you. I've heard so many great things about you. Donald Buker is may full name, sir. I usually go by Don. I just came by to pick up the fliers. It was a real pleasure. See y'all later." Don Buker left on his mission to recruit more possible White Wings.

"I know you've heard the news. What do you think my chances are?" Cartwright asked him candidly.

"The way I see it, they're pretty good. Most of the men want someone who is in a position of power and not just in our organization. That's you. You have more of a power position than any of those other boys you're up against," Jamison promised.

"That may be, Tommy, but you know how popular old Kingston is. He's from plantation money too. Kingston's family has been in Louisiana since the 1700's."

"So what? Your family come here in what? The early 1800's or something? You've been the king of your Krewe, twice. You're a judge. That alone is going to be worth a lot of votes for you. Since the integration of our schools a couple of years ago, no one has been happy with this no violence stand. I think everyone knows that you'll be willing to give the signal for more violence." Tommy wasn't sure how Jefferson Cartwright stood on the violence issue but he desperately needed to know before he cast his vote. Tommy Jamison had long advocated more violence. He actually preferred the beliefs of the Klan but he was Catholic.

"I think this integration thing has gotten way out of hand. I was glad Barbie only had to go to school with the Coloreds for one semester. I don't know how they expect for the Coloreds to keep up with the White kids anyway. The cities are trying to ensure that more and more of the Coloreds are allowed to vote. That's why the federal government is squirming so damned much," Judge Cartwright commented.

"Ain't it the truth. You think if we help to keep the Coloreds at home during voting times it would make a difference?" Jamison urged. Jamison wondered, short of asking the judge, if he was going to find out where Cartwright stood on the violence issue.

"Keeping them home won't change the statistics none. Uncle Sam will still know how many of them could eventually vote. Keeping them home during voting might just encourage old Unc to come and stick his nose in more of our state's business."

Tommy nodded, rubbing his chin. "I see where that might have that effect. What if we let the Coloreds know whose boss during the other times. Don't you think that would keep their voting down?"

"I suppose so. I don't advocate random violence on their people. I say we should use it when necessary but leave the women and kids alone."

That was what Jamison was waiting to hear. Cartwright was a little weak in his belief for violence but there would be no backlashes from him if those advocating it used violence. He would urge his hanger to vote for Cartwright.

"Well now, Jefferson, I don't see any problem with violence on any of their kind if they step out of line."

"I suppose not," Cartwright murmured. Cartwright had the distinct feeling that he was being sized up.

"I'll be glad when the vote comes back. I'll be mighty nervous 'til then." Cartwright admitted.

"With Bill Leaverton's passing away, it will be quick. They'll want to fill the Pegasus position by the end of the week," Jamison said decisively.

Tad decided to drop out of college. He was majoring in journalism anyway. He didn't need a degree for what came naturally to him.

Tad's father had been in the army during the last World War. He had told Tad that there was nothing that compared with serving your country. Tad decided he could serve his country and be a freelance journalist.

Once he made up his mind, Tad immediately signed on with the Army. With any luck he'd get sent to that conflict in Vietnam. More and more people were starting to squawk about it so there would definitely be a market for his work. That would be a great series, he told himself, a soldier's point of view.

Tad was so excited with his idea that he hadn't even talked to Janiene first. He decided to tell her at lunch. Maybe she would wait for him, maybe she'd still marry him when he got back.

Janiene had already gotten her food when Tad arrived in the cafeteria. He grabbed something quickly and went to join her.

Tad shared his exciting news with her.

Janiene's whole face seemed to drop. "Please tell me you're kidding, Tad. This isn't funny at all," Janiene pleaded.

"It's not meant to be funny. I thought you'd be happy for me. I found what I want to do. This could be Pulitzer Prize stuff. I'm talking a soldier's point of view. It will be fantastic," Tad said enthusiastically.

"And what will you write with? Your gun? Who will you write about? The people you kill?" Janiene asked sarcastically.

"Gees, Janiene, don't be so morbid. This is a small conflict with a very small country. It's not even going to last that long. I'll be lucky if the war is still going on when I get out of boot camp."

"Lucky? You have a strange sense of what constitutes luck. I can't believe you didn't talk to me first. Did you forget? We are promised. I would think that you might care what I would have to say about the whole thing."

"I do care. It's just that the army recruiter was here on campus. The idea came to me like a lightening bolt. I just did it. I didn't want to waste time. Even if I had talked to you first, you wouldn't have talked me out of it. Maybe I would have waited a few weeks or months but ultimately I still would have chosen the same path. What if the conflict is over by then. I'd resent you for taking the opportunity from me. If the conflict wasn't over and I joined then you'd resent me for betraying you. This was the best way."

"You think I don't resent the fact that you didn't talk to me first? You men are all the same. You think about your needs and damn anything or anyone that gets in your way. You can go to Vietnam, or Hades, for all I care." Janiene gave him a weary look.

"Oh, Janiene, I'm sorry if I hurt you. I didn't mean to. Truly I didn't. I thought I'd write to you every week and if you'd still have me when I got back then we'd get married."

"No, no, no! Tad, I will not wait for you. If you want to marry me, you will have to do it before you leave." Janiene thought she was not going to lose him too. She never loved Tad in the way she loved John Jackson but he was still her best friend. He was her even keel. She needed him.

"You're kidding, right? I would love to marry you right now. I didn't think you'd go for that."

"When do you leave for boot camp?"

"I don't know yet. I'll know in a couple of days."

"I better get home and share the news with my family."

"I'll follow you. I don't have to worry about making my English lit class anymore," Tad said with a smile.

Janiene's parents had been less than thrilled. Even so, her mother had dug out the dress she had worn on her wedding day and laid the dress gently across Janiene's bed.

When Tad finally left, Janiene's mother asked her daughter to her bedroom where she then made a gift of the gown to her. Janiene had shed a few tears of joy and shared a hug but her mother could not hold back her questions or concerns for her daughter any longer.

"I don't understand this, Janiene. Why can't you wait until the boy returns home? That is if he ever leaves home. What's the rush?" Jean Jeaneaux asked her daughter.

"I love Tad. I want to marry him now. It's funny that someone who ended up eloping should talk about things being rushed," Janiene told her.

"You know that was different. I was engaged to another man. My wedding dress was made for that wedding. My parents did not approve of your Papa. In the end, I felt it was better to disappoint my parents for a little while than disappoint myself for a lifetime."

"There you have it then. I'm just following my own happiness."

"It's not the same. Your Papa and I are not against this match. We wish you every happiness. We only fear, well we think, uh, that you are not over John yet."

"What difference does that make? I can never have John Jackson. I love Tad. I really do. Maybe it's not the same type of love I felt for John Jackson but it's still love." Janiene, not meeting her mother's eyes, fingered the tiny pearls on her mother's wedding gown.

"Maybe you would like to wait until Tad came home. Once you're over John, you may be able to love Tad like you love John."

"I don't want to wait. I don't want to lose Tad. What makes you think I still love John Jackson anyway?"

"Your eyes, your posture, your whole being speaks of the love, and the pain, you feel whenever John Sommier is mentioned."

Tears stung Janiene's eyes. "It doesn't matter how I feel about John Jackson. All that matters now is how I feel about Tad. I love Tad and I will make him a good wife."

"There has never been any doubt about you making a good wife. Any man would be blessed to have you. We just want you to be happy, to be sure of what you're doing."

Janiene smiled at her mother. "I do know what I'm doing. This is the first thing in a very long time that has brought this much happiness," Janiene paused as he looked at her wedding dress. "Now, can we please plan a wedding, Mama?"

"Of course," Jean Jeaneaux said softly.

Tad went back to school after his meeting with the Jeaneaux family. He had to take care of the paper work for dropping out of school.

After visiting the registrar of classes, Tad decided to have a snack over at Loyola. He had already shared his good news with everyone he'd seen at Tulane. There were plenty of people he knew that went to Loyola.

Tulane and Loyola Universities practically sat on the same ground. They both fronted St. Charles Avenue across from Audubon Park. Only the Holy Name Of Jesus cathedral separated the two. Well, the cathedral, and a religion. Loyola was the largest Catholic university in the South.

Tad made the short walk over to Loyola sharing his news with anyone he knew.

Tad was even sharing his news with people he hadn't talked to since high school. That's how he came upon Don Buker.

"That's great news, Overthall. Congratulations," Don Buker grinned.

"Thanks. I know I just keep popping this news on everyone but I'm just so damned excited about the whole thing," Tad said quickly.

"Don't worry about it. I know I'm happy for you. I'm glad you told me. Here you may be interested in the pamphlets I have here. You'll probably be planning to have children soon. You'll want to keep the world a safe place for them." Buker handed Tad the information.

Tad cringed when he saw the White Wings insignia on the pamphlet cover. "I don't think I'd be interested in this, Buker. When did you get involved with the Wings?"

"I'm a new recruit. I think if you read the material that you'd agree with us. We can't just let the inferiors take over the earth. That's not what God intended—"

"There I have to agree with you. That's not what God intended. God did not make inferior people. God did not intend for us to hold other people back due to their race. It's wrong. I can't believe you're involved in all this," Tad said with shock.

"Come on, Overthall. Have you met a smart Negro? And you know it's not only that, you can't trust their kind."

"This is foolish. What are you basing your ideas on? Of course, I've met smart Negroes. So have you. In high school, a good friend of mine was Negro."

"See, we only went to high school with them for one semester. They've already got you calling them friend. What's next? You gonna be best man when one of 'em tries to marry a White girl?"

"Calm down, Buker. I'd lay odds you liked the boy I was friends with. I saw you talking to him many times."

"I never liked one of 'em. Never. You never saw me hang out with no nigger." Buker looked nervously to the other new recruits that were handing out materials with him.

"I think you did." Tad whispered the Negro boy's name to Don Buker.

The blood in Don's face drained. "I never liked him. You know I didn't hang out with him."

"Whatever you say, Don. I won't be needing these." Tad handed the propaganda back to the young recruiter.

Judge Cartwright was pacing the floor waiting to hear the news. The hangers for lower Louisiana were voting that night. The hangers for northern Louisiana had voted the day before.

"Jefferson, why don't y'all have a drink and relax," Judith Cartwright said to her husband.

"I don't feel like sitting down. This could be the most important decision ever made. And it's being made for me! I know I'd be the best damn Pegasus they'd ever had. What is taking so damn long, anyway? Judge Cartwright continued to pace.

Judith poured herself a drink. "You know you're way ahead after the vote last night. You'll have to win."

"I wish it were that simple. There are many more votes in lower Louisiana. Tonight's vote is far more important."

"If you would just relax. The time would seem to pass faster. Have a drink, Jeff."

"Fine. If I have a drink will you get off my damn back?" Jefferson roared at his wife.

She played with the ice in her glass careful to avoid eye contact with her husband. "I'm sorry, Jefferson. I was only trying to help."

"Well don't. Just sit over there and keep your mouth shut." He hadn't meant to be so harsh with his wife but he couldn't remember the last time he felt this wound up.

The telephone rang. Cartwright raced over to answer it.

"Yes, I understand," Jefferson Cartwright said and placed the receiver on the hook.

"Well? What's the news?" Judith eyed her husband's solemn face.

"Judith, I will fly to heights that only the Pegasus can."

Judith still looked at him with apprehension. "Does that mean that you're the—"

"I'm Pegasus. White Wings will sail to new heights under my direction. My first step is to replace myself as The Eagle. Excuse me, Sugar. I need to call Tommy Jamison." Cartwright escorted Judith to the doorway, planted a big kiss on her cheek and closed the door in her face.

Judge Cartwright's mind was buzzing with ideas. He hadn't been sure if he'd be elected Pegasus. It was what he had wanted since college. He had wanted to be Pegasus more than anything. The only thing he had ever wanted more was a son. So he didn't have a son. He had a grandson. And now, finally, he was Pegasus.

Cartwright poured a tall bourbon and water. He dialed the phone to give the good news to his friend.

"Jamison, I just heard. I've got it. I'm Pegasus," Judge Cartwright boomed.

"Great! I knew you would be. Have you thought about who will be your replacement?"

"Whoa there. Am I already being hit up for special favors?" Cartwright teased his friend.

"I'll take all the special favors I can get," Jamison admitted easily.

"Well, it won't be no special favor to appoint you to The Eagle. You deserve it. Of course, I can't announce it until I've been sworn in as Pegasus. I'd appreciate it if you'd keep it hush hush until then," Cartwright told his friend.

"I won't tell a soul," Jamison paused as a smile crossed his face. "Jefferson, I just want to congratulate you again and say thanks."

Cartwright hung up the phone. He had to start planning. He had to get a 'flock' together soon. He needed to meet all of his men personally.

A flock was a gathering of all the White Wings for the state. The flock was usually held in the backwoods up north or swamplands down south. Since the White Wings of Louisiana numbered into the thousands they had to meet somewhere large yet discreet.

Cartwright had heard the Negroes were planning a march in Washington DC next month. He wanted to make sure they covered that at the flock. He didn't want individual pilots and copilots deciding what should be done with the Negroes who were planning on attending.

He wanted to make sure White Wings did not offend the federal government. That would give them a lot more room to maneuver when the time came.

Chapter Nine

Everything was business as usual at Past Into Present. Barbara was sure she had worried for nothing. Henri still treated her the same. What's more, he was spending more time at the other stores. Barbara was reading the journal faster than ever.

Barbara needed the journal now. It helped her escape from the problems at home. Everything had been going so well at home. Why had John agreed to let Lacy's son come to work with her? He should have known she wouldn't like it. He probably did know. Damn him!

Barbara didn't want her son playing with Negroes. What if he started talking like them. She had asked John that. John had been sarcastic. He told her that it would be great, they would have the first seven-month old that could talk. She had told him she was talking about Jammy's accent. John told her not worry about it. He said kids tend to have the same accent as their parents which was why Jammy had the accent he had, not because he was Negro. She hoped that he was right. Still, she'd rather be safe than sorry.

She was trying not to mention Jammy too much lately. John was starting to go into those black moods like when they were first married.

Barbara had actually been surprised at how smart Jammy was. He probably wouldn't grow up that way. Barbara's Daddy had told her how many stupid Coloreds came though his courtroom everyday. She wondered how many stupid Whites went through it. Oh no, Barbara thought. Now, she was beginning to think like John. But maybe, just maybe, John had a point. Jammy was an awfully smart little boy. He was cute too.

Barbara pulled the journal out while it was still slow.

July 1845

I have been greatly honored this day. Today was the reading of Uncle Jean's will. He has left me all of his property with exception being made to his town house in New Orleans. He left that to a person known only to his lawyer. Aunt Marie thinks it was left to his mistress. I fear she is right. I was instructed to care for Aunt Marie until which time she joins Uncle Jean or she remarries. It is Uncle Jean's wish that I do not live in the main house until such time that I have wed. I think he need not worried about me compromising his Marie. She is nothing more than an Aunt to me. Yet I will be happy to live in one of the garconnieres until I take a bride. It is hard to believe Mallard's Landing is mine. Not being first born, I did not know when I would acquire property. Gustave, being first born, was happy for me but Luc who has always been not only my brother but my friend was angry with me. I will gladly share with Luc, and the girls too if Papa doesn't find good matches for them.

I cannot wait to share the news with Jean-Claude. He says that Papa is sending him to Paris next year. Papa still does not know of my friendship with his mistress' son. Jean-Claude says it would only make our Papa nervous. It is not proper for the family to formally know of the mistress or of her offspring.

Barbara paused while she got out her ham and cheese sandwich and potato salad. She stood over the counter while she ate.

Barbara found her place and continued reading.

Of all the children Papa has, I think I like Jean-Claude the best. Luc is a good man but he is not as quick witted or as adventurous as Jean-Claude. Sometimes I feel Jean-Claude is older than I and not the other way around. He is so wise in the ways of the world. I will dearly miss him when he goes to Paris.

When the little bell rang out Barbara went and helped her customer but not before she put both the journal and her lunch away.

Later that night, Barbara was rushing around trying to decide what to wear. She had thrown half a dozen dresses across the bed in her frenzy.

Her Daddy had called her at work the day before to invite them all to dinner tonight. He hadn't said who all would be there. Barbara decided it was better to be a little over dressed than under dressed.

Lacy had John Jr. dressed in his best little sailor suit. John was wearing a blue suit. They both looked like pictures off the pages of the finest fashion magazines.

Barbara felt proud that they both were hers.

Shortly after they arrived, Barbara's Daddy sent for her to meet him in the library.

"Hi, Daddy." Barbara kissed him on the cheek. "I didn't realize so many people were coming over tonight."

"Oh, I didn't tell you? Sorry, Darlin'. You look good enough to eat. You sure dressed for the occasion." The judge hugged his daughter.

"What is the occasion?"

"This strictly 'tween you and me, Darlin'. Not all of those here tonight would be pleased with the news. Particularly that husband of yours."

"Daddy, what is it? Tell me," Barbara interrupted.

"The time has finally come. I'm Pegasus."

Barbara let out a squeak from excitement. "You're kidding. When? How?"

"That old coot Leaverton died last week. I was voted in two days ago."

Barbara embraced her father. "I'm so proud of you. This is what you've always wanted."

Cartwright pushed some hair away from his daughter's eye.

"Yes, Barbie. This and a son to follow in my footsteps."

Barbara's face saddened. "I'm sorry you've never had a son. I hope I haven't been too much of a disappointment to you, Daddy."

"Oh, Darlin', you've brought me nothin' but joy. You also gave me that delightful John Jr.. He can follow in my footsteps."

"I don't know if John will allow him to follow in all of your footsteps, Daddy."

"What John don't know won't hurt him," Judge Cartwright said with a wink.

Barbara decided to let it go. She knew John would never allow his son to get involved in White Wings or any other group like it. He would die first.

"Barbie, are you listening to me?" Judge Cartwright broke her concentration.

"Uh, yes, what is it, Daddy?"

"I asked how much does John know about my involvement with White Wings?"

"Nothing. I mean he and his family know you're involved with the Klan or something but they don't know what."

"Why do they think I'm involved with the Klan or something? What have you said to them?"

"I didn't say anything to them. You can't be a member of White Wings for over twenty years and not have people find out about it. I didn't think you were ashamed of your involvement with the Wings."

"I am not ashamed. I'm damned proud. But there's a time and a place for everything. This is not the time for people to know what I'm up to."

"What are you up to, Daddy?"

"I'm making the world a safer place for John Jr. and for you Darlin'. Come on, let's join the others." Judge Cartwright kissed his daughter on the cheek before escorting her to the dining room.

Barbara surveyed the dining room as they entered it. She knew everyone there. Tommy and Betsy Jamison were just taking their seats. Judge Perez, Paul and Linda Shore and her stepmother were already seated. John was leaning against the mantle holding John Jr..

John walked over to where Barbara and her father were standing. He pulled her chair out for her before her father had a chance to. He sat down next to her, still holding the baby.

John whispered in her ear. "What's this all about? Is it some political dinner or what?" Though John had never met Judge Perez before, he had seen him many times on TV and in the papers when they were integrating the schools. Perez was a staunch segregationist.

Barbara didn't answer him. Luckily at that moment Judge Cartwright stood up at the head of the table. He began tapping on his wine glass with a fork.

"Can I get everyone's attention, please. I have asked you all to dinner to share in all that is going well in my life right now," Cartwright inclined his head toward Tommy Jamison in some private gesture before he continued. "My seat as District Judge has never been more secure. They are talking about making me King of the Krewe for Mardi Gras again. That will make three times. 'Course it's way too soon to know about that yet. Things in all aspects of my life are going well. Take a look at that big healthy grandson of mine. I just wanted to share my happiness with y'all. So, eat and drink to your hearts content. This is a celebration."

Barbara leaned over to John. "I guess that answers your question."

John adjusted his fidgety son on his lap. "Not quite. I think there's more to this than meets the eye. I think he's celebrating something in particular. I gather some of the guests know exactly what it is."

"Oh John, you're always looking for something that's not there."

"Let's just say I'd rather not give the benefit of the doubt. Especially when it comes to your father." He sounded disgusted.

The servants began serving the soup. The dining room was lit by a huge glittering crystal chandelier. The gilded rims of the plates reflected the light so that it danced upon the faces of all the guests. The dining room with its fourteen foot high ceiling and two fireplaces did not seem so overpowering in the dancing light. The dining room could easily accommodate three times the people. The baroque gilded mirrors on every wall made the gathering seemed to fill the room. Barbara's father told her when she was a little girl that it was the trick of the mirrors. They gave a large gathering a sense of roominess and a small gathering a sense of coziness.

The soup was a cream of collard greens that was both rich and creamy. Everyone was so delighted with the soup that there wasn't much conversation except the occasional 'ooh' or 'aah'.

Betsy Jamison broke the pleasure of the diners with small talk. "That's just 'bout the cutest baby I ever did see. You must be proud of him, Barbara."

Barbara swallowed her soup and wiped the corners of her mouth. "Yes, we are. John Jr. has been the joy of our lives. He is such a sweet baby. Not at all fussy."

"Did you say John Jr.? We named our son after Paul. He's a junior too. Paul Wilson Shore, Jr.," Linda Shore chimed in.

"John Jackson Sommier, Jr. is his full name. I think it sounds regal." Barbara adjusted her son's jacket while he was still seated on his father's lap.

Tommy was getting sick of the ladies small talk though he had to admit little John Jr. was a cute thing.

"You must be proud of your family, Judge," Tommy hoped to shift the conversation to the men.

Two 'yeses' chimed in together. Tommy then realized what he had done. "I'm sorry Judge Perez. I was speaking to Judge Cartwright but I'd love to hear about your family as well."

Tommy had long admired Judge Leander Perez. His views on segregation had earned him a place in the hearts of many a New Orleanian. He was a stern looking man whose hair had long since silvered yet his brows remained the jet black of his youth. Tommy thought the man had to at least be seventy years old but both his face and his voice seemed to be that of a man twenty years younger.

"Go ahead, Jefferson. I'll just enjoy some more of that delicious soup if y'all don't mind," Judge Perez said.

Judith Cartwright rang for Percy to get more soup for Judge Perez. She also instructed Percy to hold off on the second course until the Judge had finished his soup.

Judge Cartwright looked down the table at his daughter and his grandson. "A man couldn't be prouder of his family. I've got a beautiful wife and daughter. My grandson is the apple of my eye. A real pleasure, that one." Cartwright paused before he started to sound like a sentimental old fool. "How are your kids doing Lee?" Cartwright addressed Judge Perez.

The older judge scooped up his last spoonful of soup before answering. "Great. My oldest is following in my footsteps, law you know. Enough to do any father proud. Not to change the subject but I thought you invited us here to make some sort of announcement," Judge Perez inquired not too tactfully.

Judge Cartwright tugged at the knot of his tie. "I believe I have already explained why I requested your presence here tonight. Though I do have a case pending that I wanted to get your thoughts on, Lee."

That seemed to satisfy Judge Perez, who looked on while Percy served the salad.

Tommy kept looking at John. He was trying to size him up. Tommy knew Cartwright had not wished to share his promotion publicly. He wondered why he couldn't share it with his family. Maybe he could. Maybe he was only keeping silent because of Judge Perez. Paul Shore already knew. Paul had been a White Wing for nearly as long as Cartwright. That left only John Sommier and Judge Perez. He wondered which one the judge did not feel comfortable in sharing his news with.

Tommy didn't have that problem. He only surrounded himself with people who were either White Wings or sympathetic to it's cause.

The conversation around the table had broken up into small groups. Tommy took the opportunity to speak to Judge Perez candidly.

"What do y'all think 'bout this march the Negroes are planning to have in the next few weeks in Washington?" Tommy asked Judge Perez.

"I say let 'em march. It's not going to do a bit of good to try and stop 'em. The more we interfere on a state level, the more rights are taken away from us. Take our schools' integration for instance. Where was our say? The state said a emphatic 'no' but the feds said yes. So now we have integration. We have to find different ways to keep the rights of our people intact. I've had about enough of the darkies trying to push their way in here and there. If the think they can organize against us they'll learn a hard lesson. The White man isn't an animal from the jungle. If they keep trying to tangle with us they'll see that we have more to fight them with than the proverbial spear." Judge Perez sat back to allow the main course to be served.

Tommy looked over to see if John had been paying attention to the Judge's remarks. He had not. Tommy would just have to corner him when they got their after dinner brandy.

Judge Cartwright had been paying attention to Judge Perez's statements. He did not want this to turn into a political rally. There would be plenty of time for that.

"I think you'll all enjoy the herb encrusted lamb. It's always been one of my favorites. Did I tell y'all that Barbie is working now," Cartwright shifted the attention to his daughter.

"Um, yes. I'm really enjoying it. I'm helping John's father out. The Sommier's own five antique stores around town. It's fascinating," Barbara tried to handle her embarrassment. She still didn't like the idea of people knowing that she worked.

Tommy's eyes challenged John as he spoke to him. "Is Barbara working out of necessity or for pleasure?"

"I don't see where that's any of your concern, Mr. Jamison," John said coldly.

Tommy regarded John with open speculation. "No, I don't suppose it is. I was just curious if the daughter of one of Louisiana's most prominent judges had to work."

John refused to be goaded into anger. "We all know what curiosity did to a certain feline."

"Was that a warning?" Tommy was still hoping for more of a response.

"Take it anyway you please. I was merely stating a fact," John said blandly.

Paul Shore didn't know what his friend was up to but he didn't like it. Judge Cartwright was a good friend of his and he didn't like the idea of Tommy picking a fight with the judge's son-in-law.

"I hear you're tearing up Tulane, Son. Aren't you going to law school?" Paul asked to calm things down.

"I won't start law school until next fall. I'll finish my under grad studies in about half the usual time. I've taken a pretty heavy academic load. I want to get to Harvard as soon as possible." Though John spoke to Paul Shore he continued to eye Tommy Jamison.

Betsy had apparently kicked Tommy under the table. He jumped and looked at his wife with barely restrained fury.

"We are all so proud of John. With the exception of when John Jr. was born, he has perfect grades. I'm still hoping he'll reconsider Tulane for law instead of that Yankee school," Judge Cartwright told his guests.

The talk broke up into smaller conversations for the rest of the meal. Tommy Jamison did not involve himself in any of the small talk. Instead he watched his wife with a smoldering look.

When everyone finished their dessert, Judge Cartwright stood. "Why don't we all retire to the living room for brandies. I've got a cherry brandy I think the ladies will enjoy. Of course, there's a Napoleon brandy with quite a kick for any one in the mood for something stronger."

Judge Cartwright helped Judith from her seat. Everyone else followed his lead. Everyone, that is, except Tommy Jamison. Tommy waited until everyone except the servants had left the room. Then he helped Betsy with her chair. Tommy grabbed Betsy's wrist and yanked her up from her chair. "Don't you ever kick me under the table again."

Betsy squirmed to try to free her wrist. "We are guests of the judge. You were being rude to the judge's family."

"I'll decide when I'm being rude. If you ever embarrass me like that again I'll break your goddamn neck. Do I make myself clear?" Tommy growled while he continued to twist his wife's wrist.

"Tommy, you're hurting me," Betsy cried.

"No shit. I asked you a question. Now answer me." Tommy looked up and caught John Sommier's reflection in one of the mirrors. He released his wife suddenly.

"Go join the others, Betsy," Tommy ordered.

Tommy waited until Betsy had left the room before he addressed John. "Are you in the habit of eavesdropping, Mr. Sommier?" Tommy whispered in a dangerous tone.

John walked over to the table where he had been seated for dinner. He reached under the table and grabbed a bag.

"I am in the habit of tracking down the diaper bag whenever my wife needs it."

"Are you saying you didn't hear what was said," Tommy asked accusingly.

"No, I didn't say that at all." John moved to exit the room.

"Someone needs to teach you some manners, Son." Tommy moved to block John's exit.

"Maybe so but I'm sure I can't learn them from a Neanderthal who threatens women. Kindly get out of my way, Mr. Jamison." John tried to push past Tommy but Tommy wouldn't budge.

"You'd be wise not to make an enemy of me," Tommy warned.

"My son needs a fresh diaper. Either move out of my way on your own accord or I'll move you."

Tommy stepped out of the way and let John pass.

John Sommier certainly had guts, Tommy thought. Tommy hadn't decided whether he liked the kid or not. That would depend on Sommier's beliefs. Tommy wondered if John Sommier were White Wing material.

Two weeks later Tad and Janiene were married in a small religious ceremony. Even though the arrangements had been rushed, the wedding was beautiful.

Janiene, dressed in her mother's gown, looked like a picture on the cover of a bridal magazine. Tad wore a black rented cutaway and top hat. She carried a petite white rose bouquet and he wore a white rose boutonnière.

Tad stood adjusting his ascot while they smiled for what seemed like the four hundredth picture.

"Tad will you quit fidgeting around," Janiene pleaded.

"When will they be finished taking pictures? I'm ready to get to the party," Tad said bluntly.

"It's not everyday you get married. Can't you hold out a while longer." Janiene patted his hand.

"Boy, you're telling me. I won't ever get married again just so I don't have to go though all the picture taking," Tad said with a devilish smile.

"That's right, smile dear," Janiene said as she stepped on his foot.

When the last photo had been taken, Janiene and Tad got into the limousine that had been rented for them. They were whisked over to the Overthall's house for the reception.

The house was a typical ranch style house made popular by the stars of the silver screen of the early fifties and it was still a popular modern style nearly ten years later. The outside of it was decorated with green garland filled with white rose buds. When they entered the house they were surrounded by more of the same garland and flowers.

Tad's mother hugged the young couple in the hallway.

"Everyone is in the recreation room. Did you want to change first or go straight to the reception," Mrs. Overthall smiled at the young couple.

"It's not everyday I fork out ten bucks for a suit that I don't get to keep. I'm wearing mine. How about you Janiene," Tad teased.

"I'll be wearing mine too. I feel like a princess," Janiene admitted.

"You look like a princess. You took my breath away when your dad walked you to the alter." Tad's eyes misted.

Tad's mother eased her way from between the young couple.

"Are you coming?" Mrs. Overthall said as she headed to the recreation room.

Many hours later Tad and Janiene went to his bedroom. They didn't have enough money for a honeymoon. They didn't even have enough money for a hotel room.

The Overthall's had said that Janiene could live with them while Tad was at boot camp and if he got sent to Vietnam she could remain with them.

Janiene had been reluctant but her mother pointed out that a wife's place was with her husband. She was her husband's responsibility. As much as her own parents might want to have her continue to live at home it wouldn't be possible. That would be an insult to both Tad and his parents. They had, after all, opened their home up to her.

Tad's bedroom was a typical young man's room. It was dark with wood paneling and wooden shutters. The north wall was covered with shelves filled with books and little league trophies. The double bed had a brown tweed spread on it.

Tad lay down on his bed. "It's been a long but happy day. I'm glad you decided to marry me before I left. You have made me happier than you'll ever know." .

Janiene nervously walked over to the bed. "I'm happy too." Janiene sat down on the bed, "I feel a little funny about staying here in your parent's house."

Tad pulled off his ascot and his jacket. His muscles rippled under his shirt. "We're on the other side of the house. They won't hear a thing."

Janiene blushed a bright red. "I wasn't talking about that. I was just, uh, it's just that I wish we had our own place."

"We'll get our own place soon. I'll send all my money home from the army. You'll be able to pick whatever apartment you'd like." Tad reached for his wife and began kissing her.

Janiene responded to his kisses until he started to undress her while he kissed her. She panicked. She jumped up from the bed clutching her bodice together.

"What is it?" Did I hurt you? Are you okay?" Tad's eyes were filled with concern.

"Yes, I mean no. I don't know what I mean. I'm just nervous. I'm kind of scared."

"You don't have to be scared of me. We have a lifetime together. We'll take it nice and slow if that's what you want. Tonight we can just kiss if that will make you feel better, okay?"

Tears of gratitude flowed from Janiene's eyes. "Thank you. I don't mean to be frigid."

"You're not frigid. You're just a little scared. Come here. I promise we won't take it any further than kissing tonight." Tad reached for Janiene's hand and helped her back to the bed. He began kissing her again but this time he was careful to keep his hands on her back. He didn't have to rush her, she was his wife. There would be plenty of time. Plenty of time.

Chapter Ten

Two days later Tad found himself in the middle of a mix up down at the offices of the army recruiter.

"Sorry, Overthall. Regardless of what orders you originally received, you are due in boot camp tomorrow. If you don't show you will be AWOL," the army recruiter said firmly.

"But I just got married. These papers say that I don't have to leave for another week and a half." Tad held his orders out to the recruiter.

"I'm not going over this with you again. Be on that truck tonight or face the consequences. This not a game, Son. This is the United States Army." The recruiter handed Tad his new orders.

Tad drove home as quickly as he could. He needed to pack before Janiene got home from school. He wanted to spend every minute he could with her. Heck, they hadn't even consummated their marriage yet. Tad thought a week and a half would be plenty of time to ease Janiene into a complete marriage. Now he did not have time. Still, he couldn't exactly force himself on her.

A few hours later, Janiene arrived home. She had stopped by her parent's to pick up a few more things before she had gone over to the Overthall's.

Tad had already broken the news to his mother. He was sitting in the recreation room drinking a beer when Janiene found him.

"You're late. You could have called. I was starting to worry," Tad said dryly.

"Well, hello to you too. I had to stop by and get some more of my things. I'll call next time I'm going to be a whole hour late,' Janiene replied coolly.

Tad got up and hugged Janiene. He didn't mean to be so cold with her. But he hadn't wanted to lose even a minute with her. "I'm sorry. Things just aren't going like they're supposed to."

"Because I'm late? How do you think things would go? Was I supposed to have to have dinner waiting for you or something?" Janiene asked flippantly.

"No, I wasn't saying that at all." Tad went to the table and picked up his new orders. "Here, read these." He handed her the orders. "There was some sort of mix up. Those are my real orders."

Janiene's face dropped as she read the orders. "They can't do this. They said you wouldn't leave until the week after next. Tell them this wrong. Tell them, Tad."

"I've already spoken to them. They say if I'm not in that transport tonight that I'll be in big trouble. I have to go. I have to leave in three hours. Mom called Dad at work so he could come home early. They want to take us out to dinner if that is all right with you."

"Tad, what are you going to do? We haven't even, um, we haven't, you know." Janiene felt guilty.

"We could remedy that now. Or if you're still not comfortable with the idea, we can wait until I get a pass after boot camp is over."

Janiene walked to the doorway. She looked back over her shoulder. "Now. Let's try now."

Tad followed his wife into their bedroom.

Half an hour later Tad found himself in a very embarrassing situation. Embarrassing that is, only to him. Janiene was very understanding.

"Don't worry about it. It's just the anxiety about having to go away so quickly." Janiene stroked his hair.

"Damn, I can't believe this. I've had it come up at the most inopportune times. Times I didn't want it to come up. This is the first time I wanted it to come up and it didn't. I thought this only happened to old men. You are probably thinking you married a real dud."

"I most certainly am not. You are under a lot of strain right now. The last couple of days you have been more than patient with me. In that time I saw, more than a few times, what you are normally capable of. I understand." The topic of conversation had Janiene blushing deep shades of red.

"I sure as heck don't understand. I really do want you. My mind says yes but look at my body. It's like a damn noodle."

Janiene couldn't quite bring herself to look at the area in question. Two days ago was the first time she had ever seen a naked man and only in his aroused state. She was very embarrassed. "Do you want to kiss and touch some more before we have to go to dinner?" Janiene asked almost inaudibly.

"Yes." Tad melded his body to hers seeking any type of relief.

The flock had been set up for the following Saturday. All the Eagles had been contacted around the state. Even one from Mississippi, the Natchez area.

The Mississippi Eagle preferred his hangers to attend the Louisiana flocks because the meetings were usually more proximal.

Jefferson Cartwright sat in his library drinking bourbon and added up the number of attendees. He had confirmed the flock with nine Eagles. Each Eagle oversaw between ten and twenty hangers. Jefferson had gotten the exact number of hangers from each of the Eagles. A huge smile crossed the face of the judge. From what he could ascertain, there would be nearly twenty-eight hundred White Wings in attendance. If they all turned out, this would be the largest flock meeting in Louisiana in the twentieth century.

There were records of flocks numbering into the tens of thousands immediately following the Civil War. The White Wings were formed shortly before the end of the Civil War. The membership had been overwhelming back then.

Since the turn of the century the membership had been steadily falling. With the Jim Crow laws people had felt protected. They had not felt the need to join the protection of the group.

Now it was different. With the integration of the schools the membership drives had been more successful than they had been in over sixty years. More and more young people were joining the Wings. That, in itself, was a promising sign for the Wings.

It was Jefferson Cartwright's goal to have the membership numbers approach their original status. Without the large membership numbers the judge would not be able to realize his dream.

Jefferson Cartwright had spoken to the Pegasus in Mississippi. He had gotten permission for the hangers in western Mississippi to attend his flock. It was probably enough to just talk to the Eagle but Jefferson didn't want to step on anyone's toes.

He had liked the Pegasus for Mississippi. His goals and beliefs were similar to his own. The Mississippi Pegasus was on a membership drive too. The man had a tendency to be a little more violent than Cartwright thought was necessary but, still, he was a good man. Cartwright thought it would be wise to keep in touch with him. It could prove to be a beneficial relationship.

Jefferson Cartwright almost shared his plan with the man in Mississippi but thought better of it. Cartwright would need to obtain more power, much more power before he started implementing his plan. It was something that should have been done many years ago and now he had the chance to do it. He was going to make damn sure he didn't blow that chance.

Judge Cartwright found that since he'd become Pegasus, Tommy Jamison was around all the time. If he wasn't on the judge's doorstep then he was on the telephone. At first, Cartwright felt the man was checking up on him. Then he decided that Jamison was just a natural born leader. That type of man could never sit still while others took action. Cartwright knew that feeling firsthand. He was the same type.

Cartwright decided he would need a right hand man when the time came. Jamison would be that man. Jamison was the strongest where Cartwright was the weakest. The violence issue.

Cartwright didn't approve of all the violence that Tommy condoned but there might be a time when he needed to implement more violent strategies. Jamison was just the man.

Though it disgusted Cartwright, he had seen Betsy Jamison often enough to know what kind of violence Tommy Jamison was capable of. Over the years, Betsy had sported many a black eye, bruises and even broken bones. The 'accidents' only happened when Betsy dared to contradict or oppose her husband.

Cartwright could never strike a woman. Especially a woman as lovely as Betsy. He figured if Tommy Jamison could inflict that kind of damage on his own wife then he would be invaluable if the need for violence ever arose.

Cartwright had promised Jamison he would call him with the final numbers as soon as they were compiled. Jamison was, after all, going to be organizing all the combat lessons. The lessons weren't supposed to be teaching the men to take action against the Coloreds. It was to protect the White Wings from the federal government. At least that's what Jamison had said. Cartwright couldn't help but feel, given Tommy's nature, that there was an ulterior motive.

Cartwright shut the door to his library. He had heard some of the servants mulling around. He couldn't afford to let the wrong ears hear his conversation with Jamison.

He picked up the phone and dialed.

"Hel-lo," Betsy answered in a weepy voice.

"Hello, Betsy. Jefferson here. Is Tommy about?" Cartwright knew from Betsy's voice that Tommy was definitely home.

"Who the hell is this?" Tommy yelled into the receiver after snatching the phone from Betsy.

"Cartwright here. Did I catch you at a bad time? You can call me back," he said not too pleasantly.

Tommy forced himself to calm down quickly. "No, sir. It's not a bad time at all. Sorry to yell at you but we've been getting crank calls lately. I was trying to put an end to it."

Cartwright was amazed at how fast Jamison had come up with that lie. Cartwright knew that there hadn't been any crank calls. Knowing Jamison, Betsy was probably turning black and blue right at that moment. "I see. No harm done here. I was calling to give you the final numbers. It looks like twenty-eight hundred in all. It will be a mandatory Saturday meeting. Any of the boys who want to stay for your training can do so on Sunday."

"I thought there would be some combat training on Saturday," Tommy said, obviously agitated.

"I don't know how you got that impression. Even though I've been sworn in as Pegasus, the official ceremony will be held then. Then there's the whole business with the Colored's march. I have to handle that at the flock. We also have to cover the recruiting process. We need to get more Wings. I really don't see how we will have time for combat training on Saturday," Cartwright said.

"It's not just the combat training I wanted to cover. I had planned a lecture on how to spot a plant. What with all the recruiting we'll be doing, the men'll need that. You know the feds infiltrated the Klan in Georgia. We can't have that here," Tommy said emphatically.

The feds, if not handled properly, could really screw up his plans, Cartwright thought. "Yeah, I see what you mean. The entire flock needs to hear how to prevent that. Get any of the boys trained in military intelligence involved in that lecture."

"I was trained by the marines myself. I don't think I'll need any help," Tommy said indignantly.

"Right. It will be a lecture after all, but you will need help for your hand-to-hand and firearm training," Cartwright said impatiently.

"That's true. If you want to give me all the other Eagles phone numbers, I'll get it set up with other potential trainers," Tommy said.

"Already done. Wings will be contacting you soon. Oh and Jamison?"

"Yeah?"

"You better get that crank caller taken care of. A lot of the boys would take none to kindly to being yelled at over the phone." Cartwright hung up the phone without waiting for a response.

Cartwright had no idea how much he had just angered Tommy Jamison.

Jamison put the receiver down. Cartwright had a lot of nerve talking to him like he was some sort of flunky. If it hadn't been for him,

Cartwright wouldn't be Pegasus now, Tommy thought. He had really gone out of his way to influence the hangers in the New Orleans area to vote for Cartwright.

Tommy was disappointed that he hadn't been able to get all the Eagles' phone numbers from Cartwright. He needed those phone numbers.

Traditionally only the Pegasus had the phone numbers of all the Eagles. That was supposed to protect the Eagles in case of infiltration. That way only one person had the information that could link the whole group together. In case of death there was a safety deposit box held in corporation that contained all the names but only the trustee could get the list, which, of course, was given to the successor.

Tommy wanted to talk to each of the Eagles individually. That way he would be able to know which Eagles would be with him when the time came. It was time the Wings were the biggest organization in the state. Hell, Tommy thought, in the whole damn country.

Tommy's thoughts were interrupted by his wife's sniffling. Tommy went through the house to seek her out. He came upon her in the master bedroom. "Would you quit that crying, Betsy? You know I don't want to hurt you. I did it for your own good. You have to learn that you can't be goin' against me. Especially not in front of the maid."

"But I didn't go against you, Tommy. I just said that Lena hadn't had time to mop the floor yet. I didn't want her to quit because you were yelling at her," Betsy choked out softly.

"You're doin' it again. I said you went against me. You said you didn't. What's that, huh? That's going against me. I don't like it, do ya hear? I'm the man in this house. You will not oppose me!" Tommy's open hand came crashing down on Betsy's cheek.

Betsy let out a squeal. She fell back on the bed and began sobbing.

"You make me do this to you. I don't want to." Tommy smoothed his wife's hair. "Come on, stop your crying. Come on, Betsy. It hurts me more than it hurts you. I don't like to mar up that pretty little face of yours but you make me. Don't you?"

Betsy didn't answer. She just continued crying. Her whole body was shaking from her sobs.

Tommy pulled her head up by her hair. He glared into her eyes, His face twisted and distorted with anger. His eyes seemed to bulge from their sockets. "I asked you a question."

"Yes, Tommy, yes," Betsy cried.

Tommy reached for Betsy. "Come on. Give me a kiss."

Betsy knew it would turn out like this. Either like this or with her in the emergency room. Tommy was so angry tonight. He always took his anger out on her. One way or another, his anger always came out on her.

The following afternoon Barbara was completing her fourth sale of the day.

The elderly woman had selected a lovely hand painted plate by Limoges. Barbara carefully wrapped the plate in tissue paper before she wrapped it in newspaper for extra protection.

When she picked up the old newspaper, something caught her eye. It was a photograph of Janiene Jeaneaux.

Barbara placed that piece of newspaper behind the counter and reached for another. She finished wrapping the plate, put it in a bag and even helped the woman out of the store. Barbara was very anxious to see why John's old love was in the Times-

Picayune. Barbara walked behind the counter and grabbed the paper. She searched for the photo of Janiene and read the caption beneath the picture.

YESTERDAY AT THREE IN THE AFTERNOON THE LOVELY JANIENE JEANEAUX WAS WED TO THE VERY ELIGIBLE TAD OVERTHALL. The story went on to tell about Tad and his family's background.

Barbara's heart felt like it did a flip inside her chest. She hadn't been this happy since the day John proposed to her. Now John was really hers. He couldn't very well go pining after a married woman. Especially a woman who married his one-time best friend.

Barbara looked at the top of the newspaper. It was dated the previous Sunday. Barbara was pretty sure they still had Sunday's paper at home. But she decided to take the piece from the store just in case.

She had to think of a way for John to see the paper without it being too obvious. She was afraid to show him herself for fear her face would give away her elation. John would really be angry if he knew Barbara was taking pleasure from his pain.

Barbara could hardly sit still the rest of the day. She couldn't wait to see John's reaction. To think, Tad Overthall had married Janiene. Barbara was sure that the news of his precious Janiene's wedding would be enough to take the wind out of his sails but that news combined with who Janiene had married would be more than enough to capsize his boat. That just might be enough to knock Janiene from her sainthood position. John was bound to be hurt by the news. With Tad involved he would have someone other than her to take his pain out on.

Barbara wore a Cheshire smile all the way home. She had found the perfect way to share the news with John.

Barbara had made a purchase from PIP. She carefully wrapped her crystal candy dish in the inevitably damaging newsprint. She had been careful to place most of the photo across the front of the dish. She was sure John would notice it, just as she had.

When Barbara arrived home she didn't see any sign of John, Lacy or the baby.

Barbara set her package on the kitchen table. She picked up a note that was laying there.

The note said something about John taking the baby to the park. That was perfect. She would have time to bathe and change before watching the fireworks. Barbara was sure John's reaction to the news would be just like watching a Fourth of July celebration. And for her, it really would be a celebration.

She hurried into the bathroom. She was reclining, half sleeping, in the tub when John arrived home. Barbara was so relaxed that she didn't hear him come in the house.

John took John Jr. to his bedroom. The little guy had really conked out after all his activity in the park. John could hear the gentle movement of the water in the tub. He knew Barb was relaxing after a long day's work. John decided to do the same, relax that is. He went to the fridge and got a Dixie beer. He grabbed a bag of chips and was headed into the living room.

That's when it caught his eye. The wrapped item on the table. It wasn't often Barb brought things home from work. John wondered what could have caught her eye.

He set down the Dixie and the chips. He picked up the item and began unwrapping it. John nearly dropped it when he saw the very familiar face staring up at him.

He unwrapped only enough of the item to free that section of the paper. He sank down in a chair at the kitchen table and began to read.

"This can't be. No! It can't be! They haven't graduated yet." John spoke out loud to himself. He reread the article. "It just can't be."

Barbara floated into the kitchen. "What can't be, Sugar?" she asked in her sweetest drawl. She glanced to the paper in John's hands.

"Huh, oh, um, nothing," John said quietly.

Barbara was surprised by John's reaction. She took the newspaper from John's limp hands. "My, my, my. Tad and Janiene have gotten married. Who even knew they were dating?" Barbara feigned surprise.

"I knew," John said very softly.

Barbara really was surprised now. "How could, I mean how did you know?" She paused wondering if he still kept up with his old flame. "Do you still keep in touch with Tad?"

"No. He was pretty upset about us getting married." John seemed to be in a trance.

"What? Why on earth would he be upset because we got married?" Barbara was truly perplexed.

"You know why. You know it ended our friendship," John whispered dangerously.

"I really don't know what happened. I always assumed he took Janiene's side."

"Of course he took Janiene's side. That's not what ended my friendship with him though."

"What was it then?"

"You know very well that Tad was in love with you. He told me that he never did break it off with you. He didn't either, did he?"

Barbara had been thrown for a loop. When had he talked to Tad? How long had he known that Tad hadn't broken up with her?

"Yes he did. I've already told you the whole story."

"Yeah but you didn't bother including the truth in that story," John mumbled.

"John, don't say things you're going to regret. You are upset because you found out the girl you once loved has gotten married."

"Yeah right. The girl I once loved." John's words were laced with irony.

"What are you trying to say? That you still love that little tramp? Well, you can't have her! Do you hear me, John Sommier? You can't have her," Barbara's voice rose to a shrill scream.

"I've told you before, Janiene is not the one that is a tramp. By the way, thanks for the update, Barb. I know I can't have Janiene. I haven't been able to have her for nearly two years. The fact that she's gotten married doesn't change a damn thing. In case you've forgotten, I have been married, to you, for what seems like an eternity. While you may not have trusted me not to cheat on you, you could have always trusted Janiene. You may find this hard to believe but some women are actually quite virtuous," John said so icily that the room temperature felt like it was sub zero.

John thought about Janiene. He wasn't sure if he wouldn't have had an affair with Janiene had she been willing. He probably would have. Of course, his feelings might not run so deeply for her if it weren't for her virtue. She was all that was good, honest and sweet. That's what he loved so much about her.

Barbara looked into John's face. Her heart sank. John had practically admitted that he still loved Janiene. He didn't need to say the actual words. The inference that she just could not compare with Janiene had been proof enough.

The issue of his love had come up many times in the first weeks of their marriage but she thought it was different now. She was wrong. She was too hurt to strike back at the harsh comparison.

Barbara went into the living room and sank down into the well used sofa. She had been sure that John loved her. Now she knew she had been wrong. She came to the stark realization that he may never love her.

When she had so expertly trapped him into their marriage she had not thought of it as a trap. She thought she was saving him from poor White trash. She had felt sure John would grow to love her, grow to see things her way. Yet he hadn't. As it turned out, he really was trapped. No wonder he had all those black moods, she thought. He was acting like a caged animal. Sometimes he was complacent while other times he was bursting at the seams to be free from his jail, and his jailer.

The thought of John being caged caused a tinge of pain in the pit of her stomach. Like a zoo keep, she couldn't bear to see him caged but she also couldn't bear to set him free.

Barbara loved everything about John. At first she had wanted him because he was such a perfect example of manhood. Tall, dark and handsome. He had a rugged quality that made him bow to no man. Yes, originally it had been his beauty and his raw masculinity that had attracted her.

Now it was different. She loved him for so many reasons. The original reasons were still there but she had discovered that he was gentle, thoughtful, caring and absolutely brilliant. He was a wonderful father, much better than she was a mother. He was a multifaceted diamond. He shone brightly and many people were drawn by his magnetism. Just to be near him, made her happy.

A part of her wished she had left him alone nearly two years ago. If only she had never seen him. They might both be happy now. If only she had never seen him, someone like Tad Overthall would have been enough for her. Then John would be happy and so would she. That wasn't meant to be. She had seen him. And from that moment she knew she must possess him, body and soul.

Barbara felt so alone in her thoughts. She looked to the kitchen for comfort. Just to see him was a comfort. Just to know that he was hers in body, if not in soul.

John sat at the table shaking. He was shaking from the silent dry tears that assaulted his body.

He looked up to meet the gaze of his wife. It was more than he could handle. He found his life at that moment to be pathetic and repulsive.

John got up from the kitchen table. Without a word he left the house.

For the first time ever, Barbara truly understood her husband's pain. Pain that she had caused. Pain that she would continue to cause. She loved him too much to set him free. There wouldn't be much point in doing that anymore, she thought. Janiene's arms were filled by a man who really did love Barbara. At least he had at one time.

Chapter Eleven

August 1963

The flock had been held in the backwoods area below Marksville off highway 105. The site was chosen because of its central location.

Four armed men from the flock patrolled the area to keep out unwanted visitors.

Jefferson Cartwright stood on a platform looking out over a sea of men.

The men wore differing outfits since the Wings had no singular uniform.

Though they did not have a uniform, they did wear one small item that identified them to each other and, if worn publicly, to the world. They all wore a brass tie tack. It was worn on the left collar tab. The design was in the shape of a pair of wings. The shiny wings looked more like mini hands, interlocked at the thumbs with the fingers splayed outward. The tie tack was the only outward symbol of what the men truly shared.

Cartwright filled his lungs with a deep breath through his nostrils. He was the leader of all these men. It was even a more powerful feeling than being a judge.

As a judge, he controlled just one man's destiny at a time. As Pegasus, he controlled thousands and with their help, one day, millions.

The hum of the men sounded like a well oiled engine as they chatted amongst themselves. The power Cartwright felt surged though his veins like a white hot electric charge. The constant hum only added to that feeling, giving the power a sound all it's own.

Cartwright was determined to change the course of the Wings. To make them bigger, better and more powerful. In fact it was his dream that one day the Wings would be as powerful as the federal government. Actually, if things went as planned, his name would be as well known as Thomas Jefferson or Ben Franklin.

His formal swearing in ceremony had been quick. The cheers that rang out through the crowd, confirming that the men believed in their choice. The cheers had lasted longer than the ceremony itself.

When Cartwright finally addressed the crowd a hush fell over them. The Wings were captivated by every word he spoke.

A few exasperated sighs rang out when Cartwright backed the no violence stand that the Wings had always followed. Even more sighs were heard when he said there was to be no violence against the Coloreds planning that march in DC. Still, no one challenged his stand on the issue.

Even those who had sighed nodded in agreement when Cartwright explained that the risk of bringing the FBI down on them was too great. Besides, there would be about five to ten thousand Coloreds at that, so called, freedom march. Hardly big enough to merit the attention of anyone.

Jamison gave his lecture on spotting infiltration within the organization.

Cartwright noticed that Jamison gained more than a few of his own followers by the end of the lecture. Many of the men had signed on with Tommy for his full day of combat training.

Cartwright was sure that under his leadership the Wings would one day be bigger than the Klan. And more importantly, control governmental decisions.

Yes, Cartwright thought at the end of the day, one day all the Wings would wear their golden wings anytime they pleased. All of them, not just the outspoken members of the Wings. One day the Wings wouldn't have to worry about the feds breathing down their backs. One day, Cartwright thought, one day soon.

Barbara found her place in the journal. She skimmed the entries of Henri's uneventful sailing. She didn't become engrossed in her reading until Henri had finally arrived in Paris.

August 1848

My legs still shake from the sea. I am hopeful that it does not take as long for me to become re-accustomed to solid ground as long as it took me to gain my sea legs.

I am enthralled by this beautiful city. Paris is perhaps the loveliest city on earth. I have not seen much of the world but it would be hard to imagine many cities that could outshine the beauty of this gem.

I have only just arrived in Paris last night fall. I met my distant cousins from Maman's side. They are a bit arrogant but a kind people. The accent they attach to their French makes then nearly impossible to understand.

They have found me wonderful rooms near to the river. I am pleased.

I shall buy all my necessities today. I do not want to have a need for anything when I search for Jean-Claude tomorrow.

The idea of surprising Jean-Claude became less and less appealing as I journeyed. As I had no way of writing by that time, I am forced to stay with my original plan. It sounded so grand when I first thought of it. Now I realize that I have not heard from him in over eight months. I hope his address is the same though tracking a rogue like him should not prove too difficult. A man with Jean-Claude's dashing good looks must have made himself known, at least to the ladies.

Barbara found herself wondering if pictures existed of Henri or Jean-Claude. Barbara wondered if Jean-Claude was really as good looking as Henri described or if that was friendship speaking.

Maybe, Barbara thought, she could look though the boxes upstairs for a picture. Of course, there might be a photo in the family album of Henri but they probably would not have any photos of Jean-Claude unless Henri had kept one. It wouldn't hurt to look though the upstairs storeroom, if she got the chance.

Barbara suddenly felt very sick to her stomach. She rushed to the bathroom and vomited. Even though she had vomited she still felt queasy.

Barbara found her father-and-law and informed him of her illness. He insisted that she go home early.

By the time Barbara pulled the car in the garage she felt clammy and had a slight headache. Her stomach was still unsettled.

She walked though the door to find a scene that may not have bothered her on a better day. Today, however, it was totally unacceptable.

Jammy was bouncing up and down on the sofa with a chocolate cookie in one hand and a toy in the other. Crumbs were flying everywhere. Jammy's hands were covered with the gooey cookie which was also smeared all over the toy he held. He giggled with delight with each bounce he took.

John Jr. sat in his play pen. He smiled up at his mother with his face covered with chocolate goo. Apparently, John Jr. had some of the same cookies Jammy was currently enjoying.

Not only was John Jr.'s face covered with the melting cookie, his undershirt was nearly black as well as his hands. To make matters worse, John Jr. smelled like he needed a fresh diaper. By the way the smell permeated the room, Barbara thought he probably had needed a change for a long time.

Lacy wasn't in the living room with the kids. Nor was she in the kitchen.

Barbara was livid. "Lacy! Lacy? Where the hell are you?" Barbara screamed as loudly as her headache would allow. She heard the toilet flush. A few seconds later Lacy emerged from the connecting hall.

"Miss Barbara, I didn't 'pect you home so soon," Lacy said with surprise.

"That's obvious! Is this what goes on in my house while I'm not home? Look at John Jr., he's a mess. You can't tell me you changed him recently either. This place stinks to high heaven. And look at Jammy! He looks like a little street urchin. A street urchin that was bouncing on my sofa!" Barbara heard her voice echo in the hallway.

"I'm sorry. I had a bout with watery bowels. I gave the boys cookies to content 'em while I was in the toilet," Lacy admitted reluctantly.

"No wonder I'm sick. You probably brought something here from your house. I know how dirty you people are. Just look at, and smell, my own son under your care." Barbara's head was beginning to pound now.

"Now you know, Miss Barbara, that you ain't never come home to find a mess befo—"

"You have always known before when John or I was going to be home. You probably just rush around cleaning for the last half hour before we get here," Barbara interrupted her.

Lacy ignored her employer's remarks and continued. "Your house has always been clean in my keeping. I ain't been hired on as no maid either. I'm just 'posed to be a baby nurse. And my house ain't dirty 't all. Why, you could eat off my floors," Lacy sounded indignant.

"I wouldn't eat off anyone's floors. Maybe I don't know how you keep your house but I can see how you've been keeping mine, and my child. I don't like it. I don't like it at all. I'm sorry to do this to you Lacy but you—"

"Please Ma'am, please don't fire me. I need this job. This has never happened before. It's only 'cause I had bowel sickness. Please don't let me go," Lacy pleaded.

Barbara was surprised by Lacy's out cry. Barbara hadn't even thought about firing Lacy but she thought she'd use the misunderstanding to her advantage. "I'll keep you under one condition," Barbara paused.

"Yes Ma'am. Anything."

"You are not to bring Jammy here anymore. You obviously can't care for more than one child at a time."

"But I don't have no place to keep my boy and I don't have the money for no daycare."

I'll give you a week to find someplace to keep him. Why don't you ask his father to pay for his daycare? The boy is his responsibility too."

"His daddy don't care 'bout him none. He won't help."

"That's just like your people," Barbara said snippily.

"Jammy's daddy ain't one of my people. He's one of yours."

Barbara gasped. No wonder the boy was so fair skinned and so cute, Barbara thought. "Is his father poor white trash?"

"He ain't poor."

"How old is he?"

"He's old enough to know right from wrong," Lack paused before confiding in Barbara. "He's not only old enough to be Jammy's daddy, he's old enough to be mine."

"If he's some rich old man then you can threaten to tell his family about Jammy. Then he'll give you money. I assume his family doesn't know."

"No."

"Problem solved for both of us then. You get money for Jammy's care from his daddy then you can care for my son properly. Okay? Now clean those boys up. Can you stay 'till John gets home?" Barbara didn't wait for a answer, she went straight to bed.

Lacy thought about telling Mr. John. He would let her keep Jammy here. He would understand about her bowels. He knew she was good with their boy.

Lacy decided that would only bring trouble between Mr. John and his wife. Lord knew that man had enough problems with his wife without her adding to them.

Maybe she would take Miss Barbara's advice, Lacy thought. Maybe it was time for Mister High And Mighty White man to pay.

Lacy thought back to when she had first told him that she was pregnant four years ago. He had been vicious. He had told her that if she had kept her legs together like she should've then she wouldn't have that problem. He asked how many other men she had spread her legs for.

She had run away crying. She was just a girl then. He had known she was a virgin when he took her.

She wasn't a girl any longer. If it had been only her spreading her legs then there wouldn't have been a baby. No, she had spread her legs but he had put himself between them. They had both made Jammy, up until now, only one had paid the price for that.

"Things 'bout to change," Lacy said softly as she began changing the soiled diaper.

The next morning Barbara was still feeling queasy. The feeling was a familiar one. She couldn't remember when but she was sure that she had this particular illness before.

She went into the kitchen where John was reading a newspaper.

John looked up when he heard Barbara come into the room. "You don't look too good. You better call Dad and tell him you can't make it in."

Barbara was reading a very interesting part of the journal right now. She didn't want to miss her daily installment.

The thought of staying home and listening to Jammy and John Jr. did nothing to settle her stomach either.

They were expecting a small shipment in at PIP anyway. Henri might need her there. He could probably get along just fine without her there but she'd rather be there than at home.

"No, I'll go in today. I'm not that sick anyway. It's some sort of stomach thing. Lacy had diarrhea yesterday. I probably have something similar."

John looked back to his newspaper. "Come home if you start to feel too sick."

Barbara could see she did not have John's full attention. Whatever he was reading in the newspaper had his complete interest. Though he had shown concern for her health, she could see him straining so he would not look back at the article.

"What's so interesting"? You are pretty wrapped up in that paper this morning." Barbara went to the refrigerator and pulled out a bottle of orange juice.

"Huh?" John looked up and saw the juice. "Sure, I'll have some. Thanks."

Barbara grabbed two glasses from the dish drain. "Why your not even listening to me. I didn't ask you if you wanted juice. I asked what you were reading."

John looked up again. He paused for a moment while her words sank in. "Sorry. I was reading about the freedom march in Washington DC. It was the other day, the 28th to be exact. Anyway, they had estimated that about ten or twenty thousand would attend. As it turned out, there were about two hundred thousand people there. It says here that there were speeches made by ten civil rights leaders but whoever wrote this article was most impressed by Dr. Martin Luther King."

Barbara frowned. She hated when the Coloreds stirred up trouble. Why couldn't they accept their lot in life? They scared her, especially when they did things like that.

"They always complain when the KKK or the Wings have a march but then they turn around and do this. They are just a bunch of hypocrites." Barbara handed John a glass of juice.

"It's hardly the same thing. It says here that King's speech was about a dream for America and he described a nation free from hatred and injustice, of a people, the American people, working and living together in peace. I think this march was a great thing."

John drank a gulp of juice before he continued. "When the Wings or the Klan march it's to promote hatred, injustice, fear and a separate America."

"The Negroes only say they want to end hatred so that they can get a stronger position in our society. They are not fooling anyone with that. They hate us as much as we hate them."

"You know something Barb? 'We' do not hate them. You think you do but I don't think you really do. I think you've confused fear with hate. I'm sure some of the Negroes hate us. They are Americans for God's sake. They are treated like second class citizens. Not out of hate but out of fear. The Negro has been deemed 'different' from us. So we have kept him back. At times making it illegal for him to learn to read and write, implementing laws like the Grandfather Clause to keep him from voting and laws to make their schools, thus their productivity, substandard."

John searched Barbara's face to see if any of what he was saying was sinking in. Her forehead was etched with lines but the frown seemed more thoughtful than disapproving.

Her face had given him hope so he continued at a quickened pace. "It's fear, not hatred. Don't you see? If the Negro were actually inferior then why would we need laws like the Jim Crow laws or the Grandfather Clause? Why forbid a people to read and write. If they really were all that stupid then they would not be able to learn anyway."

John silently prayed that his words would not fall upon deaf ears. "You talk about the Negroes like you know them well. 'They're lazy, stupid, inferior, lethargic, etc.'. How do you know? How many Negroes do you know? I mean one's that haven't been subservient to you. Any one in a servant's position will lead their boss to think he's superior, it's part of the job, right?"

Barbara was thinking about what John was saying. In a way it made sense. Yet it made her very uncomfortable. She always felt comfort with the beliefs her daddy had taught her.

"All the Coloreds I've ever known have been servants. With the exception of Jim and Girod who do the refinishing at your father's store. I suppose they're just servants too since they work under your father."

"They don't work under my father. They work for my father. Do you think of yourself as a servant?"

"I'm not a servant to anyone. I'm a sales lady, a wife and a mother," Barbara said with vehemence.

"Why do you think of Jim and Girod as servants but not yourself? You all work for my father."

"Well, they work in the back. It's not even air conditioned back there so your father must feel the same way."

John couldn't believe how dense his wife could be. If people were to generalize about the White race based on Barbara, John feared they wouldn't fare too well. "I'm surprised you don't know more of the aspects of the business by now. The air conditioning is not on back there because the varnish and oils dry quicker. Dad tried the air conditioner to take some of the humidity out of the air but the varnish dried faster with the humidity as long as it was hot. That's why it's so much hotter back there in the winter."

Barbara was embarrassed by her assumption about the air conditioning. Now she was even more determined to point out the servitude nature of the two black men. "But look at them. Their job is so dirty and nasty. I don't think a White man would want their job."

John smiled. His lovely little racist had set a trap for herself. "Barb, there you couldn't be more wrong. Dad had mostly White applicants. Girod and Jim just happened to do better restoration work. With the money they make, you can bet a lot of White men would give their right arms to have their jobs."

Barbara's world revolved around money. She quickly took the bait that John had put out for her. "How much money do they make? Not more than me, do they?"

John raised his eyebrows and tilted his head slightly.

"They have to make less than you." Barbara gave him a beseeching look.

John knew he shouldn't take so much glee in upsetting his wife but her ideas were so pompous. "'Fraid so. Next to Dad, Jim and Girod make more than anyone in all five stores."

Barbara grimaced. Suddenly her face lit up and she smiled. "Oh, you mean their combined incomes. At first I thought we were talking about each of their incomes." Barbara let out a sigh of relief.

"Wrong again, Barb. I'm not a liberty to discuss their salaries but since I do the books I know the exact numbers. Sufficed to say, they each make more than three times what you make."

Barbara let out a gasp. Her grip was so tight around the now empty glass that her knuckles had turned white.

"You've got to be kidding. They are just a couple of Colored men."

"Here we are. We've finally come full circle to my original point. You judge them by their color. At PIP they are judged by their skill. Without their expertise, we would have only junk at PIP. The sales ladies would have nothing to sell. The book keeper, me, would have no books to keep. Without them, there would be no Past Into Present." John smiled at his wife.

"It doesn't have to be them. It could be anyone who restores furniture and repairs antique jewelry. It could just as easily be White men doing their job." Sweat broke on Barbara's brow as a wave of nausea over took her.

"Why you are absolutely right, Barbara. I'm sure you'd feel more comfortable with that. But when you stop looking at color and start looking at skill then you will get the best man for the job. That's when people start appreciating people for who they are rather than not giving people a chance because of what they aren't."

Barbara was feeling very uneasy. She looked at her watch. She was thankful it was time for her to leave for work. She grabbed her purse and car keys.

"I best get going. I don't want to be late." Barbara gave John a peck on the cheek. She was relieved to end their conversation.

On her drive to work she kept thinking about the things John had said.

Barbara hated conversations like they had this morning. She had grown up with racial discussions surrounding her but those had always been different. They had always supported a position of superiority of the White race.

The conversations she had with John or with his father were always about equality. At first she had given her standard answers for race relations. The ones she had been taught at a very early age. Now it was getting more difficult. They discussed topics in which she had no standard answer. On top of everything, they had made some very convincing arguments.

Barbara thought about what John had said. What if, just for the sake of argument, what if John were right. That would mean people like her father weren't making the world a safer place but a place filled with injustice. That would mean people weren't being kept in their place but being held back. Barbara felt a shiver go down her spine. John must be wrong, she thought. He has to be wrong!

Judge Cartwright was feeling a loss of control. The reaction to the turn out at the freedom march had not been good.

He had already taken half a dozen calls from irate Wings. They were practically blaming him for the size of the march. Even if he had allowed violence against known participants that wouldn't have decreased the size of the march by more than a few individuals, if at all.

Cartwright couldn't understand why the men couldn't see that?

The Klan was constantly being harassed. The FBI watched them like a hawk watches a snake. Hell, Cartwright thought, he had plenty of friends in Washington, it wasn't the issues that the government had a problem with, it was the damn violence.

Cartwright couldn't risk that type of notoriety. He had to get things back to how they once were. It wouldn't help to draw the attention of anyone that didn't believe in the White man's divine right.

Tommy Jamison couldn't or wouldn't understand the facts. Out of all the phone calls the judge had gotten, Tommy Jamison's had been the most disturbing. Tommy had practically guaranteed there would be some sort of retaliation for the 'nigger gathering'.

Judge Cartwright had worried about Tommy's call all morning until the phone had rung again. As a judge, Cartwright was fairly used to getting threats but this caller had been different. This caller's threats had been a little too real. Cartwright was so upset when he hung up the phone he was shaking.

He decided to kill two birds with one stone. He'd take care of the threat and let Tommy get some of the violence out of his system.

Cartwright called Tommy and told him the details of his threatening phone call. He altered the story slightly. After all he didn't want Tommy or anyone else to have the power to make the same threat against him again.

The judge was greatly relieved when Tommy agreed to rough up the person in question. Tommy assured him that by the time he was finished with the caller, that person would never call again. Hell, Jamison had said they'd probably never even pick up a phone again.

After talking to Tommy, he felt a lot better. He felt a little guilty about using violence but he had been threatened. The caller should never have threatened him.

Cartwright laughed out loud. If it hadn't been for Jamison, he would have had to pay to have this person roughed up. All he had to tell Jamison was that it was a civil rights worker. It had solved two of his problems. It made him look stronger in Jamison's eyes and it took care of that damn threat.

Cartwright put his robe back on and headed for his courtroom. Those who came though his courtroom today might get leniency. Thanks to Tommy he was feeling rather merciful.

That afternoon had not found many customers in Past Into Present. Barbara had read the journal freely since Henri was out at another location. Barbara thought about the question John had asked her that morning. How many Colored people did she know? Really know. She felt like she was getting to know one very well. A man who had been dead for nearly a hundred years.

Barbara found herself liking Jean-Claude more and more. From what John's great-grandfather had written, she had determined that Jean-Claude had been much like she herself was.

When he saw what he wanted he went after it. He used his intelligence to suit his needs. When he was in America, he had known when to play coy or stupid so that he would not offend the Whites. When he went to France he became a successful merchant in only a year.

Barbara found that she was becoming more interested in reading about Jean-Claude than Henri. Although she did enjoy Henri's romantic interludes.

Jean-Claude had shaken Henri's beliefs about a superior White race. Henri had apparently passed those beliefs down through the generations since Jean-Claude's arguments sounded similar to John's. Henri, however, didn't seem uncomfortable with changing his belief system. If it made sense to him, he changed. Barbara could not change so easily, even if she saw a flaw in what she believed.

Barbara squinted at the yellowed page. Much of the ink on the next several pages had apparently gotten wet. The ink had run together in some areas while spots of paper were swollen in others. She strained to make out the date. It looked like 'December 1848'.

It is two days from the celebration of our Lord's birth. At the Papa Noel ball I found myself being a rude oaf.

Jean-Claude and I arrived at the ball shortly before nine. It is fashionable here to be late so, as is the fashion, we were late.

The grand ballroom was a delight. Candlelight shown so brightly it fooled the mind into thinking it was the middle of the day. There were great white satin bows and ribbons draped about all the entry ways, mantles and tables. A quartet with accompaniment sounded like a full orchestra the way the music echoed off the walls and ceiling.

It was a good year for the vine in the region so the Champagne flowed freely.

Perfumes of the ladies mixed together to form a scent so sweet that a flower maid, even if she mixed a hundred flowers, could never hope to reproduce the sweet aroma.

Young ladies could be heard giggling softly while whispers of the men, probably suggesting some impropriety, danced upon their perfumed necks.

Jean-Claude wasted no time finding a drink in one hand and a lady in the other. I filled my time with small chit chat and a couple of dances with the shy maidens.

In the middle of it all my whole world stopped. A lovely, no, much more than lovely, young lady arrived. She arrived, with a handsome young gentleman, much later than is the fashion.

A hush fell over the room when she entered. Her golden hair was piled high atop her head in hundreds of delicate coils. Her eyes, the color of the sable, were surrounded by long golden lashes. Her skin was so pale, so delicate, that her golden hair almost appeared brown upon her. Her body was lovelier than even Venus herself. She wore a white silk gown with soft blue ribbons laced in various areas of the gown. More of the same ribbons were intertwined with the beautiful golden locks.

Immediately I sought out Jean-Claude for I had to know who it was that stopped my heart.

Jean-Claude said that her name is Isabelle Duchere. Her escort, her brother, Alexander Duchere. He is the first born son of a wealthy land owner.

Jean-Claude said that Isabelle Duchere is an innocent. I asked him how could be so certain. He said that he had propositioned her himself. She had refused him. Since most women do not refuse him, he was convinced that she is pure of body. He said she had not coyly flirted with his maleness either so he is convinced she is pure of mind. It was after Jean-Claude went back to his flirtation that I made the oaf of myself.

I did not realize it myself but I was staring at the beautiful Isabelle. Her brother came upon me and asked me if it was our custom in America to stare at women in such a manner.

I assured him that my thoughts were pure. That I was only admiring beauty, the likes of which I have never seen. He said since I was a foreigner I would be forgiven this once, if I apologized to his sister.

As I crossed the room to bow my head humbly, the room seemed to grow from forty feet to four hundred feet. I felt as if I would never reach her. My heart was pounding so loudly I could not hear the music.

When I finally came upon her, her brother introduced us. I apologized for my rude stares. My nervousness prevented me from telling her why I was staring. I was unable to compliment her at all. Instead I found myself committing the same act for which I was apologizing.

She drew me out of my trance by asking me if she had a boil upon her nose. As I stumbled over my words I found that she really did not know why I was staring. She is a pure beauty who is pure at heart.

Isabelle Duchere! I wish that it were Isabelle Sommier. I cannot deceive my own person, a fine lady like that is only a dream for me. I am thankful that, in this instant, that she is only a dream for Jean-Claude also.

The time had flown since Barbara had first opened the journal. It was already time for her to close up the shop. She had decided she would stop by her daddy's house before she went home. Something was bothering her. He would know what to do.

Chapter Twelve

Percy walked out the front door just as Barbara parked her car in her father's circular drive. The older lady had her coat on and her purse in hand.

"Miss Barbie child, how are you doing? How's that beautiful baby of yours? I didn't know you'd be coming by today. I'll go tell your daddy you're here," Percy said cheerfully.

Barbara noticed the black circles under the eyes of the woman who had been the Cartwright's cook for all of Barbara's life. "I'm just fine. You have to see John Jr., you just wouldn't believe how fast he's growing. You look tired, Percy. Don't bother with going back inside, I see you're on your way out. I'll tell Daddy I'm here myself. Where is he?"

"Same place he always is lately, the library. Your daddy practically lives in there when he's at home. You be sure to knock before you go in, ya hear. He don't like to be bothered none while he's in there. Child, you have yourself a good night." Percy walked past Barbara to her car parked out on the street.

Barbara took Percy's advice and knocked before she entered the room. She had to knock several times before she heard the click of the lock.

The judge pulled the door open. He was wrapped up in his own thoughts. It took him a few minutes before he recognized it was Barbara in the doorway.

He smiled. He looked around his daughter for the stroller. "Barbie, this is a pleasant surprise. You didn't bring John Jr.?"

"No, I came over straight from work. I needed your help with something." Barbara kissed her father on the cheek and walked into the library.

Judge Cartwright closed the door and followed her into the room. He took a seat behind his desk and motioned for Barbara to take one of the two seats across from him.

"What'd you need, Darlin'? You know your ol' Daddy will do anything he can for you," he promised with a wink.

"Oh Daddy, I don't know what to do. We're back to John wanting to leave again. He's going to apply to Harvard in a couple of months. He's getting everything together now. We wouldn't have to leave for almost a year from now but I just don't want to go, Daddy. Not in a year from now. Not in ten years from now. I don't want to leave New Orleans or the South," Barbara whined.

"I don't like the idea of you or my little grandson going away neither."

"Can you help me to convince John to stay here. Maybe if you talked to him, he'd listen to reason."

"You know your husband doesn't want to hear anything I have to say."

"Please Daddy, won't you at least try."

"I'll do one better than that. I've got some friends, other lawyers, up North. I'm sure they've got connections up there. With that semester that John's grades were none too good, I think I can get his application denied."

"I don't know. If John ever found out I was behind his not getting into Harvard he'd never forgive me. Never."

"Don't worry. There's no way he could find out. Just relax and let your Daddy take care of everything." The judge rose from his desk to hug his daughter.

Barbara's neck muscles loosened from relief. "Thanks, Daddy. You are so good to me. I love you so much."

The next morning Barbara was feeling very secure in her world. She had no way of knowing that the newspaper she had handed John that morning would shatter the security she felt. Barbara got her breakfast while John sat reading the newspaper.

"Please God, don't let this be." John bowed his head while he spoke.

Barbara looked at her husband's ashen color. "What is it? I don't know why you read the newspaper anyway, it's only ever bad news."

John didn't answer her for a long time. He sat there reading the article over and over again. When he finally accepted the truth, tears began to run down his cheeks.

"Barb, its Tad. It says here that he was killed in some military training exercise. God, I didn't even know he was in the military."

Barbara involuntarily released the pitcher of orange juice. Juice and broken glass covered the kitchen floor but neither she nor John noticed.

She walked through the orange juice and took the newspaper from John. "There must be some mistake. This must be someone else with the same name."

"I thought the same thing at first, but they list Tad's age and the high school he had attended. They also list his surviving family members. It's Tad."

"Shut up. Just shut up. This has to be wrong. He can't be dead. He's too young. He can't be dead."

John was surprised by his wife's apparent grief. Sure, John was overcome by grief. Tad had been his best friend from the third grade. They had been inseparable up until he had slept with Barbara.

Of course Barbara would be upset, John thought. She had once been Tad's girlfriend. She had been intimate with him. Her feelings must run deep for him.

John stood up and put his arms around Barbara. That action broke the dam. Barbara started to cry uncontrollably.

Barbara didn't cry for Tad. She cried for herself. Janiene was free again. What if she decided she wanted John back now that her own husband was dead?

Barbara's body fell limp from the thought. She felt dizzy. She felt as if the room were closing in on her.

John picked her up and carried her into the bedroom. He laid her down on the bed.

"I'm sorry. This has hit us both pretty hard. I don't know why I didn't realize that you cared so much about Tad," John said his voice husky from the tears he held back.

John thought about the good times he and Tad had. He thought of Tad's parents. They must be devastated. He thought how much he had loved to visit the Overthall's as a boy.

Barbara was still crying. John thought if Barbara was so upset then Tad's mother would be beside herself. And Tad's wife would be too. Tad's wife.

John's body was racked with pain as he thought about Tad's wife. Janiene.

He and Tad had been best friends until the ninth grade when they met Janiene. Actually, Tad met her first. Tad had tried asking her out but when that failed he settled on friendship. As Tad and Janiene's friendship grew, John was included in the friendship. The three of the had become best friends. They had even stayed best friends when John and Janiene started dating in the summer after ninth grade.

The three of them spent so many hours together people had thought they were related.

Janiene was related now. She had been Tad's wife.

John felt the urge to comfort her. The urge to be comforted by her. Only Janiene could understand his loss and only he could understand hers. He knew that could never be. He knew Janiene would not want comfort from him, would not offer comfort to him.

At the funeral two days later, John was careful to keep himself and Barbara out of Janiene's sight.

He didn't want to upset her anymore than she already was. He was afraid, if she saw him, she would ask him to leave. He couldn't leave. He had to say good bye to his friend. As hard as it was, he had to say good bye.

John looked at Janiene as the eulogy was being read. From where he sat he could only see her profile. Her skin was pale under the black veil she wore. She was being supported by Tad's father on one side and her own father on the other. She sat perfectly still staring at the closed coffin.

Tad's body had been too badly disfigured to have an open casket.

John was thankful for that. He was sure he would not have been able to hold back his tears if he had been forced to look at his friend's body throughout the service.

Later when the pallbearers carried Tad's body from the hearse to the Overthall family mausoleum, John felt a tinge of pain. After all he had shared with Tad, he felt he should be one of the pallbearers. He knew deep in his heart that Tad wouldn't have wanted that. That Tad never forgave him for sleeping with Barbara. That knowledge is what caused John the most pain.

Barbara hoped they wouldn't have to offer condolences to Janiene after Tad's body had been placed in the tomb. She had tried to talk John out of attending the funeral. He had thought she had been too upset to want to attend. He had said he'd go alone. That had been worse. She didn't mind attending the funeral, she just didn't want John there.

She didn't want John to see the woman he really loved at her most vulnerable. She didn't want John to see Janiene crying. Barbara knew how susceptible John was to tears. She had certainly used them often enough to suit her needs.

Barbara gently tugged on John's arm to head him back out to the street. He continued walking to where the family stood.

"John, don't you think we should go?" Barbara asked softly.

"I have to tell them how sorry I am about Tad," John said determinedly.

"I don't think that's a good idea. Come on let's go." Barbara tugged on John's arm once again.

Anger flashed in John's eyes. "You can go back to the damn car if that's what you want. I told you where I'm going."

Barbara didn't go back to the car but neither did she continue walking with John. She just stood there and watched as he approached the family.

John felt nervous as he walked up to Mrs. Overthall. He choose to speak to her because she was standing the furthest from Janiene and her parents.

"Mrs. Overthall, I just wanted to tell you how sorry I am. Tad was the best friend I ever had. I loved him like a brother," John said sincerely.

"Thank you, John. I'm sorry you boys never made up. He never stopped loving you, you know. But he loved you so much, he couldn't believe what you had done to him. He told me, right before he married Janiene that he was sorry that y'all couldn't be friends. He said he missed you." Tad's mother's voice caught in her throat.

John's eyes filled with tears but he managed to blink them back. "Thank you for telling me that. It means a lot to me."

John and Mrs. Overthall didn't notice Janiene's father bearing down on them.

"You have a lot of nerve coming here, John. My daughter doesn't need anymore upset," Paul Jeaneaux said sternly.

"He is here for me. Please, Paul, I don't need anymore upset either." Mrs. Overthall gently ran interference for John.

Paul Jeaneaux was silenced by his in-law. Still, he inclined his head and eyes toward the gate, imploring John to leave.

John complied with the man's wishes and turned to walk away.

He had gotten three feet when he felt a hand on his shoulder.

John turned back around to meet a woman in a veil. It was Janiene.

Though he could not see her eyes he could sense the tears that were there. Her stature was straight and hard as if to fight the pain she was feeling.

"Thank you for coming. You know you could have spoken to me. I know you loved Tad very much," Janiene said in a husky whisper.

"I'm so sorry. I had hoped you wouldn't see me. I didn't want to upset you by my being here." John looked around at all the tombs.

New Orleans sat five feet below sea level so it was impossible to bury the dead. At the first sign of rain the coffins would pop back up. The early settlers of the area solved that problem by building large ornate white marble mausoleums. Some stood as tall as fifteen feet and others were supported with beautiful columns. They almost looked like little houses. Because of that, the cemeteries in, and around, New Orleans were known as cities of the dead.

Janiene blew into her handkerchief before she spoke. "I didn't have to see you, John Jackson. I can always sense when you are around. I would have been more upset if you didn't come. You and Tad had been friends since you were little boys. I couldn't imagine you not being here."

"I thought you wouldn't understand about me being here. I mean, nobody called me. I had to read about it in the paper."

"John Jackson, I hope you can understand. Tad did care about you. I think he even forgave you but he didn't want to hurt me so he never told you how he felt. He was such a good man."

Barbara stood watching John talk with his old flame. Jealousy raced through her. She had felt the first surge of jealousy when she saw Janiene follow John. Then she had touched him. Rather than saying his name, the little tramp had touched him.

The conversation was taking too long, Barbara thought. They must be setting up some secret rendezvous.

Barbara's thoughts drove her to action. She walked over to where John and Janiene were standing. She was like a volcano waiting to erupt. When she witnessed John hug Janiene good-bye she blew her top.

"Get your hands off my husband. Your husband isn't even as cold as the tomb he lays in and you're looking to replace him,"

Barbara shrieked.

Barbara didn't notice that all conversation in the cemetery had stopped and all eyes were upon her.

John looked at the veil that separated his eyes from Janiene's. "I'm sorry Janiene."

John grabbed Barbara's arm in a vice-like grip. "Shut your mouth and let's go before you make an even bigger spectacle of yourself," John said darkly.

Barbara dug her heels into the soft earth. "I'm not going anywhere. At least not until I have a chance to warn that bitch that I'll kill her if she as much as looks at you again."

Janiene was instantly surrounded by family. Her father stood on her right, Tad's father was on her left, her mother stood behind her and Tad's mother stood almost in front of her. It looked as if she stood inside a human fortress. Janiene started to step forward but Mrs. Overthall's arm flew out and stopped her.

Mrs. Overthall stepped forward and looked at John with pity before she addressed Barbara. "This is my son's burial and you are not welcome here. My son found a good wife and you will not slander her. I know all about you, Barbara Cartwright. You best go now before I expose you for the fraud that you are."

"Me? A fraud? Why don't you ask your precious little daughter-in-law if she still loves John. Then you'll see whose really a fraud." Barbara ignored the pain John caused with his fingers digging into the sensitive flesh of her upper arm.

"I know Janiene still loves John. We all do. What people don't know is how you used Tad. You'd come over swishing and swaying and you caught my boy. He wasn't what you wanted though, was he? You never looked at him with love or even infatuation. He was a means to an end. I used to overhear all the questions you'd ask about John. I knew you were using him to be closer to his best friend. What could I do? I was only his mother. He wouldn't have listened to me even if I had tried to warn him. He was in love with you."

Mrs. Overthall looked at the deer-in-the-headlight look on Barbara's face. She knew she had been right about Barbara. The look upon the young woman's face confirmed it.

"I don't know how you seduced John but I am sure it was a pregnancy you sought. I know John would not have married you if you had not been carrying his child. I personally think that Janiene should take him back from you but she is not that class of woman. She is a lady." Mrs. Overthall looked exhausted when she finished speaking.

John pulled so hard on Barbara that she toppled out of one of her shoes. John didn't let her retrieve the shoe. He continued walking her out of the city of the dead. John looked back once more to the family. His eyes bade a silent apology.

He gently shook his head from side to side as the shock of his wife's behavior hit him full force. John opened Barbara's car door and waited for her to get in before he slammed the door.

He walked around the car, opened his door and slid in behind the wheel.

Barbara started to speak but John's stern look warned her to keep the silence.

Barbara thought the ride home was the longest ride she had ever taken. Even so, the ride could never be long enough. Barbara feared what would happen once they arrived home. Deep in her heart she knew, she knew she had gone too far.

Once home, John released the baby-sitter from her duties. He had yet to speak to Barbara. His mind kept replaying the words that Tad's mother had said. It scared him to think that what she had said might be true. Hell, he knew it probably was true. The fact that he had let his passion destroy so many relationships had always bothered him but to think the whole thing might have been planned was almost too much for John to bear.

John changed his clothes, went in the kitchen and grabbed a beer. He hadn't thought of what he'd say to Barbara. He saw her on the sofa when he went into the kitchen but he had not spoken to her.

He knew he should be angry at the inexcusable behavior of his wife at the burial. But he couldn't concentrate on that after what Tad's mother had accused his wife of doing. John went into the living room. He plopped down in the recliner that sat directly across from where Barbara was seated.

Barbara looked down at her shoe and around at the four walls. She looked anywhere that did not include looking at John.

John studied his wife's nervous behavior before he finally spoke. "Obviously, I have been thinking. I don't—"

"John, I'm sorry. I overreacted in the cemetery. I don't know what came over me. When I saw you with Janiene I flipped out."

"To tell the truth, I'm not even concerned with that at this point. Don't get me wrong, what you did really bothers me but I have been more engulfed in what Tad's mother said." John looked Barbara directly in the eyes. "Tell me the truth. What she said, is that true?"

"John, you know that I love you.—"

"I didn't ask you that. I asked you if what she said was true."

Barbara hesitated before she answered. "I'll admit I acted like a real witch at the cemetery. I was so jealous. I guess my yelling at Janiene pushed Tad's mother over the edge. I can't think of any other reason she'd say those things."

"You have nothing to be jealous of. I've told you before, I can be trusted. Besides, if I were the type to cheat, do you really think any of your screaming fits would make one bit of difference?"

John looked at Barbara who was trying to hold back tears. He didn't believe her. He agreed that Mrs. Overthall had been pushed too far but he didn't think she had lied. Then again, Barbara never said Tad's mother had lied, John thought. His wife was a sly one.

John thought about what Tad had said about never breaking it off with Barbara. Unfortunately, what Tad's mother had said fit together with what Tad had said. Just like a puzzle. A big ugly puzzle.

The next day Barbara was happy to be at work. For the first time in her short married life she was actually glad to be away from John.

He hadn't said two words to her after their conversation in the living room. Instead he had stared at her. No, not stared but watched. He had watched her like she was some venomous snake that might attack at any moment.

Barbara opened the journal and hoped the writings would take her away from the present. She was ready to drift back into the past.

January 1849

I can hardly believe my good fortune. I met yesterday, at his request, with Alexander Duchere. He invited me to partake of the family dinner last evening. I do not like nor dislike Alex but I could not pass upon a chance to gaze upon his lovely sister.

I arrived promptly at the set time. His mother was quite a lovely lady for a woman of so many years. I was informed that Alex and Isabelle's father had perished some years ago.

When we took our seats for dinner, I felt quite uneasy. Being of a big family, it was hard to sit down to a table with only three others. I spoke primarily to Alex and Madam Duchere. I avoided all contact with Mademoiselle. I was afraid I would lay my heart for all to see if I spoke to her.

After dinner, Alex and I had some strong drink while the ladies retired to the sitting room. When we joined them, Mademoiselle was in need of fresh air. I offered to accompany her and to my delight she accepted.

On our walk, she admitted thinking that I would not come for dinner. I asked if that would have upset her. She said most assuredly as it was her idea for me to have dinner with them. My heart leapt and my head began to spin at her words. I still do not know if it was the drink, the words she spoke or her beauty but momentarily my senses took leave. To my amazement I leaned down and tasted both her sweet lips.

I stopped the kiss as soon as I realized my actions. I opened my mouth to seek her forgiveness but instead words of a marriage proposal came out. I spoke of Louisiana and Mallard's Landing. When I stopped speaking a hot flush encased me as I awaited her gentle refusal. That is what has puzzled me the most. She did not refuse. She merely said we would have to court a few months before we could marry.

I told Jean-Claude and he laughed at me. I asked if this was a game she played with many young beaus. His face took on a serious look before he finally said no. He slapped me hard on the back and congratulated me. Though he does not understand why I would settle for one rose, though beautiful, when there are so many flowers to be picked.

Barbara skimmed over much of the courtship since Henri had not been as detailed as she would have liked especially when it came to the romance.

Henri had asked for and gotten Alex Duchere's permission for Isabelle's hand in marriage.

One thing Henri did make clear, he was deeply in love with Isabelle. Barbara wished that John was like that. She wished that she could not only slip into the past by reading the journal, she wished she could bring the past into present.

Barbara laughed out loud at her thoughts. Past into Present, she must have work on the brain, she thought decidedly. Barbara put the journal back and began pricing the items that had recently been brought forward.

* * *

Judge Cartwright was furious. He had received another threatening phone call from the individual that Tommy had promised to take care of. It had been three weeks since he had first spoken to Tommy about it.

Cartwright immediately called Tommy and asked him to come over. He sat impatiently waiting with a glass of bourbon in hand.

Cartwright was on his third bourbon before he heard the knock on his library door.

He answered the door with an agitated grunt. The alcohol had done nothing to calm his mood. In fact, it had worsened it.

Tommy Jamison eyed Cartwright when he entered the room. He knew Cartwright was upset. He just didn't know what he was upset about.

Tommy nodded toward the decanter of whiskey before he poured himself a double. He liked his whiskey neat and the judge always had the best whiskey.

"What'd ya want to see me about?" Tommy gulped down the rest of his drink and poured himself another.

"I got another threat today. I thought you were going to take care of that little problem for me. I told you it's a civil right's worker. We can't have their kind threatening us. Are you going to take care of it or am I going to have to get a man who's got the balls for it?" Cartwright growled.

"I don't think you ought to question my balls none. I ain't the one that's been threatened. If I were, I'd handled it myself instead of asking another man to take care of it, if you get my meaning." Tommy's eyes had taken on a real nasty glow.

"I get your meaning. I'm a judge. Shit, I'm Pegasus. I can't go out after everybody what threatens me. I've got to protect the organization. I can't afford to get my name in any type of scandal," Cartwright explained.

"And I can, is that it? I think you've forgotten. I'm the fuckin' Eagle for New Orleans. I don't think none of the boys would be too pleased to see my name in the paper."

Cartwright could see he had offended Tommy. He needed to find some way to get control of the situation. To get control of Tommy. Tommy had a nasty look about him that warned the judge that Tommy was the wrong man to tangle with.

"I wasn't saying you weren't important. Hell, I hate to admit it's the truth, but that fact of the matter is, you'd be able to handle this little problem better than I would." Cartwright noticed Tommy's facial features soften.

Tommy poured himself another drink. "I'm sorry I ain't got around to it yet but I'll take care of it. I been real busy with a few boys in Alabama. Let's just say a certain church needs to replace not only a building but four of it's little choir girls too." Tommy smiled a smile of sheer evil.

Cartwright flinched. He had read, heard and talked about the church bombing in Birmingham. It had happened in September at the 16th Street Baptist Church. The bomb had left four young Colored girls dead.

It had sickened Cartwright. He hated random acts of violence against innocent people. The fact that a bomb had taken the lives of children didn't sit well with him.

He could see knocking back the uppity colored man but, usually, even then it didn't call for anything more violent than a beating. Women and children were another thing all together.

"You were involved in that affair? They were only children; they weren't a threat to anybody." Cartwright's voice was thick with condemnation.

"Is a baby alligator any less an alligator just 'cause it ain't full grown? Gators are fine if they stay in the swamp but if they come into my backyard I'm gonna kill them, baby or no. It ain't no different with the Coloreds, if they stay in their place then ain't no one gonna bother them but when they start stepping on our toes then they need to be taught that we ain't gonna allow it. It don't matter how little they are now, just like the baby alligator, they will grow up and be a danger.

I ain't fooled by the cuteness of no twelve inch gator, I know what it will be someday and, I ain't fooled by no nigger child."

Cartwright watched Tommy pace the library. The alcohol had apparently taken affect since Tommy stumbled a couple of times.

Cartwright was unsure if Tommy had been involved in the children's murders. Tommy hadn't exactly said he'd been there, only that he condoned it. Cartwright decided he didn't want know. Tommy was so vehement and hate filled. This was a side of Tommy that Cartwright had never seen and frankly it scared the shit out of him.

Tommy felt so good from the whiskey that he didn't notice the prolonged silence. He didn't notice Cartwright watching him.

Tommy walked over to the bookcase and looked at pictures of Judith and Barbara. Judith was a fine looking woman but she could not compare to Barbara. Tommy looked at Barbara's baby pictures and her grade school pictures but it was her senior high picture that caught his eye. She was wearing a tight blue sweater that matched her midnight eyes.

As Tommy looked at Barbara's picture he unconsciously began rubbing between his thighs. He looked at her breasts and thought about what they'd feel like in his hands, in his mouth.

The combination of alcohol and sexual desire made him forget that Cartwright was in the room. Tommy nearly jumped out of his skin when Cartwright spoke.

"Are you going to warn the civil rights worker or not?" Cartwright had observed Tommy's behavior while he was looking at Barbara's photo. Cartwright wanted to get Tommy out of his house as soon as possible.

"There won't be anymore threats. I guaran-damn-tee you that." Tommy smiled.

At that moment fear swept though Cartwright. Looking at Tommy's smile was like looking into the face of the devil himself.

"I don't want there to be too much violence. Just a warning, ya hear?" Cartwright opened the door to indicate that their business was finished.

Tommy didn't move towards the open door. Instead he poured himself another whiskey.

"I'll take care of it. You'll be happy, okay?" Tommy stumbled, spilling some of the whiskey as he set his glass down.

"Thank you, Jamison. I'll see you out." Cartwright knew he shouldn't let Tommy drive in his condition but he wanted the man out of his house.

Tommy walked to the doorway before he turned back. "You know what, Cartwright?"

"What?"

"You're a very lucky man." Tommy nodded towards Barbara's senior picture. "If I had a daughter like that, I'd be the happiest man on earth." Tommy licked his lips with a smacking noise and walked out of the room.

Cartwright's stomach turned at Tommy's implication. He was sure Tommy had only said that because it really wasn't Tommy's daughter. Tommy could never look at his own daughter in that way, Cartwright thought. Could he? The thought sickened Cartwright once again and he pushed it from his mind.

Chapter Thirteen

John was fast becoming impatient. It wasn't like Lacy to be late. In fact, she had never been late before.

John searched for Lacy's telephone number but since he had never had to use it before he wasn't sure where they had put it. He knew it wasn't in their address book because Barbara hadn't wanted the 'help' listed with friends and family.

John looked at the clock. If he didn't leave for class in fifteen minutes he would miss his first class.

John thought about calling his mother but she lived too far away to get John Jr. there in time for him to make school. So he called Barbara's stepmother, Judith.

Judith had been agreeable to watching John Jr..

John raced around packing the diaper bag and getting the baby food. He picked up his sleeping son and took him to the Cartwright home.

Later that afternoon, John stopped by home before he picked his son up. He wanted to check for any messages Lacy may have left on the door. He didn't want Barbara to get her hands on them first if there were any such messages.

John checked the screen door, the door jam, under the door and in the mailbox. Lacy had not been there.

John put his books on the table and left to go pick up the baby.

Judith answered the door when John arrived. She looked worn out. Her usually neat hair was in a state of disarray and her designer dress was so crumpled it looked like she had pulled it out of the hamper before she put it on.

John thought she looked like she had been caring for John Jr. all by herself. He knew that wasn't possible as Judith and the judge always delegated that duty to Percy whenever they got tired of John Jr.

"I'm glad you're finally here. I expected you an hour ago. Where have you been?" Judith had an exasperated tone.

John thought from the look of things it would be best if he didn't tell her he had been home first. "School. I got held up. I'm sorry. Did John Jr. give you or Percy any trouble?"

"He didn't give me any real trouble but that son of yours is a compact bundle of pure energy. He wore me out near to a frazzle," Judith said without even a hint of a smile.

John looked around for his son. He must be upstairs sleeping, John thought. John wanted to get his son and get home. He was starting to feel a little tired himself and he still needed to hit the books.

"Thanks for you help, Judith. If I can get John Jr. now, we'll get out of your hair."

"He's upstairs in the playpen Jefferson bought for him. I wanted to talk to you. That's why I put the baby upstairs. Let's go in the living room."

John followed Judith into the living room. It was filled with antiques, two beautiful red velvet settees, French tapestry chairs and cherry accent tables. It was a little too formal for John's taste. Yet, thanks to his upbringing, he was able to appreciate the beauty and value of each piece.

John took a seat in one of the chairs while Judith opened an oval table that sat near a large black marble fireplace. The table concealed a bar. She poured two bourbon and waters and added a sprig of mint to each glass.

Judith closed the top of the bar and placed the vase back on top of it. She set two coasters down on the coffee table before she retrieved the drinks that she had set on the marble mantle.

Judith tried to hand a glass to John.

"No, thanks. I don't care for the hard stuff too much besides I really have to get going." John wondered what was on Judith's mind, she seemed to be a nervous wreck.

"I'll set this here. You may change your mind after you hear what I have to say. I've wanted a drink all day but with me having to watch the baby I couldn't take that liberty."

John noticed he hadn't seen Percy at all. She was the one who usually made the drinks and, more often than not, answered the front door.

No wonder Judith was tired, John thought.

"Is Percy sick today? I'm sorry about saddling you with John Jr. today. You didn't say anything about Percy being out sick when I called you."

"That's uncanny, John. Percy, well indirectly, is what I wanted to talk to you about." Judith took a large unladylike gulp of her drink. "When you called this morning I didn't know Percy would be home from work today. She doesn't start work until ten each morning. Percy was Lacy's aunt and Jammy's great-aunt. She—"

The word 'was' stuck out like a sore thumb. "Has something happened to Percy? I mean did she pass on?" John felt his muscles across his shoulders tighten.

"I think maybe you better have that drink."

John could sense something was terribly wrong. He felt like a cat on a tight rope. He hoped if he fell, he'd land on his feet.

"Spit it out, Judith. I haven't got all day." John could hear himself raising his voice but he wasn't able to control it.

"It's Lacy. She won't be coming to work for you anymore—"

"Is that all? You had me really worried for a second." John could feel his muscles loosen.

"Please, John, don't interrupt me. Percy called this morning to say she wouldn't be coming in today. She was hard to understand because she was crying. They found Lacy and Jammy's bodies in the bayou St. John. Eyewitnesses said that Lacy was run off the road by a man in a pickup truck. Percy said the police said they think the man was probably Klan." Judith drank down the rest of her drink and got up to fix herself another.

"Those sons-of-bitches. How could the kill an innocent girl and her baby? How could they?" John picked up the drink in front of him and took a swallow.

"Watch your language, please. I watched the noon news to see if they had any additional details other than what Percy told me. The authorities seem to believe that Lacy must have been out spoken about civil rights. There was even an anonymous call that the police had received. The caller said that this wouldn't have happened if the girl had known her place."

"That's outrageous! I have never heard anything about civil rights leave Lacy's mouth. She may have believed in them but she certainly wasn't outspoken. Even if she was, that's no reason to kill her. What are people so afraid of that they would kill a young woman and her toddler son?" John got up and looked around the room.

He thought about the house the Cartwrights lived in. No doubt built by slave labor. John thought it seemed ironic. The Negroes had been free from slavery for nearly a hundred years but invisible chains still held them. Chains they were trying to break. Chains their masters were trying to keep in place.

"You know, John, if Lacy was involved in that kind of thinking she should have known what she'd get. I have a hard time feeling sorry about any Colored that over steps their bounds. She should have thought about her son."

"That's sick. How could you side with a murderer? Judith, I have to go. Which room is John Jr. in?" John didn't wait for an answer. He headed upstairs.

That evening when John broke the news to Barbara he didn't know what to expect.

Barbara couldn't believe her ears. Lacy had been a good baby nurse, Barbara thought, and she now realized, she had never told her so. Jammy, Barbara thought, was such a cute little boy and so sweet too. She couldn't believe the little guy was gone.

Barbara wished she had never forced Lacy to find child care for Jammy. Only a few days before, Barbara had even thought about telling Lacy she could bring Jammy back to work with her. Barbara had found she missed seeing the little guy the few days a week when he would come to work with Lacy. John Jr. seemed to have missed Jammy too.

Barbara said a prayer for the little boy. She tried to say a prayer for Lacy but she was too mad at her.

Lacy should have known better than to get involved with any civil rights groups. Lacy knew that these were hard times. People would tolerate very little. Barbara tried to tell herself that it was all Lacy's fault. As sure as if Lacy had put a gun to her head, Lacy had not only killed herself but she had killed her son as well.

Deep down in the pit of Barbara's stomach she felt another anger. An anger for the man or men who took the life of a small boy. It wasn't fair. Why should Jammy die just because of his skin color? Barbara asked God that question. She had the answer to her question. An answer she knew all along. An answer she tried to deny for her entire life.

Jammy shouldn't have died and Lacy shouldn't have either. Not simply because of their skin color. Of course, Barbara comforted herself, Lacy hadn't died simply because of her skin color.

Lacy had died because she had stepped out of line. Stepped out of whose line? Who drew the line? Who maintained the line? Barbara questioned herself. Barbara knew that line had a name. It was the color line. Negroes just couldn't do anything they wanted to, even if it was legal. Lacy knew that. She would have to have known that. It was made clear to their people from birth. Wasn't it? Barbara thought about Jammy's smiling little face. He hadn't known about any color line or any other kind of line.

Barbara rubbed he temples. Her head ached. It was too much for Barbara to think about and it certainly wasn't anything Barbara wanted to discuss with John.

John, oh shit, Barbara thought. He had been sitting there watching her the whole time. Barbara had completely forgotten about John being in the room with her.

She had no intentions of letting John know how upset she was about Jammy. She certainly wasn't going to tell him she felt bad about Lacy too. He would probably take the opportunity to point out how often she had yelled at Lacy. Barbara felt bad enough. She didn't need John rubbing her nose in her grief.

The first words out of Barbara's mouth had shocked and appalled John.

"We will have to find a new nurse maid right away. Maybe this time we can get one that cooks dinner too," Barbara said stonily

"You know something, Barb? You're one cold hearted bitch. I have to wonder why some really good people die while the assholes live and breathe. It must be true what they say about the good dying young. I think you'll be a centurion." John stared hard at Barbara.

"That's not fair. I'm sorry Lacy and Jammy are gone. We, however, are not gone. We have to think about the everyday things and we will need a new baby nurse."

John knew Barb could be cold but her reaction had shocked him. She had seemed to be so engulfed in thought after John had relayed everything that her stepmother had told him.

John wondered what his wife had been thinking of. Maybe she was thinking about her own father's involvement in the Klan or whatever group he was with. Maybe she had thought about the possibility that her own father might have killed them. John knew he had thought about it. Maybe that hadn't been it at all. Maybe she had only been thinking about possible replacements for Lacy. John thought decidedly, whatever she had been thinking, it wasn't sympathy or a sense of loss. That was evident by her ice cold remarks.

"Barbara, I'm going to try and ignore your lack of sympathy so I can deal with you without wanting to slap some sense into that dense head of yours." John took a deep calming breath. "Do you have Lacy or Percy's phone numbers? I'll need to find out where the services are being held and where to send flowers."

"I'm not sure I know where I put Lacy's phone number. Isn't she listed?"

"No. I called information this morning when she didn't show. What about Percy's phone number, do you have it?"

Barbara chuckled. "You claim you aren't prejudice one tiny bit but you think Percy would have known Lacy just because she's Colored. Why that's ridiculous, John."

"Don't be foolish. I guess you weren't listening to me earlier. I understand, you were struck by an overwhelming grief," John said sarcastically. "I told you, that's how Judith knew about Lacy. Percy was Lacy's aunt. Judith saw the rest of the story on the twelve o'clock news," John finished.

"Oh, I had no idea that Percy had a niece. I've known Percy all my life too. Come to think of it, there's not too much I do know about Percy."

"Well, what about it?"

"What?"

"Do you or don't you have her telephone number?"

"No but I'll call my Daddy or my stepmomma and get it. I'll go and call now."

Barbara got the number for John and went in the bedroom to lay down.

The knowledge that Lacy and Jammy had died had hurt her. The fact that the Klan, a group much like her father's, had been responsible caused her more pain. Now, knowing it was Percy's family had hurt her even more so.

Barbara loved Percy like a grandmother. The kind of love that comes from knowing someone really well from childhood. Only she, Barbara thought, apparently did not know Percy as well as Percy knew her. All the same, Percy's loss would always have been Barbara's loss. In this case, unfortunately, Barbara thought, it wasn't just a sympathetic loss.

The next day John had agreed to meet with Percy after his classes. He didn't know what it was about. When he had called to get the church and house address, Percy had not given them to him. Instead she asked him to meet her at Audubon Park.

John crossed St. Charles street away from Tulane University. He only got half way across. The street car was too near to cross in front of it. John finished crossing once the street car had passed.

It was a nice day although a bit windy. The park was lush and green. It would have been a perfect day for studying in the park.

John looked for Percy but he didn't see her. He walked the park's front perimeter on St. Charles. No Percy. John looked at his watch. He was five minutes early. John decided to take a seat on a bench right up front. He had only been sitting a minute when he heard his name. His first and middle names.

John looked up to see Janiene. He stood up. "How are you doing? Are you okay? How are Tad's parents?" John realized he was bombarding her with questions but he was so concerned about her.

"I'm doing okay. Tad's dad is doing better than his mother. It's hard for all of us, you know? We all just keep thinking it's some sort of cruel joke, that Tad will come home any moment."

John blinked. "I know exactly what you mean. I've lost three people recently. All of them young. It's hard to believe they are really gone."

Janiene was having a hard time with the loss of one person. Of course, that one person was her husband. She wondered how close John was to the other people. She didn't want to ask in case it would bring up too much pain for him.

Luckily, John told her about the other deaths. Janiene had never met Lacy or Jammy but her heart went out to John and to the family of the victims. Janiene was so tired of violence. If Tad hadn't been training for war he never would have been killed.

"I'm meeting Lacy's aunt here." John looked down at his watch again. "She should be here any minute."

"I better get going. I'll be seeing you, John Jackson." Janiene got up and started to walk away.

"Janiene," John called after her.

"Yes?"

"Do you think we could get together again. I mean to talk about Tad."

Percy walked up before Janiene could answer. She had obviously overheard John's question to Janiene. Percy gave John a very disapproving look.

"Her husband was one of my best friends and he died recently," John tried to explain.

"Ain't none of my business. I don't need to know nothing about it. Just don't let my Miss Barbie child see you with that girl. From the look of you, I'd say she got a right to be jealous."

John flushed from embarrassment. He thought he had his emotions for Janiene under control. He should have known from the way his heart was slamming into his rib cage that he did not.

"I got to tell you in person 'cause it breaks my heart." Percy brought John's mind back to her. "My sister don't want you or Miss Barbie at the funeral and she don't want no flowers from y'all."

"Why? I don't understand. We have never had any bad blood between us. We've never even met her. We'd really like to express our feelings about the loss of Lacy and Jammy."

"It jus ain't possible."

"Why? What have we done?" John was puzzled

"Nothin'. Nothin' on purpose anyhows."

"What do you mean by that?"

"Miss Barbie told Lacy to make Jammy's father start paying some support on the boy. You see, he's a old rich white fella and Miss Barbie convinced Lacy that he would pay to keep his family and friends from knowing 'bout his Colored boy. So that's what Lacy did. She asked for money. Nothin' big, only what was fair. Only it didn't get her money. It got her killed." Percy blew her nose in her embroidered handkerchief.

"Wait a minute. I thought they said Lacy was involved in some civil rights group. They said that's what got her killed."

"I know they says that but it ain't so. Lacy didn't think there was any use in fighting for civil rights. She always said your type were predators. No offense not but she said you all would get your way no matter who it hurt. She used to talk about how the Indians lost their land and the Blacks built the South for free." Percy blew her nose again.

"If she felt so strongly, how do you know she wasn't involved in some civil rights group?" John questioned.

"Uh-uh, she wasn't like that. She thought that we may have to suffer here, on earth, but y'all would suffer at the hands of the Lord. The Bible says that the meek shall inherit the earth, ya know."

"But the authorities said the Klan was probably responsible."

Percy lowered her voice to a barely audible whisper, "Jammy's daddy has friends in high places. I doubt if he dirtied his hand none. It could have been the Klan that carried out the act but it was Jammy's own father that got them killed."

"I don't know what to say. I could never hurt John Jr.. What kind of beast fathered Jammy?" John really asked the question of no one but Percy had an answer.

"The worst kind. The kind that let color block reason, intelligence or even love," Percy paused. "So you see why y'all can have nothin' to do with Lacy and Jammy's burin'. I know Miss Barbie didn't mean no harm. She was only trying to help but if she hadn't given Lacy that advice, my niece and great-nephew might be alive to this day."

John was anxious to get home and lay blame on Barbara. After her cold reaction to the murders, he would enjoy seeing her suffer a little. John didn't really blame Barbara. He was sure she was only trying to help but still he wished she had kept her nose out of it.

Jammy had been fine staying at their house. John had never known why Lacy stopped bringing him. Now he knew. John guessed that the father must have given Lacy some money or she wouldn't have been able to afford the child care. Unless someone else in Lacy's family had been watching Jammy. No, John thought, the reason Lacy stopped bringing Jammy was a mystery to him. John hoped it wasn't because of something Barbara had said.

When John arrived home that evening, Barbara and John Jr. were already there.

John's mother and Oliver had been more than willing to watch John Jr. while they looked for a replacement for Lacy. The arrangement worked out very well since Barbara parked her car at the Sommier house anyway.

John mussed his son's hair and sat down on the sofa. Barbara came out of the kitchen to make small talk but she wasn't quite at ease with John.

"I talked to Percy today." John said inviting Barbara's curiosity to spring forward.

"Did you find out about the services?" Barbara picked up John Jr. who was trying to crawl up onto the sofa.

"No. Lacy's mother doesn't want us there nor does she want any flowers from us," John said dryly.

"What? Why? Has the woman gone mad with grief? Call Percy back, I'm sure Lacy's mother will change her mind."

"Nope. When I met Percy today—"

"You met with Percy? I thought you were going to call her."

"I did call but she wanted to meet with me. She didn't feel she should tell me over the phone."

"Tell you what, John?"

"That you are at least partially responsible for Lacy and Jammy's deaths." John was enjoying this. He had really been disgusted with his wife's reaction when he told her about the deaths.

"Me? How? Well, she's crazy if she thinks because Daddy is with the Wings that I had anything to do with this."

John made a mental note. This was the first time Barbara had ever said which organization her father was with. When John had questioned her before, she had always insisted that it was her father's business, not hers.

"That's not why, Barb. Did you tell Lacy that she should get some financial help from Jammy's father? To threaten to expose him as Jammy's father if he didn't pay?" John looked at Barbara knowingly.

"Well, yes, but it was only fair. He should have to pay for the child's care too. I really don't see what this has to do with anything. The police said they think its Klan related because of the tip off they got. It's been all over the news, you know that."

John kicked his feet up on the coffee table. "I was led to believe that Lacy's lover did not take kindly to the threat. Rather than pay her or continue to pay her, he decided to have her killed. From what Percy said, he has friends in some pretty high places, or low places, depending on your point of view."

Barbara felt her stomach clinch. She had been having trouble with her stomach lately. Probably due to all the recent problems, Barbara thought.

"I bet she tried to ask him for way too much money. That's probably it."

"I don't think so. Percy said that Lacy only asked for what was fair. Unfortunately, thanks to you, she asked it of a man who has no sense of fairness."

Barbara was disgusted. How could anyone order their own son's death? Barbara had never thought it would turn out like this. She was only trying to help Lacy.

No, Barbara thought, she hadn't been trying to help Lacy. She had been trying to help herself. She had been trying to get Jammy out of her house, permanently. All because he had jumped on her sofa. Jammy was dead now just because he had jumped on her sofa.

Barbara's stomach turned. She felt the burn of stomach acid and lunch rise up her throat. She tried to hold it back but she could not. Barbara raced into the bathroom with her hand over her mouth.

She barely made it to the toilet when her body purged itself of the contents of her stomach. Even after her stomach was empty, her body continued to heave, as if it could purge itself of the ugly truth.

She had forced Lacy to go to Jammy's father. How was she to know the man was a monster?

Barbara knew all the reasoning in the world wouldn't take the blame off her shoulders. Her stomach convulsed once again while an eerie guttural scream left her throat.

John had followed Barbara to the bathroom. He hadn't thought she would take it so hard.

It was true; he had wanted her to feel some pain after her cold reaction to the murders but he hadn't wanted this. The awful noises she made with her head near the rim of the toilet made his heart tighten. She was trying, like a trapped animal, to free herself. To free herself from the truth.

John knew that in the perfect truth, it was not Barbara's fault. The blame lay with Jammy's father. He could understand why Mrs. Washington would blame Barbara. She needed someone to strike out at, someone who would feel it. Obviously, Jammy's father didn't care, so Barbara was the next best thing. A White woman. A woman who had been her daughter's boss. A woman who had given her daughter deadly advice.

John soaked a wash cloth and squeezed it out. He wiped Barbara's mouth and handed the cloth to her so she could finish the job.

He picked up John Jr. who had crawled into the hall to see what noise was. John placed his son in his crib before returning to the bathroom to help Barbara up.

Barbara looked stricken. Tears flowed down her cheeks. Her face was bright red from her head being held down low and the strain of the heaves.

"It's all my fault, John. She's right. It's my fault." Barbara fell against John's chest.

John patted her hair. He was sorry now that he had done this to her. He had wanted to see her hurt but he hadn't thought it would hurt her like this.

"It's not all your fault. Hell, it's not your fault at all. So, you gave some bad advice. Lacy didn't have to take it. Lacy knew what kind of man Jammy's father was. You didn't." John kissed Barbara's forehead. "Listen Honey, it's not your fault. Lacy was a proud woman. She probably felt like she was imposing on us by bringing Jammy to work with her. I bet she asked him for money for day care."

"I know she was asking him for day care money and it's all my fault." Barbara sounded hysterical.

John hugged her tightly and tried to calm her. "How can Lacy's pride be your fault? She chose to ask Jammy's father for money. How do we even know she hadn't thought of it before you suggested it to her?"

John's comforting tone was more than she could take.

"It's my fault! I told Lacy to talk to Jammy's father because I told her that she couldn't bring Jammy here anymore!" Barbara screamed.

John stepped back from Barbara. He looked at her like she was an alien. "You did what?" John's deep voice reverberated off the bathroom walls.

Barbara braced herself against the sink. "I was sick. When I came home, Jammy was jumping on the sofa making a mess with the cookie he had. It was too much for my aching head. I gave Lacy a week to find day care for Jammy. When she said she couldn't afford it, I, uh, I told her to get the money from Jammy's father." Barbara reached for John's hand.

John snatched his hand away from Barbara's. "You know something, Barbara? Every time I start to think you're a nice person, you do something to prove me wrong. You really don't care about anyone except yourself, do you?"

"John, you have to understand. I was feeling sick that day. I was thinking the other day how I missed Jammy. How I wanted him back."

"Did you tell Lacy?" John hoped for some sort of redemption for his wife.

"Well, uh, no. I hadn't gotten around to it."

"I think that pretty much says it all." John backed out of the bathroom but before he walked away he added, "Barbara? You were right. You are responsible for Lacy and Jammy's deaths."

Though John didn't truly believe that, he knew his wife had, at least in some way, contributed to the murders of two innocent people.

John walked away from the sound of Barbara's heavy sobs.

Judge Cartwright was really starting to get nervous about Tommy. He hadn't asked Tommy about the killings in Alabama because he had been afraid of what Tommy would say. Now Cartwright had a hunch that it was Tommy who was behind the murders of Lacy and Jammy. It was true that a lot of people had pickup trucks and it was true that a lot of people were willing to kill in order to keep things the same but Cartwright just knew down in his heart that it was Tommy's doing.

The tip off to the police had given Tommy away, at least to Cartwright. The tip had said that the girl had been a 'Rebel's rouser'. A term Tommy liked to use for civil rights advocates because he said their kind always roused the true rebs of the South, good White men. Most of the newspapers had printed 'rebel rouser' but the desk sergeant who took the call was careful to point out, in a news interview, that the caller had added a 's' to rebel, though it was clear the officer thought it was done out of ignorance.

Cartwright knew that Lacy had never been involved in such activities. She wasn't the type. She always knew her place. Well, almost always.

Other things had pointed to Tommy as well. Such as the death of Jammy. Cartwright had been witness to Klan violence many times in his life. Usually they weren't the type to kill an innocent boy. More likely than not they would spare the boy so he would serve as a reminder for the family and friends of the one who had stepped out of line.

He debated whether or not he should call Tommy. He knew he would have to talk to him sooner or later. He thought about Tommy's behavior the last time he came to his house. He decided he'd talk to Tommy later.

Chapter Fourteen

"Guten Morgan, Frau Sommier," Helga said cheerfully. Helga was the nurse maid they found to replace Lacy. She was a large woman, big bones and fully padded. Her heaviness added to the sense that she was of sturdy stock. A third generation German-

American that, if you didn't know any better, made you think she had just gotten off the boat.

Helga had long blonde hair with barely visible strands of gray intermingled. She braided her long locks in two braids on either side of her head. The braids were coiled just above each ear.

Barbara thought Helga's hairstyle made her look like the character 'Heidi' of the same name book. Helga, however, did not look twelve. She looked more like fifty. Helga, obviously proud of her German heritage, always had an odd odor about her. She always smelled faintly of sauerkraut. Barbara thought the woman must rub some of the marinated cabbage behind her ears daily.

Barbara could understand taking pride in one's heritage but Helga took it a bit too far. Her strange body odor, her strong accent, the braids and always slipping German words into conversation was really starting to wear on Barbara's already fragile nerves.

"Helga, how many times do I have to tell you? Don't call me Frau. I hate it. I think it's such an ugly word. Call me Mrs. Sommier and it probably wouldn't hurt if you said good morning in English," Barbara told her firmly.

"Ja, okay. I will try," Helga smiled, "Wie gehts?"

Barbara threw her arms up in exasperation. "Helga? English, speak English."

"Sorry, Ich habe, I mean, I have a hard time remembering."

Barbara knew Helga didn't have a hard time remembering. She was just stubborn. In two weeks time, Barbara had already told the woman not to call her Frau at least fifty times.

At least, Barbara thought, Helga cooked. Some of the food like the bratwurst, Barbara could live without but the breads and pastries more than made up for the ethnic dishes that did not appeal to her palate.

The important thing was that John Jr. really liked the big woman, funny smell and all. Since Helga arrived, John Jr. was back to his old self.

In the first days after Lacy's death, John Jr. had started to whine constantly. His eyes lost their sparkle and he hardly ever smiled. The doctor had told them it was normal. He explained, using a lot of medical terms, when a baby loses a person he or she had spent most of their lives with, they mourn their loss. In other words, he missed Lacy.

Helga's big smiling face had done what his parents could not, it brought John Jr. out of his melancholy.

"Helga, I've got to get going. We've got a new shipment of fragile things coming in. There's supposed to be a Ming vase in the shipment. I'm anxious to see it." Barbara kissed John Jr. on the forehead and left her son in big capable hands.

As she closed the front door, Barbara heard Helga's loud hearty laugh and her son's faint little giggle.

Later when Barbara arrived at work, her father-in-law sent her upstairs to uncrate the fragile items they had received.

Henri seemed to be more trusting of Barbara now. When she had first started with PIP, she rarely went upstairs but lately he had sent her up there with some regularity.

Upstairs no longer held the mystery it once did for her. Things that were 'off limits' had always intrigued Barbara. Now that she could freely roam about the upstairs she no longer wanted to.

Barbara thought the upstairs could be best described in three words, dusty, musty and crusty. Walking across the floor kicked up so much dust that her shoes became covered with the stuff. She hated to touch anything up there. There was a layer of dust that it encrusted all the boxes. While the musty air was enough to give a healthy person an attack of asthma. Oh and the heat, Barbara thought, one could swelter inside of three minutes. Of course, the heat and humidity, did nothing for her hair except make her curls droop.

No, Barbara thought, the upstairs no longer held anything of interest. She really didn't like going upstairs at all but she dare not complain to Henri. He still kept the upstairs under lock and key. She knew that sooner or later she would actually need Henri to send her upstairs so she could return the journal to its neglected box of things saved from a fire nearly ten years ago. Barbara wondered if anyone would ever really notice if she didn't return the journal. It didn't matter, as soon as she finished it, she would put it back.

While the journal might not be noticed missing from the box; there was a chance it would be noticed in the lunch drawer. It seemed to her that the risk of being caught with the journal grew more and more each day. Barbara's stomach still turned whenever she thought about how Henri had almost caught her. The sooner she put it back, the better.

At lunch Barbara resumed reading the journal.

May 1849

My excitement grows as the wedding nears. I cannot believe how calm my bride-to-be is. Isabelle, though only sixteen, is so very wise. I often think she is the older of the two of us.

Jean-Claude was disappointed at my refusal of the trip to the brothel. He said he wanted to treat me to the pleasure of an experienced woman one last time before I started the drudgery of taking an inept girl to my bed.

Drudgery! Inept! I was almost consumed by anger towards Jean-Claude before I realized, he has never been in love. His pleasure is derived from experienced women. Mine shall be from the love returned to me by a woman, my woman.

I have already discovered that a simple kiss with Isabelle gives me more pleasure than would seeing a hundred female forms parade nude before me.

My anticipation of sharing the love act with her is overwhelming. I am anxious to draw her near to me to be one with me. I know that we shall not only join bodies but minds. I think that is what Jean-Claude cannot understand. He only satisfies his body. I must satisfy my mind as well.

It is a funny thing. In Louisiana, a man is expected to take a mistress. (It is also here in France as well.) Isabelle asked me if I intended to take a mistress. I promised her that I never would. I really do not understand why any man would take a mistress if he has married for love.

Isabelle asked me what it feels like to make love. She said her Maman says it can be enjoyed with some men while endured with others, depending upon their level of expertise. I am sure my skin was crimson when I told her I did not think it was a matter of expertise when there was love. She looked at me with those big doe-like eyes, and she told me she believed I was correct but then, to my great embarrassment, she asked me if I were extremely experienced. I told her that I felt our conversation had taken an inappropriate turn. I have promised to answer all of her questions when we are married. I hope she understands that I did not answer her due to modesty, and not due to lack of experience.

Isabelle shall have all her curiosity satisfied, as will I, in less than a month. Jean-Claude has agreed to stand up for me. Papa has refused to come. He says he and Maman are too old for the travel but I think it is because he has learned of my friendship with Jean-Claude.

Luc has already come for my wedding to Isabelle. I am glad he has gotten over his jealously of the terms of Uncle Jean's will. I think my making him overseer at Mallard's Landing has something to do with his change of heart. I am sure Luc has secretly loved Aunt Marie since he was a boy. It is for that reason and not for the money that I think he has befriended, me, his brother once again.

Luc met Jean-Claude for the first time two days ago. He was surprised that he liked him. Luc believes that the blood of the dark ones taint your mind so that you are inferior. He was surprised by Jean-Claude's quick wit and even said as much.

Unfortunately, Jean-Claude brought up the notion of freeing the slaves at Mallard's Landing in front of Luc. It is a notion I have been, thanks in part to Jean-Claude, toying with. Jean-Claude says it is unfair, immoral even, to become wealthy off another man's labor. To build houses off that labor, plant and breed more laborers is wrong.

I see Jean-Claude's point and I agree, but if you look at it from Luc's view then there is nothing wrong with it. It is the same thing as using a horse to plow the field because the Negro is only an animal to Luc. Jean-Claude said if God had intended for the Negro to be used as an animal then he would not have made him the same in form. He says if a man cannot spill his seed in a horse and get a horse then why does he think he can spill his seed in anything else and get anything different from himself. His seed will only grow in what is like him.

Luc said you only have to look at the skin to see it is different. Jean-Claude said it is not so different, only not accepted. He told Luc to look at Isabelle with her fair skin and blonde hair. Is she less than the red head with freckles because the red head says it's so.

These arguments went on for hours. I do not think Luc changed his mind much, if at all, but I knew that I did. Jean-Claude's arguments made good sense while Luc's did not. When I get back home, I will start a process that will eventually free my slaves but in the meantime I can not afford to set them free.

I am glad Jean-Claude has enlightened me but at the same time I wish he had not. I feel like a madam, peddling the flesh of young, sometimes unwilling, girls while never exposing her flesh and always filling her purse.

Barbara continued reading the rest of the afternoon. She read about Henri and Isabelle's wedding, the many gifts they received and their preparation to leave for Louisiana.

After school, John decided to study in the park. It was a beautiful day, not a cloud in the sky.

As he stepped off the curb to cross the street, something fell from a tree and gently tapped him on the head. John looked down on the ground to see what had hit him. Shimmering on the ground near his foot was a strand of plastic pearl Mardi Gras beads.

At Mardi Gras each year, hundreds of thousands of the beads were thrown into the crowds. The onlookers would yell 'Throw me somethin' mister' and the costumed men would throw handfuls of beads, doubloons and other trinkets, but not all the beads made it into the eager hands of the crowds. Many strands of the beads ended up intertwined with the leaves and branches of the trees. This was most common along St. Charles Avenue where the great oaks lined the street on either side. Their sprawling branches held many a treasure, especially in the first few days after Mardi Gras, but even when the city was preparing for Mardi Gras once again the trees still held some baubles.

It was considered good luck if one of the strands of beads fell on or near you, so the residents left the stands in the trees to bring good fortune to whomever the beads fell upon. In the meantime, the beads were a joy to look at. To find them in the trees they had to be searched for most of the time but sometimes, when the twilight came, they would sparkle like real treasure hidden among the Spanish moss and leaves.

John leaned down and scooped up the beads. He pulled the beads over his head. What the heck, John thought, maybe they'd give him good luck with his studying. Not that he needed it. He was easily getting through all of his classes. John crossed the street and found a grassy area halfway to the zoo. He put all but one of his books down on the grass and lay down. Rather than reading the book in hand, he used it for a pillow.

He closed his eyes and felt the hot sun beating down upon his face. A tree branch blocked the sun's path so that John's torso was shaded. The heat on his face combined with coolness of his body made him very sleepy. He drifted off in no time.

John wasn't sure what visions he had had while he was sleeping but they had been pleasant. When he sat up, shaking off the affects of his nap, he felt contented. Everything was serene, a smile crossed his face.

He was unaware that Janiene was sitting on a park bench less than fifty feet away. She had been watching him sleep.

Janiene had seen John cross the street and decided to follow him so that they could talk. Talk about the good times they had with Tad, she told herself. When she saw him lay on the grass rather than take a park bench, she chickened out.

She had taken a bench that was partially hidden from John's view by a large bush.

As he had lain sleeping she had watched. She had remembered, not the good times with Tad but the good times with John. Janiene had started to feel guilty and was going to leave but then he sat up. The peaceful look about him intrigued her but it was his smile that captured her full attention. A smile that went from his mouth to his eyes to his soul. His smile had drawn her up off the bench and towards him. As if in a trance, she slowly walked to where he was seated.

John, still groggy with sleep, was barely able to make out the colorful beads in the delicate hand. They reminded him of his own beads and he reached for his beads, lifted them from his chest and twirled them around his finger.

John squinted up into the sunlight to see who it was that was standing so near him. The sleep combined with the sunlight made it difficult for him to focus.

He looked back to the delicate hand because it was the only thing his eyes could bring into focus. He noticed an intricate wedding ring in addition to the beads.

"John Jackson, you surprise me. I believe you don't know who I am." Janiene drawled slowly as if mocking the stereotypical southern belle.

"Janiene? Janiene. I couldn't see, the sunlight was blinding me." He made no attempt to look at her face but instead studied the beads in her hand.

"Mind if I sit down? Or are you busy studying?"

"Oh, sorry. Please." John motioned at the ground next to him. "The grass is perfect, not too hot, not too cool and not damp at all." John unconsciously fumbled with his beads.

"Where'd you get those?" Janiene inclined her head towards his chest.

"Oh, these?" John looked down at the beads, "they fell on me when I was crossing the street."

"That's strange. It's not even windy. These fell near me today when I came out of the Holy Name Of Jesus. It's been over half a year since Mardi Gras, don't you think it's weird that both of us had beads fall to us on the same day?" Janiene examined the beads in her hand.

Janiene noticed a faraway look in John's eyes. He seemed to be engulfed in deep thought.

"Well?"

"Yes, I was just thinking about your question. Actually, I don't think it's strange. I think it is destiny."

"What?"

"Both of us having the beads today is our destiny."

"I don't follow you. Are you taking one of those Philosophy classes or something?"

"No, it just makes sense. It was our destiny to be together. Don't you see? The beads falling on us both proves it. We—"

"You're not making any sense. You must still be confused from sleep."

John realized that she must have been there watching him while he slept. That knowledge filled him with an indescribable warmth. "We are two parts of a whole. We were meant to be together. It's our destiny."

"If we were meant to be together then we would be together. Destiny is just that, destiny. It can't be changed or altered. A man couldn't possibly change his destiny."

"I think he can. I think that there is a preset course but that man still has free will. If a man goes against what is his natural course than he goes against his destiny. That's what I did. I changed my course but that does not change the fact that you and I were destined for one another."

"I disagree with you. If we were destined to be together than we would be together. I don't go for all that 'Romeo and Juliet' stuff. People who are so blessed that they have a destiny with another person will ultimately be with that person."

"I think we're going to have to agree to disagree on this one. I know in my heart that you were meant for me. I just chose to ignore that."

Janiene wasn't listening. She was suddenly transported to a different place, a different time. A time when she had first heard him say that she was his destiny. A time when she had believed him, even agreed with him.

During those first awkward months of when she had first started high school, she had noticed John Jackson. Heck, every girl had. He was the type of boy that made girls stutter when he was around and made them giggle when he wasn't. He was a dream, Janiene remembered.

Back then Janiene had been like every other girl at school, catching glimpses of John whenever she thought he might not notice. Just looking at him back then would make her heart race. To be honest, she thought, her heart still raced whenever she saw him.

John had never noticed her or any of the other girls who would sneak peaks at him. In spite of his extremely good looks he wasn't in the least bit vain. He always thought the looks were directed at Tad or one of the other boys that were standing near him.

It was that lack of vanity that had gotten them together, in a round about sort of way. John had noticed Janiene looking at them and thought she was beautiful. Convinced that her attentions were for Tad he had talked his best friend into asking the unknown beauty out.

Janiene had felt bad about turning Tad down but she suggested, as a way to soothe his pride, that they be friends. To her surprise, and later her delight, he accepted.

It was only natural that John be around his best friend's new friend. That had made it easier for Janiene, instead of being tongue tied around John, she could easily talk to Tad. After a couple of months, John felt like an old pair of shoes, the kind that are so comfortable that you search them out whenever you can.

Once John and Janiene had started dating, John had confessed that he was jealous that Janiene had been looking at Tad. He said that he had been watching her from the first day of school but he didn't quite know how to ask her out, especially when she kept looking at his best friend.

When Janiene had confessed that it was really him that she had been looking at, he laughed. Then John had taken on a very serious look and told her that it must be true, it was destiny.

"At least I get to stare in those beautiful eyes while you ignore me," John said in a light tone.

"Huh? Oh, I'm sorry. My mind was somewhere else." Janiene was embarrassed by the emotions the memories had stirred. She somehow knew that she had been smiling before John had stirred her back into the present.

"I was saying we are just going to have to agree to disagree. I can't believe for a second that you weren't my destiny before I screwed things up." John's voice was full of regret.

Janiene felt sorry for John and Barbara. At least, she and Tad had had the love that comes with a deep friendship. Janiene doubted if John shared any love with his wife, even the kind that friends share.

Janiene wondered, how would she know what John shared with his wife? It was true that he showed signs of still loving her, Janiene thought, but that didn't mean he couldn't love his wife too. After all, she had loved Tad even if it was in a different way. Barbara had given John a son. He must love her a little, at least because of that.

Janiene felt her heart constrict in her chest. It was too much to be around John. It was always the same, at first she'd feel joy and then she'd feel pain. Now, with Tad gone she felt one more thing. Guilt.

John sensed Janiene's unease. He thought he'd better drop the whole topic before she ended up leaving. He really didn't want her to leave, it felt so good and right to have her there with him.

"How are your folks doing?" John really wanted to ask about Tad's parents but he didn't have the nerve.

"They're fine. They've been a little overprotective since I moved into my own place. Dad is always 'just in the neighborhood' so he stops by all the time and nine times out of ten it's Mom on the telephone."

John's brows shot up. "What made you decide to get a place of your own? Don't you want to save money while you're going to school?" He knew that most of the local collage students preferred to live at home until they graduated.

"After Tad died, I felt like my life had changed too much to go home. I don't suppose I have to worry about money anymore. Tad was very thorough, between the Army and the private insurance policies, I'm taken care of for life." Janiene looked a little embarrassed by her admission.

John hadn't really thought about all the changes she must have gone through, must be going through. When he was with her, it was hard to remember the changes that he had gone through. In a way, it seemed as if time was suspended. That they were always in love and the whole world didn't matter.

The clouds shifted so that the sun was shining directly in her eyes. She squinted and her hand flew to her brow to form a visor. The beads hung from her hand in front of her face.

"Watch it." John reached out to wipe the beads. "There's grass all over those things. You'll get in your eyes."

She had apparently ground the beads into the grass when she had lowered herself to the ground.

Janiene didn't have a chance to look at the grass on the beads before John's hand had clasped the beads and had pulled them from her fingers.

John laid the beads down beside him and reached back over to gently brush the grass from her cheek.

She jumped, surprised by his touch. Her cheek felt heated by the light rubbing of his finger tips.

"Sorry, didn't mean to scare you. You had some grass on you. You still have a little right below your eye."

She wiped the area below her right eye.

"Wrong eye. Here let me get it." John reached over and wiped softly at the tiny piece of grass. "Hold still, I didn't get it yet."

She instinctively closed her eyes since his hand was so near to them.

He looked at her with her eyes closed. Her eyes were not tightly squeezed shut as a child would do but instead they were gently closed, confiding trust.

He thought she looked beautiful sitting there before him with her eyes closed. He had forgotten about the grass. Before he knew what he was doing, his lips touched hers. He kissed her lightly at first but quickly deepened the kiss.

Chapter Fifteen

Janiene felt the familiar tender yet exciting kiss. She was drawn to a different time. A happier time.

She accepted and returned the kiss before realized what she was doing.

She quickly pulled away, her face flushed. "What do you think you're doing? John Jackson, you're married," she sounded more disgusted with herself then John.

John's ears burned from the truth. A moment ago he had been kissing the woman he loved. He had been drawing a much needed energy from that kiss. He had been feeling shared love. But she wasn't his wife.

God knew that he had never shared a kiss like that with his wife. He had shared passion. He had shared lust. But he had never shared energy, never shared love. Never, not with Barbara.

"I don't know what came over me. Please forgive me. I'm so sorry." John looked ashamed.

"I guess it's not a good idea for us to see each other. It's obvious that we both have trouble with this 'friendship'. I don't think this is a friendship that Barbara would approve of anyway." Janiene could still feel the tingling from their kiss.

"I don't give a damn what Barbara approves of. We've been friends for a lot longer then I've even known Barbara. We can't just stop being friends."

"Don't you see? We stopped being friends a long time ago. I mean we were still friends but it ran much deeper then a simple friendship. It still runs deeper than that." Janiene looked off in thought. "I can't do this. The kiss was just proof that we can't afford to be around each other. It's not fair to Barbara or your son. Shoot, it's not fair to you or me either."

"It won't happen again. I swear it. Please, Janiene, please don't break off our friendship. It was all that talk about destiny. I forgot the present and kind of slipped into the past."

"That's my point. We really don't have a present together. We will always be looking to the past." Janiene paused thoughtfully, "I think that's because that's when we were both happiest. That part of our lives is over now. Since it's apparent that we can't let the past go, we have to let our friendship go," Janiene said quietly.

John frowned. His whole face was etched with the pain he felt. He knew what she was saying was true but he didn't want to admit it.

He knew that their past was what he wanted to regain. Not some new found friendship. He never had been the type to have a large circle of female friends anyway.

What did he expect her to do? John asked himself. He couldn't keep their relationship going without eventually wanting more. Only a moment ago he had crossed the invisible boundary and he still wanted more. If she allowed him to, he would end up leading her down a path of emotional destruction. A path that led straight to adultery and bastards.

Just the thought of a child with Janiene excited him. He hated to admit it but he wouldn't care if the child were a bastard as long as he had made that child with Janiene.

John loved Janiene too much to try to keep a 'friendship' going. Especially since he knew where he'd like to take that friendship. It wouldn't be fair to her, he told himself. She deserved better than that. Much better than that.

"You are right." John stood up gathering his books up with him. He looked down into Janiene's eyes. "We never did kiss good-bye the last time. Shall we consider that our good-bye kiss?"

"Yes," she whispered.

As John walked away, Janiene thought that it had been a perfect good-bye kiss, except for one thing. It had been too short. Janiene thought realistically, even if the kiss had lasted a month, it still would have been too short. How do say good-bye for a lifetime to the only person you'll ever truly love?

John walked to where he had parked his VW Bug, his stomach bunched in knots. He was, however, feeling better about one thing. The kiss didn't seem like such a betrayal to Barb when he thought of it as a good-bye kiss.

A few days later, Judge Cartwright was not looking forward to his lunch with Tommy Jamison. Tommy had been trying to put the screws to him about making the Wings a violent faction. He approached the subject at every opportunity and it was beginning to get scary. Tommy was obsessed.

Cartwright arrived at Galatoire's right on time. He informed the staff that he was waiting for a Mr. Jamison and allowed himself to be seated.

He ordered a mint julep. Cartwright checked his watch several times before the drink arrived.

He ordered another julep when the first one was being served. He had a strong feeling he was going to need it.

Cartwright looked around the place not noticing the reflective mirrored walls or the shiny highly polished brass fixtures. He was looking for familiar faces. He had purposely set the luncheon in the late afternoon so that he would avoid running into too many friends or acquaintances.

So far he had been lucky. Only a few business associates were in the place. None that required him getting up to greet them. A simple nod had been sufficient.

Cartwright had always tried to be careful when he met with any members of the Wings. Especially when they weren't upper class or at least upper middle class. He knew he'd have a hard time explaining lower class friends since he and his friends were snobs.

He never had problems from liberals the way some of his more open comrades had. And he preferred to keep it that way. Until, of course, he was ready to implement his plan. Even then, he thought, no one would have to know he was with the White Wings.

Cartwright knocked back his first mint julep and started working on the second one. He was ready to order a third but decided he might not need it. The drinks were pleasantly powerful.

They tasted like homemade mint juleps. The ones that required fresh mint, good Louisiana refined cane sugar, an ample amount Kentucky bourbon, a small amount water and, of course, time. The whole concoction had to sit at least over night while the bourbon, sugar, mint and water formed a sweet syrupy drink.

Cartwright remembered how his Daddy had once told him if you wanted to get a girl to drop her dress then get a couple of mint juleps in her. In his time, it was the only strong drink that a 'lady' would drink. Because of its sweetness, it really wasn't considered a hard drink even though each drink contained enough alcohol to make three mixed drinks.

Cartwright was thinking about just how many dresses had been dropped for him thanks to the minty whiskey when Tommy walked up.

"You look like the cat what ate the canary," Cartwright said to Tommy as he sat down.

I am, Tommy thought. But Tommy wasn't quite ready to break his news to the judge.

"Funny, I was thinking the same thing 'bout you by that expression you were wearing when I walked up," Tommy retorted noticing Cartwright's wry look.

Cartwright smiled. "I was remembering a very pleasant time in my life. What did you want anyway, that you couldn't come by the house?" Cartwright asked impatiently.

"You're the one that asked me not to come by the house so much. The way I figured it, since I wasn't welcome at your house none, you could take me out to some fancy smancy place for lunch." Tommy grinned as if he were kidding but something in his manner said he was not.

"Yeah, okay. But what did you need to talk to me about?"

Tommy was about to answer when the waiter came up to take their orders. Tommy didn't really look at the menu; he simply ordered the most expensive thing.

Tommy waited until the waiter was out of ear shot and said, "I think it's time that the Wings started pressing back the nig, uh, coloreds a bit. Teach 'em who's in charge. I think things are startin' to get way out of hand. If we ain't careful, this here President Kennedy is going to start requiring we marry our White women off to the Coloreds."

"That's a bit radical—even coming from you. What's really going on with you?"

"No, I mean it. They are pushin' for more and more rights until they push us right out of our homes, jobs and away from our women. Did you hear about the nig, uh, colored they had to lynch over in Texas 'cause he was up with a White woman. Married to her! We got to put an end to this shit."

Cartwright had heard about the man. Though he didn't know where the couple had gotten married, he was aware that more and more states were allowing interracial marriage and more and more people were turning a blind eye to it. It had disgusted him.

Tommy could see the concerned look that crossed the judge's face when he mentioned the White woman so he went with it. "Woman a lot of times ain't a bit smarter than children. There could be a lot more White women what ended up with blacks and I'm not just talking about the crackers."

"What are we supposed to do? We can't predict which one of them will try marrying a White woman. Besides, once they do step over the line then the Klan will take care of them. That is if the woman's family doesn't do it first."

"That's not all we have to deal with. I remember when you'd talk to one of their kind and they show you some respect. Now, they'll look you in the eye and practically dare you to do anything to them. I say we take that dare."

"While I tend to agree with you that they don't act like they used to; I don't think anyone's daring us to hurt them. You know what your problem is, Tommy? You can't tolerate them. You know it's our burden in life to watch out for them. They aren't like us."

"You're damn right they ain't like us. I don't have to tolerate them no how. There's more of us then them in this here country!" Tommy had turned more then a few heads with his loud voice.

"Keep it down or I'm leaving. I can't have—"

"You're not going anywhere. At least not until you hear what I have to say," Tommy whispered in a dangerously low tone.

"Say what you have to say then I am going. I don't intend to have attention drawn to me in a public place. I have a reputation to maintain."

"I'm counting on it. That's why you'll stay. You'll stay however long I want you to stay or that reputation of yours won't be worth a gator's asshole."

"What the hell are you talking about?" Cartwright boomed, his face turning purple with rage.

"Tsk, tsk, tsk. You don't want to draw attention to yourself." Icicles dropped from Tommy's mouth as he smiled. "Listen up, Jefferson. I ran into someone the other day. Kin to that civil rights worker that you were so riled up about. I got the whole story on that 'civil right's worker'. Seems you left out part of the story. Now I know why you were in such a hurry to have me take care of that little problem." Tommy looked at Cartwright knowingly.

Cartwright looked cautiously from side to side. He was afraid someone would overhear Tommy.

Tommy read his friend's mind. "Ain't no one going to hear me. Besides, I want to keep this information all to myself, unless, of course, you make me use it."

"You sonofabitch! I'll kill you if you ever tell anyone! Don't forget what happened to the last person that threatened me with that."

Tommy threw his head back and laughed a grating, bone chilling laugh. "I haven't forgotten. Remember I'm the one who took care of 'em. You won't kill me; you don't have it in you. You'd be wise to remember just what happened to that 'civil rights' worker before you go threatening me."

Cartwright looked into Tommy's eyes and was reminded of the night in his library.

The man was sheer evil. He wished he could kill this son-of-a-bitch but he knew that Tommy was right. He didn't have it in him.

"Why don't you come by the house so we can discuss this further. I just got a case of Markman's bourbon in." Cartwright worried about eavesdroppers.

"While I'd really enjoy some of your fine whiskey, I don't think you want to run the chance of that pretty little wife of yours overhearing."

"How do I know that you know anything? You could be bluffing."

Tommy leaned in so close to Cartwright that they looked like lovers. His voice was so soft that Cartwright could barely hear him. Tommy eased back away from the judge with a grin on his face. He had left no doubt whatsoever that he definitely was not bluffing.

"What the hell do you want?" Cartwright fought to control his shaky voice.

"I want you to give the go ahead for violence against the niggers. I ain't asking you to do it at a flock. Only for the Wings here in New Orleans."

"You don't know what you're asking. The feds will be all over us if we start attacking them. If you'll be patient, I have a plan."

The waiter delivered their food and filled their half empty water glasses. Cartwright took the opportunity to order another mint julep. By the look of his unsteady hands, he knew he'd need it.

"Screw your plan. If I know you, it's just something that slaps the nigger on the hand. They've been slapped on the hand so much their hands are callused. It's not getting through to them anymore. They need something stronger."

"This is too risky. I don't think—"

"That's right, don't think, just do it. I'm having a meeting with all the local hangers and I want you to give the go ahead."

"I don't know if I can do it. This isn't smart. The White Wings have kept out of the lime light for over a hundred years because we haven't endorsed violence."

"Times are a changin' and we have to change with them. You'll do it. You don't have no choice."

Cartwright thought about how the tables had changed. For years Tommy Jamison had looked up to and even feared him. Now, while Cartwright definitely did not look up to Jamison, he certainly feared him.

Cartwright had started to fear Jamison shortly after he appointed him Eagle for New Orleans but what had really stirred him was how Tommy had handled his problem for him. Cartwright hadn't wanted anyone killed.

Cartwright looked at Jamison. He didn't even look like the man Cartwright had once called friend. His hair seemed greasier, his teeth yellowed and his eyes were as cold as stone. On retrospect, Cartwright had to admit the man's eyes had always been like stone.

Tommy knew he was in charge now. He knew Cartwright would do whatever he asked. Before this tidy bit of information, Cartwright never would have allowed him to use the word 'nigger' around him in public. Tommy was glad the judge had buckled under so easily. He would have hated to have to hurt Barbara or Judith.

Cartwright was a fool to think he would actually ever tell anyone the truth about the civil rights worker, Tommy thought. He was, after all, the one guilty of murder. He couldn't risk a sniveling Cartwright telling about his involvement, and that's just what Cartwright would do if any scandal ever ruined his precious reputation.

Tommy looked up to see Barbara being shown to their table. "Right on time. I had your secretary phone her to tell her to meet us for lunch— in case you got difficult."

Cartwright didn't have a chance to respond before Barbara got to their table.

"Hi, Daddy!" She kissed her father on the cheek then nodded politely to Tommy, "Hi, Mr. Jamison."

Barbara looked down at the plates of food. "I wasn't late, was I?"

"No, Darlin', I forgot I had a lunch date with Jamison here. I thought we would have our business out of the way before you got here, and it looks like I was right." Cartwright sighed when he looked at Tommy's full plate. There would be no way to get rid of the man.

"Business is finished, now there's just pleasure." Tommy leered at Barbara's breasts but quickly looked at his food before she noticed him.

"The food does look wonderful," Barbara said, misinterpreting Tommy's remark.

"Your Daddy got a call just before you got here. He's got to get back to the court but I'd be happy to have you join me for lunch, so I won't have to eat alone." Tommy shot Cartwright a warning glance.

Cartwright didn't know what Jamison was up to but he didn't want to take any chances so he went along with the lie. "Yep, sorry Darlin'. The jury just got back in. I best get going. Order whatever you'd like, I'll have them put it on my bill." Cartwright bent to kiss his daughter good-bye.

"I understand the mint juleps are pretty good. Your Daddy had a couple of them. You want me to get one for you?" Tommy asked in a slow drawl.

"I don't think so. I have to go back to work after lunch and I don't think Henri would like it if I had been drinking." Barbara forced a smile.

She never had liked Tommy Jamison. If she hadn't been absolutely famished, she would have gone back to the shop and eaten her sandwich.

She had known Jamison for many years but she didn't like the way he had started looking at her when she started Jr. High School. Once, one of her friends told her that he wanted 'to jump her bones' but she knew the girl was teasing her. It was ridiculous, Mr. Jamison was nearly her father's age. Still, there was something in the way he looked at her that made her uncomfortable.

"How's that babe of yours? Looking at you now it's hard to believe he wasn't fatter then he was the last time I saw him."

"Why is that?"

"Bottle fed babies is usually fatter. He never was at the tit, was he? "Tommy grinned.

"Yes, Mr. Jamison, he was breast fed until he was six months old, not that I think that is any of your business." Barbara was incensed by a man asking her about breast feeding especially in such a crude manner.

"Well, he sure never suckled you. A wet nurse, huh?" Tommy shifted his eyes from her face to her low cut bodice.

"What?" Barbara felt herself turn red from her cleavage up to her hairline. "Well, yes, John Jr. did have nurse."

"I knew it. A man knows those sorts of things." Tommy openly admired her bosom.

The waiter came and took her order. Barbara ordered a salad hoping that it would be quicker to prepare. The sooner she got away from Jamison, the better. She was sure he had only been making conversation but the conversation had made her extremely uncomfortable.

Later that night Barbara decided to asked John about Jamison's observation. She wasn't sure how a man could tell if a woman had breast fed or not. Certainly not if a woman was wearing a brassiere.

"Can you tell if a woman has breast fed or not?" Barbara asked seriously.

"I can only tell if she's currently breast feeding. What you look for, is half a baby sticking out from under a blanket that the mother is using to shield herself from unwanted stares," John said teasingly.

"I'm serious, John. I'm mean did Lacy's breasts look any different than mine?"

"Forget it; I'm not walking into that one."

"Really, I want to know. I know breast feeding can cause sagging but can you tell when a woman is wearing a bra?"

"What's brought this on? In case you've forgotten, you have nothing to worry about, you did not breast feed."

"I know that. I just want to know if you could tell that from looking at me. Someone at lunch today said he could tell that from looking at me."

John's ears perked up on the word "he". "Who? Who said he could tell that you did not breast feed," John said tightly.

"Don't go getting jealous or anything. It was only Daddy's friend, Mr. Jamison." Barbara ignored the anger on John's face. "He said a man could tell whether or not a woman had breast fed. He was sure that I did not breast feed John Jr.. How could he tell? I mean—he knew for sure."

"He couldn't, not for sure. There are some women who have such perfect breasts that you might assume they didn't breast feed. Then again, a sagging pair of breasts doesn't necessarily mean the woman breast fed."

"What were you doing with Jamison anyway? I don't want you around that man. He's a real bastard."

"Daddy invited me to lunch and had forgotten he had a meeting with Mr. Jamison."

"So you, your father and Jamison talked about the lack of decline of your breasts?" John asked tersely.

Barbara was hot from the blood rising to her cheeks. "No, Daddy got called back to court. I had lunch with just Mr. Jamison."

"And you thought your breasts would make good lunch conversation?" John asked accusingly.

"Don't be an asshole. Mr. Jamison brought up the subject when he asked about John Jr.. I changed the subject soon enough."

"Stay away from that bastard. Trust me when I tell you he was probably giving you the once over."

"John! That's disgusting, he's Daddy's friend. I'm sure he meant no harm."

"Well, I'm not. I don't trust any man who would discuss your breasts with you."

"Gees, John. You really are jealous. That's so sweet." Barbara bit her lip in thought.

"You're damn right. I don't want any man discussing any part of your body with you."

"What about you?"

"What about me?"

"Do you want discuss my body with me?"

John crossed the room to where Barbara was seated. "No. I prefer to explore it."

"A man of few words, huh?"

John crushed her lips under his. He didn't wait to take her into the bedroom. He felt a primal need to prove that she was his. She may not have been his first choice, he thought, but she belonged to him.

When Barbara awoke the next morning she was sick once again.

John went into the bathroom when he heard her throwing up. "Are you okay?"

Barbara rinsed her mouth out. "I guess. It's probably from staying up all night," Barbara said sexily.

"I'd like to think my lovemaking doesn't make you sick. You've been sick off and on for several weeks, why don't you go to your doctor?"

"I hate going to the doctor. It's probably nothing but the flu."

"Then go and get a flu shot. Being sick so long has got to be hard on your system. I don't want to risk John Jr. getting what you've got either."

"All right, all right, I'll go. I'll make an appointment right away."

John pushed his fingers through his hair. "I've got to get to school. Are you going to be all right without me?"

"Helga's here, isn't she? I'm sure I'll be fine after I get that shot."

Helga was feeding John Jr. by the time Barbara came into the kitchen. She was teaching him the German words for the strained fruit and cereal he was eating.

"He doesn't even speak English yet. You're just wasting your time."

"Guten—good morning Mrs. Sommier. He will remember my words when he starts to speak. I remind him each day."

Helga looked at Barbara's very casual attire. "You're not going to work today?"

"No, not until later. I got my doctor to squeeze me in."

"Gut. You're finally going to see the doctor about the baby. I was starting to worry."

"What are you talking about? Is John Jr. ill?"

"No, he's fine. I was taking about the unborn baby, the one who makes you so sick."

"That's not morning sickness, Helga. I get sick at all hours of the day. Besides, when I was pregnant with John Jr. I was never sick."

"Morning sickness doesn't only come in the morning. You can be sick one pregnancy and not the next. You've been sick a long time now. You must have known."

"Helga, I am not pregnant. Do you understand? I'm not. I haven't missed even one of my monthlies and I've been sick for several weeks."

"Oh, I'm sorry. I have never been wrong before. I read it in the eyes, you see, and your eyes have told me you were pregnant from the day of our first meeting. I don't understand it. I have never been wrong before."

"Well, you're wrong this time," Barbara said testily.

Helga hung her head low. "Ja, I'm sorry. I did not mean to interfere."

Barbara felt for the older woman. "How could you have known for sure with me? You had never seen my eyes before so you had nothing to compare them to."

Helga perked up. "Ja, das ist true. It must be that your eyes will scream to me when you are pregnant."

On the way to school, John kept replaying his conversation with Barb in his mind. He had said he didn't want to think she would be sick from his lovemaking. Yet she could be sick from his lovemaking.

John thought back to the night Barbara had gotten drunk and been so wild. She had demanded that he leave the condom off. She had said she wanted to feel him completely.

God, John thought, she really could be pregnant.

John had a hard time concentrating at school. His mind kept drifting back to Barbara. The last time she had told him she was pregnant, he had been an asshole. He hadn't thought of the baby, he had only thought of himself. This time, he told himself, he would make it up to her. He was so excited with the possibility of another child he could hardly contain himself.

That evening, John didn't allow Barbara to fully step through the door before he posed a barrage of questions to her.

"What did the doctor have to say?" John asked expectantly.

"Do you mind if I sit down?"

John moved so that he no longer blocked her path. "Well?" John could not contain his excitement.

"What are you so happy about?"

"Oh, nothing. C'mon, what did your doctor say?" John was smiling from ear to ear now.

"No, you first. I can tell you have some good news."

"Okay, okay, I think I know what the doctor told you. You're pregnant, right?"

"Did Helga tell you that? I should fire that smelly old bat."

"It just added up with you being sick so much," John paused. "You told Helga before you told me?" John sounded hurt.

"No, I didn't tell Helga anything. She had the silly notion that I was pregnant. She thought all this sickness was because I was with child. I told her, and I'll tell you, that I haven't missed a single period."

"I guess my mind went into a frenzy when I thought that you might be pregnant. If you're not pregnant, what did the doctor say." John sounded disappointed.

"He gave me a shot and said I'll be sick for a couple of weeks. It's just a hormone imbalance. Nothing to worry about. I'll be fine."

Barbara thought back to what the doctor had really said. Her heart pounded in her ears just to think about it.

Barbara had yelled at the doctor, "That can't be! I haven't missed any of my monthlies!"

The doctor had patiently explained, "It's not entirely uncommon for a woman to continue menstruation for the first three months of pregnancy. The uterus can become distended and a section continue with menses while the rest of it supports the embryo."

"If you'll let me do a pelvic exam today, I can give you a pretty good idea of just how far along you are. That and the blood work will let us know with a certain degree of accuracy." The doctor continued, "I'll give you a shot for that vomiting. Your hormones are not in their usual balance when you are pregnant."

Barbara had been scarcely able to drive when she left his office. She had been so upset. Two and a half months. The doctor had said she was probably two and a half months along.

Barbara hadn't wanted Helga to know that she wasn't going to work. Helga probably would have guessed the situation.

Barbara had driven straight home. Changed into a suitable dress for work and drove straight to her father's house. She had called in sick from there.

Barbara knew that Percy would be able to help her. She had offered to help the first time. It had been different then, Barbara needed to be pregnant then.

Percy had misunderstood the reason Barbara's visit. "Congratulations, child. I'm so happy for y'all."

"You're not listening to me, Percy. I didn't come here to break the 'good news' to you. I came because I need your help."

Percy's eyes went wide with understanding. "Does your husband know what you up to?"

"No. And he better not ever find out, ya hear? Now are you going to help me or not."

"I don't know. You should talk this over with the mister. You may decide you want to keep it. You know, if it's money you worried 'bout, your Daddy would help you."

"It's not money. And I'm not talking this over with John. Percy please, you were willing to help me the last time."

"That was different. You didn't have yourself no husband then. Now you do. I don't think I would feel good 'bout myself if I was to lead you to an abortionist without your husband knowing."

"Fine. Just fine. I'll find someone without your help."

"You don't know where to go, Child. You'll get yourself killed. Some of these back alley jobs will-

"I don't have much choice, do I? You refuse to help me."

"I don't like it. I don't like it at all, but I'll set it up for you. This gal, she's real busy so it will probably take two or three weeks to get you in. How far along are you?"

"A month and a half," Barbara lied.

Chapter Sixteen

Barbara heard John stirring in the kitchen. He had seemed excited about the possibility of her being pregnant. He had surprised her. After the way he acted the first time, she thought he disliked the idea of children as much as she did.

Deep down in her heart she knew that John's reasons for not wanting a child the first time was not because of his dislike for children. It was because of his dislike for the woman whose womb his child was growing in. He would have been pleased back then if his child had been growing inside Janiene.

Barbara's heart skipped a beat when she thought about John's excitement now. John's new attitude made her feel a little sad about not having the baby. For a moment she considered keeping the child. Maybe, she thought, it would bring them closer together. As Barbara thought about another baby growing inside of her she thought of all the things that went with that experience. Weight gain, hemorrhoids, water retention, back aches, and so on. No, she thought, her first plan was much better.

Even though John had suggested abortion with her first pregnancy she knew she couldn't discuss it with him. After all, she had been the one who had been so against it at the time. She couldn't risk him finding out her real reasons for her decision then. And now, with his elation at the thought of another child, she hoped Percy could get the whole thing set up fast. It scared her to think what he might do if he ever found out.

Barbara put her hand on her stomach. She couldn't feel anything. Well, she thought, the sooner the better.

Judge Cartwright didn't have much choice but to concede to Tommy's plan. He did, however, set it up so that he would meet with each individual hanger in the greater New Orleans area. He didn't like the idea of a big meeting for all the hangers in the area.

The less attention he brought to the situation the better. Most of the long time Wings wouldn't care too much for him changing such a basic policy. But the new Wings, the younger ones, would be all for it.

He had listened closely to all the small talk when they had had the flock. Much of the talk, though whispered when he neared, was about becoming a violent group. Mainstreaming, that's what the men were calling it. The men felt it was necessary not only to control Colored people but also make the White Wings a group that was known and revered. He had heard many of the men say they wanted to be more like other groups of divine supremacy.

Fools, Cartwright thought. It was fine for groups like the Klan to be known. Those who didn't want their faces known were safely hidden in the folds of bed clothes. While not many of the Wings wore their brass tie tacks in public, none of the Wings hid their faces behind sheets or anything else.

Why couldn't they see that? Their faces would be known, not only to those they attack but to their attackers as well. If they weren't careful, the federal government would have them all indicted for conspiracy to commit murder or some other heinous crime.

Cartwright went straight from the courthouse to the hanger. It would be his sixth meeting in as many days. Tonight he couldn't afford to let any of his ill will towards Tommy show. Tonight he was going to the hanger that Tommy once piloted. These were Tommy's strongest supporters. Tommy had even set it up so that they were meeting at his house tonight. If Cartwright could gain their trust by praising Tommy then he might be able to use them for his own purpose in the future.

Cartwright sat in his Lincoln Continental finishing the final touches on his speech he was going to deliver tonight. His stomach turned a little at each of the statements he had written about Tommy. It disgusted him to be brown nosing someone he considered to be insubordinate.

He and Judith used to laugh at all the times Tommy had obviously been flattering the judge. Look where it had gotten him, Cartwright thought. He certainly could do it for awhile if it got him what he wanted.

He felt a little guilty about his speech. He couldn't help thinking that even though these men were aligned with Tommy they really didn't know what kind of man he was. Yes, he thought, these men, most naive college recruits, are laying with the devil himself, but he was the one who would be tucking them in.

Cartwright staggered a little when he got out of his car that was parked in front of Tommy's house. He had made it a point to have a few drinks in him before he got there. He had a hard time facing Tommy without at least a drink or two.

Cartwright pounded hard upon the front door. Betsy opened the door.

"They're in the back room already. You want me to bring you a bourbon?" she asked sweetly, her eyes batting seductively.

His eyes roamed freely over her body. She looked lovely, as usual, except for the heavily applied make-up under her right eye. Cartwright wondered if what was under the make-up looked as bad as he thought it would.

Betsy was such a sweet woman. He had noticed the way she had made eyes at him before. He had always figured to take her to bed one day. He thought if Tommy's heavy hand was any indication of his lovemaking, she would welcome a lover like him again and again. Cartwright pushed the thoughts from his mind. That was not a pleasure he could partake of. Sleeping with another man's wife always had its risks but sleeping with Tommy's wife would be like playing with a stick of dynamite near a blazing fire.

"Sure, honey, I'll take a bourbon. I'll show myself back to the meeting." Cartwright swatted Betsy on her nicely padded pear-shaped bottom. He had been doing that for years, just because he couldn't have her in bed didn't mean he'd have to stop all his flirtations.

He walked down the short hallway past the kitchen into the back room. Though it was still light outside, the dark tweed curtains blocked out all light. The small hanging lamp with its four bulbs hidden by red flutes provided little light while adding an air of secrecy. The white washed fold-down wooden chairs were arranged in five rows of five chairs, nearly all occupied, stretching from the front of the room to a long table in the back. A few men stood near the back table.

Cartwright was surprised at the number of men in attendance. There hadn't been many cars parked out front so he had only expected ten or so men. But, it was a full hanger, twenty-five men eagerly waited.

Cartwright walked up to Tommy who was busy handing out addenda. "Big group."

Tommy grinned. "These boys are some of the most dedicated Wings that there are. They always attend the hangers. Even if they have to walk to get here."

Cartwright took the drink that Betsy had brought back for him. He smiled and watched her walk out. He had no way of knowing that his admiration would earn her a few more bruises that night.

"She didn't offer to get no one else a drink," Tommy commented hostilely.

"She didn't offer, I asked. I'm sorry, I didn't mean to cause any problems." Cartwright attempted to ease the other man.

The judge's remark surprised Tommy, he wasn't aware he had spoken out loud. Didn't matter if he did ask for it, Tommy thought. He didn't like the way Betsy looked at Cartwright and he sure as hell didn't like the way Cartwright looked at her.

He couldn't really blame Cartwright though, Tommy thought. Whenever the judge was around, it seemed that Betsy stuck her tits out further and swished her ass more. Tommy would take care of that later but first he had a meeting to concentrate on.

The pilot called the meeting to order and introduced the 'finest Eagle the state of Louisiana has ever seen'. Cartwright was about to stand when he realized the man was talking about Tommy.

Tommy slapped a few backs as he walked from the back of the room to the front. He was acknowledging as many men by name as he could before he reached the front of the room. This slowed his pace considerably since the room was just an average sized recreation room in a three bedroom-two bath tract home.

Cartwright was thankful Tommy didn't come from money. The man was a born politician. If he had had money, Cartwright had no doubt, he would have been in public office. Tommy was just the type of man who would lead you to your own destruction because he couldn't see the big picture. He wasn't aware of the fact that no matter how big you got, there was always someone bigger. Always someone who would hold you accountable.

"Gents, it's good to see y'all here tonight. I ain't let the cat out of the bag to none of you boys 'cause I wanted you to hear it straight from the Pegasus." Tommy stopped smiling and his voice became deadly serious. "The main thing I want to tell y'all, is that, what you're about to hear is not to leave this room. It's not to be discussed with other Wings unless it's at a hanger. That means you don't discuss it at flocks, you don't talk with your wife about it and you don't ever mention it in public. Trust me, when I say there will be hell to pay for the man that breaks those rules. Ya hear?"

The men looked puzzled but anticipation mixed with excitement filled the room.

"That was kind of you, Jimmy, when you made the introductions." Tommy looked disgusted with Jimmy. "But, I think y'all will agree when I say the finest Eagle ever is in this room all right, but it ain't me. Y'all know him, not as The Eagle, but as Pegasus. I give you Judge Jefferson Cartwright."

Jimmy turned a little red with the realization of his unintentional insult.

The room started to echo with clapping and cheers as all faces turned back to look at Cartwright.

Cartwright stood and followed same path Tommy had taken. He mimicked Tommy actions. Cartwright had paid close attention to Tommy as a lot of the boys were new and, up until a few minutes ago, he didn't know their names.

Cartwright shook Tommy's hand when he finally reached the front of the room. He pulled out several three by five cards while Tommy took his seat in the back of the room.

"Good Evening, Wings. It is my pleasure to announce some changes that will be taking place for your hanger. I will basically be going over the addendum. Your Eagle will give those of you wishing to participate additional information. Open your addendum and look it over. Memorize the contents, Gentlemen, tonight. At the end of this meeting, the addendums will be collected and burned. As you can see, that's not the kind of information we want getting out."

Just like the other five meetings in the past week, Cartwright heard several gasps, a few expletives and a couple of 'it's about damn time'. He waited a few moments until the initial excitement died down then he explained the new order of business. Violence.

Barbara was thankful it was a slow morning at work. It gave her a chance to think about her conversation with the strange woman that Percy had put her in touch with. It would also give her a chance to read the journal.

The woman was from some island in the Caribbean, Barbara couldn't remember which one. She had a funny accent and kept talking about moon phases.

Barbara had been furious that Percy had given the woman her home phone number. Although the woman had been discreet when Helga answered the phone; Barbara didn't like taking a chance that John might discover what she was up to. Barbara was relieved when the woman had said she wouldn't need to contact her again.

She had nearly fallen off the bed when the woman told her the cost. She thought five hundred dollars was an exorbitant rate. Especially for a Colored woman who had no formal medical training.

When she conveyed her feelings to the woman, the woman had asked her what reputable White doctor would perform it for less. Barbara knew there weren't any reputable doctors who would perform an abortion for less because a reputable doctor wouldn't perform an abortion.

Due to some moon phase thing, the strange woman set the appointment two weeks out.

Barbara had pleaded for an earlier date. She had even told the woman the truth about how far along she was. But that didn't help. The woman claimed she already knew the due date, May 8, 1964. Barbara's spine tingled when the woman corrected herself, she had said that there truly was no due date since it was the child's destiny to remain unborn.

Thinking about it gave Barbara a creepy feeling. It was probably knowing the due date, Barbara thought. The doctor hadn't given her a due date yet. He had said he wanted to wait until all the blood tests had come back so he would be sure. Somehow putting a due date with the baby was like putting a face with it. That, combined with the unborn remark, had Barbara feeling a little guilty.

Barbara carefully searched for her place in the journal. More of the pages in the back had been water damaged. All the pages were fragile due to their age but the water damaged pages crumbled like delicate wafer cookies.

Barbara had accidentally destroyed three pages of the journal when she first got to that extremely brittle section. Three pages that had represented nearly four months of Henri P. Sommier's life.

Barbara noticed, as Henri got older his entries became more methodical. He made an entry nearly every month not just when something memorable or intriguing happened to him, though there were still those types of entries as well.

September 1850

I am pleased with our newly completed town house. The workmanship is almost enough to turn a gentleman into a braggart. It is a splendid sight, so big and bold, on the Rue Royale.

Isabelle chose the intricate scroll patterns of the cast iron gallery rails. If one looks closely, the initials HSI are in the center of each scroll. Isabelle says we shall be locked together for eternity thanks to those scrolls.

Isabelle is anxious to get the town house furnished so that we may move in. She says she wants to have a house of her own. I explained that Mallard's Landing was mine but she refuses to listen. She said my Uncle erred when he left Mallard's Landing to me. She said Aunt Marie is the rightful owner.

Luc is thankful that he has a chance to buy Mallard's Landing. He is to wed Aunt Marie in a month. I shall have to leave off "Aunt" and start calling her by only her Christian name since she will be my brother's wife.

Luc fought me a little when I told him that all slaves giving birth were having only free children on Mallard's Landing. When they come of an age to work, they will be paid for their labors. Luc and I did agree upon one thing, not to tell our neighbors or even those slaves who are giving birth if they are loose with the lip. Children born to mouthy slaves shall be given their freedom papers at age ten.

As a loyal Southern gentleman, I tend to agree with the states rights issues but somewhere along the line, my brethren have forgotten individual rights. If I were to publicly free my slave babies, I would have to fight off all sorts of insults and innuendo. It is my hope this gesture, though a private one, is pleasing to both the people who shall be free and to God.

Work has me busy all day and Isabelle keeps me busy all night. She is so anxious to be with child that it hurts her. I told her to be patient, we have only been married a little over a year. I fill her nightly with the seed. I am certain a baby will grow from it soon.

A letter posted to me from Jean-Claude brought with it sad tidings. A lady acquaintance of his has perished. She had been attempting to end the attachment of Jean-Claude's bastard to her womb. Unfortunately, the grist of blood she lost in the process proved to be too much for her. Jean-Claude feels personally responsible since he provided her the funds to take such an action.

I did not tell Isabelle of Jean-Claude's letter for fear she would ask me all that it said or worse, want to read it for herself. Isabelle would not understand why anyone would not want a baby even if the woman were unmarried. To see a baby brings her instant elation. She fawns all over the slave babies and has even started midwifery with Marie in the slave births.

I fear Isabelle would blame Jean-Claude for the young woman's death and she would never forgive him for the death of his baby. In truth, I blame him myself but I do not hold any animosity towards him. It was tragic, to be sure, but I think he will learn from his mistake. Isabelle does not understand the needs of a man. Jean-Claude has not understood the needs can be fulfilled in marriage. Perhaps, now, he will settle down.

Carl Atkins has called me to duel. Though I did not gravely insult his person. He has insisted upon satisfaction under the code duello. His purpose, as he has made known to several of our shared colleagues, is an attempt at justified murder. He has made it known that he fancies Isabelle for himself. He has made several attempts in the past to defame me but I allowed not one remark to penetrate. I knew his purpose long ago so I have made him wait until he could stand it no longer. Since he is the one that called for a duel, I have privilege of weapons. He is half bear and a wonder with the pistol so I have chosen the rapier. His disappointment in weapons was upon his face for all to see. I am confident I shall prevail. Although he is a nuisance, I will only attempt a flesh wound. How can I truly fault him for loving the only perfect woman in God's creation?

Barbara thought about the town house that Henri wrote about. She knew it was the same house that her in-laws lived in now. She'd have to remember to look in the cast iron railings for Henri and Isabelle's initials on either side of the initial for Sommier.

She leaned back in her chair to relax when the door to the shop opened. She was surprised to see John standing in the doorway.

John pretended not to notice as she scurried to put the journal away. No wonder she got caught, John thought, she's so careless.

"John, whatever are you doing here? I thought you didn't have to do the books until next week." She walked with an ease she didn't feel.

"I came to see you. I wanted to talk to you."

She felt a knot form in the pit of her stomach. She feared that John might have found out the truth about her pregnancy. It just wasn't like John to visit her at work.

John observed his wife's nervous behavior. "You haven't had lunch yet, have you?"

"No, but your father won't be back for another fifteen minutes so I can't leave the shop. Can't you talk to me here?"

"I'd rather do it over lunch. We'll go as soon as Dad gets back."

She sighed with relief. If he had found out, he wouldn't be able to remain calm for very long. She was anxious to find out why he had come all the way down for lunch.

"I'm going to the back to say hi to the fellas. They are in, aren't they?" John didn't wait for an answer. He opened the door that separated the refinishing area from the showroom and he slipped behind it.

As Barbara looked over the store she noticed some smudged fingerprints on the tiffany lamp that sat near the register. She went behind the counter to get the spray bottle of glass cleaner and a cotton cloth.

She bent down to reach the glass cleaner on its floor level shelf. She couldn't see it so she got down on her hands and knees to look for it. She was so absorbed by her task, she didn't hear the bell ring.

"That's an interesting position, one I rather enjoy." Tommy Jamison leaned his full torso over the counter to see Barbara on the floor. His gaze followed the small of her back down to the to the rounding curves of her buttocks. Her dress was stretched tightly around her hips due to the position she was in.

Barbara scrambled to get up, scraping one of her knees on the hardwood floor.

"Mr. Jamison, I didn't hear you come in. May I be of service to you?"

Tommy slowly undressed her with his eyes. "Definitely."

Barbara was beginning to think that John had been right. There was something very sexual in his manner. He's probably like a lot of older men, she thought, he's just admiring a young woman.

"What sort of thing were you looking for? Furniture? Curios? Jewelry?" Barbara edged from behind the counter.

"I'm just looking." Tommy's tone left no room for misunderstanding.

"I'm sure you'll find something to your taste. If you need to know any prices in the show cabinet, I'll be happy to assist you." She tried to ignore the lewd look in his eyes.

"No, thanks. I've already found what I'm looking for. That's you."

Before she had a chance to reply, Tommy grabbed her by the waist and crushed her against him. His mouth came down hard upon hers and he forced his tongue between her clenched teeth.

She pounded on his chest and turned her head from side to side to escape his probing tongue. Tommy grabbed one wrist and forced it behind her, holding it firmly with one hand. He forced her other wrist into that same hand, her wrists crossed behind her back. With his free hand, he snatched her hair at the nape of her neck and held her head steady for his harsh invasion.

Tommy was not prepared when she simultaneously bit down on his tongue and stomped on his foot. He roared out in pain.

"You bitch! You'll pay for that. After you hear what I have to say, you'll gladly give me your kisses and more. But right now, I'm gonna teach you some manners." Tommy pulled back his hand to slap her but something caught it.

He turned to see John's rage filled face.

"Hitting your wife not enough for you?" John's fist made hard contact with Tommy's jaw. "Let's see how you fare against someone more your size." John's other fist crashed hard into Tommy's nose, breaking it.

Tommy fell backwards. A small wine table broke under the force of his fall.

Tommy, his lip split and blood oozing from his nose, looked up into John's twisted purple face. Two of John's veins, one on either side of his neck, were bulging and throbbing. Tommy thought it would be better to control his own rage. He hadn't lost many fights in his life but he had a feeling, if he continued this one, he'd end up in the intensive care unit.

Tommy tried to ease himself off the floor.

John yanked Tommy the rest of the way up. "Don't you ever touch my wife again or I'll kill you."

"You'll pay for this Sommier. You don't know who your messing with. I've got friends all over this state. Maybe not today and maybe not tomorrow but I assure you, you will pay."

Tommy looked around John to Barbara who was timidly watching the whole scene. "As for you, I ain't finished with you yet." He swirled his tongue over his blood covered lips. "Even through all this blood, I can still taste you. Mmmm, sweet."

Barbara walked out from behind her husband. "You bastard! Daddy will hear about this. I don't think—"

"Your daddy is a spineless jellyfish."

John roughly dragged Tommy towards the exit. "Well, I'm not. I mean it, touch her again and you're a dead man." John opened the door and released Tommy's arm. "Now, get the hell out and don't you ever set foot in one of our shops again."

Tommy stepped out of the shop prepared to reply but he wasn't given the chance. John slammed the door in his face.

John turned to face Barbara. "You okay?"

Barbara, white as a sheet from the ordeal, rushed into John's arms. She couldn't manage a word. It was all she could do to hold back the tears. Her whole body was shaking with fear. She couldn't believe her father's friend had attacked her in such a cold brutal way. She had to tell her father but she didn't quite know how. It was so humiliating. So degrading.

John didn't say a word. He simply held her. She was grateful for that. She was almost able to gain her complete self control. She would have too, if Henri hadn't walked in the store and seen the grief on both of their faces.

"What is going on here?" Henri looked at John. His eyes were drawn to the splintered wooden pile on the floor.

Barbara ran out of the room to the bathroom not only to hide her tears but also to empty her stomach. She could no longer hold back the wave of nausea that assaulted her.

"What is going on here?" Henri repeated.

"That bastard, Tommy Jamison, paid Barbara a little visit. I guess he thought she was all alone in the shop. I'm not sure what all he did to her but I'm pretty sure he kissed her. I had been in the back talking to Girod. She must have fought like a wildcat because I heard a man scream out. When I came forward, he was getting ready to hit her."

"I saw Jamison on the street when I was walking up to the shop. It looks like that table over there isn't all that got broken."

John smiled with masculine pride. "Yeah, I think he'll think twice before he messes with me or my family again."

"I wouldn't count on that. The man is ruthless. Be careful."

"You know Jamison that well?" John asked.

"No, he was a few years behind me in school but I know of him. He has had an ugly reputation since he was in grade school. There was even talk that he had raped a Negro girl when he was still in junior high school. Nothing ever came of that so I don't know if there's truth to it or not. I know one thing for certain, he's not a person to tangle with."

"How does he know Barbara? I assume he does know her, doesn't he?" Henri asked.

"He's one of Judge Cartwright's friends. I've seen him at a couple of the judge's parties. I'm not sure how they became aquatinted."

"Of course." Henri nodded his head knowingly.

"Of course, what?"

"Cartwright must know him through that white supremacist group he's involved in. I know Jamison belongs to one. He's one of the boys that tried to recruit me long ago."

"Oh shit. That's what he meant by his having friends all over the state." John mummered under his breath.

"What was that?"

"Nothing, Dad, nothing. Hey, I better get this mess cleaned up before a customer comes in." John walked to the back room to get a broom and trash bag.

Barbara came back from the bathroom while John was cleaning up the mess. Her face was still waxy though she had some of her color back.

"Dad is in the back. He said we can take lunch whenever you're ready. He also said that you could take the rest of the day off."

"I can't. It wouldn't be right. Do you know how many days I've been out sick lately?"

221

"Don't worry about it, Dad understands. C'mon, let's walk over to the Central Grocery Company. I'll split a muffuletta with you."

Barbara loved the big round Italian sandwich with its ham, salami, mortadela, provolone cheese and special olive salad. Usually, one sandwich was more than enough for two people but Barbara had found, that when she was upset, she could easily demolish one of the meaty treats all by herself.

"I want a whole one, and extra olive salad too."

"Deal, I'll go tell Dad we're on our way."

John couldn't bring himself to bring up the subject he had come down to see her about. She was really enjoying her lunch but she still was visibly shaken by what had happened with Jamison.

He didn't press her for facts about the occurrence. He felt sure she would tell him once she felt more comfortable.

With the exception of an occasional smacking noise, they sat in complete silence on an iron bench overlooking Jackson Square while they ate their lunch.

Maybe in a couple of days, John thought, he would talk to her about what he had come to see her about. A baby. He had decided he wanted to have another baby. Hopefully, they would have a girl this time.

Chapter Seventeen

Barbara convinced John that it would be better for her to talk her father alone about Jamison. He hadn't readily agreed yet, eventually, he had agreed. She knew it was something she would have to handle alone. John and her father had never gotten along well and, with John's attitude, her father would only become defensive if John was involved. John was nearly blaming her father as much for what happened as he was Jamison.

She arrived at her father's house a couple of hours before he was due home. Thankfully, Judith was out at one of her many charity meetings, so, with the exception of the servants, she had the house to herself.

She headed for her old room to take a nap but suddenly felt uncomfortable. The big house which she had spent most of her life in, just didn't feel like home. She went into her father's library instead.

She walked around the big room filled with all types of books. She looked at the north wall which was covered from ceiling to floor with law books. The big tufted burgundy wing-back swivel chair behind the massive mahogany desk had been a favorite place to play when she was a little girl.

The library had always been off limits when she was a child. Which, of course, made it the most desirable room in the house in which to play. Barbara remembered how she used to play in the big chair pretending that she, like her father, was a judge.

The big chair rolled back easily when she pulled on it. The area rug that covered the highly polished hardwood floor did not extend beneath and behind the desk so it did not interfere with the rollers on the chair.

She sat down in the chair feeling a great relief. The memories of her childhood had brought her not only comfort in the now unfamiliar house but also comfort from the ordeal she had been through at the hands of a family friend.

Barbara thought about how she would tell her father about Jamison. She knew he had been close to Jamison for a long time. The Jamison's had been coming to family parties for years.

Her mind went to Betsy Jamison. She thought Betsy was a pathetically weak woman. Everyone knew that Jamison beat her. Barbara had never understood why Betsy would stay with a man like that.

Barbara loved John more than she loved life itself but if John ever laid a hand on her she would leave him. Of course, Barbara thought, John never would lay a hand on her. Unless, of course, she hit him first. That's what comes from knowing how to choose a good man. Betsy had chosen her problems, Barbara thought, she deserves them. But, Barbara had not chosen Jamison and she refused to put up with his abuse.

Barbara, exhausted, fell asleep in her father's big chair. She slept peacefully until she was awakened by loud deep voices reverberating off the hallway walls.

One of the voices was her father's and the other one, she couldn't quite make out since it was muffled behind the door, sounded very familiar.

The more she listened the more she realized the voices were clashing in anger. She heard two sets of foot steps nearing the library. Without thinking, she climbed under the big desk just like she used to do as a child when she wanted to avoid being caught in the library.

When the door opened, she recognized the other voice immediately. It was Tommy Jamison.

"You had better keep that damn son-in-law of yours away from me, Cartwright!" Tommy's voice was filled with rancor.

Barbara heard her father's heavy walk come behind the desk. She pulled her legs to her chest as she eased herself as far away from the chair as possible. Barbara realized she took up a lot more space than she did when she was a child. If her father sat down with his legs under his desk, he would be sure to bump into her. She felt so nervous, she nearly wet on herself.

Cartwright sat down, his chair squeaking under his heavy form. Luckily, she thought, he didn't bother scooting his chair under the desk.

Barbara heard Jamison take the seat on the opposite side of the desk. She was thankful the desk only sat an inch off the floor, there would be no way that Jamison could see her.

"I asked you before, what you did that John felt it necessary to do that to your face?" Cartwright was secretly pleased to see Tommy's face looking more like Betsy's after a bout with her husband.

"Fine. I'll tell you but I don't want no lip out of you, ya hear? You just remember, I got the power to break you."

"How could I forget?" Cartwright sighed. "Now, why did John beat the hell out of you?" Cartwright couldn't resist the jab to Tommy's masculine pride.

"He didn't beat the hell out of me. He got in a few lucky punches, that's all. I spared him because he's your family."

Cartwright unconsciously rolled his eyes. He knew that Tommy would have taken great pleasure in beating John to a pulp but he didn't have a chance against John. Even though John was still a young pup, he was built like his father, a mountain. A mountain of muscles.

Tommy took in the judge's expression and decided to let it go. "Sommier did this because I visited your daughter's shop."

"You did what? Why?" Cartwright knew there was more to the story than Tommy was telling. He could feel rage within him as his paternal instincts rose up inside.

"That Barbie of yours is a fast little thing." Tommy looked at the anger building in Cartwright's face. "Could be I read her wrong but the other day at lunch she asked me to stop by the shop sometime," he amended.

"What does that have to do with John?" Cartwright was scared that Tommy had done something to Barbara.

"Well, I took the little filly's advice and stopped in. She was all batting lashes and leaning over the counter to afford me a better view of what she's got to offer a man when her husband came in and started pounding on me."

Barbara had heard more then she could take. She moved to get out from under the desk when her father's legs blocked her exit. He had moved his chair so far under the desk that his legs pinned her against the front of the desk. One of his feet was firmly planted in her side. She had no doubt that he knew she was under the desk; she just wondered how long he had known it.

"I think you must have misinterpreted my daughter's behavior. She's very much in love with that boy and wouldn't intentionally flirt with any man." Cartwright knew he was speaking the truth but he felt cowardly for not asking Tommy to tell him the whole story. He knew John wouldn't have attacked a man for just flirting with his wife. The man would have had to be doing a lot more than flirting.

"Like I said, Cartwright, could be that I read her wrong but the point is that husband of hers. You best warn him off of me or you'll be the one who's sorry."

"I'll talk to him but it would probably be best if you stayed away from Barbara."

Tommy could see that Cartwright didn't believe him. He wanted to tell Cartwright to turn his daughter over for his pleasure but he knew how protective fathers could get. He had no doubt, if it came down to Cartwright choosing his reputation or his daughter's well being, he would choose his daughter.

That's why Tommy had gone directly to Barbara himself. He was going to tell her that he would ruin her precious daddy's reputation if she didn't start doing some real personal favors for him. He was sure she would have done it too. But when he saw her, down on all fours with her derriere rounding up at him so nicely, he hadn't been able to control himself. Hell, he had gotten hard just by having lunch with her. He had lost control of his senses before he had a chance to talk to her and strike up a bargain. Still, if Sommier hadn't been there he still would have been able to talk to her and make her a somewhat willing partner.

Tommy wasn't sure when he'd get the chance to talk to her now. He was sure Sommier had told his own father about the incident. Tommy had seen the man walking toward the shop shortly after he had been thrown out. It wasn't too likely that Henri Sommier would leave his daughter-in-law unprotected, at least not for a long time.

Tommy had to find a way make her his. He had never found any woman so desirable in all his life.

"See to it right away. You tell him if he doesn't want men looking at his wife, he'd be a damn sight wiser to control her wanton behavior than trying to control all the men attracted to it." Tommy was annoyed. Just thinking about her had his loins aching once again.

"Now you see here—"

"No, you see, I won't hesitate to destroy that reputation of yours if you can't control your family. That includes Sommier, ya hear?"

Tommy had been so upset he had forgotten to help himself to some of the judge's fine bourbon. He remedied that, took a Cuban cigar and headed towards the door.

Cartwright didn't move. "You don't mind if I don't see you out? I've got some pressing business to attend to."

Cartwright watched the door to the library shut and listened for one of the servants to let Jamison out before he pushed his chair back.

"What the hell are you doing under there?" Cartwright demanded as he offered his hand for assistance.

Barbara slowly climbed out from under the desk. Her back was sore from the position she had been forced to sit in for so long.

"I was waiting for you in your chair. I must have fallen asleep because the next thing I knew, I heard people coming in the library. I guess I panicked and climbed under the desk." She stretched her arms over her head.

"Why didn't someone tell me you were here?"

"I let myself in and came straight to the library."

Barbara walked around the desk to take the seat still warm from Tommy Jamison. The warmth of the chair made her cringe.

"I came to talk to you about that awful man but before I do, I have to know something, how long did you know I was under your desk?"

"From the moment I came in the room. Of course, I had to do a double take 'cause I couldn't quite believe my eyes. I've been in the habit of checking under my desk when I come in the library since you were a little girl. You used to always hide there—"

"But you never caught me under the desk."

"I never let you know you had been caught. I liked the idea of having you with me, sometimes for hours, while I worked but since you were hiding you had to keep silent."

"Why Daddy, that's terrible. Do you know how many times I was trapped under there when I had to go to the bathroom?" Barbara started to laugh and her father chimed in with a hearty laughter of his own.

Cartwright's face took on a serious look when he remembered the situation with Tommy. "What's really going on with Jamison? Did you invite him to the shop?" Cartwright studied his daughter's face for any indication that she had been hurt by the man.

"Daddy! That's revolting. Surely you don't think I would—"

"No, Darlin', I know you wouldn't intentionally lead him on but men like Jamison take the smallest thing to be an invitation."

"Well, I did tell him if he was ever in the neighborhood that he should stop in. I didn't think he would, Daddy. I was just being sociable."

"It's best not to be sociable with men you don't know." Cartwright lectured.

"Men I don't know? Daddy, he's your friend! He's been coming to the house for years. I thought if you trusted him then I could too. Boy was I wrong." Barbara felt the weight of the whole ordeal fall back onto her shoulders.

"I don't trust him. I never have. I suppose there was a time when I trusted him more but the man has changed. You stay away from him."

"I came to ask you to keep him away from me but you sounded scared of him. And, what's this about him destroying your reputation?"

Cartwright avoided her question. "What did he do to you and how was it that John came to rearrange his nose?"

Barbara told her father the entire story leaving out the lewd comments that Jamison had made to her. She was also careful exclude how forceful he had been and the fact that the man had almost hit her. Somehow she knew if she told her father everything Jamison had said as well as what he had done that Jamison would be a dead man before morning.

By the time she had finished telling her father the story, she had sipped down two glasses from the bottle of white wine that her father had had Percy bring in to help calm her nerves. She had completely forgotten about the threat Jamison had issued to her father.

"I'm glad you came to me, Barbie but I think that maybe Jamison merely read you wrong. I'm sure he won't bother you now that he knows you aren't interested." There was no conviction in his words. "You will be staying to supper, won't you?"

"No, I've got to get home. I haven't seen John Jr. since this morning and I think John will be worried about me if I don't get home soon."

Barbara left her father in the library and headed for the front door when Percy blocked her path.

"You got it all set up, Child?" Percy's face was filled with concern.

"Percy, would you keep it down? I don't want anyone to find out." She pulled Percy over to the front doors. "Yes, it's all set."

"You be careful, now. You pay her what she ask and don't be trying to short change her none. She kin be a real dangerous sort if she crossed and she don't like White folks no how."

"Why'd you send me to her if she doesn't like Whites?"

"'Cause, Child, out of those I know of that does that, she be the best. You be safest with her."

Barbara didn't like the way Percy had said 'safest'. It made her feel like she wouldn't be safe with any of them.

"Percy, I've got to go. Please don't bring this up at Daddy's house anymore. As a matter of fact, don't bring it up period," her whisper took on a deadly hiss.

The next day provided Barbara with little peace. Jim, Girod or Henri were always peeking up front to check on her.

She moved the slipper chair nearer to the counter so that they could see her head and shoulders when they peeked through the door but they could not see the journal in her hands.

August 1855

I am glad the summer is near to an end. I begged Isabelle to take summer at Mallard's Landing where the heat does not suffocate and the threat of yellow fever is not so great. She says she remains because I remain but I know that is not so. She just cannot stand the pain of her barrenness.

Since Marie and Luc had the twins we hardly ever take our month long visits to the country. It has been nearly two years now. Isabelle is already making excuses for not attending the boys second birthday celebration.

I know she loves the boys but the pain of seeing them is so great. She resents Marie for giving Luc two healthy sons when she is so much older than Isabelle and Isabelle has been fruitless. She speaks to Marie always kindly but now there is so much coolness to her where there was once warmth.

For six years we have been without child. I do not think we shall ever have children. Isabelle refuses to take in a poor abandoned child as our own. She said the child must be blood. At one point, she suggested that I ask Luc for one of his sons.

She is losing all of the light that once shone so brightly in her eyes. Her golden locks have dulled as she does not take care of herself. Her ribs show through her skin and her breasts are not as full as they once were.

As it has been for the last four years, our lovemaking is still methodical and unsatisfying. Perhaps, if our lovemaking had not once been so very pleasurable for the both of us then I would not miss it so much as I do now.

I, though it shames me to admit it, went to a quadroon ball to find myself a mistress so that I might enjoy some satisfaction of the flesh but I could not choose one, though many were lovely. It was not guilt I felt but rather lack of desire. I am worse than a eunuch.

It is not a mistress or a whore I seek. It is Isabelle, my sweet dear Isabelle. She seems lost to me forever, not only her body but also her mind. She wallows in her pity and does not see that her pain also causes me pain.

She is enough for me. If she would only go back to how she used to be, I am sure that we would be happy again. I do not need a son so badly that I would sacrifice Isabelle. Why then, does she not give up this dream and come back to me?

Carl Atkins was at the states rights meeting on Monday. He still blames me for his lame leg. How many years must I remind him that he chose the duel? If he had not charged at me, I would not have cut the sinews of his thigh. Even if we had never dueled, I would not like the man. His temper flares too quickly and he is sure he carries God's own righteous indignation.

Atkins views on states rights are always linked to slavery. He is adamant about all new states coming into the Union being able to choose whether they be slave or free, with a vote. That way we can insure a slave state even if we have to stuff the ballot box. He has said as much in public.

I, too, feel the need for a state to be able to choose its own path but there must be some union or we all become little countries rather than states. We must have unity or we will become weak without the strength of the other states. Unfortunately, but especially, with the states to the north of us.

The Northern states have the industry that we lack. They do not depend upon the free labor of the Negro so their economy is more secure. Even without the moral issue, it is easy to see that slavery is an outdated system.

My thoughts return to Isabelle. Even with the heated discussions of secession, Isabelle troubles me more than anyone or anything. I have begged God for his mercy. I must have faith.

Barbara felt a twinge of guilt. Here she was getting ready to have a child aborted and this woman, John's great-grandmother, had suffered so many years wanting a child. But she did have one, Barbara thought, or John wouldn't have been born.

Barbara skimmed through the last twenty pages of the journal to find out if Isabelle returned to her normal self after she had a baby but the information was not there. Barbara carefully reread the last entry.

November 1859

We leave for Paris in a fortnight. War is inevitable but my heart is torn. I cannot side with the North but I do not side with the South. I still consider myself a democrat though I do not think any party represents my view fully. There is no party that supports abolition while supporting the rights of the individual states.

I hope travel to a different country will give me a new perspective on my own country. A country which may be split in two by the time I return home.

I am anxious to hear Jean-Claude's views on the matter. He is always so level headed. It will be good to see him again. He still is the man ever with the ladies so we will stay with Isabelle's family.

It is my hope that a reunion with her family will bring her some joy. She has finally accepted the uselessness of her womb but rather than accept happiness in life, it seems she waits for death.

I would give my own life if it would bring her happiness but only a child would do that. I do not question God's plan for us but it seems such a terrible waste that Isabelle could not bear our children. She would have made a wonderful mother.

It is hard to believe I am near the end of this first journal. Uncle Jean had inscriptions placed on both volumes so that they could not be confused. When Uncle Jean gave me the two journals over twenty years ago, I thought one of these thick books would be more than enough to hold the memories and thoughts of a man but it seems that he knew best. I shall start my fresh journal in Paris.

It was always my hope to pass my journals on to my son or grandson so that he would know who I really was. But, as it is, I still hope to pass the journals on to family, now more than ever. Since I probably will not have any children, let alone sons, these writings shall be my immortality on this earth.

I pray that Volume II is not only a fresh journal but it will bring with it freshness to my life. I pray with this new start there will also be a new start for Isabelle and the tireless love we once shared.

Barbara looked at the watermarked signature of Henri P. Sommier. She couldn't believe that there was another journal. She hadn't seen two journals when she had been going through the box but then she hadn't really been looking.

The curiosity of what happened between Henri and Isabelle was almost more than she could stand. She hoped the other journal would be easy to find. What if, she thought, the second journal had been destroyed in the fire or if it was never handed down. No, she thought, she was sure it was handed down and if it was around she was going to find it.

Later that night, Barbara kept dreaming about Isabelle's unhappiness. Her dreams turned from recollections of the journal to nightmares.

In her nightmares she saw Isabelle's distorted face begging her for the baby she was about to murder. She kept hearing Isabelle's haunted voice saying, "A baby to love. A baby to love".

Barbara woke with a start. She knew she couldn't go through with it. She knew she couldn't abort her baby. John's baby.

With her new decision, she returned to a peaceful sleep with beautiful dreams.

The following morning Barbara called the abortionist to tell her of her decision. The woman had not taken the news well. She demanded that she be paid anyway. Barbara refused. The strange woman had threatened her. She said she had two days to pay her or she would cause her many problems.

The woman had ended the conversation by saying that she might as well come in now because this child was in the ranks of the unborn. It would not be born anyway. Barbara assumed the strange woman meant that she would change her mind. But, Barbara knew she would not. Something had changed within her, she wasn't sure what had happened during the night but she now wanted this baby more than anything else in the world. Anything, that is, except John.

Four days later, John was in an uncontrollable rage after intercepting a call meant for Barbara, or so the woman had said. John was sure that it had been him that she had wanted to talk to.

Helga had answered the phone four times that morning, only to be hung up on. She had finally refused to answer the phone which is why John had taken the call.

He could hardly believe the demands of the woman with the Jamaican accent. At first, her thick accent and loud ravings had made her nearly impossible to understand but he had been able to make out Barbara's name.

When he finally convinced her he would hang up if she didn't speak more slowly, the pieces of the puzzle started to come together. Helga had been right. Barbara was pregnant, or at least she had been. The island woman was demanding the payment that Barbara had tried to cheat her out of.

John was furious knowing not only that she had gone behind his back to have an abortion but she had also lied to him. Not only had she told him that she wasn't pregnant when he had asked her, she had also told him long ago that she was not the type of woman who could 'kill her own baby'.

Yeah, he thought, abortion had not been an alternative when they were still in high school but now it was. John could see the walls closing in around him as he realized that she had trapped him into marriage. Tad's mother had been right, she had used Tad to get to him.

His mind was whirling. He didn't know if he was angrier because she had taken Janiene away from him or because she had taken a child of his away from him.

Trust. That was the problem. He had tried and tried to trust Barbara but she had always proved herself unworthy. The woman was a liar.

John wondered how many other things she had lied about. And how had she gotten pregnant anyway? She was supposed to be on the pill again. But, of course, that's how she had gotten pregnant the first time. She had said she was on the pill. Or had she been telling another one of her lies?

John had to know the truth. He went into the living room to find the address book. Helga must have sensed his fury because she quickly scooped up John Jr. and took him to his bedroom.

John thumbed through the pages until he came upon the name and number of Barbara's personal physician. Even though Helga had left the room, he thought it would be better if he made his call behind the privacy of a closed door.

Once inside their bedroom, he immediately dialed the doctor. The doctor was out so John sweet talked the nurse until she gave him the information he had been looking for. Before he hung up the nurse congratulated him on the 'new bun in the oven'.

He hadn't even thought to ask about that. He knew Barbara had known she was pregnant, hence the abortionist, but he had not thought that she had consulted her doctor.

The nurse had confirmed his worst fear. Barbara had not been on the pill in high school. In fact, she had only inquired about the pill after John Jr. had been born.

John had felt trapped many times before in his marriage but before he had always seen the trap as one he had set himself. One in which a sin of the flesh could be blamed. But in truth, he had been trapped by a huntress, a seductress. She didn't care about him, she only cared about her prize.

Half of John hated her for aborting his child and the other half was glad she was no longer with child. No child deserves a mother as conniving as she is, John told himself. But the truth was he had felt more for her when she was big with John Jr. than he had ever felt for her. He didn't want to care for her. He wanted to see her for who or what she really was. A lying, self-serving woman who had seduced him away from his one and only true love.

Chapter Eighteen

John informed Helga that he was going out and did not know when he'd be back. When she asked where she should tell the misses he had gone, he didn't answer. He couldn't answer since he didn't know himself.

John's mind was racing as he slid behind the wheel. He didn't head in any particular direction. He was just trying to sort out his thoughts. He was trying to figure out what kind of woman he had really married.

He thought about the first night he had made love to Barbara. No, not made love, had been seduced. A carefully planned and skillfully orchestrated seduction.

Her distraught phone call had been a lie. Her supposed break up with Tad, a lie. She had laid the bait with that phone call and foolishly he took it.

He should have noticed that night that she was up to something. The way her robe clung to her full breasts. The way she had insisted they go into her bedroom. The way she had very nearly exposed herself once they were in her bedroom.

She had used his sympathy to get him near her, to comfort her. To make it look as though it was all his fault or at least the fault of his damn male hormones.

And he had believed it too. He had believed he had taken advantage of her weakened emotional state. He believed that she was truly distraught, and in her anguish, had sought his comfort. He had believed that she had accepted his advances because she needed that comfort so badly that she was willing to take it in any form it was being offered.

John thought about how he had tried to stop himself from taking advantage of her by claiming that he had no protection. But, in fact, he had had protection. Most of the guys in high school had carried a condom even though most were not even sexually active, and never had been. It was just one of those guy things. Always trying to impress the other guys.

But he hadn't carried the condom from only peer pressure. Before he started dating Janiene he had dated an older girl who had taught him 'the ropes'. He had always worn a condom with her. He started carrying a condom then.

It hadn't been Barbara's assurance that she was on the pill that broke his resistance because he knew he had the condom with him. It had been the knowledge that he could make love to her without the sheath. He had heard many of the guys say that sex with a rubber was like trying to cool off in a pool with a wet suit on. He had wanted to feel what it was like without the 'wet suit'.

His curiosity had been his snare. And once in that snare, he had gone to her again and again. He tried to remember how many times he had made love to her before he and Janiene decided to get back together. What had it been? Two weeks? In that time, how many times had he shared her bed, or, as was often the case, the back seat of her car? John tried to remember but couldn't. One thing he was sure of though. Barbara had been trying to get pregnant and she had succeeded.

He knew that her trap could not have succeeded with out his willing consent but that knowledge didn't stop him from placing all of the blame upon his wife's shoulders. It had been the blame that he had carried solely on his shoulders for nearly two years. Now, he thought, it was her turn, and rightfully so!

He knew now that Mrs. Overthall had been right. Tad had been used by Barbara. She had wrapped Tad around her little finger so that she could, eventually, wrap her legs around John.

John had to hand it to her, she was a clever one. He wondered how long she had planned his seduction. She had started dating Tad shortly before Janiene had broken it off with her. How long would she have used Tad to get to him? She couldn't have known Janiene would break it off with him, could she? Could she?

John was beginning to wonder just how clever his wife was. She had used Tad knowing that she could get near him. She had used her body knowing it would be difficult, if not impossible to refuse. She had used her pregnancy knowing that honor would force a marriage. What else or who else had she used? John wondered where Janiene had gotten the idea that she was not good enough for him. That had been the reason she had broken it off with him.

John was numb with increasing rage. Barbara refused to consider abortion then. John had come to realize that she had been right. He pictured his son's little round smiling face. He wouldn't trade that face for anything in the world, not even for Janiene. But, it had been Barbara who had said she wouldn't kill her baby. It had been Barbara who had looked at him incredulously.

John unconsciously pressed harder on the gas peddle as he thought about her abortion. She didn't even tell him, he thought. She killed their baby and then tried to stiff the abortionist. Didn't she think he'd find out? Didn't she think the abortionist would come looking for her?

John wondered if he would have had another son or if it would have been a daughter this time. He pushed the thoughts from his mind. He would have neither. Not now, his scheming wife had taken his son or daughter away from him.

John pulled up to the curb and parked the car. He had unknowingly driven to Janiene's place. Not her parents' house or Tad's parents' house but to her new place. The reality of it surprised even him.

He had driven by her new address a couple of times after she told him she had moved out of Tad's parents' home. He had looked her up in the phone book when he first heard about her move. At first he hadn't able to find her in the phone book even though the books were newly issued, so he called directory assistance to obtain her address. It wasn't until they had given him her parents' address that he realized he was checking under the wrong name. Still, he had not found a listing, so he had followed her home one day.

After following her home and driving by her place a couple of times, John had felt like a real weirdo. He had been getting obsessive and he vowed not to drive by her house anymore.

He knew he should drive off. He knew he shouldn't risk letting Janiene see him sitting out in front of her place but he couldn't leave. He wanted to go inside. He needed someone to talk to.

Since he had lost Tad's friendship and Janiene's love, he had gotten much closer to his father. He talked to the man about all kinds of things he would have never shared with him if he still had Tad or Janiene. But this, he couldn't go to his father with this. How could he tell his father that his daughter-in-law had tricked him into marriage with one child but, now that she was married, had aborted another child? His own grandchild.

John swiveled his head violently when he heard a tap on his window. He looked to see Janiene bending down looking in his window. He rolled down the glass that separated them.

"Are you going to sit there all day or are you coming in?" Janiene could clearly see that he was upset.

"How did you know I was out here? I guess you really can sense when I'm around." John tried to make his tone sound light but failed.

"Not this time." Janiene nodded toward the grocery bag sitting on the ground near her feet. "I pulled up behind you. I gather you were pretty wrapped up in thought not to notice me pull up. Have you been waiting long?"

Janiene decided, given John's state of upset, not to ask him where he had gotten her address.

"Actually, I just kind of ended up here. I wasn't really waiting for you." Confused thoughts and feelings assaulted him.

Janiene wondered how much of a coincidence it really was that John ended up in her neighborhood but, still, she could see his words were genuine.

"Well, you're here now. I need to get my groceries in the house. Why don't you come on in?" Janiene didn't wait for an answer, she picked up her groceries and headed across the street.

He had never known for certain which apartment was hers. He rolled up his window, jumped out of his car and ran across the street to catch up with her.

"Here, let me take those," John said as he took the bag of groceries from her arms.

She didn't say anything until they were both inside her spacious apartment. "Have a seat. Can I get you a Coke or something?"

He looked around the apartment which was much bigger than the apartment he and Barbara had lived in when they had first gotten married.

All the furniture was Victorian or Early American in style. It was obvious that most of the pieces were reproductions. But a couple of pieces like an old rocking chair she had placed in the corner of the room was rustically authentic.

John took a seat on the sofa. "I'd love a beer if you have it."

"I think I do have some beer but I'm not sure how long it's been sitting in the fridge. Is that okay?"

"That'll be great. I don't really think it matters too much how long alcohol sits around."

"You have a point." Janiene popped the top off the bottle. She knew John would want it straight from the bottle but she asked if he wanted a glass, not only to be polite, but to put some distance between them.

John took the bottle and polished it off in what seemed to be one large gulp. He started to get up to throw the empty bottle away but Janiene took it from him. She offered him another one and he readily accepted.

"Since you don't have the pot belly that beer guzzlers get, I assume that you normally don't drink like this. Something is bothering you. Do you want to talk about it?"

John thought it would be unfair to bring Janiene in to his problems but he had to know just how deep Barbara's deception had gone.

"Tell me something, and I want you to be totally honest with me. Why—"

"I am always totally honest with you," Janiene said indignantly.

"I know you are. I just mean that I need to know not only your reasons but how you came up with those reasons."

"What reasons? What are you talking about?"

"Why did you break up with me?"

"Oh, John Jackson, aren't you going to ever let that go? I wasn't the one who forced you into Barbara's bed. Can't you accept her as your wife and be happy with your family. I can't keep dwelling on something that happened back in high school. You need to let this go."

"I have, well, I had. I need to know something. I am hoping I am wrong about my wife but I am beginning to think that Barbara set a very clever trap to get me to marry her. In the process she used Tad, she hurt you and she tied me into a marriage I didn't want. I could accept all of those things if they weren't planned but it's beginning to look as though it was all contrived."

"What a thing to say! That is so arrogant. You really think that Barbara would want you so badly that she would have used people to get you?"

"Yes."

"John Jackson, I can't believe you. Take responsibility for your part in this whole affair and then let it go. Things are how they are."

"I have been taking responsibility. I used to blame myself. I knew I shouldn't have had sex with Barbara that first night but I was lonely and hurt because you had dumped me. Then when I was with her she made me feel so good for those two weeks."

Janiene's eyes got big with that. She had thought it had been just one night. She had never thought of John as really having a relationship with Barbara until after he and Barbara had been married.

"Two weeks? You had sex with her every day for two weeks?" Janiene sounded stunned.

"That's not important now—"

"Yes, yes it is. Barbara came to my parents house early in your marriage and told me that she had been a virgin and didn't believe that she could get pregnant the first time. She told me that she never meant to hurt me. She made it sound as if you had talked her into it."

"She said what? She was no virgin! Tad could have told you that." He noticed Janiene blush with that. He supposed no woman wanted to hear who her husband had once been to bed with, even if her husband

241

was deceased. "Sorry, I didn't mean to be crass. I didn't talk Barbara into anything, she was more than willing. She told me she was on the pill. I found out today that she never took birth control pills until after we were married but she stopped taking them because they made her sick."

John thought for a moment. "I need to know how far her deception goes."

"I don't understand."

"You remember what Tad's mother said at the cemetery? About how Barbara had used Tad to get to me? Mrs. Overthall was under a lot of stress at the time and Barbara was just adding to it so I thought Tad's mom was lashing out. What good would it have done Barbara to go out with Tad if she really wanted me? You and I were going steady when she first started dating Tad. How could she have known we would break up? Unless, of course, she planned it."

"How could she plan that, John Jackson? Barbara didn't tell me to break up with you. I did that all on my own."

"Did you? Did you suddenly decide that our backgrounds were too different or did someone help you along?"

"No one—" Janiene paused and realization came into her eyes. "Chauncey. Chauncey told me that I was holding you back. That we would end up only hating each other. Your family having so much money and my family being blue collar. But Chauncey was my best friend, she would never do anything to hurt me. She gave me that advice for my own good or so she thought."

"Yeah, but who gave her advice?"

"What are you saying?"

"For nearly three years we were dating and Chauncey never had any advice about us before that. Did she?"

"Not like that. Before that she used to tell me how lucky I was to have you and then she'd say that you were lucky to have me too. She had always been encouraging."

"Can you reach her? Is Chauncey still in New Orleans? I have to know if Barbara talked to her." John ran his fingers through his hair. A muscle in his jaw had begun to twitch.

"She went to Tallahassee to Florida State University. We usually write each other but I have her phone number. I can call her now, if you'd like. Are you sure you want to know, John Jackson?"

"No, I'm pretty sure I don't want to know, but I have to know. I have to know what kind of woman I made my wife."

"I'll call for you. I'll used the extension in the bedroom if you don't mind. The kitchen phone can sound a little scratchy especially the few times I've use it for long distance."

John watched her walk out of the living room. He wanted to make sure that he had all the facts. He had known since he first found out about the abortion that he was going to file for divorce. He wanted all the facts so that she would acknowledge that she had never wanted John Jr.. That she had only had the baby to trap him.

He had to make her think that he was leaving her and John Jr.. It was a risk but he was almost certain that she would demand that he take their son. If he let on that he wanted the boy then she would try to use him as a bargaining chip.

When Janiene returned from the bedroom her face told John all he needed to know. Her eyes were red and her eyelashes were clumped together from the tears she had wiped away.

"Poor Chauncey, I think she is more upset then I am. She blames herself. I wish I had never called her. She feels so guilty."

"Then it was Barbara who put the ideas in her head."

"Yes, but I was the one who believed them. It can't all be Barbara's fault. If Chauncey and I hadn't felt so insecure about our backgrounds than Barbara never would have succeeded."

"That doesn't change the fact that Barbara carefully planned this whole relationship. She didn't care who she hurt or who she used as long as she got what she wanted. Well, let's see how she takes it when she is the one being hurt." John's face turned to stone.

"What are you saying, John Jackson? You couldn't hurt a flea, at least not intentionally." Janiene had to admit that he looked like he needed a punching bag. She just hoped he wasn't capable of using Barbara in that capacity.

"I'm not talking physical abuse." John gave her a you-know-me-better-than-that look. "I'm not even talking deliberate emotional abuse. I'm talking divorce."

"You can't get divorced—"

"Why the hell not?" He yelled in a harsh, raw tone.

"Lower your voice, please. You can't get divorced for a number of reasons. Think about John Jr.. Barbara must love you very much to have gone through so much planning and trouble to get you."

"Love had nothing to do with it. I was some sort of prize she wanted. Lady Barbara thinks whatever she wants she can have. Well, she's wrong, dead wrong. I can and will divorce Barbara."

"Have you forgotten? You're Catholic. You won't be granted a divorce."

"I think some heads may look the other way on a divorce or maybe they'll even grant me an annulment when they find out that Barbara has had an abortion! And I didn't even know she was pregnant. No, I take that back. I suspected she was pregnant and asked her point blank and she lied to me."

"She had an abortion? When? Why?" Janiene's voice was barely a whisper as she took in the shock of John's announcement.

"I don't know when exactly, within the last few days. I got a phone call demanding payment for the procedure. As for why, I can only guess that she never wanted children in the first place. She used that first pregnancy as bait. Now that she's got the fish, she doesn't need anymore bait."

"You haven't talked to her then? You have to talk to her. Maybe there as some other circumstances involved that you are unaware of."

He looked into Janiene's big brown eyes. So expressive, he thought, so sweet. Here was the woman he should have married trying to make sense of the actions of the woman he did marry. So loving, so forgiving, he hoped those two qualities would be there for him after he divorced Barbara.

"Will you marry me?"

"John Jackson, the first time I heard those words from you I was so excited and so happy to say yes. But then you married Barbara because she carried your child; which was the right thing to do. Don't ask me now to marry you because Barbara doesn't carry your child. You are a married man. You cannot ask for my hand or any one else's because your hand is already intertwined in another. Go work things out with your wife."

"I love you. I told you, I'm going to divorce her. I want—"

"John Jackson, go home. Go talk to your wife. Get her side of the story. Get to know her better. I still say she must love you an awful lot to go through so much to get you."

Janiene got up and went to the front door. She held it open for John. "Go home."

Janiene was glad that he had left without argument. She had to get him out of her house before temptation took the place of good judgment.

Her heart had leapt when he said he was going to divorce Barbara but, almost as quickly, she was filled with guilt. If she tried to talk to him about divorce she may end up no better than Barbara, serving her own needs without considering anyone else. No, she thought, it was not something she could be arbitrary about.

John drove around looking for the address the abortionist had given him. He decided to make good on his wife's debt. He wanted to ask the woman some questions too. He wondered if she knew whether the baby had been a boy or a girl.

The address was in a bad area across the river in Algiers. He was extremely cautious when he got out of his car. John was sure that this wasn't an area that many White people ventured into anymore.

He saw a couple of children playing but most of the faces he saw belonged to black males. Not real friendly looking either. Maybe they feel as uncomfortable having a white face in the neighborhood as he felt taking his white face there, John thought.

John skipped up the steps of the run down double shotgun house. It had once been whitewashed but that must have been years ago. Only flakes of paint here and there remained. The rest of the cypress wooden siding was dark and warped from exposure.

John knocked lightly on the wooden screen, paint chips stuck to his knuckles. When there wasn't an immediately answer he knocked again, only much harder.

He heard a mumble from the inside but couldn't make it out until the voice neared the door.

"Hold ya horses. Just waitta minute."

When the door was pulled open he saw a brown woman with a scarf wrapped around her head, island style. She was a thin woman but she still had good curves to her. Though her face didn't have any lines, John guessed she was about forty-five or fifty years old.

"The way you be lookin' me over, me tink you got de wrong house, mon. De ho lives on de next street," she said in a heavy Jamaican accent.

It took a few seconds for John to comprehend the strange accent but he knew it was the same voice he had spoken to over the phone.

"Sorry, I didn't mean to stare. You phoned me this morning about my wife owing you some money."

"Ah, ya, mon. Come in. Come in." The woman stepped aside so that John could pass.

John was surprised by the interior. It was on the small side but it was very clean and decorated with some very expensive modern pieces. The sofa and loveseat were bright orange and an angular looking lime green chair sat in a corner. There were two six foot tall aluminum palm tree sculptures on either side of the sofa. Mirrors covering the entire back wall made the room seem nearly double its actual size.

"You are surprised. Most of de outsiders are. You never hear of de saying 'can't judge de book by de cover', hmm?" The woman disappeared behind a curtain of orange plastic beads that separated the living room from the rest of the house.

John felt uncomfortable so opted to stand near the door rather than take a seat. He had a hard time picturing Barbara driving through this area, let alone parking her precious Cadillac here. John was glad his VW bug wasn't much of a find.

"You did not call first so you have to wait a bit. I be very very busy now." She noticed John's eyes get big and guessed his thoughts, "no,

I am not separating a babe from de womb. I have to cook. I have de guest coming wouldn't ya know," she said in a sing song voice.

She poked her head out of the beads. "Have a seat, notting gonna happen to ya, mon."

John hesitantly sat down in the lime green chair. Though abstract in looks, the chair proved to be very comfortable.

"You have de money wit ya?" The Jamaican woman yelled from the other room.

"I have a check, if that's okay." John raised his voice so that he could be heard throughout the house.

The woman reappeared through the curtain of beads. She had a slight smudge of flour on her forehead, centered right above her eyes. At first John thought it must be from the cooking but the location and size of the streak made it look as if it were put there deliberately.

John felt there was something very creepy about this woman. He was anxious to pay her and be on his way.

"A check, will it be okay?" John pulled the check book out of his back pocket.

The woman eyed John up and down. "I spose de check will be good. If it's not, I will use de spell I already prepared for de wife. I told her she had to pay, even if she changed her mind."

John stopped writing and looked up. "She changed her mind? You mean she didn't have an abortion?"

The Jamaican woman knew she had spoken too much. He must not have understood her over the telephone, she had clearly told him that she had to be paid even though she had not performed the separation. She knew from his face that she would not get paid if he knew that there had not been an abortion, regardless of how much black magic she threatened with. But, she was no liar.

"You child is most definitely in the ranks of the unborn."

John sensed that she was playing a game with him. "I know that. What I want to know is if you performed an abortion, if my child will ever be born."

"No, sir. De child will always remain in the ranks of the unborn. I must have my payment now and you must go! I don't have time for dis. I be a busy woman."

He didn't need to know she didn't perform the abortion, the woman thought. She knew she would do the job in time. She or someone else like her. She had known from the first time she talked to the woman called Barbara that the child within her womb would die an unnatural death.

Something about the look in the island woman's eyes and her manner told John that she was telling the truth. He finished writing the check.

Chapter Nineteen

Barbara had only been at work three hours when she was forced into the bathroom by waves of nausea. She had vomited for nearly half an hour but, still, she had no relief. She wasn't sure when she would have relief, if ever.

The vomiting she had experienced the first weeks of her pregnancy were unlike the sickness she felt now. Before it had been a physical reaction to a hormonal change, at least, that's what the doctor had said. Now her illness, though certainly physical, was caused by an emotional change. A change that affected not only her emotions but her whole life as she knew it.

Barbara gripped the sides of the toilet seat as she gave way to yet another wave of nausea. She wished she had never seen that second journal, wished she could erase the truth from her mind, from her body.

Shortly after Barbara had arrived at work that morning she had gleefully put some curios in the upstairs storage room as Henri had requested. She took the opportunity to return the first journal and search for the second one.

She put the first volume back into the box in which she had found it. She looked in that same box for the second volume. Volume II of Henri P. Sommier's journals hadn't been hard to find. As a matter of fact, it had been right on top. Almost, she thought, as if it had been placed there for her to find. Of course, she reasoned, she hadn't noticed it the first time because she hadn't been looking for it. She hadn't been looking for anything in particular; she had just been looking.

She had quickly tucked the volume under her arm and returned to the showroom where she could read it in peace. The lack of customers in the morning had provided just the quiet time she needed.

January 1860

It was a shock to Isabelle to learn that one of her favorite opera sopranos is carrying Jean-Claude's bastard. It was a bigger shock for her to find out that they are to put the babe, as soon as it is born, into the local orphanage.

Isabelle and I spent many hours in the deep of the night talking of this child. We have decided, with the permission of Jean-Claude, to adopt this child. Isabelle said that the blood of the child is also my blood so it will not be a lie when we tell people he or she is our own. Since we will be so long in France there will be no one to know that the child did not grow is Isabelle's womb. We will tell anyone who is surprised by the birth, after all our childless years, that the air of France was good for us both.

Isabelle does not care that the child will be, in part, Negro. In truth, neither do I but my practical side must rule me. I have told Isabelle that we will remain in Paris long enough after the baby's birth to make sure there is not a darkening of the skin or a kinking of the hair.

Jean-Claude only has a slight tint to his skin and his hair is roguishly wavy. The singer has skin like the petals of the lily in the early spring. If there is no outward sign of his Negro blood than we shall take the child back to Louisiana to raise as our own.

No one would ever have to know that the child is not ours. No one, of course, except Jean-Claude, the child's mother, Isabelle and me. It is only we that share in the knowledge of the young opera singer's condition. She has told her troop that she has taken ill and must go to a sanitarium to regain her health. They all assume it is consumption that she must have.

In a way, I am saddened that I cannot share the truth of this with Luc but he would be the first to shout inferior. Though I am sure he would keep our secret from the public, for more his own sake than ours, he would scorn our child at every turn.

A beautiful irony is that Papa will love this grandchild though he never truly loved the son who produced it. He will love the grandchild because it is his grandchild, his White grandchild. If he knew this child came from the loins of not this son but his darker son, his feelings would not be those of love.

I have always thought of myself as more of a son for Papa than Jean-Claude was. It was only because that was how Papa felt. Jean-Claude has helped me to see that Papa has been unfair in his love. We both are his children, equally. The seed from which I grew might have just as easily been spilled in his mistress as Maman.

I think it only fitting that Papa show love to his grandchild since he did not show it to his son, Jean-Claude. He showed responsibility but never love. All because of his skin, no, his blood. His Negro blood.

Isabelle wants to take the child even if there are outward signs of its Negro blood. I do not think that would be wise. I did not tell her so. Her spirits were higher than I have seen them in years. It is best to wait and see what is to be rather than argue over what may never be.

After our talk last night, we made love. Isabelle responded to me like she did when we were first married. I was so excited by her new warmth that I was unable to contain myself. She was not disappointed, we simply made love again.

I think this child will not only bring a life to us to raise but bring life back into our hollow marriage.

Barbara quickly read the next several entries as her heart slammed fiercely into her ribs and her stomach gave way to a queasiness.

After several entries she came upon what she was searching for.

August 1860

Little Jean-Claude still shows no outward signs of his blood. Since he did not have any mongoloid marks at birth, I took that as a good sign. His skin is a healthy pink with his little blue veins showing themselves easily through his pale color.

His hair is black as coal and plentiful. It does not show any signs of curling. But, as I pointed out to Isabelle, he is only two months old.

Many of the slave babies on the plantation have straight hair for the first six, nine or even twelve months of their young lives.

Isabelle is anxious to get back to Louisiana. I had hoped to wait and see how little Jean-Claude, or J.C., as we call him affectionately, turns out physically. I do not think that is possible now.

From all accounts, the South sits on the verge of secession. If a Republican is voted into the Presidential seat, South Carolina has promised to secede. I do not think Louisiana would be far behind them.

I have booked us passage to leave next week. It would do no good to wait. Isabelle is so attached to J.C. that I think she would leave me rather than leave him. I could not tolerate that. I will just have to hope and pray that J.C. has mostly straight hair.

No matter how J.C.'s hair turns out, I will teach him pride in his blood. Not only his Creole blood but his Negro blood as well. If I have learned anything from my brother, Jean-Claude, it is, that there is no race that is held back due to their intellect, or supposed lack thereof, there are only other races that hold one another back. Usually due to greed. The usual reasons given are merely excuses to help ease the guilt of the rapacious.

Barbara had scanned several other entries to find out if Isabelle had had any children of her own. To her dismay, she found that Henri P. Sommier had been seriously wounded fighting for the Confederacy. He returned home a impotent man, or at least he claimed that was the reason Isabelle remained barren. They had only one child. A son, J.C.. Not their son at all, but son of a Negro!

Barbara had been unable to hold back the queasiness when she realized all the ramifications of the words she had read. She had rushed into the bathroom to empty her stomach and relieve herself of the disgust she felt. After half an hour neither had been accomplished. She was still throwing up and she was still disgusted.

Her own son was a Negro, she thought. No, no, what were the laws in Louisiana? His blood must have been thinned out enough by now.

She had to think. J.C. would be John's great-grandfather, no, his grandfather. What was Jean-Claude? Had he been a quadroon? No, half, he was a half breed.

Barbara thought furiously as she sat on the floor near the toilet.

That would make J.C. a quadroon, she thought. My God, she thought, that makes my father-in-law an octoroon. Then John would be one sixteenth Negro and John Jr., one thirty-second. No, she thought, no state would think of her son as a Negro. Maybe no state would, but that didn't change the way she felt.

Barbara thought of John. She thought of the way she had tempted him, had lain with him. With that she felt another wave of nausea and placed her head in the toilet yet again.

He must have known, Barbara thought. All of a sudden her father's face flashed in her mind. "Daddy, I didn't know. I didn't know!" she said to the porcelain bowl.

She couldn't tell her father, he would kill John. He would be devastated to find out that the grandson he doted on is really a Negro. She knew it wouldn't matter how many generations away from the Negro blood John Jr. was. Her father believed that one drop of Colored blood made you Colored. She had heard him say often enough that the mixing of the white and black races only made more blacks. He'd say, 'you can't take good White blood and mix it with Colored blood and hope to get a White man. Their blood is so contaminated that it taints the blood for all generations after it. No amount of White blood mixing in will ever bring it back to pure. It's like mixing vinegar with water, it may look like water but it sure don't taste like water.'

Barbara felt confused. She was inclined to agree with her daddy but she knew that John not only looked and acted like a White man but so did her father-in-law.

John, too, was highly intelligent. He was probably a lot smarter than her own father. And John Jr., he was way above his learning curve. He was just about the smartest baby that Barbara had ever seen. Even her father had said so.

How could that be? Either they were different from most Negroes or her father had been wrong. Barbara didn't care which it was. The thought of her husband and her very own son being Negro was too much for her.

Barbara left the bathroom and made a phone call. She knew the woman on the end of the line had not believed her lie but she had given her the information she needed anyway.

Barbara left the store not bothering to tell anyone where she was going or even that she was going. She left the journal out on the counter top. She was sure when Henri saw that, he'd know exactly why she had left.

Barbara didn't have a chance to knock, the door was opened before she could raise her hand.

"My mother called to say you were on the way over." Janiene motioned for Barbara to enter.

Janiene's mother had called her twenty minutes earlier saying that she had given her address out to someone who claimed to be from the journalism club. Her mother had recognized the voice but she couldn't put her finger on who it was until she had hung up. She immediately called her daughter to warn her.

Barbara took a seat on the edge of the sofa. She wasn't quite sure why she had come here. She had told herself it was to tell Janiene that she was lucky she hadn't married John. To tell Janiene of John's background. But somehow, she hoped the knowledge of his background would make Janiene hate him. Make it so that she was no longer a threat to their marriage. Why, she thought, did she still want John?

"I think I know why you're here. John only came here today because he was upset. Really, Barbara, you have nothing to worry about. He needed someone to talk to and with Tad gone, I guess I'm the first one who came to mind."

"John was here today? Why? Why would he come here to talk to you?" Barbara's tone was nasty.

"I thought you knew. If that's not why you're here then what is it? Why are you here?"

"Oh no you don't! You tell me what my husband was doing at your house in the middle of the afternoon?" Barbara stood up to look Janiene in the eyes.

"I think you better talk to John about that." Janiene could feel Barbara's breath on her face. It smelled of stomach sickness. She walked to the rocking chair and took a seat. She had no intention of smelling the foul breath longer than she had to.

"Barbara, please, have a seat. Why don't you tell me why you came here today?" Janiene tried to keep her voice calm.

Seeing Barbara like this and knowing what she had done made her heart go out to John. Maybe, she thought, divorce would be the best thing for them.

Barbara reluctantly sat back down. "I want to know why John was here." She pursed her lips in a childish pout.

"Fine, but first, tell me why you've come."

"I don't know an easy way of telling you this." Barbara paused. She was going to enjoy seeing Janiene go through the anguish she had gone through all morning.

"Come right out and say what you have to say. I've always found that is the easiest way to communicate."

You would, Barbara thought. It was obvious Janiene had little breeding. "Okay, if that's the way you want it. John is a uh, uh, Negro."

Barbara didn't see any of the shock she had expected to see. "I said John is a Negro. Your John, I mean my John. John Sommier, he is a Negro."

Still there was no shock on Janiene's face. It was clear she didn't believe her though the look on her face was not one of disbelief.

"Didn't you hear—"

"I heard you. How did you find out about John's Negro blood?"

"I was reading—" Barbara stopped talking. The realization of Janiene's knowledge came to her. Janiene knew. She already knew.

Barbara was filled with outrage. "You knew John was a nigger and you never told anyone! How could—"

"John is not, I repeat, not, a nigger. I don't particularly like that word used to describe anyone."

"You knew! How could you let an unsuspecting White girl, one of your own kind, marry a Negro."

"Somehow, Barbara, I just can't bring myself to think of you as unsuspecting. Anyway, how was I to know that they didn't tell you."

"They, they who? Who told you?"

"John and his parents, of course. Who told you?" Janiene silently hoped that John had not told Barbara just to get back at her for the abortion. Janiene didn't like Barbara but neither did she like pettiness.

"I read, uh, I was reading. Uh, well, it doesn't matter. What does matter is that John never told me. I had his little black offspring and he never told me."

"Is that how you think of your son? Little black offspring? Maybe I was wrong to send John home. Maybe you don't love John like I thought you did."

Waves of panic swept over Barbara. Worse than the ones she had felt when she discovered the truth. Had John wanted to stay with Janiene?

"Why would John want to stay with you? Are you trying your little tricks on him, you slut?" Barbara knew she had gone to far but the anger that gripped her hadn't allowed her control of her tongue.

Janiene stood and walked to where Barbara was seated. She didn't care about Barbara's halitosis. She only cared about making her point and with every point she made she pushed her finger deeply into Barbara's chest. "Not everyone is like you. Not everyone would use a man's best friend, sleeping with him in the process, to get to that man. Not everyone would lie and say they are on birth control pills when they are not. Not everyone would get pregnant on purpose to trap a man. And last but not least, not everyone would swear they were against abortion but then go and get one without consulting their husband!"

Barbara hadn't even felt the push of Janiene's finger as the truth hit home. At first she assumed that Janiene was guessing but how could Janiene know that she was pregnant, know that she considered an abortion?

Barbara tried to defend herself. "Even if everything you said were true, I couldn't have succeeded if you yourself hadn't dropped John. How could I know—"

"Funny you should ask. That was the same question that was plaguing John. At first I couldn't remember but then it came to me. Chauncey talked me into breaking it off with John."

"Well, I certainly don't see how that—"

"I called Chauncey while John was here. She seemed to remember a certain Barbara Cartwright telling her that mixing the class structures would never work. As it turns out, Chauncey figured it out long ago but she didn't tell me because she didn't want to see me hurt anymore. It was a relief for her to get it out in the open."

"That doesn't prove anything."

"Barbara, I'm going to tell you what I told your husband. Go home. This is none of my business. You obviously only came here with some twisted attempt to hurt me with the knowledge of John's ancestry. It didn't work. So please, just go home."

Barbara wasn't ready to leave. Janiene had brought up abortion and Barbara had to know why. Percy, her doctor and the strange Jamaican woman were the only ones who knew she was pregnant. Unless, unless John had found out some way and told Janiene.

Perhaps that was the reason he had been to see Janiene. After all, he had asked her point blank if she was pregnant and she had denied it. Maybe the doctor's office had called and he assumed she had been considering an abortion.

"How do you know I'm pregnant again?"

"You're pregnant? You are pregnant!" There was shock and then relief in Janiene's voice.

"What the hell are you talking about? You knew I was pregnant. You're the one who brought up getting an abortion behind my husband's back."

"That's because I thought you had already gotten the abortion. John said—"

"John? What did John say about an abortion?" Barbara's voice had turned shrill.

"He told me that you had an abortion and skipped out on the abortionist without paying her. She called him and demanded payment."

"She did what? That crazy black bitch! I'll kill her. I didn't pay her because she didn't do anything. I never met the woman. We only talked over the phone."

"She told John that you had an abortion and you owed her money for the service. I think John said he was going over to pay her."

"What else did he say? Was he very upset?" The panic over the possibility of losing John was far stronger than the panic she had felt over his bloodlines.

"I think you better go home and straighten this out right away."

"I demand to know what he said. Now!" Barbara used the haughty tone with the long drawl she had heard her mother and then her stepmother use on all Whites that they felt were inferior to themselves. It wasn't like the condescending tone they used with Negroes, no, the tone used with Negroes was similar to the tone they used with children, only it lacked the affection. Those Whites deemed to be inferior were, at least, shown a slight modicum of respect.

Janiene was unfazed by Barbara's mannerism. "I told you, this is none of my business. You won't solve anything by talking to me. Go talk to John."

"But you know how angry John was. I need to know. You know how he can be such a hot head. I want to know what to expect." Barbara tried the damsel-in-distress tact.

Janiene knew that Barbara was going to have a rough time with John. She herself had never earned John's wrath but she had witnessed it several times. In high school he had run interference between the blacks who were integrated, many against their will, and the rednecks who didn't want any changes.

Janiene walked to the door with a sense of déjà vu. She wondered how many hours had passed since she had asked John to leave. "Furious is the word that best describes his emotions while he was here. Now, would you please leave?"

Barbara thought about the irony of the situation. She had stopped by to torment Janiene but she was leaving as the tormented.

Barbara looked at her watch. It was past five. She needed time to think, to turn everything around, to make John go on the defensive.

By the time Barbara walked through the front door she was prepared to meet with whatever accusations John threw at her. What she wasn't prepared for, however, was the letter sitting on the kitchen table. Her name was scrawled across the front of the envelope in John's familiar hand.

She ripped the envelope open with a sense of foreboding. Her hands turned clammy and beads of sweat formed on her brow as she read the letter.

Barbara could only see one word in the whole of the letter. One word that echoed in her mind. Divorce. He wanted a divorce.

Barbara left the house with her mind whirling. She needed time to think. She needed time before John came back home, if he came back home.

Barbara drove to the Jamaican woman's house. Though she hadn't gone to the woman for her services, she had kept her address. Kept it in her car where John wouldn't find it.

Her fury prevented her from noticing the deterioration of the woman's neighborhood, prevented her from seeing the black skin of the people there and prevented her from feeling the fear she normally would have felt.

She skidded to a stop when she found the address that matched the one she had written down. She ran to the door and bombarded it with her fists.

"Who you?" The Jamaican woman said harshly through the closed door.

"Barbara Cartwright, would you open this damn door?"

The sound of chain could be heard before the woman opened the door. "Don't you curse at me girl. Ya hear me? I knew you would be back but I do not have de time for you now. I will have to check de calendar."

"Are you crazy or something? I told you, I don't want the abortion."

The woman frowned. As a medicine woman she had been called crazy many times but she had never learned to brush it off. "What you want den?"

"I want to know why you called my husband and why exactly you told him that I had had an abortion." Barbara's eyes seemed to harden to a clear blue glass.

"I told you that you must pay whether or not you have the clearing out."

"So you lied to John so that he would pay you on my behalf?"

"I lie to no one." The woman crossed her arms and lifted her chin a fraction of an inch.

"But you told him I had the abortion!" Barbara glared into her eyes.

"I do noting of de sort. I only tell de mon de truth. He pay me and he leave. Now unless you want me to get de calendar, you better leave too."

Barbara felt every muscle in her body release it's tension. So John knew that she was pregnant. He must have written his letter before he had seen the woman.

Barbara had the advantage once again. He would never leave his babies. And if he tried, she'd threaten to expose him.

Chapter Twenty

Henri hastened to the showroom when he heard the frantic clanging the customer was causing. The antique brass bell which sat right next to the register was rarely ever used, unless, of course, the clerk had the day off or was in the back room.

He thought Barbara must have gone to the bathroom again. With that old vent fan on you couldn't hear a thing outside the tiny necessary room.

The customer had taken a long time in deciding upon a purchase, asking many questions, looking at a variety of items and finally settling on a little antique perfume bottle.

She said it was for a gift. She wanted a little piece of historic beauty for someone who loved the past. That's when Henri had explained the double meaning of the shop's name. By purchasing antiques, not only could you bring the past into the present thus keeping it alive, you could also turn the past into present, as in gifts. Henri pointed out that she was doing both. The woman had liked that and said though she had never been there before she would come again. She said it would be impossible for her to think about antiques now without thinking about Past Into Present and its meaning.

Though Henri had enjoyed waiting on the lady, and he always liked explaining the meaning of the shop's name, he had some refinishing he was working on in the back. He was angry that Barbara had not come forward the entire time the customer was in the shop. He was growing a little tired of her always being sick.

He needed someone dependable, especially since he couldn't be at that location everyday. That's why he had hired her in the first place, Henri thought. He had needed to replace a clerk. He would have to remind her of that. Family or no, the job had responsibilities that had to be met.

Henri walked to the register to complete the record of sale in the books. Everything was itemized and therefore had to be recorded after each sale. That way, at the end of each quarter, they had an accurate accounting of the net profits.

As Henri was recording the sale he noticed something out of the corner of his eye. He looked directly at the object in question. It was his grandfather's journal, the second volume!

He didn't need to check the bathroom or any place else in the shop, instinctively he knew Barbara had left. She knows, Henri thought, she finally knows.

He had tried to get in touch with John to warn him of Barbara's newfound knowledge. When Helga answered the phone she hadn't known where John was or when he'd be home.

Henri didn't hang up the receiver, instead he cleared the line and called home. He told Catherine about the journal. She had remained very calm. She said it would be better to discuss it when he got home rather than over the telephone. She had been right, of course. You never knew who would walk in on a phone call or who could be listening on the line.

He had anxiously waited for closing time. Henri wasn't feeling the calm that his wife had conveyed. He didn't like the idea of the daughter of a White supremacist having that kind of information about his family, even if said daughter were a part of his own family.

When five o'clock rolled around, he rushed out the door and locked it. He had put the jewelry and the days profits in the safe an hour earlier. He hurried down the narrow brick streets towards home.

Henri was surprised to see his smiling grandson at his feet when he walked through the door.

"John Jr., where'd you get yoself to, you? John Jr.?" Oliver called from down the hall.

Henri picked up his grandson. "I think I have what you're looking for, Oliver." Henri carried the baby down the hall with him.

"C'est bon. I have been looking all over de house for 'em. I was afraid he headed for de stairs again. I will take him, yes?"

"No, he's fine right here. Aren't you?" Henri planted a big kiss on the little guy's pudgy cheek. "Oliver, where's Mrs. Sommier?"

"Madam, she is in de drawing room. I think she is relaxing after a few hours of play with that one. He could zap the strength from Superman hisself, yes he can." Oliver tickled the baby's wiggling toes. "I'll go see 'bout de supper, M'seur."

Henri carried his wriggling grandson into the drawing room. After he pulled the pocket doors closed he set the baby down on the carpet.

He crept quietly over to the sofa. He assumed Catherine was lying down there since he couldn't see her in the room but he could smell the faint scent of gardenias. He leaned over the back of the sofa and saw his wife's lovely face, peaceful in slumber.

He rubbed her cheek softly and kissed her forehead. She barely stirred. He walked around the sofa and dropped to his knees. He bombarded her lips with whisper soft kisses. Catherine was awaking slowly until she heard a peal of wild laughter. She bolted upward.

"It's okay, Catherine. John Jr. has apparently found something quite funny about your shoes." Henri looked to the boy who was beating the soles of the shoes together and laughing intermittently.

"Oh, Henri, get those filthy things away from him before he puts one in his mouth."

"He's fine. All kids eat their share of dirt. Let him play. He seems to be enjoying himself much more with a pair of shoes than he does with all the toys that we or the Cartwrights give him." Henri turned up his nose at the thought of the Cartwrights.

He hoped John was right about Barbara. John had said that when Barbara found out about the family's true heritage that she would never tell her father because she'd be too ashamed.

Henri hated knowing that Judge Cartwright could and would turn on his own grandson if he knew the truth. Much like his great-grandfather had turned on his father when he found out the truth. But there was a big difference then, Henri thought. His father had chosen to tell his great-grandfather. His father had been a young man, proud not only of the people he knew as his parents but also proud of his biological father, a half Negro, Jean-Claude. There had been another difference too. His father's grandfather had sired Jean-Claude.

Although Henri didn't like to admit it, it was clear that John Jr. favored his maternal grandfather over any of his other grandparents. It was easy to see why, Cartwright absolutely doted on the boy. John Jr. couldn't have that relationship turned from love to hate. He was too young, he would never understand.

His father had been old enough to understand. His father had even been warned of how his grandfather might behave. His own father had understood the risks but had chosen to taken them anyway.

It was from his father's experience that Henri knew that Cartwright would turn on his own grandson. His father's grandfather had never spoken to his father again after learning the truth. He did, however, remember him in his will. A token like all the other former slaves and servants had received. It had been his final snubbing of his own grandson.

Of course, his father's grandfather had come from a different time. But then again, Henri thought, his father's grandfather had never belonged to the Wings or the Klan.

Henri picked up his chubby grandson. John Jr.'s meaty little fingers were wrapped tightly around one of Catherine's shoes.

"Henri, don't look so worried. Everything will be fine. Even if Barbara does know our family's past and even if she does tell her father, what can he possibly do to us without also exposing his link to us?"

Henri kissed John Jr. on the forehead. "It's not us that I'm worried about."

Catherine knew Henri was thinking of his father. "Just because your Papa was snubbed by his Grandpere doesn't mean that it will happen to John Jr."

Henri looked at her with disbelief. "Do you really think Cartwright will feel the same about John Jr. once he knows the boy has Negro blood? He's a White supremacist! Do you really think he'll continue to think of John Jr. as his flesh and blood?"

"He does absolutely adore," Catherine paused knowing that if she could not convince herself that she certainly couldn't convince Henri. "No, Henri, no. But John Jr. is just a baby. This really doesn't have to hurt him that much. We will keep him protected."

"From who? Maybe if it were only Cartwright we could explain that away. Plenty of kids aren't close to their grandparents from birth. But how do we explain his mother? Every child wants its mother."

"My God, Henri. What are you saying?"

"Barbara couldn't have been raised by a White supremacist without picking up at least some of his views. I'm not even sure that she ever cared about John Jr.. Look how she's had someone caring for him since he was only a few days old."

"Henri, that's not fair. I had Oliver helping me with John from the day he was born—"

"But you did not have someone breast feed for you."

"You know Barbara had a medical problem. That's why she didn't breast feed. Besides which, many mother's are choosing not to breast feed at all these days."

"Even if I'm wrong and she does care about John Jr., how do you think she'll feel knowing that her own son is of Negro blood? Knowing that the man she married is not the man she thought he was?"

"John is still the same man. John Jr. is flesh of her flesh. She'll come to terms with that. She has to."

"She doesn't have to come to terms with anything. I'm not sure that she could come to terms with this even if she wanted to. My great-grandfather never could."

***

John sat alone in the house waiting for Barbara. He had sent Helga home after his mother had agreed to watch John Jr.. He had taken his son to his mother's and come straight home. He hadn't wanted an audience when he confronted Barbara about the abortion.

He knew she had already been there since the letter he had written her was crumpled up on the kitchen table. He didn't know where she had gone or when she'd be back but he would wait. No matter how long it took, he'd wait.

A haze settled throughout the living room as dusk approached. The minutes seemed to tick by at a slow but even rate.

He wasn't aware how long he had been sitting on the sofa. He was trying to come to terms not only with the death of his unborn child but also with the fact that his marriage was a lie. An elaborate scheming lie.

By the time John heard the jingle of keys in the lock the room was completely dark. He didn't move a muscle when the door swung wide open and the figure encased by darkness entered the room.

"John?" Barbara's eyes hadn't adjusted from the street light but she sensed a presence in the room with her.

"Shut the door," John said darkly.

Barbara did as she was told. She walked to the end table to switch on the lamp.

"Don't touch that light. Sit down. We have to talk." John's voice barely restrained all the anger he felt.

Barbara was glad she had left the journal on the counter top before she had left PIP. She knew Henri must have seen the journal and warned John. She was sure that her contacting that Jamaican woman would be the furthest thing from his mind now that he had been exposed to her for what he really was.

She was surprised by the way he was acting. She was sure he couldn't be angry about her almost having an abortion, not after finding out that she knew of his bloodlines. In Barbara's opinion, one could not compare with the other. Yet she knew from his tone that he was angry. She had expected him to be ashamed, embarrassed or at least surprised by her discovery. She had not expected anger. What did he have to be angry about? Her secretly reading the journal certainly couldn't compare to the secret he had been keeping.

"Didn't you think I'd find out what you'd done? No, of course you didn't think I'd find out but you're not nearly as clever as you think you are."

Barbara was incensed by his tone. "I wasn't trying to be clever. I wanted you to know. I can't believe your audacity! You sound as if you are actually angry with me over that. Like I'm the one who has something to be ashamed of. I saw Janiene and she already knew."

John wondered if she had gone to see Janiene or if it were the other way around. But at the moment, that was not nearly as important as what she had tried to pull, as what she had done.

"You are one cold bitch. You damn well should be ashamed. After what you've done you should be a lot more than just ashamed. So what if Janiene knows? Who else was I going to tell? I went to see her right after I found out this morning."

"You're lying. You knew before this morning. Janiene told me so herself."

"What the hell are you talking about? How could I know?"

"Quit trying to deny the fact that you knew. It won't change anything."

"There I'm going to have to agree with you. Like I said in my letter, I want a divorce. It really doesn't matter when I found out. The point is that I did find out and I can't live with your deceptions."

"My deceptions? My deceptions? I think that what you tried to hide is far worse than what I did."

John couldn't quite follow what she was talking about. Whatever it was she was trying to communicate just didn't matter anymore, he was too tired to deal with her anymore.

"I'm moving out tonight. I know you don't give a damn about John Jr. so don't try to fight me for custody." So much for pretending he didn't want the boy, John thought.

He walked out of the room. He pulled a small suitcase from the hall closet and went into the master bedroom.

Barbara panicked. Even if John was part Colored she still loved him. She wasn't willing to give him up. Besides no one knew about his tainted blood and she sure wasn't going to tell anyone.

John looked so stern while packing. Barbara could think of only one way to keep him there. She was glad she hadn't been able to go through with it.

"How can you walk out on me and your child?"

"I told you, John Jr. is going with me." John dumped a drawer full of clothes on the bed to facilitate packing.

"I'm not talking about John Jr., I'm talking about the child I'm carrying."

John stopped packing. The muscles in his neck turned to rods of steel. "What do you take me for? The world's biggest idiot? What have we been talking about? I know what you've done."

"It doesn't matter to me. Don't you see? We'd never have to tell anyone."

"The hell with everyone else. I'd know. I can't live with what you've done."

"John, I will not let you turn this into to something about me. My reading your family's journal can hardly be compared to your hiding your true blood from me. This isn't even about me. I can understand your shame but I do not fault you for your blood."

John was taken aback. No wonder the conversation had been confusing in the living room. While he had been talking about her abortion, she had been talking about his bloodlines. He had never said the word abortion because just to think about it had made him sick to his stomach. He wondered if that was the same reason Barbara had never said the word Negro.

"Let's get one thing straight. I'm not at all ashamed about my grandfather. I knew you'd read about it sooner or later. We knew you had the journals."

"A minute ago you were trying to convince me that you only found out this morning."

John resumed his packing. "A case of crossed wires. It seems while you were talking about my family history, I was talking about my family's future. Or, rather, lack of it thanks to you."

Fear was causing Barbara to tremble. "We have to have a future. You know I'm with child."

"While I am sure you could get some recent document that will validate your claim, I've got five hundred dollars that says your not."

"Wh-what?"

"You should have paid her yourself and I never would have found out. What happened to 'I could never kill my baby'?"

Barbara looked at him dumbfounded. "Why should I pay for something I never received? She charges the same thing whether or not she does her dirty deed."

John spun around to face his soon to be ex-wife. "Her dirty deed? She may have performed a duty but you are the murderess."

Barbara was stunned by his accusation. "She said she told you the truth, you know I didn't go through with it."

"C'mon, Barb, I know what you did. I paid the woman."

"Did she tell you that I had the abortion or did she just demand payment?" Barbara had to find a way to get him to believe her.

John thought about what the woman had said. She had seemed like she was manipulating her words but he had believed her. Besides, even if Barbara were telling the truth now she couldn't possibly explain how someone who had been so dead set against abortion would see an abortionist. She couldn't possibly explain away her elaborate trap in which she had snared him.

John pulled the wedding band off his finger and tossed it on the bed. "I'm sure you wish you were still pregnant, so that you could trap me once again."

"Trap you? Trap you? How the hell did I trap you? It took two to make John Jr., just like it took two to make the babe I now carry!" She trembled with anger and fear.

"I talked to your family doctor and I know all about your birth control pills. I know you never took the pill in high school."

Barbara thought fast and furiously. She had to get herself under control. She should have known that island bitch had lied to her. She had to find a way to make John believe her. After all, she really was pregnant. If she could make him stay then mother nature would do the rest to save her marriage.

"I didn't go through my family doctor for the pill. I couldn't risk Daddy finding out. I know I told you I was on the pill for hormonal reasons but that wasn't the truth. I didn't want you to think I was easy."

"Didn't you? Then why did you open your door that first night with only a flimsily silk robe on?"

"You know I was upset! To be honest, I wasn't even aware of what I was wearing."

"Spare me the amateur acting hour, okay? When I suggested an abortion back in high school you looked at me as if I were the devil himself. You set up the entire situation so you would get pregnant. You knew exactly what you were doing, what you were wearing, you had it all planned."

John turned to looked into his wife's eyes. All the anger he had felt only a moment ago was gone. The only emotion he had left for her was disgust.

"Don't you even care for the child I'm carrying? You can't leave! How many times do I have to say it? I'm pregnant."

"It doesn't matter how many times you say it, Barb. Saying it won't bring the baby back. Tell me something? Was the thought of carrying my child too much for you?"

"No, John, please listen. I was doing it for you!"

"For me? How the hell could you be doing it for me when you never even told me that you were pregnant?"

"I didn't want you to have to worry about another mouth to feed with your law school coming up. Since you won't take any money from Daddy and you insist upon working like a nig, uh, you insist upon working when you don't have to."

"I insist upon working like a what? Like what? Huh, Barb, what is it that I insist upon working like?"

"You know full well like what. I will not be goaded into calling you that degrading name. I told you no one has to know what you are. You must have enough White blood in you anyway."

"Why is that? Because I don't look Negro? Because I don't sound like the Negroes you've heard? What exactly has all my precious White blood saved me from?"

"You aren't stupid and you aren't lazy."

"I'm getting out of here. You make me sick." John pushed in the locks on his suitcase and picked it up. "John Jr. will be with me at my parents house."

Barbara couldn't believe what was happening. "What about the baby?"

"Give it up. There is no baby. My family's lawyers will contact you."

"You can't leave me. I love you. Why I was even willing to stay with you even after I found out about your nigger blood." Barbara opened her eyes wide with horror as she realized the admission she had made.

John put his hand on the front door knob. "Good-bye."

"If you walk out that door, I tell the world what you really are. No respectable White family would ever go to your law firm. You'd have to go up North with all the other nigger lovers. Don't forget about your family's antique shops either. Why they'd probably be boycotted right out of business—"

John's suitcase dropped with a thud. He wanted to grab Barbara, to make sure she heard every word he said but he didn't trust himself. He wasn't sure that he could touch her without breaking bones.

"You won't be telling anyone. This coin has two sides, honey. You tell on me and you'll be telling on yourself. How do you think your Daddy or his friends would take the news that you not only had given yourself to a Negro but you bore him a son as well? What would that do to the all powerful Judge Jefferson Cartwright?"

"I don't care! If you leave me pregnant like this I will tell. I'll tell the whole damn world. The Wings will skin you alive."

"Yeah, right after they have their way with the White girl who put out for a Negro, right? Or don't you remember what happened to that White woman in Houma who befriended a Negro man? They said at least five Wings had forced themselves on her."

"That was never proven. Daddy told me that the Wings had no part in it."

"Somehow I don't think your Daddy would admit his part in a rape, even if his only part was condoning it."

John picked up his suitcase and walked out the door. The last thing he heard as the door closed was Barbara screeching, "Don't you understand? I'm pregnant!"

Chapter Twenty One

John arrived at his parents' house, suitcase in hand. He remembered his key and let himself in. John didn't feel like reiterating the whole story to his parents so he headed up the dark stairs to his former bedroom.

"I told you about de stairs little one, yes. I'm gonna get you." Oliver had heard the cracking noise on the stairs.

"I think I'm old enough to maneuver these stairs, even in the dark, Oliver." Even in his low mood he couldn't resist the tease.

Oliver pushed in the switch at the base of the stairs. The stairwell and downstairs hallway were instantly lit. "I didn't hear you come in. You usually ring the bells, no?"

Oliver looked at the suitcase in John's hand, he said, "You want that I make up your room for John Jr.?"

John wished he had slipped into his room without detection. Oliver would want all the details if he told him even a small part of the situation. Maybe, John thought, it would be better to get it over with now.

"I'd appreciated it if you'd set the room up for both of us." John took two more steps. "Oh, would you tell my parents I'm here? I'll be down to talk to them in a few minutes." John rushed up the rest of the stairs.

He knew Oliver hadn't asked anymore questions because he would get his information soon enough. Oliver was a good man but nosy to a fault. So nosy that he didn't even bother trying to hide the fact that he had been eavesdropping the numerous times he had been caught. John had no doubt Oliver would hear the entire account just as his parents would and at the same time his parents did.

John put the suitcase down on his bed. He switched the desk lamp on. The room seemed small to him. His twin bed, which had gotten uncomfortable, due to its length, his last two years of high school, looked unbearable now. His shelves, once filled with books and football trophies, were empty now. He had taken everything with him when he had moved.

John's eye was drawn to the only thing left on the shelving above his bed. He picked up the face down picture frame. He gently wiped the glass with his shirt cuff. He sat next to his suitcase and studied the photo, Janiene's senior picture. He had forgotten about it. When he had been moving he couldn't stand the thought of her watching him so he had put it face down. There hadn't been any point in him taking it with him, so it had been forgotten.

John got up, put the photo on his desk, turned out the lamp and headed down the stairs. He saw light coming out from under the drawing room doors. He knocked.

John Jr.'s laughter was the only 'come in' he heard. John slowly slid one of the doors open. "Mom? Dad?"

"Over here. Give me that shoe, give it to me."

John could hear his son's laugh once again at his mother's words.

He walked around the sofa to see not only his mother but also his father sitting on the floor with the jovial baby. "I see he has you playing games his way." John's light sounding tone didn't fool either of his parents.

"I take it you've seen Barbara and know that she's read the journal," Henri said with concern. "How did she take it?"

"I don't give a damn how she took it. She can go jump in Lake Pontchartrain for all I care. I've left her."

"John, you watch your mouth in front of the baby. Just a minute, let me take John Jr. to Oliver." Catherine didn't have far to walk since Oliver was right outside the door. She asked him to put the baby in his playpen because she didn't want John Jr. to overhear in Oliver's arms either.

Henri put his hand out for Catherine when she walked back in the room. He escorted her to the sofa and they sat together.

"What's this about leaving her? Has she kicked you out, Son? I knew she would not take this information well," Henri said.

"I left her; she did not kick me out. I can't take living with that conniving little bitch anymore," John said tersely.

"Watch your mouth in front of your mother—"

"It's okay, Henri. He's obviously very upset. What happened, John? Has she told her father yet?" Catherine watched her son pace in front of the antique chairs.

"I doubt if she'd ever tell her father but, then again, I don't care if she does. We'll be divorced soon anyway."

"Divorced? You can't get a divorce in our church, you know that. I think you and Barbara can work this through unless, of course, she's taking it that badly," Catherine said seriously.

"This isn't about my blood. It's about her trapping me. It's about her manipulating ways." John paused in thought, and then said, "how do you know she found out about Grandpere?"

"I had to help a customer because Barbara was no where to be found. It was then that I saw the second volume, atop the counter, and I knew she had read it." Henri looked up at John who had stopped pacing.

"What is this about 'trapping you'? I've told you before, John, you are just as responsible for making John Jr. as is she." Catherine unconsciously shook her head with pity.

"There's more to it then that. I found out today that Tad's mother was right. Barbara had used everyone in sight to get to me, including Janiene's best friend. She actually used Janiene's friend to instigate a break up. No wonder she called me when she and Tad supposedly broke up. Thing is though, Tad said they didn't break up until after I had slept with her."

"Even if that is all true, though it is terrible, nobody forced you into her bed. I taught you about condoms before you started high school yet you must not have used one. You cannot blame her for everything. If she is willing to stay with you, now that she knows your bloodlines, you must be willing to try to work things out with her," Henri told his son.

"Your father is right. It may not seem like much to you, but I'm sure that Barbara finding out her husband is, in part, Negro was a real blow to her. I, myself, had to come to terms with your father's history. But if he had never told me, and I had found out through the journal, I am sure that shock would not have been the only emotion I'd have felt. It is no small secret that you kept from her," Catherine admitted quietly.

"My secrets are nothing compared to hers!" John turned his bitter glare on his mother.

"Son, even if she used each and every one of your friends to get you in her arms, I am sure she would not have done so if she had known the truth about you. It is not only a question of which deception was worse but, also, which came first," Henri said.

"She is your wife, she gave you a beautiful son and if she is willing to try to live with you then you must give her a chance. Understand, this is hard on her." Catherine pleaded with him.

"If she's so wonderful then why did she kill my child? Do you have an answer for that, Mom?" John hadn't meant to tell them about the abortion but his mother's empathy for Barbara had pushed him too far.

"Kill your child? What are you talking about? You can drop that tone you used with your mother, right now!" Henri wrapped his arm around his wife in a protective gesture.

"I'm talking about the abortion she had last week. I asked her straight out if she was pregnant and she said no. You know all those days she was sick at work, Dad? That was because she was having morning sickness."

"That can't be. When you suggested that vile action to her she said she didn't believe in it." Catherine stared at John in shock.

"I have been trying to tell you that. It was all part of her trap. She told me she was on the pill, she wanted to get pregnant. She knew I never would have married her if she hadn't been pregnant."

"How do you know she had an abortion?" John's father shared his mother's shock.

"The woman who did it called because Barb had stiffed her. She wanted her money, I paid her. The woman told me herself that Barbara had aborted our child."

"Have you talked to Barbara? That doesn't sound right. Why would Barbara go to all the trouble of setting up an abortion without your knowledge and then not pay the woman? Over the months, I have gotten to know Barbara and she is a lot of things but stupid is not one of them." Henri scratched his chin.

John finally sat down in a Louis XIV arm chair. "Yeah, I've talked to her. She's a liar."

"What did she say? Why did she do it?" John's mother looked directly at him.

"She said she didn't do it. She said—"

"That explains why she didn't pay the woman," John's father broke in.

"Dad, she did it. She would say anything to keep me with her. I told you, the woman who did the job confirmed it."

Catherine exchanged a disturbed look with her husband. "You believed a woman you've never met before over your own wife? Tell me what Barbara said."

"She claims she was only doing it because she knew we couldn't afford another mouth to feed. She said she couldn't go through with it. That's just bullshit. She's trying to hang onto me, that's all."

"I think it says a lot about her character to consider an abortion to help you out and it says a lot more that she couldn't go through with it. Not to mention, her willingness to stay with you even though it must go against some very basic beliefs for her," Catherine said.

"You can't tell me that you believe her! Well, I don't. It's believing her that got me tied to her in the first place. I could have used a condom the first time but when she said she was on the pill, I wanted to find out what it really felt..." John turned bright red with his admission. He talked about sex with his father but never with his mother.

Catherine had to fight back a smile at her son's embarrassment. "There is an easy way to find out if she telling the truth. Have her take a pregnancy test and if the rabbit dies then you had better reconsider your actions."

"I'm sure she could get false results from somewhere. I wouldn't put it past her to—"

"She can go to our family doctor. I'll set it up. I'm with your mother on this one. I believe Barbara is telling the truth."

"And if she's not pregnant?" John stood up.

"I'll be the first to talk to our priest about an annulment," Catherine said easily.

The next day Barbara didn't feel like going to work. Hell, she didn't even feel like answering the door when Helga had come. She told Helga that they wouldn't be needing her for the next few days but Helga had forced her way in anyway. Helga had gone in the kitchen and Barbara went back to bed.

Barbara had put on the white silk robe and cried herself to sleep the night before. She couldn't believe that John wouldn't believe her. She couldn't believe he had turned the truth about his family history into something trivial.

She wanted to tell her father, wanted him to fix everything but she knew he couldn't. And, if he knew the whole truth, wouldn't even try.

Barbara heard a knock on her bedroom door. She pulled the coverlet over her. "Yes?"

Helga came in carrying a tray pilled high with all sorts of pastries, bacon, eggs and a singular glass of some thick caramel colored liquid. She put the tray down on the empty side of the bed.

"Frau Sommier, you must eat, not only for yourself but also for the baby."

"Helga, I told you before that I'm not pregnant."

"Ja, but das ist not true. I see it not only in your eyes now but in your belly and your bosom is like the lusty beer maidens during Octoberfest. You do carrying another life within you, ja?"

"Okay, okay, you're right. I'm pregnant, are you happy?"

"Ja, of course, aren't you?"

No, Barbara thought, how could she be happy with her husband gone. Her black husband. Barbara hated to admit it but her heart had ached early that morning when she hadn't heard John Jr.'s little laugh.

Helga picked up the thick liquid and handed it to Barbara. "Drink up, it will cure the doldrums. It is the hormones that make you so sad. Go on, drink."

Barbara eyed the contents in the glass. "What's in it?"

"If I told you that, you would not drink. It is good for you and the child you carry, drink."

She crinkled her nose as she brought the glass to her lips. Barbara was surprised to find it had a sweet fruity and rich nutty flavor. She drank it down in two big gulps.

She looked at the pastries on the plate. "When did you make these?" She picked one up and took a bite.

"This morning, of course, everything ist very fresh."

"I didn't see you carry anything but your purse in. Surely you didn't have time to make these here."

"Frau Sommier, I have been here over three hours. I started baking right away." Helga walked over to the dresser and started dusting it with the dish towel she had pulled from her apron pocket.

Barbara rolled over and looked at the clock. It was already ten-thirty a.m.! It seemed like she had let Helga in only half an hour earlier. She couldn't go to work but neither could she wallow in self pity.

She finished all the food but two pastries on her breakfast plate. "Thank you, Helga. I'm going to shower. Maybe that drink of yours really does cure depression. You take the rest of the day for yourself, don't worry, I'll pay you for a full day.

Through the noise of the shower faucet and her happy little song, Barbara hadn't heard the phone ring. Helga had already left. After ten rings the doctor's office had given up hope of confirming the appointment that Henri Sommier had set up.

Cartwright was doing his best to monitor Tommy's actions. It was proving to be more difficult than he had expected. It seemed that all the Wings that condoned mainstreaming thought of Tommy like he was their true leader and all the men who preferred the old ways of the Wings steered clear of the man.

A lot of the new recruits had been at hangers where Cartwright had given the okay. Cartwright found that they treated him with almost as much reverence as they did Jamison, almost. It was through one of the youngsters that Cartwright had heard about the meeting of Tommy's former hanger and three other hangers from surrounding areas. Tommy hadn't said a word to Cartwright even though there would be close to seventy-five men in attendance. It was true, Cartwright thought, that technically Tommy didn't have to get any meetings smaller than one hundred men approved but Cartwright still had a feeling that Tommy was trying to be sneaky.

The meeting, being held in the upstairs ballroom of the Orleans Hotel, was guarded at the entrance by two Wings wearing suits. Cartwright felt sure that both men were carrying guns, either that or each man had a strange way of holding their left arm.

"Let's see it," one of the men said gruffly.

All of the meetings held outside the home of a member went through the same routine, the man had to show his brass wings before he could be admitted.

Cartwright took exception to be treated with so little respect, he was, after all, Pegasus. He flashed his brass tack, a tiny winged horse and brushed passed the man.

He felt fingers dig into his shoulder and he turned to see the face of the guard staring hard into his own. "I think you have wrong meeting, Sir," the guard said with a nasty hiss.

"What? Since when can you or any other member prevent me from attending any meeting I damn well please?" Cartwright was careful, as he always was in public, not to mention the name of the group or his position in it.

The man began pulling on Cartwright, twisting the top of his suit jacket in his huge hand. "Listen you, I can make it easy or I can make it hard. Are you—"

"Get your hands off me, Boy. You fool, don't you know who I am? What do you think it was that I showed you?" Cartwright was unable to contain the volume of his voice.

"I don't know and I don't care." The man addressed the other guard, "Billy, can you manage by yourself? I'm gonna escort this one over to the stairwell and I'll even help him down a few." The guard pulled back his fist to hit Cartwright.

"Stop it, Roger. What the hell do you think your doing?"

"Stay out of it, Buker. I'm in charge of the door. Just go on in and let Billy and me handle the riff raff."

"What are you, a complete idiot? He's the Pegasus." Buker lowered his voice to a whisper when he realized he had an audience, "who the hell did you think he was?"

"If he's Pegasus, how come he ain't got the wings, huh?" Roger didn't bother lowering his voice.

"Because he has the Pegasus, you fool," Buker said with disgust.

"Get your hands off of me, Roger is it?" Cartwright started brushing himself off and straightening the wrinkles in his suit. "I'm gonna talk to your direct superior, count on it."

Cartwright straightened his jacket and motioned for Buker to walk with him. Buker whispered something to the other man and stepped in stride with Cartwright.

Buker waited until they were deep inside the ballroom before he spoke. "I'm sorry, Sir. Some of these boys are so new that they don't know all our symbols and codes."

"What the hell are they doing manning the doors then? You'd think they'd know who the damn Pegasus is, wouldn't ya? After all, I spoke to all the hangers in New Orleans in the last two weeks."

"Roger is out of Plaquemine Parish. He's not from New Orleans but he goes to Loyola."

Rage ran hot through Cartwright. Tommy had no right to call together the hangers of any area he pleased. Tommy was the Eagle for New Orleans only, besides, Cartwright had given the go ahead for mainstreaming only in New Orleans.

"Help me out here, Buker. I can't remember, how many meetings on mainstreaming have y'all had with other hangers?"

"This is the second one, the third, if you count when you talked to us."

Tommy had promised to keep the violence issue quiet between the hangers. Each hanger was supposed to think that they were the only ones that were allowed to use such means. That had been the only reason Cartwright had given the go ahead. Well, Cartwright thought, not the only reason, but even with Tommy's threat hanging over head, Cartwright had been emphatic about each hanger being sworn to secrecy. That way, no one hanger would think that it was the policy of the Wings to commit random acts of violence and no one hanger would become flagrant in their violence.

Cartwright looked around for Jamison. He didn't see the man. He decided it would be best to leave. If he stayed, it would show the men, as a whole, that Pegasus supported this new stand. That Pegasus was changing the long standing beliefs of the Wings.

Cartwright stopped to talk to, the now humble, Roger, on his way out. He struck up a bargain with the younger man. He promised not to tell his pilot how he had treated the Pegasus as long as Roger agreed to let Cartwright know whenever a meeting was to be held and to give him all the details after such a meeting.

Cartwright lied and told Roger that his busy schedule kept him from attending all the meetings while his bad memory kept him from remembering them. He told him that he preferred people not know his memory was so bad, so they'd keep the updates their little secret. Roger had been agreeable.

Since the evening was early, Cartwright decided to drop by Barbara's. He didn't see enough of that John Jr., he thought.

Barbara seemed surprised when she opened the door and not pleasantly so. Maybe, he thought, he should have called first. Hell, he was her Daddy why should he call first? He chuckled to himself when he realized she was only wearing a robe. No wonder she was annoyed.

"Darlin', did I catch you and John at a bad time?" He walked towards her until she stepped aside and let him in. He looked around for any sign of John. He figured he was probably in the bedroom getting dressed.

"No, Daddy. I just thought I'd turn in early."

"Uh huh, your momma and I used to turn in early when you were a baby, every time you'd fall asleep," he said with a wink.

"Geez, Daddy, where's your mind? John and the baby aren't even here." Barbara hadn't meant to tell him that but that sleeping medicine had her feeling confused.

"They aren't? Where are they? If they'll be back soon, maybe I'll just wait for them. I was hoping to see that little cutie pie of mine."

Panic crossed her face. She wasn't ready to tell her daddy that she and John were separated. Besides, even if John didn't believe her about the baby now, he would have to believe her, and come home, in a month. By then, she was sure that there would be no denying that she was pregnant, she'd be showing.

"You gonna offer your daddy a drink? I'm a bit thirsty."

"You want some water?" She saw him lift his brows and she added, "with your bourbon, of course."

"Naw, make it neat. Don't go to any trouble. You look pretty wiped out, tough day at the shop? That Sommier probably has you doing more than your fair share of work."

"John's dad is really nice, he is. Anyway, I didn't even go to work today." She handed him his drink and sat down in the chair across from him.

"Are you still sick? I can call and get you in to see the doctor tomorrow. You can't afford to be sick, not with a baby in the house." The judge took a swig of his drink. He scrunched his face up, they sure didn't buy the good stuff.

"I'm fine but I'm not going to be working for Dad anymore. I thought I'd start spending more time at home with John Jr.. He had a hard time after Lacy died and, though he's adjusted to Helga, I think it'll be better if I stay home part of the time. I'll keep Helga on part time, if that's okay." Barbara didn't see any need to have Helga there full-time without John Jr. there but since her daddy paid for Helga's services she had to tell him something.

"What do you mean John Jr. had a hard time with Lacy's death? He's a baby, what could he know about it?" He swirled the liquid in his glass before he finished it in one big gulp.

"He knows she isn't around anymore. The doctor says it's normal for a baby to mourn the loss of someone. Besides, I think he missed

Jammy, that was her boy." She got up to refill his empty glass. She made it a double so she wouldn't have to get up again.

He took the fresh drink and sucked half of it down in one swallow. He frowned as the cheap bourbon went down. "You saw her boy?"

"Of course, he used to come to work with her sometimes."

"You let John Jr. play with a Colored boy?" His eyes showed his surprise.

Barbara shifted uncomfortably. She hoped she wasn't about to get a lecture on the evils of mixings races, even for play. "I didn't want to but she didn't have anywhere else to take him. And you know what, Daddy? He was a smart little thing and cute too."

He stiffened and shook his head disapprovingly. "They can seem like they're smart when they're kids because they start out like us but their intelligence doesn't develop the same way ours does."

Barbara worried about John Jr.. What if her daddy was right? What if John Jr.'s brain stopped developing before he became an adult. But, that hadn't happened to John, and it hadn't happened to John's father and they both had more Negro blood than John Jr..

"You say he was cute, huh?" Cartwright walked the short distance to the kitchen to pour himself some more. No wonder they call it firewater, he thought. The low quality bourbon did have a mean burn to it but, he had to admit, it also had a pretty good kick.

She waited until he sat back down on the couch before she answered. Her head couldn't take any yelling tonight. "He was a doll. He wasn't as dark as Lacy, though she wasn't all that dark, 'course, you know that. Anyway, he had the softest, silkiest looking curls, not at all kinky. And you know what, his daddy was white!"

"She tell you that or did John?" he asked coolly.

"I didn't know John knew. How did John know?"

"I told him. He wanted to know all kinds of things before he'd let her work for y'all. What other kinds of things did Lacy tell you? I guess I never realized she was such a loose—lipped nigger. That's why she's dead, niggers with big mouths dig their own graves."

It wasn't often Barbara had heard her father use the word 'nigger'. The few times he had used it were because he was either furious or he was with a small group of his friends. It was easy to see why he had used it, twice, this time, he was obviously besotted.

She knew it was pointless to argue with him when he had been drinking but she had been angered by his remarks. "I know Lacy didn't have a big mouth. I don't care what the papers said, she wasn't in that Colored rights movement."

"How do you know so damn much about her, huh? Did you suddenly start being friendly with Coloreds or was it just Lacy? Did she tell you things to make your ears burn? She must have told you something that changed your mind enough about Coloreds to let her boy come and play with John Jr.." His tone had turned vicious.

She hardly recognized her father. He must be worrying that she'd become a bleeding heart like John. She had never been treated so hostilely by her father before. Then again, Barbara thought, she had never defended a Negro to him before.

"Lacy and I didn't talk much at all, Daddy. After she died, I realized she meant more to me than I thought she had. It's the same as Percy, I know I'll miss her when she's gone. Won't you?"

He set his empty glass on the table and got up. He didn't feel like waiting anymore. "That depends."

"On what?"

"On whether or not Percy becomes a nigger mouthpiece."

Chapter Twenty Two

Tommy didn't like being spied on, he didn't like it one bit. He had seen Cartwright at the meeting, seen him pull Roger aside and seen him give Roger a piece of paper. Immediately following the meeting Tommy had talked to Roger. Roger had reluctantly told him about his awkward meeting with the Pegasus and the Pegasus' need to be reminded of things.

Looked like he was going have to show Cartwright, again, who was boss, Tommy thought. That was the problem with men like Cartwright, they've been driving the wagon so long, they don't know how to give up the reins.

Tommy spoke to Judith and found that Cartwright, even though it was Saturday, would be at the courthouse all day. He called the courthouse and found, as expected, Cartwright's secretary had the day off. Cartwright himself had finally answered the phone, after numerous rings. He had hung up on Cartwright without identifying himself. Tommy had always found the element of surprise to be a great advantage.

Tommy didn't bother knocking. He walked through the secretary's office directly to the judge's door. He stood slightly off to the side of the door; the top half of the door was privacy glass. Tommy paused long enough to listen to the silence from the inner office.

He turned the door knob and pushed the door open widely. "I guess you didn't 'pect to see me today."

Cartwright looked up from a stack of papers. "What do you want? I'm busy."

Tommy looked around the room, his eyes searching for a whiskey decanter, when he didn't find one, he took one of the chairs across from Cartwright, the one nearest the window.

"I don't take too kindly to spies in my organization. I handle them in the usual manner all organizations handle spies. So before you ask someone to spy on me you better make damn sure he's real good or he's someone you didn't like all that much anyways." Tommy's eyes had narrowed to slits.

"Don't be so damn cryptic. What the hell are you talking about?" Cartwright pulled his private stock out of the bottom desk drawer, dumped the water from his glass in the trash can and filled his glass three fingers.

He hadn't wanted to drink before he finished studying his cases but his nerves always got an edge to them around Tommy and he needed to smooth out that edge. He had planned on talking to Tommy anyway, he just hadn't thought of how he was going to handle him yet.

"You thought you were being slick asking Roger to spy on me but I saw you with him. Rest assured, Roger won't be attending any more meetings of major importance." He eyed the bottle and added, "got another glass?"

Cartwright shook his head no to the glass. "I'm the Pegasus, I have a right to know about everything what goes on in the Wings. I don't have to explain it to you or anybody else. Besides, I have some questions of my own for you. For instance, why were there hangers from outside your area in attendance? And why have you had two meetings, with several hangers in attendance, on mainstreaming?"

Tommy leaned across the desk and grabbed the bottle. He tossed the screw cap on the desk and took a swallow. "I didn't like the way you wanted it handled so I changed a few things."

Cartwright saw some of Tommy's saliva floating on top of the amber liquid when the man put the bottle back down. "You can't go changing things whenever you want to. You are going against some very basic beliefs of the Wings. Besides, I told you, in order for my plan to work, we have to keep a low profile."

"Screw your plan, you think your plan is gonna work better than mine? My plan—"

"I hadn't planned on sharing this with anyone outside Washington but looks like I'll have to if I'm to get your cooperation. I got several Wings I'm in contact with in DC, lawmakers, if you know what I mean. They say that there are literally hundreds sympathetic to our cause already holding office. If we continue to grow, keeping a low profile, within the next five or ten years we could have a caucus so large we could shape the federal government."

"What the hell difference is that gonna make? It's the feds what has us chasing our goddamn tails as it is. They ain't gonna listen to us." Tommy took another gulp of whiskey.

"What do you think 'a government for the people, by the people' means? It means, if we get enough to follow our cause we can vote the right people into office, control the way they vote, hell, we'll control Washington. I'm talking about a divine White right. We'll have the constitution amended so that it spells out the inherit inferiority of the minority, thus increasing our control over them. No more of this 'separate but equal' bullshit. That's how they got integrated into our damn school system by saying they were equal but their schooling wasn't! If we get the truth put right into the constitution, there won't be anymore of this 'our schools don't get the same kind of funding therefore Negroes don't get an equal education'. It will be understood that we won't spend the same on their education, why should we? They are mentally inferior, they can't obtain a better education anyway."

Tommy liked the judge's plan but it was too far off in the future. "If we go with your plan, we gotta wait some five, ten or more years and, though we got the niggers controlled, we still got all the niggers. If we go with my plan we won't have any uppity niggers left. Those what keeps their mouths shut will be able to continue living as niggers should, as maids, gas jockeys and the other jobs ain't suited for White folks."

"You're talking genocide! It's our duty to take care of all the animals in God's kingdom, that includes Coloreds. I don't want to sit before God and have to answer for mass murder of the creatures in his kingdom." Cartwright was incensed.

"God made a mistake when he made the nigger. I'm just planning on helping correct that mistake."

Cartwright crossed his arms, he didn't talk about God without reverence and didn't like it when anyone else did. "God doesn't make mistakes."

"Oh yeah? Then why is the nigger so stupid?"

"God has his reasons for everything. If you're going to question that then you'll have to start asking why dogs walk on four legs instead of two and why some animals have feathers while others have scales."

"But there ain't anything else in all the world that is as much like us, except maybe the ape but it can't talk. Explain that." Tommy slapped his hand on the desk for emphasis.

"God had his reasons. Maybe they are a test for us or our burden, who knows? I do know that we are given power over everything on earth and we have to do right by it."

"Next thing you'll be saying is that all the humans was created equal, that the word 'man' in the Bible don't specify no color. Pleeease, don't try feeding me that bullshit. Niggers are mistakes, plain and simple. They're good for mule work and the women are good for screwin' but what else are they good for?"

Cartwright noted the nasty glow in Tommy's eyes. "If you believe that then why did you join the Wings? You went through orientation, hell as pilot, you've taught it. You know we believe in the divine right of the White man but we also believe in the necessity to care for the darkies, you know that."

"That's a bunch of hogshit! If my fuckkin' family hadn't raised me up as a damn catholic, I woulda been Klan or some other group with backbone. But the Klan wouldn't even give me a chance 'cause of that, and hell, I ain't set foot in a catholic church, except for funerals, since I was a teen. They didn't care about that though, they acted like I was born to it like the Jews are, like it was a race not a religion."

"Why didn't you lie to get in? You've got to be crazy if you think I'm gonna let you turn the Wings into the catholic faction of the Klan," his voice was severe with no trace of sympathy in its hardness.

"I'll do what ever I want, ya hear? Don't you forget what I have on you. If I tell you to bend over, I expect to see your trousers around your ankles, ass bared, no questions asked. I ain't playing games here, you may be the Pegasus but I'm in charge. You got that?"

"Drop dead, Tommy. I've gotten to the family of the one you took care of for me. They're sitting on a nice chunk of change, they won't talk. I explained to them how it was you came to kill their kin, you know, how I was complaining about the threats demanding money and you took it upon yourself to take care of it. Told 'em you thought you were helping me out. I even told them about your involvement with that Birmingham thing, so if anything happens—"

Tommy jumped up, his eyes bulging from the sockets. His face was so red that it didn't look like there was any skin to it, only blood. "You muthafucker, I'll kill you. I'll kill those niggers too. Don't fuck with me! I'll cut your fuckin' dick off and feed it to you."

Cartwright stood up to stare the man straight in the face. "Sit down and shut up! I have placed an accounting of your actions, as well as a complete explanation as to my relationship to the party you killed, in my safety deposit box, to be read in the event of my death. I've even included a statement linking you to the church bombing. So don't even think about threatening my life, you kill me, you blow yourself straight to hell."

Tommy fell back in the chair. He grabbed the whiskey and nursed the bottle like a baby. "I shoulda known I couldn't trust you."

"Trust? What do you know about it anyway? It's trusting you as my right hand man that got me into all this trouble in the first place. Did you really think you could change the Wings basic policy just by getting a grip on the balls of the Pegasus? What'd you think the Wings in the other states would have to say? You didn't think about that, did you? They'd have us both ousted so fast we wouldn't know what hit us."

"You can't change it now. You've already given the go ahead." Tommy's tone had taken on a whiny sound.

"The hell I can't. I'll talk to all the groups individually again. Remember, when I spoke to them, I told them that their hanger, and theirs alone, would be allowed the new privilege. I'll explain that the feds are on to us. If anything gets out of hand, you'll be the fall guy. Several hangers, at once, have heard you speak on this issue, not so with me." Cartwright sat back with his hands behind his head.

"You sonofabitch! You can't do this to me. The new recruits won't like this; they won't like it at all."

"You take all the new recruits, the ones who share your beliefs, and start your own group for all I care. Violence, though necessary at times, is not what the Wings are all about."

"Maybe I will, maybe I'll do just that." Tommy stood to leave. "How safe are those papers in your deposit box? What if you had a car accident or somethin' and I didn't have nothin' to do with your death?"

"I know all about you and car accidents. And if anything does happen to me that truly is an accident, you better consider finding yourself a new identity."

Tommy let out an audible sigh. He walked to the door that he had left open.

"Tommy, here, take this." Cartwright screwed the cap on the half empty whiskey bottle. "Oh, and Tommy stay away from Barbie, ya hear?"

Tommy snatched the bottle from Cartwright's hands. "You can't stop me from doing a little antique shopping now and then," his tone was blatantly sexual.

"Barbara doesn't work anymore, so do all the antique shopping you want to."

"Really? I never really liked antiques anyway. I've always preferred young, uh, new things." One corner of Tommy's mouth twisted up wryly. Tommy strolled out of the office with an air of confidence.

Cartwright slammed his office door. Even though he had gotten back the upper hand, Tommy had made him feel like it was only an illusion. That Tommy would strike at any moment.

At least he knew Barbara was safe, with Helga there all day and John there all night, Tommy wouldn't have a chance to do anything to her.

Cartwright picked up the phone on the first ring. His mind was too preoccupied with Tommy to get back to his pending cases.

"Oh good, Judith told me I could get you there. You're not busy are you?"

"Barbie, hello darlin'. I'm glad you called. You're not mad at your ol' daddy for being so gruff the other night, are you? I guess I had a bad day. Tell John and the baby that I'm sorry I missed them."

"Don't worry about it. Are you in the middle of something right now?" her voice was apprehensive.

"Not right now. Why do I get the feeling that you didn't just call to say hi?"

"Well, I do have something that I'd like to talk to you about."

"It's not about that damn Tommy Jamison is it?" he said in a hard tone.

"No, Daddy, why would you think that?"

"Never mind. What did you call for then?"

"Have you eaten lunch yet? If not, I could bring you a po-boy and a Dixie, or two, and we could have lunch on the levee or in the square."

"Make it a fried oyster po-boy, dressed, and meet me in St. Ann's garden and ya got yourself a deal. How's about an hour sound to you?"

"See ya there."

An hour later, bag in hand, she saw her father approaching. Judging from his size and his heavy breathing at his slow gait, Barbara thought some cottage cheese and fresh fruit would probably be better for him than a po-boy dripping in grease and slopped with mayonnaise.

"C'mon, let's walk around to the square," he said as he approached her.

St. Ann's garden bordered the backside of the St. Louis Cathedral, while the square, Jackson square, bordered the front.

They walked silently along the side of the Cabildo until they reached the square.

Barbara led the way through the iron gates and took a bench that viewed the backside of the Andrew Jackson monument. "You didn't say how many Dixie's you wanted so I brought a six pack." She reached in the bag, got out his sandwich and handed it to him. "Here, here's some Tabasco, if you want it."

He took the hot sauce, balanced the sandwich on his knee, opened the paper and started shaking the sauce all over the oysters. When he finally stopped shaking the little red bottle, his oysters had gone from a golden crispy brown to a soggy looking red.

"You might need all those Dixie's to put out that fire."

"Nonsense, this is the way it's supposed to be eaten. You ought to try it."

"I like Tabasco but I don't like to drink it."

He took a bite from his mouth peeler and turned to talk to his daughter, his mouth full. "What was it that got me a free lunch?"

Barbara took a drink of the Coke she brought for herself. "You know how I asked you to make sure that John doesn't get into—" She looked from side to side to make sure there was no one within earshot. "to Harvard?" she whispered.

"Yeah, I told you not to worry. You worry too much, you know that. I'll take care of it all right." He pulled his key ring out of his pocket so that he could open the beer bottle. He searched through the mass of keys for the mini bottle opener.

"No, Daddy. That's what I wanted to talk to you about. Don't do a thing. If he ever found out that I had done anything to prevent him from getting into Harvard, I think that would be the final straw."

"Final straw? What are you talking about? He won't find out, there's no way he could."

"I used to think that about a lot of things. Please, Daddy, don't do a thing. Besides, I think when he finally believes that I'm pregnant, he won't want to go there anyway."

"You're pregnant? Pregnant! That's wonderful news, Darlin'." He drew his brows together. "What's this about Sommier believing you?"

"Oh, it's a long story—"

"I've got the time," he said coolly.

Barbara thought he looked like he was ready to strangle John so she told him the same version of the abortion story that she had told John. She decided it still wouldn't be a good idea to tell him about John leaving.

"Well I'll be damned. I'm afraid I'm with John on this one, Darlin'. You never should have considered that in the first place. Those things aren't safe. I'm sure glad you didn't go through with it."

"Me too." She took another sip of her Coke, she whispered, "Not a word to anyone to prevent John from getting into Harvard, okay?"

Tommy had remained in the French Quarter after he had seen the judge. He met Buker at his employer's, a small print shop on St. Peter. Buker had gone in while the shop was closed to run off a stack of papers for the Wings. Since Buker wasn't busy, the two men had decided to get some coffee and beignets at the Cafe du Monde. They walked along St. Peter, towards the river, and were walking between the Pontalba Apartments on their right and Jackson square on their left when they saw them.

It was Buker who spotted Barbara. "She is one pretty lady. All the right curves, in all the right places. I went to high school with her but she didn't have the time of day for me." Buker pointed at the direction she was sitting. "Hey, isn't that the Pegasus with her?"

Tommy looked at the pair on the bench. They were only fifty feet away so Tommy stepped up next to a banana tree, a couple of fronds blocked his body from their view.

"Yeah, that's him." Tommy wondered if the two of them were talking about him. Damn, he thought, he was becoming paranoid.

"That's pretty sweet, a man his age getting a young lady like that."

"You didn't know her at all, did you? He's her Daddy, I don't think he's the type to get it from his daughter," Tommy said, his tone clipped.

Buker's head snapped back as if he'd been slapped, he hadn't meant any disrespect. "I didn't know. I guess I should have put two and two together, Barbara Cartwright and Judge Cartwright."

"She is one fine piece of work. I wouldn't mind being wrapped in some of that." Tommy unconsciously licked his lips, he added, "She ain't Barbara Cartwright no more. She married a real asshole, don't like sharing his piece of the pie, if you know what I mean."

Buker thought Tommy looked a little crazed. "What man would want to share his woman, especially if his woman looked like that?"

"Not Sommier, that's for damn sure."

Don Buker eyes went wide with surprise. "John Sommier?"

"Yeah, what of it?" Tommy watched the young man carefully.

"They must not know. There's no way the Pegasus would let his daughter marry their kind. No way. They couldn't possibly know." Buker's face was chalky and full of disbelief.

"Know what? What the hell are you talking about?"

"He's a nigger."

"Who's a nigger?"

"Sommier."

"What the hell? Are you crazy or something? I know Sommier and he ain't no nigger. Maybe a nigger lover but he ain't no nigger."

"Yeah? I wouldn't have thought so either, heck I used to hang around with him in high school. Anyways, I heard it straight from his best friend's mouth."

Tommy frowned. "Why would Sommier's friend tell you that?

"I think he was trying to convince me that they, the niggers, are the same as we are. It was back some months ago, at the beginning of the semester, when I was recruiting on campus that I found out. This guy I knew from high school, Tad Overthall, was telling everyone he was getting hitched so I gave him a pamphlet, you know, thinking he'd want to protect his future for his kids, he got peeved when he saw the material. He started telling me that I hung out with Negroes and I liked them. He said that in front of everyone! I told him that I wasn't no nigger lover and he said one of my friends was one of them. He got real quiet and whispered that John Sommier's grandfather was a quadroon. Tad was Sommier's best friend all through high school, if anyone would know, he would."

Every muscle in Tommy's body stiffened with anger. "She's givin' it to a nigger and she had the nerve to push me away! I think I'll show her what a real man feels like."

The tiny hairs stood up on the back of Buker's neck. He was scared of Tommy, scared of what he was capable of. "I'm sure she don't know he's got nigger blood. I know the Judge wouldn't allow that, even if she was willing. No, I just can't believe she knows. You can't hurt her for something that she really didn't have a say in."

Tommy's faced twitched. He was deep in thought. His eyes glowed with anticipation. He had wanted to take her to his bed since she was a young teenage girl. If her daddy hadn't of been so powerful he probably would have had her, one way or another, long ago. Tommy smiled; at least he was going to get her while she was still young. It's too bad, he thought, he couldn't have had her before she had the baby. "Tonight," he mumbled.

"What?" Buker's young face was etched with worry lines.

"I said you're right. I can't very well hold anything against her but that won't stop me from putting a bullet into her nigger husband's head," Tommy's tone was unreadable.

"I don't know if that's such a good idea. The Sommier's are powerful folks around these parts. I'm sure there ain't any proof that their blood is mixed or else someone would have found out long ago. If we do anything to any of them, they would have the Wings jumping through fire hoops, not only would the feds be all over us but the state would be too. I don't think any of the boys are going to want to do this one. It's too dangerous. It'd be stupid, and, with him being the son-in-law of the Pegasus, who's going to believe it?"

Tommy grabbed Buker around the collar, he whispered in a deadly tone, "You think I'm stupid? I was doing recon missions in the war when I was your age. I don't need yours or any of the boys help with this one. I'll be in and out before they know what's hit 'em, just like the war. They'll get what they deserve and no one will ever think it was the Wings, including the Pegasus."

Buker's bottom lip was trembling. "You ar-aren't going to, uh, um, hurt her are you?"

Tommy released the young man. "Not at all." He added under his breath, "It won't hurt at all if she cooperates."

Buker instinctively turned his head, like a dog trying to pick up the direction for a sound. He hadn't been able to make out the words but the tone was unmistakable. The man sounded like the grim reaper, only this reaper wasn't so grim.

John was reluctantly helping out at the shop that afternoon. His father hadn't found a replacement for Barbara and John had the distinct feeling that he wasn't looking either.

John hadn't clerked since his father had taught him how to do the books, over three years now. He didn't like waiting on all the tourists though he didn't mind the families who lived in town. But all the people he knew who had come in the shop in the last few days had wanted to see Barbara. Barbara, John discovered, was a well liked sales lady and her customers were very loyal to her.

His father was even loyal to her, always pointing out the way Barbara did this or that or how Barbara would display some item and how Barbara really had a flair for the business.

"John? Would you run these to Mrs. Van Patten, you remember where she lives, near City Park, don't you?" Henri came from the back with two small plant stands in his hands.

"Sure, I remember." John moved to take the stands but his father pulled his hands back.

"Have you heard anything from the doctor's office yet?"

"Yeah, I talked to them. They said they haven't been able to get in touch with Barbara so they had to put off the scheduled pregnancy test. I think Barb is avoiding them."

Henri set the stands down next to his son. "How can she be avoiding something she doesn't know about? We set up the appointment without her knowledge."

John shrugged, embarrassed by his mistake. "Well, she does know where John Jr. is but she hasn't called, not even once. I think she is avoiding talking to or seeing her son."

"I think she's is embarrassed, plain and simple. You are staying with us, Son. That has to be hard for her knowing that we know your side of the story, I'm sure she thinks we hate her now."

"Don't you? I thought you never liked her in the first place."

"I didn't like her ideas but she is a smart articulate young woman. I have grown to accept her in this family, grown to love her."

297

John was caught off guard by his father's avowal. "So you think I'm being unfair in this whole thing?"

"I think, and your mother agrees with me, that you should find out if Barbara is carrying your child. Neither of us think that it is good for a pregnant woman to be alone in her condition, after all, it takes two to make a baby."

"What, exactly, do you and Mom propose I do?" He crossed his arms and half rolled his eyes. It was hard to believe that his parents were behind Barbara after the things she had done, even if she was pregnant.

"Go over there and talk to her. I know you should be able to tell if she's pregnant, even this early. There are things to look for like her breasts being larger, her eyes glowing, well you know what to look for, don't you?"

"Yes, but if she just had an abortion her body would still probably show signs of the baby that had been there, don't you think?"

"Could be, but I still think you should talk to her. She's your wife, can't you tell if she's lying?"

John hated to admit it but he couldn't. He had never taken the time to thoroughly get to know his wife so he didn't know what to look for when she was lying. "If it will make you feel better I'll go see her tonight."

"Good!" Henri had a huge grin on his face. He picked up the plant stands and handed them to John. "You don't need to come back in after you deliver these, and John? Tell her we miss her down at PIP."

Chapter Twenty Three

Tommy decided he'd wait until after the dinner hour to make his attack. If John and Barbara ate like most Southerners then he would have a real advantage over John who would probably be feeling a little sleepy from his heavy meal.

Tommy looked up their address in the phone book, drove to the house and checked it out. He noted the closeness of the houses and the number of cars in the surrounding driveways. He saw only one car in the Sommier's drive. He recognized it to be Barbara's sixteenth birthday gift. He wondered if John's car was in the garage or if he hadn't arrived home yet.

Tommy looked at his watch, eight o'clock. He was sure Sommier had to be home. He parked his car three streets over, away from the street light.

He had carefully taped over parts of the numbers on his license plate, changing the eight to a three and the four to a one before he had left home just in case anyone saw him. He checked his .32, it was loaded and ready, safety off. He looked around at the houses before he got out of his car. He wanted to make sure there weren't any curtains askew, he couldn't risk a nosy neighbor making him.

He got out of his car, dressed in black and pulled the black ski mask down over his face. He held the door handle up while he gently closed the door. The neighborhood, though obviously new, was crowded with oaks. Probably land from some former plantation, Tommy thought. He was glad for the trees as they added to his stealth.

He walked silently along the sides of houses, noting which houses had dogs and which did not. He had brought a supply of raw meat wrapped in plastic in case he encountered any unfriendly animals. He needed to make himself known to the animals now so that when he passed back through they would know his scent and welcome him. He was slow and thorough with each dog, petting each one several times around their snouts.

Nearly fifteen minutes later he arrived at the Sommier's house. He pulled his black gloves on, he didn't want to leave any prints behind. He was pleased that most of the Sommier's neighbors chained their dogs rather than using fences, it would make his getaway easier, especially if he had to rush it.

Tommy slowly walked around the entire house looking into each of the windows. The house was built about two feet off the ground so he had to pull himself up at the each of the window ledges in order to peer in.

He couldn't make anything out in the bedrooms since the lights were out. He had seen Barbara in the kitchen but he hadn't seen any sign of John. He decided to give it ten minutes or so, maybe John was in the bathroom. Tommy crouched down in some shrubs near the front porch.

After ten minutes had passed he checked the windows again. Barbara had moved to the living room but there was still no sign of John. He decided he'd go in through what was most likely the baby's room since he could see what appeared to be a mobile hanging from the ceiling.

He quietly removed the screen from the window. He had glass cutters and tape with him but he tried the window first to make sure it was locked. He smiled, it wasn't. He eased the window up, hoisted himself and slipped into the room.

He had been right; it was the baby's room. He didn't bother looking in the crib, he'd take care of the baby later, he wouldn't even have to waste a bullet, he could smother him.

He crawled to the door, which was already open, he could hear Barbara singing to the radio. He came up off his hands and knees but remained crouched down. He edged along the hallway wall. This was going to be easier than he first thought. If John was already in bed, he'd pop him and then he could take as long as he wanted with Barbara, do whatever he wanted to her.

He slowly made his way into the master bedroom. He stood up slightly in order to see the top of the mattress. The bed was still made. He checked the master bath and found that it, too, was empty. He noiselessly walked back down the hall to check the other bathroom. He could have kicked himself, he was careless not to have checked it in the first place.

He was coming back out of that bathroom, also empty, when he met her head on. She screamed and ran back down the hallway through the living room to the front door. She had almost opened it when he pulled her backwards by her hair. She fell to the floor. He pulled the gun from the back of his pants.

"Scream again and I'll kill you," he said viciously.

Barbara scooted along the floor, away from him. "Keep away from me, you're crazy if you think I don't recognize your voice Tommy Jamison. My daddy will bury you alive if you touch me."

He had forgotten he still had the ski mask on. He pulled it off and sighed, no wonder he was so hot. "Where's your husband?"

"He went to the store, he'll be back any minute, and he'll kill you if your here," she lied.

"No, I think it's me who's gonna do the killin' around here. We'll just wait for him and after I kill him," he crossed the room to where she was seated on the floor, he reached down and squeezed one of her breasts while pinching her nipple, "I'll give you what you've been missin'."

She struck out at him pushing his hand away from her breast. "Don't touch me, you filthy pig!"

"Me? A filthy pig? This from a nigger's wife. I'd think you'd be glad to get some white meat. It may not be as big as an ape's but at least I know what to do with it."

"I'd take John over you every time and I'll have you know he's a wonderful lover. You're disgusting." She spat in his direction.

Tommy had expected her to say something about being called a nigger's wife. Maybe she thought he was just saying ridiculous things but then maybe...

"You and your daddy both had nigger babies 'cept your daddy wasn't dumb enough to own up to his nigger baby."

"What? What are you talking about? Daddy's only child is me and I am most certainly not black!"

"But that child of yours is, isn't he?"

Barbara paused too long giving the truth away. "No, uh, you know John's the father; you know he's not a Negro."

"That's not what Sommier's best friend says. He says—"

Barbara jumped up off the floor. "He can't say anything, he's dead. You're lying."

Tommy backhanded her. "Shut up, nigger's whore, you knew and you gave it to him anyway. Like I said, you're just like your daddy. He likes dark meat too but he ain't stupid like you. He got his piece and tossed it aside, he didn't try passing his bastard off as White."

Blood trickled down the corner of her mouth. Instinctively she stuck her tongue out to lick her wound. "I don't know what the hell you're talking about."

"Sure you don't. You had your daddy's black whore nursing your son from her titties that were wet because of your daddy, well, because of your nigger half-brother really."

"What? You're crazy!"

"I don't think so, I'm the one who ran them off the road after your daddy got a few calls from her, probably wanting money. See, he wasn't quite straight with me. Gave me this line of crap that she was a rights worker and she needed to be silenced. After I took care of them I checked out the story, went to the funeral, acted all sympathetic and what not and found out that the honorable Judge Jefferson Cartwright had him a little thing with this girl when she was still a virgin."

"That's a lie! Daddy would never do anything like that!" Barbara was disgusted by the thought. She was disgusted, too, that they hadn't been allowed at the funeral but the killer had attended. The family had welcomed him.

"Oh, I think you know I ain't lying. Why would I? Why that Percy told—"

"Percy? What about Percy?"

"She and the girl's momma were the one's who told me all about your daddy. Seems Percy blamed herself 'cause she used to take the girl to your house sometimes to teach her how to cook but it seems the girl would wander off and Percy would have to find her. Needless to say, she didn't bring the girl back no more after she found the girl spread eagle with your daddy's fat ass between her legs but, it was too late, the girl was with child."

Barbara thought about what her daddy had said the other night when he had come to the house. At the time it hadn't made sense, his need to know what Lacy had told her, his being upset over Jammy having spent time there and his declaration that he'd only care about what happened to Percy if she was tight lipped.

She couldn't believe he would have his own son killed. Even if he wouldn't recognize him as his son. Oh God, Barbara thought, Jammy had been her half-brother, her son's uncle. How could he be her brother, her family? He was Colored. She might be able to reconcile John's blood but this was too much. She had kicked her own brother out of her house but it was her father who had them killed. Her head was spinning.

"I don't believe you. Daddy would never kill anyone." Barbara tried to fight back the churning of her stomach.

"Yeah, but that doesn't keep him from sending his Wings out to do his dirty work." Tommy reached out to touch her face.

She jumped back like he was the devil himself. "I said don't touch me."

Tommy steadied the gun in one hand and reached for her again. She clawed at him, her fingernails scratching deeply down his right cheek.

"You fuckin' bitch. You don't have your nigger here to protect you now." He backhanded her but before she toppled backwards he caught her by the front of her sweater. He ripped the sweater open with his free hand. He tried to slip his hand down her bra but she bit him. He was about to pistol whip her when he heard the key in the lock.

John pushed the door open. "What the hell?" John took in the whole scene and moved to strike Tommy.

Tommy raised his gun and fired. Barbara used her body to shield her husband. She fell back on John causing them both to fall to the floor.

John looked at her white bra that was quickly becoming red. Her cleavage was filled with blood. She was starting to gasp for breath.

"John, the baby, don't let the baby die too. Make them keep me alive until the baby's born." She struggled to get out every word.

"Shh, don't talk. You and the baby will be fine. What do you think, a girl this time?"

"Shut up, Sommier. I want a piece of her while she's still warm." Tommy stood with his gun pointed at John's head.

Before John could move a shot rang out. John saw the singular hole between Tommy's eyes and watched him fall backwards. His eyes went to the door, he saw Cartwright standing there shaking.

Barbara turned her head and saw her father. "Daddy, Daddy?"

The big man rushed to his daughter's side. "Hush now, Darlin'. John's callin' for an ambulance." He looked at her blood soaked brassiere and sweater, his face was stricken with grief.

"Daddy, Tommy told me all about Jammy. Why did you want him killed? You always wanted a boy. I know he was Black but he really was smart"

Cartwright sighed. "I didn't want him killed, or Lacy either, Tommy did that on his own. I only wanted to warn Lacy off me."

"But he was your son," her voice pleaded with him.

"Don't you see? He wasn't like a real boy. He could never have followed in my footsteps."

"No, I guess you never could have taught Jammy to hate his own race." Her words were growing softer and slurred.

"We don't hate them, Darlin'. We're just superior to them." His often recited words had little meaning to him with his daughter dying in his arms.

"John?" She coughed softly and then said, "John?"

John sat down on her other side. His eyes were filled with tears. "Right here." He squeezed her hand.

"I'm sorry, for everything. I love you and John Jr. more than anything. You tell Janiene to be a good momma to my son and our new baby too."

"I love you too. Now, be quiet, you're going to be fine." Tears rolled down John's cheeks. He realized that though he wasn't in love with her, he did love her.

The faint sounds of sirens became more and more piercing until the glow of swirling red lit the room.

John hoped against hope that they would save her life. He told the doctors that she was three of four months pregnant. They had promised to do everything they could.

"Mon Dieu, John, how is she?" Catherine rushed into the waiting room with Henri right behind her.

"I don't know, Mom. They said the bullet went into her left lung, it's lodged near her heart." John's eyes were red from the tears he held back.

"Where's Cartwright?" Henri asked.

"I don't know, probably with the police, he shot Jamison. I'm not sure what all Jamison was planning but I'm sure he intended to rape her."

"How did Cartwright come to be there, with a gun?" Henri paced the floor.

"I don't know that either. What I do know is Barbara is lying in there right now with a bullet that was meant for me. Jamison was aiming at me when she jumped in between us. Mom, she saved my life. Do you know how terrible I've been to her lately and she saved my life." He wrapped his arms around his mother and let a few tears fall.

"She loves you, John. You would have done the same for her."

"But she's pregnant." He slumped further into her arms.

Henri sat down beside them. "You finally believe her? What changed your mind?"

"That was the first thing she said after she'd been shot, that they had to keep her alive until she had the baby."

Catherine let out a strangled cry of one mother feeling for another. Barbara had been deprived of seeing her son for nearly a week. "Henri, go get John Jr.. He should be here when she wakes up."

Henri passed Cartwright in the hallway. Henri wasn't able to update the man since he brushed right by him without even glancing his way.

Cartwright stormed up to the nurses' station. "Where's my daughter?"

John went out in the hallway when he heard the man. "Judge, no one can see her, she's in surgery. Why don't you come wait with the rest of the family and I'll relate everything the doctor has told us thus far."

Cartwright looked at John like he was a speaking another language. "Whose family? Judith, is she here?"

"No, I didn't call her. I thought you would. My mother is here and Dad went to go get John Jr.."

"If you think I'm going to let you or any of your family near Barbara, you're crazy!" Cartwright's face was twisted with a murderous gleam.

"She's my wife. I have more of a right to be here than you. You're upset, why don't you try to relax a little. We're all in this together."

"She's here, maybe dying, because you lied to her."

Cartwright wrapped his fingers around John's arm and walked to a empty area down the hall, he said, "Buker told me all about your bloodlines. Buker said it was that what pushed Tommy over the edge. Thank God, Buker had the sense to warn me when he suspected Tommy was up to something. Tommy never would have done this if it hadn't been for your bloodlines!"

John wondered how Buker knew about him but it wasn't important now. "I'm not so sure about that. Tommy came into the shop a few weeks ago and attacked Barb. The man was an animal—"

"You're the animal mixed with jungle blood! There's no way Barbie knew about you. To think she wanted you to be kept out of Harvard so she could be with you! She couldn't have known, could she? Did she?"

John looked at the other man with pity. "It doesn't make much difference right now."

"The hell it doesn't! I'll ruin you, Sommier. I'll ruin your family. I'll see you hanging from an oak if you tricked my daughter—"

"It's Barbara who uses the tricks. I would never have been with your daughter in the first place if it hadn't been for her manipulations. I don't know what this business about keeping me out of Harvard is about but I'm sure it another one of her deceptions—one you were in on."

John lowered his voice so that even Cartwright had to strain to hear him. "As for ruining my family, don't even try it. I was there tonight, remember? I may not know the whole story but I now know who fathered Jammy. I also know, directly or indirectly, you had something to do with Lacy and Jammy's deaths. I'm sure the police would be interested in that. Maybe even the FBI would want a piece of this one, I heard Lacy was a civil right's worker."

There was a loud squeal behind them as John Jr. spotted his favorite grandfather. Henri walked up to them with the small boy fidgeting and trying to get to the other man.

"Someone's sure happy to see you." Henri held the baby out for Cartwright to take.

Cartwright looked at John Jr. with both sadness and disgust; he turned and walked away from the three Sommiers.

"He knows," John said to his father. He took his small son and walked back to the waiting room.

***

The day of the funeral was cold and wet. It was the first day in the fall season that hadn't topped sixty degrees. The rain wasn't heavy, just a drizzle, a long non-stop drizzle.

The service was huge; all of old-money society was in attendance. Whispers about the newspaper story filled the church. The official report was that Barbara had been attacked by a family friend intent on raping her, her father had been in the neighborhood when he sensed something terrible was happening and he had rushed to help her. He shot his daughter's attacker but not before his daughter had been shot. She had died, four months pregnant, after six long hours of surgery.

The sincerest of condolences were offered to Cartwright, who, though he couldn't save his daughter, had brought justice to the man who had shot her. He was depicted in story after story as a hero. A father among fathers.

John had decided upon an open casket. Barbara's bruises were not so bad that they could not be covered by the mortician's skillful hand. John knew Barbara would have wanted to show off her beauty at least one more time. He picked a high collared, the wound and subsequent surgery wouldn't allow anything else, white lace dress. He had her favorite locket, the one with his and John Jr.'s photos inside, placed around her neck. Her blond hair was done in curls that framed her perfect face beautifully. White lilies were laid out all around the coffin and a bouquet of them was laid in her arms. The total effect was that of a resting bride rather than a young bride resting in peace.

John held his son firmly throughout the service. John Jr.'s 'Ma Ma Ma' had wet the remaining dry eyes when the boy first spotted his mother's peaceful looking body.

John looked behind him and around him. He wasn't sure what he was looking for but he kept looking anyway. He looked at Judge and Judith Cartwright sitting on the opposite side of the church. The Judge hadn't talked to John since the day at the hospital except to demand that Barbara be buried in the family mausoleum. John had reluctantly agreed. He knew if she were laid to rest with the Sommier's that Cartwright would never pay his respects to his daughter.

After the service, John received many words of sympathy and pats on the back but only one touch held electricity and only one offered absolute empathy.

"Janiene, thank you for coming. It means a lot to me."

"I wish there was something I could do."

"You are doing something." John switched the baby from the right side to the left side.

He reached out to take her hand. She squeezed his hand gently and released it. They walked down the stairs of the church together. She offering the love of friendship, he demanding nothing more.

Would you like to see your manuscript become a book?

If you are interested in becoming a PublishAmerica author, please submit your manuscript for possible publication to us at:

acquisitions@publishamerica.com

You may also mail in your manuscript to:

**PublishAmerica
PO Box 151
Frederick, MD 21705**

www.publishamerica.com

LaVergne, TN USA
01 March 2011
218293LV00002B/19/P